The Art of Deceit

The Art of Deceit

Fabiola Joseph

www.urbanbooks.net

Urban Books, LLC
300 Farmingdale Road, NY-Route 109
Farmingdale, NY 11735

The Art of Deceit Copyright © 2018 Fabiola Joseph

ISBN 13: 978-1-64556-007-4
ISBN 10: 1-64556-007-4

First Mass Market Printing February 2020
First Trade Paperback Printing December 2018
Printed in the United States of America

10 9 8 7 6 5 4 3 2 1

This is a work of fiction. Any references or similarities to actual events, real people, living or dead, or to real locales are intended to give the novel a sense of reality. Any similarity in other names, characters, places, and incidents is entirely coincidental.

Distributed by Kensington Publishing Corp.
Submit Orders to:
Customer Service
400 Hahn Road
Westminster, MD 21157-4627
Phone: 1-800-733-3000
Fax: 1-800-659-2436

The Art of Deceit

by

Fabiola Joseph

Dedicated to Maude Henderson-Dafney and her daughter, Natasha Dafney-Neal.

I cherish the connection you two shared with The Art of Deceit.

I lovingly hold this in my heart and will do so for the rest of my life.

And as Maude would say . . . , "That damn Tangie!"

"Hate What You See?"
(Letter to the wise from Tangie)

Don't look at me like you hate me.

Hell, most of you want to be me.

I'm that bitch that you buried deep down inside.

The one in that dark place who you don't have the balls to ever let come out.

Shit, I do the things that you sit and daydream about.

I say the things that make you tongue-tied when they try to come out.

I'm that slick bitch,

That rich bitch,

That fine bitch who walks up to your man and walks away with his heart.

I'm that chick Tangie you need to start letting out.

Don't roll your eyes at me as if you can't stand me.

Hell, you wish you had my personality.

I'm that bitch who holds her head high,

although I may have just done something to make others cry.

I just say, "Fuck it." I move to my own flow.

I'm the one who will fuck your man just to get what I want,

Even if that means lying on my back and using my cunt.

Even when I care,

I'll never let you know,

And when I love,

I never let it show.

I know that I am the Tangie in you that you refuse to let out.

See, what most people don't know,

I used to be just like you.

Maybe around seven or eight,

But my mama set me straight.

I no longer walk around with my pussy tucked tight.

Held away like a game that nobody can play.

Hell, how in the fuck do you think that I bagged Mr. Too Fine Tay?

So y'all bitches go ahead and keep your nose up high,

'Cause I'll be making damn sure that your man's hand is creeping up my thigh.

And while you continue to act like you don't see me,

I'll let him slip his finger inside me and slowly finger fuck me.

Don't ever bring your eyes down to face your harsh reality,

'Cause as you continue to hate everything that you see in me,

It doesn't matter if it's my beauty, my diamonds, or my blatant sexuality,

The Art of Deceit will always live and thrive inside me.

In the end, the sad part will always be,

I'm the Tangie you couldn't and will never be!

Prologue

Now was the time for me to put my acting skills on blast. I ran over to where the DVD was being played, and I yanked the plug out of the wall. The screen went blank, and so did everyone else. I thought that Black had lost his mind for a moment. He just stood there, so still, with glazed over eyes. Then he just charged Shamika like a football player on Super Bowl day, and no one made a move to stop him. Everyone knew and felt that she needed her ass whipped. Finally, Carl stepped up to stop him, but Tay held him back. He was mystified by what Shamika had done.

When Tay looked at me, I put an "Oh, my God" look on my face. One of the guests from the party stood up and pulled Black off Shamika before he killed her. She lay on the floor, bloody and hurt. Carl went over and helped her up out of pity.

"You fucking bitch! I'm going to kill your ass. Let me go!" Black screamed as the guest held him back.

I walked over to her and acted like I was going to help her as I told Tay to call for a car. I pulled her hair back and handed her a napkin for her bleeding lips.

"Now, pull yourself together, Mika. Everyone is watching. Don't let them see you break down," I said in a whisper. "Tay'von is calling a limo for you. I want you to go back to the house and get your things packed."

She looked at me as if she didn't want to leave Miami just yet.

"Now, you know that you can't stay anymore," I told her. "Black is going to try to hurt you if you do. Just give him some time to cool off and get his mind right. But there is one favor I need you to do for me. After all that has happened, there's just one thing that I want you to remember—"

She cut me off before I could make my grand statement. "But, Tangie, I don't know how this got out. I didn't make a copy or anything. The only one who could have put this out is you-know-who."

I put my arms around her and got real close to her. "You may not know how this got out, but I do."

She looked at me with shock on her face. I wanted to spit in it, but that was too low class for me. I released her from my embrace, then gripped one of her arms tightly.

"Come on, Shamika. Don't look so surprised. Try to look like we're having a normal conversation. If you don't, I won't tell you what I know."

She tried her best to keep it together, but her body was shaking uncontrollably under my hand.

"Look at me, Shamika, 'cause I'm responsible for the tape getting leaked. That's right, bitch. I did it."

She tried to pull away from my grip, but I held on tight.

"It fucking hurts, doesn't it? I have been setting this up since we were on the road. You fucked me over, so now I'm fucking you with the biggest dick I can find. Tell me, how does it feel? Because I'm feeling damn good!"

"You bitch!" she screamed, but I wasn't moved. I kept the concerned look on my face, and I also looked confused and hurt.

"Calm down, little Mika. Don't be so mad. You got to admit that you've had this coming. I'm the last bitch that you should have fucked with. You messed with my life, so now I'm ruining yours. I hope that you never find a man who will spend another dime on you again. I hope that life gets so bad for you that you'll need to borrow money just to get a sandwich off the dollar menu at McDonald's. Rot in hell, you dirty bitch. And may you never rest in peace."

She was speechless as I let her arm go. The thought of me getting her first had never crossed her mind. It had just hit her that she had gravely underestimated me, and that mistake was to her disadvantage. She had lost the game that she thought she played all too well.

That was why my motto had always been "Before you sit down to play a game, you must not only know the rules to the game, but you must also know all your opponents, even if that means skipping a hand or two just to make sure you know their skill level. Having this knowledge gives you an upper hand every time, and an upper hand always wins the game."

Chapter 1

Mission Accomplished

Life is so funny. Here I am in my big house filled with imported furnishings, original artwork, and millions of things that I really don't need. I have all the clothes, jewelry, and accessories that I could ever want. I have six cars, which were paid for with cash and are all under my name. I also have a husband who has millions of women screaming his name as soon as he hits the stage. Yet I really don't think that I am happy. People have always said that I am hard to please, and I just don't think that this is normal. Maybe it's because so many times in my life, I have worked too hard to get to where I am. Divorce is out of the question. They get way too messy. Plus, I would end up with only half of what I have now. Even though I have my own business, Tay's money still looks too good

*next to mine on a bank statement, and I'm not
ready to give that up.*

I started out as your typical video ho. Well,
that was what they called us. I was approached
while walking down the streets of New York and
was asked to go to a model call for a hip-hop
video. I had done about eight or nine videos
before meeting this hip-hop singer at the video
shoot. He would turn out to be my future husband, and at the time, his first album was out
and was doing very well just off the first single.
That particular shoot was for his second single,
and I couldn't wait to meet him. I showed up,
and there were about fifty girls there. I didn't
have to stand around and wait to see if I had
made it in the video, because I had already been
cast in the lead role.

After makeup and wardrobe, I walked out to
the set, and there he was, Mr. Too Fine himself.
The world knew him as Tay'von, but he had been
dubbed Mr. Too Fine because of his very clean-
cut, handsome appearance in the sometimes
roughneck rap industry, and he looked even
better in person. We ended up doing the video,
and as soon as we were done, I got my things
together so that I could leave. I never tripped

over myself to meet the celebrity that I was working for, because they would always come after me, and that day was no different. Tay'von walked right up to me and asked me for my real name, thinking Tangie was just a stage name. I told him that Tangie was my only name.

He looked me over one good time and took my hand. Then he led me to his trailer, just like I knew he would. Once in there, I didn't speak. I waited for him to say something or make a move, but he didn't. He just sat down and left me standing there. He opened a bottle of Hennessy and just stared at me. He finally handed me a cup and poured some alcohol in it. And although I hate Hennessy, I drank it down. I didn't know what it was about this guy, but I never said a word. Frustrated with my mute approach, he got up, walked around me, and asked me if I remembered him.

"Why would I? I've only seen you on TV."

He started to laugh, then said, "About two years ago, I rapped a hook on a singer's song. You may remember the video shoot for the song 'What More Do You Want.' I'm sure you do, because I remember you."

"Really? I do remember working that shoot, but I don't remember you being there."

He shook his head, as if I was wrong for not remembering him. "Why would you remember me? I wasn't the main nigga in the video, right?"

I looked at him with a serious smirk on my face. The quick temper that I was well known for started to rise. "So you brought me in here to cry about me not noticing you two years ago? Isn't that some talk show–type bullshit?"

"I just wanted to see if my theory was right. It seems that all it took to get you in here was the thought of fucking a star. You didn't notice me back then, but since my song is number one now, you didn't even think twice about coming back here with me. Did you think that I wouldn't remember you turning me down in front of everyone the way you did? You're just a star fucker, and I have proved my point."

I thought that Tay had lost his mind. I couldn't believe that he had held on to this for two years. Then he had the nerve to bring me back to his trailer just to force me to remember some bullshit, and when I didn't, he got mad. He had to be off his rocker.

"Look, you took *me* by the hand and brought me back here. I didn't ask to come here with you, so if this is all that you have to say to me, well, fuck you very much, and I hope things go better for you the next time around."

I put down the cup that he had given me, and I turned around to leave.

"Bitch, please, you walk into every video shoot as if you're the finest thing to ever walk the earth. You got your nose so high that you're the only one breathing fresh air. All of them other girls out there look just as good as you, so get off of yourself."

By then he was holding on to my arm, and I hadn't decided if I should just pull away and walk out or if I should smack his ass for grabbing on to me the way he had.

"Come on now. I didn't see you turn me away when I came in for the audition," I retorted. "From what I hear, you're the one who decided to make me the lead in *your* video. And we all know why you did that. It's 'cause I am the baddest bitch around, so why don't you just get off of yourself and admit it?"

I had gotten in his face to make my point. His grip on my arm had got tighter once he realized that I would not back down. His face at first had been full of anger, but a smile had started to break through.

"You have got to be the most conceited, most arrogant, and boldest girl I have ever met, and I have to admit that it turns me on."

Wait, he had lost me. He had to have multiple personalities.

"Fuck you, Tay'von. How do you go from calling me a bitch to telling me that I am turning you on? Just let my arm go, so I don't have to be in here with your disrespectful, foulmouthed ass any longer."

I didn't care who he was anymore. He had taken things too far for me to care. I no longer wanted to get to know him, and if he didn't let me go, I was going to hit his ass. But I didn't get that chance. He pulled me really close and kissed me. It seemed like with that one kiss, all my anger melted away, and I fell deeper into both the kiss and him. I didn't know what it was, but there was definitely a fire between us. Maybe it was the fact that the whole time we were going at it, I couldn't take my eyes off his sexy lips. Men had always been my weakness, and Tay'von was no different. He was six feet three inches tall, with light brown skin. He had pretty long cornrows and the brightest green eyes I had ever seen. And his body, his body was one that I couldn't wait to get on top of.

Time went on, and I ended up doing another one of Tay'von's videos, which caused us to spend more time together and get close. He still saw other people, and so did I. He hated the fact that I wasn't just at home, waiting for him to call. I wasn't the kind of girl who let a man run around town while I stayed home, hoping that he would grace me with his company. I had told him, "I'll share my ass just as long as you share yours." He thought that it was all jokes, but he had something coming his way that would force him to choose me.

The night of an album release party that was being held for a label mate of Tay'von's, I devised a master plan. I knew he was going to the party with some low-class ho whom I had seen around. What he didn't know was that I would be attending the bash with a big-name director named Sims. I knew this would get under Tay's skin because I had met Sims when he directed some of Tay's videos.

As soon as I walked into the plush club where the party was being held, all eyes were on me. I had known they would be. I walked over to the bar as Sims walked around, shaking hands. I had men throwing all kinds of game at me, but I was not there for that. I was on a mission, so I told them all to fuck off. I had on a little dress that was tight and hugged me in all the right places. The ice that glowed around my neck and on my ears and fingers added the finishing touches to my outfit. After I finished my first drink, I rejoined Sims.

We walked around, mingling with other partygoers, and two hours later I was ready to go. On our way out, I made sure that we walked by Tay's table, although I knew that he had been watching me all night. I looked Tay dead in his eyes, winked, smiled, and kept on walking. I watched him look down at Sims's hand on my ass, and I saw anger in his eyes. Minutes later, while Sims and I waited for our limo to pull up, I felt someone standing behind me. I turned to find Tay'von standing there, smoking a cigarette. He said nothing, and neither did I.

Tay'von waited for the limo to pull up, then came and stood beside me. He took a long drag before saying, "You know that you're not getting in that limo, right, Tangie?"

I looked at him and waited for the driver to open the rear passenger door. Once the driver was back behind the wheel, Sims said nothing as he held the limo door open so that I could get in.

I went to step off the curb, but Tay grabbed my arm and said, "I already told you that you are not getting into that car. Didn't you hear me?"

Sims must have realized that if I didn't get in the car, he wouldn't be getting a piece of me, so he finally spoke up. "Let her arm go, Tay. She didn't come here with you."

"Fuck you, Sims. She ain't going nowhere unless I tell her to," Tay said while pushing me out of the way and getting in Sims's face.

Now, this was feeding my already large ego big-time, but I still had to play it off. I stepped in front of Sims and got in Tay's face.

"What in the hell do you think you're doing, Tay'von? I saw you in there with your dirty-ass groupie, but I didn't say anything to you. Why don't you go back and join her so that we can go on about our business? And stop cockblocking. It doesn't look good on you."

Tay'von looked at me dead in the eyes and dared me to go against his word. "Like I said before, you're not leaving with him, Tangie. All he wants to do is fuck you, and I'm not letting that happen. Ever since he met you, that's all he's been talking about."

"Oh, like you're any better? You must think that I'm fucking dumb, Tay. Every other day you're in some new pussy, yet you want me to stand here and think that *you* are not just fucking me too? Hey, you wanted to fuck, and you did. Now step aside and give another man a chance."

There was a level of danger in Tay's eyes that was about to boil over, and that was what I had been hoping to see. I knew he had a mouthful to say, but before he could get anything out, Sims spoke up.

"Yeah, that's right. Tangie, tell that nigga to let me have some of that pussy that's got him out here crying."

That was all that Sims was able to say. Tay knocked him down with a quick right jab to the chin. The next thing I knew, one of Tay's bodyguards came out of the doorway and held Tay back before he did any more damage. I never even saw him standing there, but he was just in time to do his job. While Tay was being held back, I could hear Carl, another one of Tay's goons, calling for the limo. I just stood there, pissed, not because Tay had hit Sims but because Tay thought that he could control me and tell me what to do.

Tay's limo pulled up a minute later, and I thought that I was free to go, but Carl just pushed me into the waiting car. I didn't try to get out, because things were going according to my plan. As we pulled off, I looked back and watched Sims's limo driver helping him to his feet. Months later I found out that Tay and Sims had words when Tay found out that I was going to the party with his favorite director, so things were never the same between them after that night.

No one spoke while we were in the limo. I looked from Tay to Carl, who happened to be fucking me with his eyes. I was so used to this happening, so I didn't even bother to make a slick remark. Despite all the time Tay and I had been spending together, I had never been to his house, so I was hoping that this night would be the night. Once I noticed that we were headed to Jersey, I knew that we were going to my prince's castle.

Once there, the driver opened the car doors, and we stepped out. There was a maid waiting for us at the door. I was very impressed with his place. There were people whom money didn't change. They may be rich, but when you walked into their place, it looked like they had filled it with overpriced trash. Tay had done well, and everything looked pricey and tastefully done.

I was taken to what looked like a game room and was told to have a seat. There was a pool table, all sorts of video games, and collector arcade games. The maid brought us the drink of our choice: mine was vodka and mango juice, while Tay had Henny straight. Tay then brought over two hand-carved boxes that looked like they had come straight from Africa. He made sure to let me know he had picked up the boxes, which were made of black bird's-eye maple and bubinga, an African hardwood, in Ghana, on his last world tour. The maid left the room, and Carl opened the boxes. One was filled with weed, and the other with coke. I knew that Tay smoked, but I had never seen him sniff anything.

Carl rolled up the weed and handed each of us a jay. I waited to see who would do the coke, and right as that thought left my mind, Carl took out a small roll of money that had a rubber band around it. He lined up the white powder on a mirror and sniffed up two lines. After doing so, he handed everything to Tay'von, who did a couple of lines himself, and then Tay walked over and held the powder out to me. I shook my head no and pushed it away. I had done coke before, but I wasn't in the mood now.

"Come on, Tangie. It's just a little coke. Hell, I'm sure you've done worse," Tay said with a smile.

I did a line just to make him happy. Then he walked back to the couch, where he had been sitting, and just stared at me.

"Why are you looking at me like that?" I asked him.

"You have got to tell me what in the hell you thought you were doing tonight." His statement made me smile.

"I was fucking with your head. I wanted to show you that there are plenty of men out there who want me and can have me. You're not the only one."

Maybe it was the drugs, but he laughed. "That's why I like you, Tangie. You are so confident, even a little too confident at times, but that's okay, 'cause I can tell that it's not an act. You really do think that your shit doesn't stink," Tay said and then he took a second to laugh at his own joke. "But like I said before, most of them other niggas just want to fuck you. They are not trying to get to know you. All they see is that phat ass, and they don't give a shit about anything else."

I got up and stood in front of him. "Now, listen to Mr. Too Fine. People would think that you were different. The way you sound, it's like that thought never ran through your mind when you first met me."

Both his and Carl's eyes were on me. I put my hands on my hips and slightly spread my legs. "Why don't you take a good look at me, Tay'von? Who wouldn't want to fuck me? Any man would sell his soul to the devil just to get a taste of this."

I took one hand off my hip and ran it through my hair, then from my hair down to my chest, then down between my legs.

"Take a look at Carl. He's damn near drooling," I said when I noticed the hunger in Carl's eyes for my sex.

"You like what you see, huh, man?" Tay asked Carl.

"Man, that's one bad bitch," Carl answered.

"See, Tay? Even Carl can see how much of a woman I am. I just don't understand how you would rather be with them low-class bitches, like the one you were with tonight. Let me guess. You had to take her shopping, 'cause all the clothes that she wanted to wear looked fucked up, right?"

He laughed, because he knew I was right. "Come on, Tangie. That girl didn't mean shit to me. You see that I just left her ass at the party to go after you. Hell, I don't even know how she's getting home tonight. Maybe Sims will take her."

We all laughed at Tay's joke.

Then I sat on his lap, facing him, and said, "Well, you need to wise up, Tay, because the best is in front of you. You won't find better, trust me."

With that, I took his lips with mine. My tight dress became even tighter as it stretched against my thighs. I wound my hips back and forth as I felt his dick begin to grow. He pulled my strapless dress down and exposed my breasts. He took one of my nipples into his mouth as I took his blunt and sucked in some smoke. I watched him work my nipples with his tongue, and I loved every minute of it.

A few minutes later I pulled myself away from him and stood up. With total disregard for Carl, I pulled my dress all the way off. I stood there with one hand on my hip and the other one still holding Tay's blunt. I continued to smoke as Tay climbed off the couch and crawled over to me. He leaned up on his knees and kissed and licked my stomach. He pulled down my red G-string and started to work on my pussy. He sucked and licked all the right places. I looked over, and Carl was holding his crotch. Hey, if Tay didn't mind going down on me in front of him, then why should I?

I felt like my legs were about to give out, so I pushed him down and sat on his face. He ate my pussy so good that my moans turned into screams of passion. His maid came in to see if everything was okay, but when she saw me sitting on her boss's face, she turned beet red and left. My body moved with each stroke of Tay's tongue. Carl walked over and played with my nipples. This, plus the hot head that Tay was laying on me, sent me to cloud nine.

"Oh, baby, don't stop. You are making me feel so *good*," I moaned.

I then exploded in Tay's mouth, and he licked me clean. I slid down until we were face-to-face. I kissed him, tasting myself on his lips.

Carl went and sat on the recliner so that he could get a better view of my pussy. I licked my way down to Tay's dick and made sure that I took my time on the head before shoving it down my throat. I enjoyed hearing Tay pant like a bitch from my head game. Maybe it was the moment or maybe it was the drugs, but I did nothing when I felt Carl squeezing my ass cheeks. When I felt his finger slide into my wet pussy, it turned me on to the max. I moaned with excitement once I noticed that Tay hadn't even realized what Carl was doing. His eyes were glued shut, and his mouth was wide open.

Carl removed his finger from inside me and said, "Don't even think about letting this one go. Even her pussy looks pretty."

Tay didn't respond. He just lay there, enjoying my head game. I knew that Tay would not be able to go too much longer without cumming, so I jumped up and sat on his dick. I made sure to slide it all the way in slowly. I rode him as if he was my little pony. I gave it to him good so that he could see what could be his if he played his cards right. I gave him my all, and when we were done, we collapsed on the fur rug, totally satisfied.

He rolled over to me, all doe eyed, and said, "What are you trying to do, Tangie? You talked, and I heard you. You have to tell me what you want to do, because I'm trying to make this happen."

I smiled when I heard the golden words come out of his mouth.

"I'm trying to be all about you, baby," he added.

He kissed me, and at that very moment, I could tell that I had him 100 percent. I stood up after asking where the bathroom was and headed there to shower.

"Good choice, man," Carl said out loud, then mumbled the rest of his thoughts to himself, but I could still hear him. "Even her pussy taste good."

I was so good that not only did I have the sex act that I had just performed on Tay's and Carl's minds, but they were also captivated by my whole being. Mission accomplished.

Chapter 2

The Sexiest Snake That I Have Ever Seen

Looking back, it seems like I had a one-track mind. Find a man with money and keep a man with money. I never stopped to think of love or falling in love. All I knew was that my life would have to be a comfortable one, no matter what. When I think about things today, I don't know if I ever loved Tay'von or if it was just lust and greed. When I look at him, he isn't even Mr. Too Fine to me anymore. Now I lust more for other men and sometimes . . . for women. I spend my days running my business, taking care of my home, and shopping for shit that I already have. When I get horny, I play with myself or I get someone else to do it for me. I can no longer keep count of the number of people that I have slept with who are dangerously close to Tay and me. And to think that I was the one who used to trip about him sleeping with other women, including that bitch Connie. I don't know. Maybe it wouldn't have bothered me so much if at first, I wasn't meant to be used only as arm candy.

Now our relationship is to the point where I lie in bed and watch him pack to go on tour and can't wait for him to leave. It's not that I hate him; it's just not the same as it was a couple of years ago. Normally, I would be packing my things to go with him, but no more. I should have known that things would end up this way.

Two weeks after I completed my first mission, Tay'von was going out on tour, and I was staying behind. I would be left alone. And we all know that when a girl like me got bored, there was only so much left to do.

"So what are you going to do while I'm gone, baby?" he asked me as he packed.

I rolled over on the bed to face my oh, so sexy man. In the past two weeks, I hadn't left his house. Our days had been filled with sex, shopping, and dining, while our nights had been filled with parties, clubs, and more sex. I didn't think that it could get any better than what it was.

"I don't know, to tell you the truth. I'm sure that I'll find something to do."

"I am leaving you one of the platinum credit cards, and there is cash in the safe, so just make sure you get whatever you want."

"Okay, but what do you want me to do when I'm wet and you're not here?" I asked in a sexy tone.

He stopped packing and looked at me hard. "You fuck yourself or you wait," he said with a serious look on his face.

"And I take it that you will also be waiting, right?"

My question came out sarcastic, and he didn't like that much. He smiled and said nothing. I lit a blunt and stared into space. He walked over to the bed and ran his hand through my hair, while his eyes were glued to my exposed breasts. He took his other hand and rubbed my nipples. I closed my eyes, took a puff, and moaned. Then I felt his hand getting tighter around my hair to the point that it hurt. He yanked me up to my knees so that I was face-to-face with him.

While he held on to my hair and still rubbed my nipples, he said, "Like I said before, you better fucking wait. Don't worry about what I will be doing. Just make sure you do as I say."

"Who do you think you are? My daddy?" I asked, again using a sarcastic but sexy tone.

He kissed me long and hard. The cover that was wrapped around the lower half of my body was now on the floor. He pulled away from me and looked at my body. He came close and pushed me down, then yanked my legs and pulled me to the edge of the bed. He rubbed my clit with his fingers, making me wet. I just lay there, puffing on my blunt, while he slipped his finger in me.

"Let me tell you something, Tangie. If you are going to be with me, then never question me."

He took the blunt out of my hand and put it out. By then I was soaking wet. He flipped me over and pulled me up on my knees. He finger fucked me from the back while unzipping his pants. He ran his dick from my ass to my pussy, making me silently beg him to put it in, but he made me wait. He continued to rub himself on me while he spoke.

"You're going to be staying in my house, spending my money, and you're asking me what you should do if you get horny?"

He rammed his dick inside me hard. I screamed out, feeling both pain and pleasure. He pushed himself all the way in me hard and fast.

"Yeah, that's right, bitch. Take that dick. I want you to remember this." He leaned on my back and bit it hard but good while he reached over and played with my clit. I was grabbing on to the sheets, trying to get a hold of myself, but I couldn't. He paid me no mind and continued to talk. "Don't you ever ask me anything like that again. I am going to make things crystal clear to your ass for good."

Sweat was dripping off his body and onto mine. He was fucking me so hard that it felt like his dick would go up to my throat. It was hurting so good that I thought I was going to black out. He flipped me over and jammed his dick back in me. We were face-to-face and eye to eye. He bit my lips, drawing blood, but all I did was moan.

He looked me dead in the eyes and said, "You're mine, Tangie, and if you ever deceive me, I'll kill you."

He closed his eyes and came inside me. Then he rolled over onto his back and put his hands behind his head. "Now, get up and clean me off."

I looked down at his still rock-hard dick and then tried to get up and go get a towel, but he pulled me back down.

"Clean me off with your mouth."

I had never seen this side of Tay'von before. This made my insides burn with fire from the lust that I felt for him. There I was, thinking that he was soft, but he had turned around and shown me that he was a man, after all. So I leaned down and tasted some of that big brown dick of his.

"Tangie, don't fuck this up. Know the best when you have it."

Twenty minutes later he came in my mouth, but I kept on sucking, moving from his dick to his balls. We lay there, me sucking and him finger fucking me until I creamed on his fingers. He took them out of me, pushed them into my mouth, and I licked them clean.

He got up to take a shower, and without looking back, he said, "Now what are you going to do when you get horny and I'm not here?"

I lit a cigarette and said, "Wait."

He showered and dressed without a word. I was still in bed, too ashamed and satisfied to move. I didn't know if I should hate him or love him for what he had just done to me. Carl came in and told Tay that it was time for him to leave.

Tay kissed me on the forehead and said, "I've thought about it, and I am going to have Carl stay here with you. I'll take Tony with me and get some other guys to take Carl's place."

Tay smiled devilishly and walked out of the bedroom. Little did he know that Carl had had his fingers all up in my ass the first night we came back to his house. I was sure Carl was surprised to still see me here since I had got down like a true ho that night. I also knew that Carl wanted to keep more than just an eye on me, and I was thinking about letting him do so.

I stayed in the house for the next couple of days. Carl tried to get me to go out, but I told him no. I didn't know what to make of Tay'von's last act on me. Had he felt threatened by my words, or had he just looked at me like every other jump off that he kicked to the curb after he was done with them? Well, if that was the case, then he had another thing coming.

When Tay called me, he sounded like he was having the time of his life, so I got up, refusing to stay in the house any longer. I went to the spa, got my hair and nails done, and also got a full body wax. I was feeling good and looked even better. When I got back home, I told Carl that we were going out. I dressed to impress, and I told Carl to do the same. When we got in the car, I told the driver to take us to Per Se, one of my favorite restaurants in New York.

Once there, I ordered a bottle of Armand de Brignac, because I was about to celebrate.

"So, Carl, tell me, how much money does Tay pay you to guard his life?"

"He pays me well, and that's all you need to know."

I laughed to piss him off.

"What's so funny?" he asked on cue.

"Carl, please. Tay'von is making millions, and you're getting paid pennies. I saw the check he gave you for this month. Six thousand dollars. I can make more money than that by shaking my ass in a day." I laughed even harder and downed my champagne.

"Look, Tangie, the money that I have in my pocket has nothing to do with you."

"Oh, am I getting under your skin already? If so, the next couple of months are going to be tough for you."

"So are you trying to tell me that you are going to make my life hell until your so-called man gets back?"

Damn, that burned. *My "so-called man"? Okay, I see that he wants to play hardball, and I am up for the game*, I thought.

"So tell me, Carl, what were you thinking about when you had your fingers all up in me?"

He damn near choked on his drink. I must have touched a sore spot. He cleared his throat, then answered. "Well, how was I supposed to know that you would still be around? I have seen a lot of girls go through that house. You're just lucky, that's all."

"Oh, no, no, *lucky* is not in my vocabulary. I make things happen. I just don't sit around and wait for luck. To tell you the truth, I think that *you* are lucky that Tay didn't see the finger action that you laid on me."

He looked at me as if I was tripping. "Girl, please. You're the one who wouldn't be here, not me. Plus, it didn't look like it bothered you, anyways."

"So you think that Tay would kick me out and keep you on, right? Carl, you don't know my game, so stop trying to step onto the court, baby. I hope that you stay long enough to see what I am capable of doing. But, hey, maybe you are right. After all, you have been working with him for a long time, right?"

I acted as if what he had just said to me had no impact, but I made sure to store it so that I could use it against him another day.

After dinner, we went to the hottest club in the city. It was a new club by the name of Fire and Ice—fire for the dance floor, and ice for the relaxed lounging area. I planned on challenging Carl's loyalty to Tay, and in seconds I saw a tasty-looking brother on the dance floor. I left

Carl at the bar and made my way to Mr. Tasty. I slid my way between him and the light-skinned girl whom he was dancing with and leaned into him. He smiled, and I turned around and pushed my ass into him. He leaned in and asked me my name, but I didn't answer. He was just a pawn in the game that I was about to play.

We bumped and grinded all over the dance floor while his hands roamed over my body. I watched Carl out of the corner of my eye, and he sure as hell was worth the money Tay was paying him. He hadn't taken his eyes off me. When the song was about to end, I pulled Mr. Tasty in and kissed him. Out of the corner of my eye, I saw Carl rushing over to the dance floor.

"Okay, Tangie, it's time to go," Carl said as he hovered over me.

"Come on, Carl. I'm just starting to have a good time. Don't be a tight ass."

He yanked my arm so that we could walk off the dance floor, but I pulled away from him.

"Don't you dare pull on me," I growled. "Who in the hell do you think you are? You're a fucking bodyguard, so step to the side and guard."

If I were a man, I was sure Carl would have kicked my ass for screaming at him the way I did. But he just turned and walked away. *Good. I have him just where I want him*, I thought to myself. I walked after him and grabbed his hand.

"Come on, Carl. Don't be like that. I was just having a little fun."

He turned to find me smiling like an innocent little girl. He knew that I was dangerous, but he just couldn't resist. So I played nice and made sure to dance with him for about an hour; then he was putty in my hands.

"So how much are you going to let me get away with?" I asked him as we headed back to the limo.

"Not much," he answered with a smile.

It was then that I noticed how handsome Carl was. Six feet four inches tall, 230 pounds, and just plain sexy, but in a powerful way.

"Can I ask you something, Carl?"

"Sure. What's on your mind?"

"Do you think that I'm sexy?"

"I really don't think it matters what I think."

"Okay, let me put it like this. What did you think of me when you first met me?"

"Well, did you ever see that movie *Natural Born Killers*?"

"Yeah. Why?"

"Do you remember the part with the old Indian guy and the story that he told? You know, the story about the old lady who took in a sick snake and nursed it back to health? Well, one day when she went to go feed it, it bit her. While she lay on the floor, dying, she asked the snake why it had bitten her. The snake looked at her and said, 'Bitch, you knew I was a snake when you took me in.'"

I had to smile at this. "So are you saying that you think that I will end up biting the person who takes me in?"

He smiled and looked right at me. "What I am saying is that you are a snake, and I will do whatever it takes to make sure that you don't bite me."

We both laughed, but for different reasons.

"Well, do you at least think that I am a sexy snake?" I asked, still trying to get him to answer my question.

"Well, since you put it like that, I think that you are the sexiest snake that I have ever seen."

"Do you want to fuck me, Carl?"

We got in the limo and took our seats before he reached into his pocket and lit a joint. He smoked it halfway before handing it to me and answering. "Tangie, I watched you fuck Tay'von like a pro. I felt and tasted the wetness that you left on my fingers. So, truth be told, I would fuck the shit out of you, but that's all hypothetically speaking."

I realized that the weed he had just smoked was a truth serum, so I handed it back to him.

"Well, Carl, I really think that you are sexy too, but you seem so cold with me at times. I just can't make you out."

He said nothing, so I moved closer to him.

"You know that Tay is going to be gone for long periods of time, and it will just be you and me," I said. "So let me ask you this. Who do you fuck when you're horny?"

He started to look nervous, and I knew that I had to make my move soon. I waited for him to suck in the weed smoke; then I covered his lips with mine. He pulled away, but I climbed on his lap and faced him.

"Come on, Carl. I just want a shotgun."

I lifted the hand that held the last of the joint up to his mouth, and he took a long pull. Again, I covered his mouth with mine, and when he blew the smoke into my mouth, I slipped him my tongue. He tried to pull away, but I pushed into him harder. He had nowhere to go, so he kissed me back.

I reached down into his pants and felt his whole body stiffen, but I didn't stop. I had to smile when I felt the size of his dick. Tay'von had nothing on him, although he could still hang with the big boys. By then things were getting wild in the back of the limo, and we were all over each other. He was sucking on my nipples, and I still had my hand down his pants. Right when I was about to undo them, the limo came to a stop, and the driver put down the privacy window. I got off Carl, and the driver told us that we were at the gates of the house.

Carl straightened his clothes and laughed.

"What's so funny?" I asked him.

"I'm saved by the bell," he said.

He got out of the car once we were in front of the house. He leaned his head back into the car, then let me know his true feelings.

"You're a real fucking snake, Tangie. A real damn snake."

He walked away, leaving me sitting in the car. He laughed all the way to the front door, but little did he know that I would have the last laugh, after I bit his ass.

Chapter 3

Once I Have Him,
Then You Can Have Me

I went straight upstairs and took a long bath. Wrapping Carl around my little finger was going to be harder than I had thought. I was sure that if we hadn't got to the house so quickly, I would have got his ass. As I sat in my hot bath, I tried to figure out what his weak points were. I knew that he wanted to fuck me, but how could I get him to do it?

A knock on the bathroom door shook me from my deceitful thoughts.

"Tangie, Tay is on the phone for you."

Carl walked in and held the phone out to me. I stepped out of the tub. Soaking wet, I took the phone and stood directly in front of him.

"Hey, baby. What's going on?" I asked Tay.

Carl tried to hand me a towel, but I took it from him and threw it in the tub.

"I hear that you and Carl had a late night tonight. I also heard that you have been on your best behavior."

"Did Carl tell you that?" I asked.

"Yes, he did. That's why he's there. So that I can know everything that you do."

If only Tay knew what was about to go down, he would have shut the fuck up.

"Well, I'm sure that you have the right person to keep you up to date on what is going on here," I said as I started to play with myself.

I opened my legs wide so that Carl could get a good look. I rubbed my clit and talked to Tay at the same time. "Oh, baby, I miss you so much. I wish that you were here with me right now. I would fuck the shit out of you."

I watched Carl as he watched me. I could see his dick hardening under the sweatpants that he had changed into. The brain in his head was no match for the weaker yet strangely stronger one in his pants.

"I wish that I was there too, Tangie, but you know that I have to do these tours, 'cause touring and endorsements are where my real money comes from. You'll see me soon, so in the meantime, why don't you play with yourself for me?"

This made me laugh. It was almost as if he was watching me.

"Nah, I'm not in the mood to do that right now," I told him as I leaned on the sink and closed my eyes. I was really starting to make myself feel good.

"Yeah, okay, but just remember that I will be home soon enough, so you know what you have to do, right?"

I was tickled to death and was forced to let out a short chuckle. "I know, Tay. I have to wait," I said out loud, but in my mind I was thinking that I had to wait only until I hung up the phone with him.

Tay asked to speak to Carl, so I put the phone on speaker and held it out to him, making sure that he had to get closer to me to get it. As soon as he got close enough, I wrapped my legs around him, making sure that he couldn't get away. He tried to pull away, but my legs were strong, forcing a straining sound to escape from his lips.

"What the hell are you doing?" Tay'von asked as I inserted one of Carl's fingers inside me.

"Nothing. I just had to bend over and pick something up, and you know a nigga's getting old," Carl joked and chuckled nervously. But he was no longer pulling away.

His dick was about to burst through his pants as he started to finger me on his own.

"Look, man, I need you to really watch this girl for me. I like her and all, but there's something about her that I just don't trust yet."

"Yeah, I got you. Whatever you want, man," Carl answered, and I loved every minute of this betrayal.

Just the thought of Tay's words and our actions turned me on even more. Carl was finger fucking me while my—wait, how did he put it?—my "so-called man" was asking him to be loyal and keep an eye on me. That was truly ironic in itself.

Carl hung up the phone, stopped moving his finger, but still left it inside me. "I'm getting the hell out of here," he announced. He pulled his finger out of me and left the bathroom.

By the time I got myself dried, lotioned up, and dressed for bed, the dead of night had crept up on me; but I wasn't done with the cat and mouse games I was playing with Carl. I had gone to the closet to look through my clothes and admire some of my new things when I came across a box with handcuffs in it. An idea popped into my head, and I couldn't wait to get things poppin'.

I headed to one of the guest rooms, the one in which Carl was sleeping, and popped my head in. The door was wide open, so I stood there and watched him sleep. His right arm was thrown across his forehead, making what I was about to do a lot easier. I walked over to his bed and leaned over it quietly. I quickly put the handcuffs around his wrist, and before he could react, I attached the other end of the cuffs to the headboard and locked it. He opened his eyes and tried to pull his arm down, but that was a no go.

"No, no, nigga, you ain't going nowhere," I said.

He had a look of shock on his face, and it turned me on. I climbed on top of him and sat on his boxers. He had one hell of a body, and I wanted it in every way possible.

"Get the fuck off of me, Tangie," he said as he tried to pull his arm down again.

"Relax, Carl. You don't want the cuffs to get too tight around your wrist, now do you? Plus, you didn't want to give it to me, so now I have to take it."

I kissed his lips, and although they were cold and closed, I continued, anyway. I licked his lips and moved to his neck and ears. Then I moved down to his chest and licked one of his nipples. I felt his breath coming in faster and his dick hardening under my touch.

"Get these fucking cuffs off of me, Tangie. I'm not playing."

Although his mouth spoke those words, he was no longer pulling at the cuffs. I paid no attention to his words and continued on my way down. Once I reached his belly button, I licked around it while pulling his boxers down to around his ankles. I acted like I was about to suck his dick, but I pulled myself back up.

"Now, it wouldn't be right for you to let me go first, now would it?" I asked.

I didn't let him answer. I sat on his face, but I didn't feel his tongue.

"If you don't fuck me with your tongue, then I'll fuck your whole face," I told him as I started to rub my clit back and forth on his nose.

He did nothing, so I rubbed my pussy from his forehead to his chin. I whined and moaned until I felt his tongue in my ass and his free hand playing with my pussy. He was doing this so well that I started to pull away.

"Wait, wait, let me turn around," I told him while almost losing my breath.

I did so and came face-to-face with his massive dick. I power drove all of his thirteen inches into my mouth, and he fucked it with force. I deep throated it until he came in my mouth. I got up, leaving him gasping for air, leaned over, and kissed him, pushing the cum that I held in my mouth into his. His eyes widened with shock, then went back to normal as I heard him swallow. I uncuffed him so that I could see what his reaction was going to be.

"So what are you going to do now, big boy?" I asked in a teasing way.

He lay there like a bitch and said nothing. I let out a taunting laugh and then turned to leave. I heard him move, but before I could turn around on my own, he did it for me. He put his gun to my head and pulled me close.

"You nasty-ass bitch. Do you really think that you are going to turn me out with some head?"

"Well, Carl, it looks to me like I just did. Don't be a crybaby about it, honey. Just accept it."

He just stood there with a look of confusion and lust in his eyes. I took my hand and moved the gun down slowly.

"Don't take it so hard, Carl. You should be proud. That was the best head I have ever got in my life."

I moved the gun farther down, toward my pussy. He let it slide down, wondering if I was crazy enough to do what he was hoping for. Making sure to leave his finger on the trigger, I pushed the other end of the gun into my still soaked slit. Again, he was shocked by my actions and looked like he was about to pass out from pure fantasy fulfillment.

"Come on, Carl. You don't want this gun to go off in me, do you? Let it go so that I can replace this steel with that big dick of yours."

He let go of the gun and gave me a wet kiss. I pulled the gun out of me, and I held it up to his head as I pushed him away forcefully.

"You are the nasty-ass bitch," I told him. "Don't kiss me. We're not making love. Now, get your ass over here and fuck me."

He rushed over to me and pushed me against the wall hard. He lifted me up, and with my back against the wall, I wrapped my legs around him. He pushed all of his thirteen inches inside me and let out a loud moan as I held mine in. He fucked me fast and hard, as if he had something to prove.

"Yeah, that's right, motherfucker. You know that you want this," I said as I fucked him back.

I bounced on his dick as if I were on a pogo stick. I heard him whine, as if he was about to lose control.

"Damn, why you got to do this to me?" He repeated this over and over again. His cries became louder and louder as he came inside me. He fell to his knees as I landed on my feet. He was drained and broken.

"Bitch, you knew that I was a snake when you took me in," I answered, towering over him.

I shot him an evil grin and walked away.

Early the next morning, I snuck back into his room and fucked him slowly and lovingly. I knew that I had totally broken him down the night before, and since he was a man who lived by a certain law, I knew that he would be taking everything that had happened hard. I had made him forgo all the rules he followed, so now I had to build him back up into what I wanted him to be. I had perfected the art of fake lovemaking on him, and by the look on his face, I already had him falling for me.

Later that day, he came into the kitchen as I was sitting at the table, eating brunch. He sat down but ate nothing.

"Just calm down and eat. You need to replace all the strength that you used up last night. After all, you were hired as a muscleman, right?" I said without taking my eyes off my newspaper.

Like a good little boy, he got up and made himself a plate. Once seated again, he spoke. "So, is this how it is going to be?"

I looked at him as if I was confused.

"You know what I mean, Tangie. We have to talk about what happened last night and this morning. I need to—"

I cut him off. "That will be all for now," I told the maid once I noticed that she was more interested in our conversation than in cleaning up. I waited for her to leave the kitchen; then I turned my attention back to Carl.

"I really enjoyed last night. You made me feel good both inside and out. But you know what I am about, Carl. You put it best last night in the limo, remember?"

"So is that why you damn near raped me? Did what I say really bother you that much?"

I moved closer to him before answering. "Come on, Carl. I made love to you because I wanted to, not because of what you said. Plus, it was hardly rape. You enjoyed it too much for it to be considered rape."

"Well, what are you going to do now that we have slept together?"

This man was really sounding like a little punk, and that was just what I wanted.

"Well, I'm not going to do anything, Carl. I am going to continue to be with Tay'von, and you will continue to do what you are paid to do."

He looked like he was about to lose his mind once I made my comment.

"Well, I am not getting paid to sleep with you, so we do have to figure something out. It's not in my contract to fuck Tay's girlfriend."

"There is nothing to work out, Carl!" I yelled. "You need to tell me if this is going to be a problem. I do not want this affecting your job, because at the end of the day, that's all you're here for."

"My job? You're asking me if this is going to affect my job? I fucked my boss's girlfriend!"

"So quit!" I yelled without a second thought.

If this motherfucker thought that he was going to mess up what I had going on, then he would have to quit, or I was going to tell Tay to fire his ass.

"So this is your solution to this? I should quit?"

"If that is what it will take for you to keep your fucking mouth shut, then yes, you should quit."

"You really are a coldhearted bitch, Tangie. I hope you know that."

"Yes, Carl, I do know, but tell me, what you are going to do? Are you going to start acting like yourself, or are you leaving the job?"

"Fine, Tangie. If that's the way you want it, then that is the way you will get it."

Before he could say anything else, I declared, "Good. Now eat up. We have a big day ahead of us."

After a long day of shopping, I lay in bed, watching TV. Carl had barely spoken to me the whole day. He had just held my bags and stayed to himself. I wasn't sure what I was going to do with him yet. I thought that maybe my plan was working a little too well. But if fucking him would make him keep his mouth shut, then I would have to keep on doing it. Sexing him wasn't going to be that bad. It was going to be a win-win situation, one that satisfied both of us. The phone rang, and it was Tay'von interrupting my thought process yet again.

"So what city are you in tonight?"

"I'm in Atlanta, but I am thinking about coming home for the weekend," he revealed.

"Oh really? I would love that. What time will you be in?"

I really did want him to come home. I would be putting the finishing touches on the plans I had for Carl.

"I don't know yet, but I will call you on Thursday to let you know."

"Okay, baby. I'll be waiting for your call." We hung up the phone, and I realized that I had only three days before Tay's weekend trip home. So that meant that the time I had to push Carl over the edge was minimal.

The next day Carl paid me no attention, but I made sure to make him as horny as possible. I gave the servants the day off so that I could walk around the house naked. I made sure to bend over when I saw him and to sit with my legs slightly open. I even played with myself while watching TV, making sure not to even look his way. That night we went out to dinner, and I still acted like nothing had ever happened between us. This was driving Carl up the wall, and he had to speak on it.

"Are you really going to push what we did to the side just for your greed?"

"Please, Carl, I am trying to enjoy my dinner. Don't start this now."

I had to put an end to the conversation before things got nasty, but I knew that he would bring it up again. I just hoped that he didn't do it at the wrong time, like when Tay was home.

When we got home, I slipped into a red nightie and relaxed on Tay'von's big bed. I had left the bedroom door open, and Carl walked in, like I expected him to.

"Carl, you just can't walk in here. You should really know your place. You're not my man. You're Tay'von's bodyguard, so chill the fuck out."

"Don't think that I'm sweating you, Tangie. It's just that this shit is fucking with my head."

Poor thing. I knew that this would happen. I had stripped him of everything, and now he was lost. How could he look Tay'von in the face when he got back? Oh shit. I didn't even tell him that Tay was coming. Oh well. he was going to find out soon enough. I pulled the covers off me and patted the bed for him to sit down.

"Don't worry about anything, Carl. I loved sleeping with you, and like I said before, you're the best lover I have ever had. But what you need to understand is that I am thinking of bigger and better things right now. It is only after I get everything that I want that I can start to think about us."

"But life is not all about material things, Tangie. Think about—"

I had to cut him off. "To me it is. That's why I need you to be on my side, Carl. Yes, I could be with you. Hell, I could even fall in love with you someday, but I need Tay right now. Can you understand that? Once I have him, then you can have me."

Damn, I was good. You should have seen the look on his face. I had him by the heart, and I was not about to let go. He gave in, and he told me this with a deep kiss. He pushed himself on top of me, but I stopped him.

"Come on, Tangie. I just want to make love to you."

"Well, Carl, I just want you to eat my pussy."

Carl ate me out like his life depended on it. After he was done, I told him that I wanted to sleep alone. He crawled out of Tay'von's bed and went to his own.

That night, I bet that he went to bed asking himself how I was able to take his manhood away. He had always been the one to drive women crazy, and now he couldn't even sleep due to the imprint I had left on his mind. As for me, I went to bed thinking about my man coming home and about how this Carl thing was going to play out.

Chapter 4

Well, I'm Sorry For
Giving A Fuck

Yeah, I really thought I had everything together back then.

"What in the hell was I thinking?"

"What was that, honey?" my hairdresser asks when she hears me speak out loud.

"Oh, nothing. I was just talking to myself."

So much time has passed, yet I am still kicking myself in the ass over some things that I have done.

"I know what it is. You're thinking about that fine man of yours, aren't you?"

Tasha is just one of so many people who think that my life is perfect.

"And I'll tell you one thing, I will even settle for that sexy-ass Carl, Tay has guarding you," she adds.

I cringe when she says "Carl," of all people.

"Yeah, well, that's just what you would be doing, settling."

We both look over at Carl, who is sitting in the waiting area, reading an Essence *magazine. Even after all the time that has passed, he is still sexy as hell. But I have already had him, and I have been having him for some time now. He has become a leech to me, still wanting to have me, still wanting me to love him. And to think that he still gets mad when I tell him that he will never have me. He's just plain weak to me, and anyone who knows me knows that I just can't stand a weak man.*

"Yeah, I see that look in your eyes. Don't even try to play it off. I know you want some of that brother," *Tasha says.*

"Girl, please, there's nothing happening there. He doesn't make enough money for me."

"Okay, say what you want to say, but I see it, and if I'm wrong, then you're a damn fool."

"Oh really? Why is that? I have everything I want."

"Money can't make you cum, Tangie."

"Really? Just the thought of it makes me cream."

We both burst out laughing.

"Come on, Tangie. On the real tip, I know that when you get horny and Tay ain't there, you have to be going crazy."

I just smile, because I don't even have a chance to get horny anymore.

"I just don't know how you do it, with Tay gone so much. Then to have Carl walking around the house . . . Shit, I would have jumped on him a long time ago."

"Well, Tasha, some things just are not meant to be jumped on."

And we both just leave it at that.

Early Saturday morning I was awakened by a warm body next to me.

"Car . . . Tay'von, baby, what are you doing here so early?" I jumped into his arms, praying that he hadn't heard me almost call him Carl. I noticed a funny look on his face, but it faded away quickly.

"I caught an early flight. Plus, I have a big surprise for you." He took my hand and led me downstairs. When we passed by Carl's room, Tay stepped in to chat.

"What's up, nigga?" Tay asked Carl as he gave him some dap while Carl sat up in bed. As Tay held my hand and talked to Carl, I noticed that I was still wearing the red nightgown that Carl had eaten my pussy in the night before, and a chill ran through my body—a good one.

"Get your ass up, Carl. I don't pay you to sleep," Tay joked.

"Damn, Tay. You should have told me that you were coming home."

"What? Tangie didn't tell you?"

"No, I didn't. It never really came up, to tell you the truth," I said, as if it really had slipped my mind.

Carl shot me a quick hateful look, which was missed by Tay.

"So how was my girl while I was gone? She didn't do anything bad after the good news you gave me, right?" Tay asked with a smile on his face.

Carl laughed before answering, but only he and I knew what was so funny. "Nah, man. She's been your perfect little angel."

I had to put a stop to this before Tay caught on to the sarcastic tone in Carl's voice. "Come on, baby. I can't wait anymore. You can talk to Carl after you show me the surprise you got me."

"Okay, baby, let's go. Come on, Carl. You have got to see what I got my baby."

Carl got out of bed and followed us to the front door. Tay put his hand over my eyes and walked me outside. He took his hands away from my eyes, and I saw one BMW 7 Series and one white Range Rover.

"Oh my God, Tay. Are both of these for me?" I asked as I walked toward the fire-red convertible with the big black bow around it.

"I got the other one so that when you're going out with your friends, you'll have more room," Tay said about the white Range Rover.

All I could think was that I didn't really have that many friends, but I wasn't going to tell him that.

"You like them, right?"

"Yes, yes, yes, Tay. I love them."

I ran over to the BMW and got in it. It was all decked out. He even had had my name put on the headrest. Tay'von told Carl to get the camera so that he could take pictures of me in my new cars. I sat on the hood of the convertible, and my red nightgown melted into the red paint. As I posed for the camera, Tay talked to Carl in a low tone so that he wouldn't rain on my parade, but I could still hear what he was saying and took notes in my mind to use later on, if I had to.

"Look at her, man. She's like a big kid that just got a new bike." Tay smiled and continued to speak as he realized that what started out as a publicity stunt had changed and formed itself into something real. "She's happy as shit, and to tell you the truth, it makes me feel good as hell."

Carl held in his feelings about the situation and forced a smile on his face as I walked over to the next car and started to pose with it.

"You don't think that I am moving too fast, do you?" Tay said.

"What do you mean?" Carl asked, knowing exactly what Tay was asking.

"As far as buying her the cars and letting her stay in my house?" Before Carl could respond, Tay continued to speak. "She is just so in your face, and you know how much I like a bold bitch. I have never met a girl like her before. And you know that I have had my share of groupies and all, but there's just something about her. Just look at her, man. I can't help but to fall this fast for her. She got a nigga hooked, and there's nothing that I could do about it."

Carl stopped snapping shots and looked at me. The look on Carl's face told all his secrets. He looked envious, like he wanted to be the one in Tay's place. As if he wanted to be the man who was making me so damn happy.

"Nah, man, you did the right thing. Look at her. She's so excited. Just follow your heart and try not to break too many on the way. Speaking of broken hearts, what are you going to do about Connie?"

Tay shook his head. "Man, I don't know. I still got love for her too, but this is different. I'll deal with that once I've got an answer to your question, because the truth is that I still don't know. But I will still need you to watch her. The cars don't mean shit to me. If she's not who I think she is, then I'll put her and the cars out. And then I'll go back to what I have with Connie."

While they spoke, I wondered who Connie was. I had never seen him out with a specific female. He was always seen with random industry girls.

"Okay, I'll keep an eye on her, but you really have to think about what you're going to do. Connie is a good person, and if you choose to be with Tangie, well, you should let Connie know before she sees that shit in some magazine or on TV," Carl replied.

"I feel you on that one, but this is just a fucked-up situation. You know I got love for that girl, but Tangie, Tangie is—"

"I know, Tay. I totally understand. She seems like one badass bitch."

Before Carl walked back into the house, he looked back and saw Tay in between my legs. I kissed Tay softly as my heart filled with gratitude.

I wondered if Carl's heart was filled with jealousy and rage. The look on his face sure did make it seem like it was.

***

Later on, I got dressed in a short gold Dior dress and matching shoes. I wore my long hair down, and I made sure not to forget my ice. Tay'von hadn't told me where we were going, but he had told me to pack an overnight bag. I stood in front of the bathroom mirror and looked at myself. My bluish-gray eyes shined like twinkling stars. Most people thought I wore contacts, and they usually were pleased when they found out that my eye color was real. My island tanned skin set off my long, wavy jet-black hair perfectly.

My mother had always said that even when a woman had nothing else to offer, she should always have her looks. She had made sure to live that way until the day the private jet that was taking her to a modeling gig crashed and killed her. Many people said that I was the spitting image of her, except for the color of my eyes. That was the only thing that I got from the Brazilian photographer my mother had fucked. After he had found out that she was pregnant, he never spoke to her again, nor did she ever try to make him. In the little time that she had to raise me, she had made sure that I knew the value of a good life and myself.

"Try to live a life that is worth more than you are. That will be hard, because you are worth the world," she would say as I sat and watched the makeup artist do her face.

These words had always stuck with me. Even when I didn't have a penny to my name, I always made sure that I looked like a million bucks.

"Damn, baby. I'm going to have to keep you close tonight. You look good as hell," Tay said when he peeked in the bathroom and saw me.

"You know that's right. As fine as I am, every man will want to snatch me up."

"I'll kill a man before I let you go. Besides, I am going to have a hard time selling your cars with your name being on the headrest and all."

We both laughed and headed downstairs. Tony, another one of Tay's bodyguards, and Carl were already in the car, waiting for us. I wondered what Tay had planned as I stepped in the limo.

"So where are we going?" I asked after Tay got in and lit a blunt.

I didn't get an answer. Tay just smiled that sexy smile of his and passed me the blunt. My mother also used to say that there was nothing worse than a woman who was dressed up and smoking, but hey, I loved my weed.

A little while later, we arrived at the airport, and my heart skipped a beat. Although I had traveled a lot, it still didn't stop that feeling I got when I had to get on a plane. I always thought of my mother and her horrible crash whenever I was near one. Once we all stepped out of the car, an airport worker took us to a side entrance, ushered us inside, and got us checked in quickly. They did that so that they didn't have a madhouse when people recognized Tay. As soon as we were done checking in, we headed outside and started walking toward the private jet, and I came face-to-face with the thing I hated the most. I didn't know if anyone else noticed it, but I started to have a panic attack. I felt like my lungs were closing up, and I started to see little red spots.

"Tangie, Tangie, what's wrong?" I heard Tay asking me from afar, but I couldn't answer. I just kept my eyes on the jet until I blacked out. When I woke up, I was sitting on one of the airport's golf carts.

"Are you okay, baby?" Tay asked as he handed me bottled water.

I had to look around to realize that I was still at the airport. I looked at Tay, then at Carl, who looked even more concerned than Tay did. "I'm fine. It's just that—" I stopped myself.

This wasn't the time to disclose what scared me, especially to a man who could possibly be gone within a month. None of my conquests ever lasted too long. We'd spend time, they'd spend money, and soon enough, it would be over. I wasn't the type to let men get too close, and I wasn't about to start.

"I just need to go to the bathroom. Do we have enough time?"

I got up but was still a little dizzy. Tay'von grabbed on to me so that I didn't fall over, but I pulled away from him.

"I told you that I'm fine, didn't I?" I snapped.

"No you're not. Carl will go with you."

I wasn't into Tay being so sweet and helpful. He was trying to get too close, and me keeping him at bay was the only way to keep my head on straight and get to the money. Carl held on to me, and we walked to the bathroom so that I could get myself together.

When he thought that I was alone in the bathroom, Carl walked in, and I really was not in the mood for that.

"Hey, baby. Are you okay?" he said.

Baby? Oh, this dude is trippin'.

"Is there something that you need in here? If not, get out."

"I just came in to make sure you were okay, that's all."

"Well, for the last fucking time, I'm fine!"

He got pissed off and started to walk out. "Well, I'm sorry for giving a fuck," he said as the door closed behind him.

I tried to get myself together enough to get on the plane, but I was still shaky. I stuck my head out of the bathroom and told Carl to get Tony. A couple of minutes later, Tony walked into the bathroom, and I locked the door behind him.

"You have got to give me a little candy, Tony! Or I will not make this flight."

"Girl, are you crazy? I can't give you anything in here."

"Come on, Tony. I won't be able to get on that jet without it. We can go in a stall, and no one will know. Hell, you went through the airport with it, and you didn't get caught, so please . . . It's the only way."

Tony must have felt really sorry for me, because he took my hand and walked me into one of the stalls. He gave me the little bag of cocaine, and I stuck my nose in it and took a long, deep breath. It hit me hard but good. I gave him back the bag and closed my eyes as I felt the drug rushing through my body.

"So are you ready to go now?" Tony asked me, looking all nervous and shit.

"As ready as I will ever be," I said as I held on to his arm and we wiped my nose. I walked back to where Tay and Carl were waiting, with a big shit-eating grin on my face.

Once we were seated on the private jet, Tay leaned over and asked me why I had sent Carl back for Tony.

"I needed something sweet to sniff," I answered.

"Starting the party early, I see."

"You know me. It's always a party when I'm around, but since we are now on the plane, can you please tell me where we are going?" I said as the effect of the drug I had sniffed hit me like a ton of bricks.

"Vegas, baby," Tay said with a smile, and all I could think of to say was, "Sounds fun."

I had done Vegas so many times with so many different rappers that it wasn't a big deal to me.

By the time we landed in Vegas, my high was gone, and I was ready to get off the plane. Our reservations were for the best suite at the Palms Casino Resort Hotel. Once there, we put our things in the Dream Suite Penthouse C, and I freshened up so that we could all go down to the casino together. Once down there, I played so many different games that I lost count. I had never really been a gambler, but the free drinks that they gave you made you think that you could eventually win at something.

Tay'von had given me twenty-five thousand dollars to blow, and before long I was down to my last ten. I took it hard every time I lost a game, and I got angrier and angrier. Tay thought that it was so cute that I was a sore loser. He even found my temper tantrums funny.

"Aw, don't get so upset, Tangie. You just have to find your game," Tay said when I lost another thousand.

I realized that poker was not my game, so I moved to the blackjack table with Tay. Carl and Tony stood to the side and watched us play. Carl had been looking so down that even Tony had noticed. He walked over to Carl and had a conversation with him, which he thought I couldn't hear.

"What's wrong with you, nigga? You look like she's losing *your* money or something."

"I'm just sick of standing around while this bitch blows through Tay's money," Carl responded.

"Well, I don't give a fuck, and you shouldn't, either," Tony said.

"I just don't understand how Tay can be so blind. First, he buys her those cars, and now he brings her to Vegas and hands her a grip of money. I know that she's fine and all, but he doesn't even know her that well."

"Carl, just stay out of Tay's business. It's always better that way. He's a grown-ass man, and I am sure that he knows what he is doing. Just do what you are getting paid to do and stay out of it," Tony said as he and Carl looked over at me. "But she is fine, though. I bet she's turning Tay's ass out every chance she gets."

"Oh, trust me, she is. I mean, she has to be for him to be acting the way he is," Carl answered while catching himself.

They stopped talking, and I downed one drink after the other while blowing most of my money away. By the time we made it back to the suite, I had only three thousand dollars and could hardly walk. Tay assured me that there would be more money to gamble with the next day.

"Tony, I need a little more candy," I said as I took off my shoes and sat on the couch.

"Damn, girl, you're going to put a third hole in your nose with all that shit you're sniffing," Tay'von answered as he rolled up his weed.

"The same hole that you're putting in your chest with all the shit you're smoking," I said with a smile.

Tony brought over the coke, and I lined it out on the coffee table. The four lines disappeared into my nose; then I let out a sneeze.

"I hope that you're not doing that much coke while I am out on tour," Tay said with a disapproving look on his face.

"As hard as you've got Carl watching me, I can't even wash my ass without him telling you.

So I'm sure that you know the answer to that question."

"Well, I am happy that you know that Carl is watching, because he's my third eye," Tay replied.

I looked over at Carl, and he seemed uneasy and stiff. Tony and Tay'von both laughed.

"Well, you better get a fourth one," I said while laughing.

I didn't think that Tay got what I was saying, but it looked like Tony did.

"Shit, with Carl, I don't need a fourth eye. With him by my side, I know that I will always have all the info that I need," Tay observed.

I didn't want this conversation to get any deeper, so I turned to one of my tricks. "Is it hot in here, or is it just me?"

"Here. Smoke this. It will mellow you out," Tay said as he handed me his blunt.

"Nah. I need to take this damn dress off. You all don't mind, do you?"

Carl and Tony both looked at Tay'von.

"Go ahead, baby. These niggas are cool. I'm sure that they don't mind."

"Hell, no, we don't mind," Tony said with a smile.

"Yeah, okay. Just remember that all you can do is look," Tay warned, yet in a joking tone.

I pulled off my dress, and I sat there in my thong, since I didn't have on a bra. I picked up the coke and handed it to Tay. He shook his head no, but I needed him to get really high for what I was about to do.

"Come on, Tay. You're not going to let me party by myself, are you? Just do two lines and I'll leave you alone."

I sat in his lap and lined up the coke. I got up, held the hundred-dollar bill up to his nose, and he sniffed up the powder. Thirty minutes later he had matched my number of lines and was high as hell. He reached for the remote and flipped on the TV. He came to the adult movie channel and left it there. I could tell that he was starting to get turned on, so I leaned in and nibbled on his ears and neck.

"You better stop, or else we're gonna end up putting on a freak show for these niggas," Tay said with closed eyes, but I didn't stop.

I licked his neck and moved my hand down to his chest. He kissed me, and I got on his lap again and wrapped my legs around him. He kissed me slowly before I pulled away and put my nipple up to his lips. He kissed around my nipple before licking it and making it hard.

"Damn, baby. I have missed you so much," I said and let out a moan as he licked me hungrily.

I felt his fingers run down my back, and then he squeezed my ass as if it were putty.

"Uh, you want us to leave, man?" Carl asked, looking like he wanted to leave, anyway.

"Nah, you're cool. We're just fucking around." Tay may have thought that we were just fucking around, but I planned on fucking him in front of Carl. I just didn't know when I would get the chance, but luckily for me, this trip came up fast.

I slide myself off Tay and got on my knees in front of him. I undid his belt and unzipped his pants. I pulled his dick out and jerked it off slowly. His body moved with my hand as I got his dick fully hard.

"Are you watching this shit, man? This chick is crazy," Tony whispered as he hit Carl on the arm.

"Man, I ain't trying to watch this. They should take this to the bedroom," Carl said.

"Man, fuck that. I want to see what this bitch can do," Tony said as he started to get into my little show.

Tay and I both heard them, but neither of us cared. Carl said nothing after that; he just stared, looking as if he was trying to control his anger. I put Tay's dick in my mouth and enjoyed the taste and feel of it. I put all of it down my throat as he let out a loud grunt.

"Damn, Tangie. That shit is feeling good as hell."

"Come on, Tay. I want to taste that cream, baby," I said after removing his dick, which had been crammed into my mouth.

But before he could cum, he pulled my head up. I stood in front of him, and I put one of my feet up on the couch.

Tay'von didn't even take my thong off. He just pushed it to the side and plunged into my pussy. He sucked on my clit and fingered my pussy at the same time. I pushed his head deeper into me until I came in his mouth. I pushed his head away after I was done, and pulled his pants off. I sat on his dick, facing Tony and Carl. At first, I fucked only the head of Tay's dick. But then my cum ran down his dick, making it easier for me to slide all the way down on it. I fucked him nice and slow while Carl and Tony watched my every move. I looked into Carl's eyes and smiled when I realized how mad he looked. Now he realized that all of this was for him. How could he have let himself fall into my trap? I silently asked myself.

I started to move my mouth, and then I silently mouthed words to Carl as I fucked Tay. "You want me, don't you?"

Tony caught the whole exchange.

Carl saw me but acted like he didn't, so I said it out loud.

"You want me, don't you?"

"Yes, yes, baby, I want you," Tay'von answered.

"I make you feel good, don't I?"

"Yeah, baby, you make me feel real fucking good," Tay answered yet again, not realizing that I was talking to Carl.

I started to fuck him even faster, making him lose control.

"You love me, don't you?"

No answer, but I continued to look directly into Carl's eyes.

"I asked if you love me."

As Tay'von came, his filter was gone. I had him open, and he couldn't help himself. "Oh shit. I love you, baby. I love you."

Again, I creamed on his dick and said my own "I love yous." "I love you too, Tay. I love your dick, I love your kiss, and I love everything about you." I got up and sat on his lap again, facing him, and kissed him passionately. "I really do love you, Tay'von." I looked into his eyes, and I saw softness there, and for a second, I even saw true love.

"Yeah, I got much love for you too, Tangie." He looked at me and smiled. I smiled too.

Later, he would tell me that in me, he saw a soft little doll-like woman who needed to be loved. He would also say that he saw a woman who thought that she was in love, but he made a decision at that moment to make me really love him. He needed me in more ways than I could ever understand, so my loving him was a plus.

"Damn, girl. You got me all fucked up. I'm really going to have to watch out for myself and make sure you're just not running a good game on me," Tay said after a moment.

"You don't have to watch out, Tay. I am really trying to be all about you." I turned around, lit a jay, and looked at Carl. "There is nobody who can change my mind about that. Plus, no one else could afford me," I said in a joking tone, but Carl knew that I was talking to him. I was hoping he would remember the comment I had made about him making pennies and would put two and two together.

"You've got that right, 'cause you ran through my money like water tonight," Tay'von said, sounding as if he really didn't give a damn about the money I blew.

I could almost see steam coming off Carl's head, while Tony just sat there as if he was watching *One Life to Live*. And to be honest, I liked Carl, but I hated his paycheck, and that was all I cared about at the moment.

Chapter 5

Even Though He Was
Knee-Deep In The Act
Of Betrayal, He Knew She
Had A Heart Of Gold

I know that at this point people must think that I am one fucked-up individual. To some, sex is something that should be done in bed between two people. Some people may have to love or even like the people they sleep with. But at that time in my life, money, sex, love, and hate were all the same. I still have to ask myself at times if I'm really satisfied with just being Tay'von's wife. The money is wonderful, but as far as having him as my man, well, it could have been any ballplayer, rapper, or actor, to tell you the truth. I loved and still do

*love Tay'von, but that love was built on the
paychecks he received and spent on me.*

*After getting my hair done, I walk up to the
counter so that I can pay. Tasha comes up to
me and gives me a last-minute reminder.*

*"Just remember that the ride in the car is not
the only ride Carl can give you."*

*I share a smile with her as I think about all
the rides I have gotten from Carl over the years.*

*"Okay Tasha. I'll see you in a couple of days.
This time let's make the appointment at my
house."*

During our trip in Vegas, we did it all. We
shopped, gambled, did drugs, had sex, and
ate at five-star restaurants. This was such a
welcomed trip, since I had been missing Tay so
much. I decided to lay off Carl until we got back
home, giving him a chance to recuperate. I gave
Tay'von all my attention since he would be with
me for only two more days. I had been thinking
about things, and I really did not want to be left
behind this time. I was sure that Tay was having
a lot of fun without me, but it was time for me to
have my own fun.

While we lay in bed after another round of
mind-blowing sex, I brought it up.

"Tay, how come you never ask me to go on the road with you?"

"I just never thought that you would want to go. Plus, that is the fastest way to fuck up a good relationship."

I looked at him as if he was trying to run game on me. "Come on, honey, you can do much better than that. If you have another bitch or two who are on the road with you, then just say so."

Tay'von sat up and picked up the jay that was on the nightstand. He lit it, then spoke. "What makes you think that I am fucking other people?"

He must have realized how dumb his question was, because he started to smile as soon as the words left his mouth.

"Come on, Mr. Too Fine. Who do you think you're trying to fool? You have the number one song out right now, you're sexy as hell, and you're out on tour without your girlfriend. So don't ask me why I think that you are sleeping with other women. I am not new to this game, Tay."

By then, Tay was laughing so hard that he had started to choke on his blunt. He had always known that I was smart, but he had thought that I would be naive about his indiscretions.

"Look, all I am saying is that I don't want to mess things up. But if you really want to come with me, then, hey, do you. But just know that it will not always be about partying and getting high. There will be times when you won't see me or be around me. There will be a lot of girls and people around, period."

He looked at me, hoping that his words would make me change my mind, but there was no way that I would back down and decline his invitation.

"I'm going, and I will even make a deal with you. You can do whatever it is that you have always done when I wasn't there, and I will not get in your way."

He looked at me as if he was trying to read my thoughts. He wondered if I was telling the truth or if I was just saying this so that he would really let me go with him.

"You mean to tell me that when I get up to go out, you're not going to question me about where I am going?"

I got on top of him, kissed his neck, then started working my way down, way down.

"You can do whatever you want, Tay, but there are some things that you will want me to be there for, don't you think?" I asked as I moved my head down to his dick.

By the time he came from my feel-good head, I had a yes as an answer to whatever question I asked. After a fast few days in Vegas, we headed home.

We went to lunch the next day with Tay's friend and fellow tour mate. He had called the house and had told Tay that he had some good news, so we had all decided to make an outing of it. Before lunch I was running late, as always, so I had told Tay to go ahead and that I would meet him at the restaurant.

A half an hour later, I showed up at La' Tre. I walked in the place as if I owned it, and all eyes were on me. I was shown to the table where Tay; his friend Black Dialect, as he was known in the rap world; and Black Dialect's girlfriend, Shamika, were sitting.

Black was the first one to stand up, and his girlfriend noticed. He had a smile on his face that told me that he was stunned yet pleased, and so was I. I had seen him in his videos and knew that he was fine, but I had always thought that he was too short for me. He stood at a tall six feet and was the spitting image of the rapper Common. Just as light, just as bald, and just as sexy. I wondered if I would ever get a chance to ride what I knew was his well-hung dick. I caught the look on his girlfriend's face, which lasted only a few seconds. She hated me already.

"Well, this is Tangie. She's fashionably late, as always," Tay said as he stood up and pulled out my chair.

"I'm sure that she always has a good reason, unless she wakes up looking this good," Black gleefully said with a friendly smile on his face.

"Yeah, well, she's here now, so let's order," Shamika spit out, with her attitude showing through the fake smile that was splattered across her face.

I really wanted to tell that hood rat that I could speak for myself, but I let her slide. She was just trying to take all the attention off me, and I wasn't going to let that happen.

"This is Shamika," Black said, introducing his trash box to me, and I wasn't impressed.

I held my hand out to shake hers, but she just looked at it. She was just used to saying, "What's up?" to everyone she met, without shaking their hand. I left my hand out, refusing to be ignored, and she finally took it and shook it hard. I took my time to look her over and had to stop myself from laughing. That day I had on Louis Vuitton—all black, with diamonds to shine—but that bitch had gone overboard. She had on every designer in the world. I could tell right away that she was a total label ho. Her hair was a bright red, and she had on way too much makeup. When it came to her bling, or the lack thereof, she had on gold, silver, and even a wooden anklet. The only thing good that I could say about her was that she looked like she might have a cute face under all that makeup and that her bright weave was glued in right. I couldn't look at her anymore, so I turned my attention back to the men.

"So did I miss the big news, or did you all wait for me?" I asked.

"They waited," Shamika said while rolling her eyes.

I reached over and put my hand on Black's arm. "Well, I'm ready to hear the good news if you're ready to tell me," I said as I slid my hand off his arm slowly. I winked at Tay, letting him know that I was just doing this to piss Shamika off. He smiled, and I assumed it was because he had noticed the change in Shamika's attitude after I walked in. She deserved everything that was coming to her, and he knew it.

"I wanted to tell Tay that I just got picked up to do *All Bases of Hip-Hop* full-time. I will no longer be a guest star who just shows up at certain cities, but a headliner, just like him." Black beamed.

"Get the fuck out of here. That's some real good news, man," Tay said as he stood up and gave his friend a man hug.

"Ever since my single hit number four on the hip-hop charts and the album hit number two, it has been on and poppin'."

"I think that is wonderful," I said as I reached over and touched Black's arm again.

Tay ordered champagne and then told everyone that I would be joining him out on tour. Shamika had always gone on the road with Black, so my news was nothing new to her.

"Girl, being on tour ain't shit. Most of the time you're by yourself, and the other half you have to put up with them hoes and niggas that just want to hang around a rapper," she informed me.

The table got quiet. A minute later Tay and Black got up to go to the bathroom, leaving Shamika and me at the table. I picked up my glass and sipped my drink. I hoped she would keep her mouth shut until they came back, but I should have known that I was asking for too much.

"So you really want to go on tour with us, huh?" she asked.

"Yeah, that is what you just heard, right?" I answered in the same tone she had asked me her question in—sarcastic as hell.

"Look, Angie, Tangie, or whatever your name is, I just want to let you know that it takes a special kind of girl to go the road with these rap niggas. Just know that who they are at home is not who they are when they are on the road."

"You may be right, Jameeka, or whatever your name is. Not just any kind of girl can hang. I am a woman who is well aware of what goes on while the men are on tour. It wasn't so long ago that I was one of them girls who were out to land a rap star, so I'll be okay."

Shamika just laughed. She looked me up and down, then continued to give me her unrequested opinion. "Look at you, Tangie. You're not hood enough to handle them bitches. I bet if it wasn't for you hanging out with Tay and them, you wouldn't even know what a rap song was. Come on, how many of them hoes do you think is going to know where to put the napkin at dinner or which fork to use for a salad? As soon as you walked in, I knew that you were a stuck-up, wannabe high-class ho."

I looked at her as if she had lost her mind. "So are you saying that I have to act like a ghetto, hood-rat chick in order to go on the road with Tay?"

"No, I'm not saying all of that, but we will see how long you're going to be acting all ladylike when some half-dressed, ready-to-fuck ho is at your man's dressing-room door."

"We will see, Shamika. We will see," was all that I said. That low-class hooker just didn't know that I was twice as good, if not three times better, at the game we were all playing.

A year later, Tay would recount the talk the two men had shared in the bathroom that day.

"Man, your girl is something else. How is she just going to come out and say some shit like that?" Tay asked as he shook his head.

"Don't pay her any mind. That's just how she is. She's been holding me down since back in the day. She even used to do my runs with me, so you know how that is. You just can't leave them behind, just 'cause you make it big."

Tay'von could understand. That was how things were with him and his last and somewhat current girlfriend, Connie. Tay let his thoughts linger on her for a second. She had always been a good woman. She had even fronted him the money to make a demo when his first record deal went bad. Things had been good until she went out on tour with him and he chose fame over her. It took a long time to patch things up with her after that, but he made sure she forgave him. Even though he was knee-deep in his act of betrayal, he knew that she had a heart of gold.

"My question to you is, where did you find Tangie? She's fine as hell."

Tay smiled proudly at his friend. "Man, if I told you, you wouldn't believe me."

"Try me."

Tay went over every detail of our first days together. By the time he was done, Black was standing there with his mouth open. He was amazed and wanted to know even more.

"So you've been kicking it with her ever since?"

"Yeah, after having to kind of push Connie aside. I really wasn't looking for a girlfriend, but Tangie just kind of fell in my lap. And I have to say that I am cool with having one. She's not a ghetto chick, and she's fine as hell. Plus, she's a real freak, and I love me a girl that's classy but knows how to get down in the bed, ya feel me?"

Black nodded. "Yeah, I hear that. Well, if you don't change your mind about her going on tour with us, how about you ask her to help Shamika out? I love her and all, but I just want her to be a little more refined. The ghetto shit was all right for the hood, but you can't act or look like that everywhere you go. Just see if Tangie can help her out with her attitude, but mostly with her style."

They shared a laugh. Tay was happy that his friend could see that his girl needed some help, because he was thinking the same thing. He promised Black that he would ask me for my help, and then they left the bathroom.

About an hour later we finished our lunch and said our goodbyes in the parking lot. I headed to my car, and as I leaned over to put the rest of my lunch on the backseat, Black could no longer control himself. He just had to sneak a look at my ass. Tay saw him, and so did Shamika. She seemed pissed off, while Tay'von loved the attention I got. Having both his friends and strangers gawk at me meant that he had a five-star chick on his hands, which made him proud. As Black looked as if he was thinking about what I might look like naked, I thought about the road ahead and what or whom it would bring my way.

Chapter 6

Winner Takes All, And

I Was Born A Winner

"*So where are we headed?*" *Carl asks as we enter the car. He has been so cold these days. I wonder if he's finally fed up with the head games that I have been playing all these years or if the wound goes deeper. I have in my possession the only two other things besides myself that Carl would kill for. I do not keep them away from him out of spite or hate. I keep them from him because that is how it has to be. Besides, I'm not even sure if they really belong to him. So, why wake the sleeping monster when life is peaceful while he hibernates?*

"*Well, since I just got my hair done, maybe you should take me out to lunch.*"

He just nods his head and says okay. Days change, but some things will always stay the same.

***

"So what was that all about?" Tay asked as we headed back home from the restaurant. He had left his car at the restaurant so he could ride with me. His bodyguards would retrieve it later.

"That bitch Shamika had it coming. You saw how she was looking at me. She hated me from the minute I walked into La' Tre's. I can't help that she came in there looking a hot mess."

Tay'von laughed as if his sides hurt.

I went on. "What in the hell is he doing with her, anyways? Did you see all the things she had on at one time? I hope he knows that he can't take her anywhere serious."

As the words came out of my mouth, I started to really think about it. There Black was, a man who could be Common's twin, and he was with a low-class Keyshia Cole–looking chick.

"I asked him the same thing in the bathroom, and he told me that she has been with him since back in the day. You know, on some street shit," Tay'von replied.

"Have you ever seen her before?"

"Yeah, but it's always been in passing," Tay answered.

"Well, I don't give a fuck that she was down with him or for how long. That bitch needs a stylist."

That one sent Tay into a deeper laughing fit. But I wasn't joking. What was she thinking when she left the house, looking like that?

"Aw, come on, Tangie. Play nice. She didn't look that bad. Her clothes are crazy, but she has a cute face and a nice body. She just needs help with her presentation. Oh, and by the way, Black asked me to ask you to help her out with that."

"Help her out with what? That bitch is rude as hell! Plus, she's a grown-ass woman and should be able to help herself."

"Come on, baby. Just do it for me. You do know that since you're going to be out on tour with us, she will be everywhere you are. Do you really want to be seen with her if she's dressed like that?"

Tay thought that he was so slick, but what he said did have some truth to it.

"Fine. I'll help her out, but if that bitch says anything nasty to me, I am going to fuck her up."

Tay'von knew that I meant what I said, so he then said he prayed that Shamika stayed cool. He didn't want me to put my foot up her ass, which would create tension on an easygoing tour.

After Tay and I got home, Carl and Tony went back to the restaurant for Tay's car. I took a nap before the maid came up and helped me pack. By eight the next morning, we were dressed and ready to go out on tour together.

The first stop was Maryland. That was one of my favorite states. It had a vibe to it like no other. I could never get enough of that place. Once in Silver Spring, we checked into the best hotel the city had to offer. As soon as we got settled, the tour manager called the suite and reminded Tay that he had a sound check at six that evening. I sure as hell was not going to any sound check, so I told Tay that I would meet him at the concert. Plus, I had to get my shit together. There were always major players at those things, and you never knew. Maybe I could trade in a used man for a new and better one.

It was around eleven o'clock in the morning, so I called the front desk and asked an attendant to set up an appointment for me at the best spa in town. About five minutes later the attendant called back and told me that the spa that I wanted was booked solid. I asked her for the spa's number and called it myself. It was the only spa in town that really knew how to take care of black people, and I wasn't taking no for an answer.

"Hello. Body and Soul. How may I help you?"

I told the woman about the hotel calling for me, said that I needed an appointment for that day, and explained that I just couldn't wait for them to fit me in.

"Well, we're sorry, miss. We cannot fit anyone else in today. How about Monday?" *Monday? Monday is two days away. That just won't do.*

"Well, how about I let you speak with my boyfriend? I'm sure you will have some room then."

I took the phone over to Tay, and he knew what was up. I had used him before to get what I wanted. That was the upside of fame. People would kick their own parents out of anywhere just to get you in. All I had to do was put him on the phone. He gave the woman his name and told her to call the hotel back to verify that he was telling her the truth. Once people in service realized that it was really Mr. Too Fine, they always changed their tone. And if they didn't, he would threaten to tell his celebrity friends how unaccommodating they were. This always worked, as it did that day. By the time he hung up, I had an appointment for a full treatment that day at no cost.

I decided to take a nap before my appointment, so that I would feel my best later on. An hour later, as Tony shook me awake, I heard Tay whisper to him to tell me that he was going out

with Carl. By the way Tay said this and then ran
out the door, I knew that something was up. But
I wasn't going to say anything. A promise was a
promise, so I had to keep my mouth shut. I got
up to go to the bathroom and get ready for the
spa, but before I took a step, Tony grabbed my
arm gently and turned me around.

"Tangie, there's something that I need to talk
to you about."

Okay, I had to think for a minute. There I
was, just waking up, and Tony wanted to talk
to me? He hardly ever spoke to me. I wanted
to hear this, so I sat down on the bed, with no
expression on my face.

"So talk," I told him, halfway annoyed.

"Nah, you go ahead and get ready. Tay would
kill me if you were late tonight just because I
wanted to talk to you."

I didn't even look at him. I just got up and got
ready. I wasn't going to rush him.

By two o'clock, we were in the car, heading
to the spa, and since I didn't want to seem like
I was pressing him, we just drove quietly for ten
minutes. It seemed like he was having trouble
saying what he wanted to say, so I waited some
more.

Finally, he spoke. "Look, I'm not trying to get
all up in your business, but are you with Tay

'cause you really like him, or are you just along for the ride?"

"Now, why would you ask me that, Tony?" I asked. I had got caught off guard by his question.

"Well, let me ask you what I really want to ask. Now, just sit back and don't get mad. Just tell me straight up."

I kept quiet and smoked my weed, waiting for his question.

"What is going on between you and Carl?"

We were at a stop sign, and I could see him looking at me through the rearview mirror. Tony trying to catch my reaction made me not give him one.

"Carl just watches over me while Tay is gone, and that's all. Why are you asking me this?"

"Well, that's the question of the day, isn't it? Why do I ask? Well, maybe it's because of that night in Vegas. I saw you mouthing words to Carl—"

I cut him off. "No, you saw me mouthing words to Tay. I was talking shit to my man while fucking him, that's it. You do remember who my man is, right? You know, the one who pays you?"

I was trying the same shit that I had always used on Carl, but Tony just laughed.

"Damn, baby girl, relax. I'm just telling you what I saw. I have been working with Carl ever since Tay blew up, so I know him as well as I know the back of my hand. I know when something is up."

"Well, if you really do know him that well, then you wouldn't be sitting in this car, asking me these questions. You would already know the answers."

"Well, how do you know that I didn't ask Carl and that he didn't tell me the truth about you two? Maybe I am just asking you as the icing on the cake."

"Look, Tony, I am with Tay, not with you or Carl. So let me just make it clear. My pussy belongs to me, and I can give it to whomever I please. So don't ever ask me about who I am fucking again. If it's not you, then it's none of your business."

"Did you ever stop to think that maybe that house has cameras? How do you know that everything you have done in that house isn't on a tape somewhere?"

My heart skipped a beat, but I didn't show it. "If there was a tape, then you wouldn't be asking me this, because you would already know that there is nothing between Carl and me. So just shut the fuck up and drive."

Tony just kept on laughing, and that was making my stomach do flips. I was going to end up feeling sick for the rest of the day. What would I do if there really were cameras in the house? Tay would leave me for sure. I would have to come up with a plan to find out the truth so I could take the right course of action to get rid of any evidence.

Two hours later I walk out of Body and Soul, feeling a little more relaxed than how I had felt walking in. I was just happy that Tony kept his mouth shut as we drove back to the hotel. Once we made it to the suite, I saw that Tay'von was still not back.

"Do you have any candy, Tony?" I asked as I lay back on the couch.

Tony shook his head yes as he pulled a ziplock bag of the drug out of his pocket. I took the bag from him and cut the drug into two thin lines on the coffee table. I asked Tony if he wanted to join me, but he said no. I sniffed up my two lines and pulled off my pants. I threw my legs up on the couch, and although I was wearing a gold thong, you could clearly see the shape of my phat pussy lips through it.

Tony smiled and said, "Is this how you got Carl?"

"Why? Is this how I can get you?"

"Hey, I see your angle. You're young, sexy, and clearly dangerous. I'm not hating or anything, but just know that your moves are not on the same level as mines. Okay, so you take off your pants and sit with your legs spread." He smiled and shook his head and continued. "Do you know how many girls I see while on the road with Tay who play the same games that you do? These games aren't anything new, Tangie."

I stood up and put my hands on my hips. "Well, if my game isn't up to par, then where are all the other girls, Tony? Why is it that I am here and they are not?" I asked as I put one of my legs up on the arm of the chair that he was sitting in.

I pulled my thong to one side and got closer to his face. "Nigga, you haven't even seen my game, so what do you know?"

I spread my pussy lips so that he could get a better look at my cave. "Take a good look, Tony. This hole doesn't look like them other bitches' shit that you are used to seeing. I do everything I can to keep my shit tight, so don't put those other bitches' game up against mine."

Tony reached up and touched me. He played with my clit, then put his finger in me. I closed my eyes and enjoyed it. He slid a second finger in, then tried to put in a third. I held my pussy tight, and he couldn't get it in.

"Yeah, okay, you got a tight little cat, I'll give you that, but look at you."

He kept on fingering me, then pushed my leg down and stood up. He then pulled the same leg up and held it while pulling me closer to him. He used his thumb to rub my clit as he used a finger to fuck me.

"Look at you, Tangie. You're just like the rest of them. Here you are in your superstar boyfriend's hotel room, and you have his bodyguard's hand in your pussy. Is this what having a tight game is?"

He laughed but continued to finger fuck me until I came. It was feeling way too good for me to stop him and slap him, so I finished getting off before doing so. But he didn't just take it. After I slapped the taste out of his mouth, he grabbed me close and slid the fingers that he had just had inside me into my mouth. This was turning me on, so I sucked them.

"Yeah, you're a nice little ho. I know that Tay is fucking your ass good, and I also know that Carl is too." He smiled like he knew all the answers to his own questions. "Who's next?"

I made sure I licked his fingers clean, then told him the truth. "It's not you, so don't worry about it."

He touched my breasts, then moved down to my ass. We stood there in what looked like a hugging position while he put his lips to my ear.

"Bitch, it's just a matter of time before Tay'von sees you for who you really are. And when he's no longer blinded by your fat ass and your tight little pussy, you'll be out, just like the ones who were here before you. Then you'll be here fucking me, hoping that I can hook you back up with Tay. But it will be too late, and I'll just fuck you and move on. That's how it always goes down, Tangie, and your story won't be any different."

"So do you really want to play this game with me, Tony?"

Again, he laughed. "Well, you know what they say, don't you? Players are always going to play, right?"

"Well, game on, then, muthafucka. I sure hope that you're ready to really get down, 'cause once you take a seat at my game table, there's no second place. Winner takes all, and I was born a winner."

And with my last warning, he left.

After what had just gone down with Tony, I needed to take a nap. He had just worked my last nerve, and I was not in a happy mood. I rested for about three hours, then woke up and took a hot shower. I couldn't wait to see who was going to be at the show. I was sure that I was going to be one of the hottest bitches there, and I was ready to strut my stuff.

After my shower, I lotioned up and put on some of my Donna Karan Cashmere Mist perfume. It was soft and sweet and always made me feel like a true woman. That night I was wearing Gucci from head to toe. I put on tiny black shorts and very high heels. For my top, I put on a see-through black cupped shirt that had gold sparkles around the neck that dripped all the way down between my breasts. I added a gold Gucci belt and clutch as finishing touches. I looked at myself, and I was happy with how I looked, so I made my way down to the waiting limo.

Pulling up to a concert was always crazy. You had your pure rap fans. You had your half-dressed ladies who were hoping to bag a star or at least to sleep with one, and then you had the people who came just to see the famous people. Tony took me past the waiting people, but before we could make it all the way into the stadium, this white guy took my hand and asked me if I was the girl from Tay'von's video. I told him yes, and then he asked me to take a picture with him. After doing so, Tony took my hand and we went inside.

The walls were lined with reporters, women, and the rappers' entourages. I got jealous looks, but I pushed my nose up in the air and walked with my head held high. There was this one fat girl that I noticed, and she was looking at me extra hard. She was tall, about five feet four, and weighed about 250 pounds. The more we looked at each other, the more I noticed how pretty she was. Whereas my skin had a light Indian tan look, she had a darker tan complexion. Our hair had almost the same texture, but she wore hers in big curls. Her makeup was flawless, and she was dressed to kill, even for her size. Even her strong presence matched mine.

I could feel her from a mile away. I felt like we were two bulls staring at each other, waiting for the right time to attack. She possessed as much arrogance as I did, and neither of us would be the first to look away. Who was that bitch? It was as if she had all the right in the world to be in there. Black walked up to me just then, and by the look on his face, I could tell what he was thinking about.

"Hey, Tangie. Looking good," Black said to me as he gave me a hug.

I hugged him a little longer when I saw Shamika come out of his dressing room. She stopped and talked to the big girl while they both eyed me.

"I am always looking good, Black. Who is that girl Shamika's talking to?"

He turned and looked at Shamika as if he wanted to kill her. He kind of got this funny look on his face but quickly tried to hide it.

"Oh, that's just an old friend of hers. Why do you want to know?"

"I am just asking since she is the only one that looks almost as good as me." I said this in a joking tone, but I really did mean it.

Shamika walked over to us and flashed a fake smile. I stood there and looked her over. This chick had on a bright pink halter dress that she had to keep pulling down to stop it from riding up and showing her ass. Her hair was jet-black, with hot pink highlights, and this time it was a wig. She was just a pure mess.

"How are you doing, Shamika? I must say that you are looking really nice tonight."

I barely got that lie out without laughing. I pulled Tony's hand and started to walk away so that I wouldn't laugh in her face. I heard her thank me as I walked away. Everyone within earshot had got my joke except for her. When I walked into Tay's dressing room, there were about ten people in there.

"Damn, baby. I'm surprised that you made it on time," Tay joked.

"I'm sure you are," I answered while giving all the women in the dressing room evil eyes.

Tay sat down in the chair that had his name on the back of it, then patted his lap, telling me to sit on it. As I walked by the men, they all let out a loud damn!

"Ya niggas better cut that shit out. This is my girl, Tangie, I was telling you all about."

"It's okay, Tay. Your friends are just letting you know that your girl is the shit," I joked.

All his friends laughed and shook their heads in agreement.

Time was flying by, and it was almost time for Tay to hit the stage. We walked backstage and watched Black finish his set. He rocked the crowd and left them wanting more. This was what an opening act was supposed to do—get the crowd hyped and ready for the main act—although Black considered himself a headliner like Tay. The announcer let the crowd know that Tay'von "Too Fine to Be Rapping" was about to come out, and they went crazy. He kissed me, then ran out on the stage.

In the corner of my eye, I could see that fat bitch pitching a fit about something, but I ignored her. I watched Tay for about thirty minutes, before I turned around to head back to his dressing room. As I pivoted around, I bumped into someone. I had had no idea that anyone was standing behind me, so I was a little annoyed . . . until I saw him.

I said, "Oh, I'm sorry. I didn't know—"

He cut me off with a wave of his hand. "It's okay. I have been waiting for you to turn around, so if it took you bumping into me for me to see your face, then so be it."

I just smiled.

This man had a presence that was full of power. He was at a hip-hop concert, yet he was wearing a tailored designer suit. He had set off his suit with a nice arrangement of diamonds that sparkled just as bright as all of mine. He was as big as any well-built male model, just as tall, and just as fine. He had a nice milk chocolate complexion and nicely shaped up facial hair. His hair was cut short and flowed with waves. He looked like he was a sexy twenty-five-year-old, but he later told me his true age was really thirty-three. He extended his hand to me, and I shook it. He made my body quiver the same way Blair Underwood did in *Set It Off*. His face looked like a genetic copy of Blair's, and it took me back to that sex scene he had with Jada, and I wanted to stay there.

"Hi. I'm Carmello. And you are?"

"I'm Tangie."

After shaking my hand, he held it and spoke. "Where are you going in such a hurry, Tangie?"

I took my hand back from his reluctantly. "Oh, I just need a pick-me-up."

He smiled as if he knew what I was talking about. "Are you here with anyone?"

"Yes. He's out onstage," I answered.

There was a brief look of shock on his face; then it went away when things clicked in his head.

"Do you mind if I join you?"

I smiled. "I go to parties. I don't throw them. So unless you are giving out goodies, there is no need to even come." I wanted to let him know that I was not going to share my drugs with him. Everything that I had was for me alone.

"Come on, baby. Do I look like a tagalong? You should be able to tell that I am the one who throws parties."

I took his hand and walked toward Tay's dressing room. I looked around to see if I saw Carl or Tony so that I could tell them where I would be, but they were nowhere in sight. The only one I saw was that big bitch, and she was watching my every step.

"Why don't we go to my car instead of this dressing room?" Carmello asked once we reached Tay's door, but I wasn't that crazy.

I knew that Tay would be taking a five-minute break soon, and I didn't want him to flip out if he couldn't find me. So I walked into the dressing room and sat on the couch. Carmello got my hint and walked in after me.

"So what are you into, Miss Tangie?" Carmello asked, taking a seat on the couch.

"What do you have?"

It turned out that this man was a walking drugstore. He had everything any drug head could ever want, but I stuck to my weed and coke. We chilled for a while, and I got high as hell. He had some top-notch shit. I saw him reach into his pocket and pull out some pills.

"Are you into Ecstasy?" he asked.

"It's okay. I just hate that it makes me grind my teeth."

"Well, I have a trick for that, if you are willing to try it."

We had done a lot of lines, and we had smoked a lot of weed, but I said, "Fuck it."

He handed me the pills but told me to do another line of coke first before swallowing them. I did as he told me to, and thirty minutes later the pills kicked in. Damn, I was fucked up. My whole face was numb, but the rest of my body felt really good.

"So, how close are you to Tay'von?" he asked.

I looked at him like I did not understand what he was asking.

"I'm just asking because normally, a stranger can't walk into a rapper's dressing room while he's not in it, so you have to know him pretty well," he explained.

"Oh, well, I live with him, so you can think of me as his girlfriend, I guess."

"You're his girlfriend? Wow! You don't find too many girlfriends on the road. They usually stay at home and shop," Carmello joked.

I just smiled at him, and he continued to ask questions.

"You and Tay must be tight, then?"

"You can say that."

"How are you dealing with his fame?"

"I'm dealing. He's not the first famous guy that I have ever been with."

"Oh really? Well, is he happy at his label?"

"Well, I haven't really asked him that, but I don't hear him complaining," I replied.

"Oh, I see. Well, do you think that he will renew his contract with the same label—" He stopped talking.

Tay'von and Carl were standing in the doorway, and neither of them looked happy. Tay told Carl to go and tell the show conductor to prolong his five-minute break. Then Tay shut the door and looked at me, then at Carmello.

"What the fuck is going on in here?" he snarled.

"Aw, come on, Tay. I was just having a conversation with your lady here," Carmello said.

"Man, don't give me that. Why are you here? And don't give me that bullshit about you and Tangie having a conversation, 'cause by the looks of it, there's more drugging going on than talking."

"Baby, he is just chillin' in here with me. We didn't do anything—"

Tay'von cut me off, refusing to listen to what I had to say. "How am I supposed to know that, Tangie? And you know what fucks with me? It's the fact that you're in my dressing room, getting high with some man that you don't even know. And when I ask him what he is doing here, he can't even answer me."

"Look, man, I just wanted to come by and check out the show, and I was hoping that we could finish our conversation that you walked out on," Carmello interjected.

"You're checking out the show, yet you're in here with Tangie. Come on, man. You and I both know why you are here, and I already told you that I want no part of it."

"Damn, Tay, you're making this shit way too hard on yourself. One day you are going to need me, and by then I won't want to help you. You'll see. They always come to me when they need help, and you will do the same," Carmello said as he got off the couch. He stomped out of the dressing room.

"Yeah, whatever, nigga," was all that Tay said as he shut the door behind Carmello.

Tay turned and stared at me. "What in the hell were you thinking, Tangie? You don't even know that man. How are you going to bring him back here without even thinking about how I would feel about it?"

"Baby, we just came back here to smoke and do some lines. He seemed nice, and he talked as if you two were friends, so I thought that it would be okay."

Tay just stood by the door, clenching his teeth. He finally said, "Did you even ask him his name, Tangie?"

"He told me that his name was Carmello. Why? Should I know anything else about him?"

Tay looked at me as if I was dumb. "Come on, Tangie. As much as you have been around the music biz, you should know who that is. That's Carmello Green, from Green Note Records."

My mouth dropped open. He was one of the biggest black record label owners in the business. I had heard about him but had never met him in person.

"So what's your beef with him? He looks like he is getting paid," I said.

Tay'von looked at me as if he wanted to hit me. "Why do you want to know? All you care about is getting high and how paid niggas are. Do me a favor and don't bring any more strays back to my dressing room."

With that, he left the dressing room. I smoked the rest of the blunt that I had put out, and then walked back out into the hallway. Carmello was still out there, leaning against the wall, looking just as fine as he had when I first bumped into him.

"He didn't come down on you too hard, did he?" Carmello asked me with a devilish smile on his face.

"No, he didn't, but you could have told me that he didn't like your ass."

"Would it have made a difference? We were just getting high, right?" he asked as he reached out and caught me as I stumbled a little to the right.

He went into his pocket with his other hand and pulled out a business card. "Look, Tangie, I've got to go, but take my card. Maybe you will need it one day."

I took it from him and put it in my purse. He said goodbye and let me go. I watched him walk away, and for a moment I thought about how good he might be in bed. As I snapped out of my thoughts, I saw the big girl in the same spot, still looking at me. I wanted to tell her to fuck off, but if she was there with some other celebrity, then I didn't want to get Tay in trouble. But who cared, anyway? She just wanted to be me. She just wanted to be in my shoes, so I let her stare. Maybe then she would know what a real bad bitch looked like. If she was in the next city, I would just work my shit and rub it in her fat face that she would never be me, that she could never be in my position.

"That's right, bitch. Envy me, because I'm not thinking about you," I said aloud in a low tone while wondering if I would ever see Carmello again.

Chapter 7

Get Your Head out of
Them Clouds
and Wacth Over Your Shit

When I woke up the next morning, my head was pounding. I remembered Tay being so upset the night before, but things were hazy. He had even told me that I fucked up his show. I remembered getting to the hotel and him pushing me on the bed and ripping off my shorts like some kind of madman. He had pushed himself inside me with no lube and had started to call me all types of names. When I'd told tell him to get some lube, he just spit on his dick and fucked me even harder. The last thing I remembered before passing out from the pain he was inflicting on my ass was Tony and Carl. They had stood in the doorway, watching as Tay yelled at me, telling me not to ever disrespect him.

It was only eleven o'clock in the morning, and my body was sore as hell. I didn't even feel like getting out of bed. Carl came into the bedroom with hot coffee and looked at me as if I was a wet, homeless dog. I didn't need him feeling sorry for me, nor did I want to hear any of his bullshit, so I got up and headed to the bathroom. My ass felt like Tay had ripped it open. Even my pussy was sore. As I walked, my legs trembled.

Carl came over to help me walk because I just couldn't hold my emotions in anymore. Tears ran down my face from the pain. Once I got in front of the mirror and saw myself, that was when I really lost it. I had love marks, bite marks, and a whole bunch of other bruises all over my body.

Carl gave me a sympathetic look. "Tangie, come and sit down. Just don't look at yourself."

"What in the fuck happened to me, Carl? Tell me, what did Tay'von do to me?" I yelled as I pulled off my shirt. I was stunned at the marks on my body. I looked like shit. There were even places where Tay had drawn blood.

Carl wrapped his arms around me as I continued to cry. "Tell me, Carl, why did Tay do this, and why would you just stand there and watch him do this to me?"

"I tried to stop him, Tangie, but he was crazy. No matter what Tony or I did, he just wouldn't stop. But I really don't think that he was in his right mind. Tony told me that he saw Tay and Shamika smoking and that it smelled like it was laced."

I didn't give a shit what Tay had been smoking. I was still hurt and pissed that he would do this to me, high or not. I swore that bitch Shamika was going to get hers, no matter what.

Carl sat me down and drew a hot bath for me. He went to his room and got this oil, which he rubbed all over my body. He then sat me in the tub and told me that it would help with the pain. With the massage, the hot water, and the oil Carl had rubbed on me, I felt halfway better by the end of my bath. While I was drying off, Carl told me that if I felt worse by nightfall, he would take me to the hospital. Every time that I asked him if he knew where Tay was, he made this funny face, then said that he didn't know. He put me back in bed after having the sheets changed, then told me that he was going to order up some food for me. But first I asked him to roll up some smoke for me.

"Tangie, have you ever thought of cutting down on all the drugs that you do?"

I thought for a second or two before I answered. "Well, to tell you the truth, Carl, after last night I really am happy that I do, do drugs. I know that it makes it sound like I am dependent on them, but sometimes I am."

"Come on, Tangie, I am being for real. Don't you think that if Tay wasn't smoking last night, maybe he wouldn't have done this to you? And you know that I am not just talking about weed, Tangie. What about all that powder you're putting up your nose? It seems like you're doing more and more every day."

What Carl was saying was right. With all that had been going on, I hadn't really taken the time to stand back and realize how deep I had fallen into coke.

"Okay, Carl, I do need to cut down on sniffing coke, but I don't think that I'm just going to stop smoking anytime soon."

"Okay, fine. I just don't want you sniffing that shit all day."

I smiled to myself as I watched him roll up a blunt for me. He really was a sweet man. It was good that we could sit and have a conversation without going at each other, like we usually did. I loved that he took the time to care for me.

***

"Tangie, Tangie, are you up?"

I thought that I was dreaming. I heard Tay's voice, but it sounded far away. Then I felt a warm body beside me and a warm hand running through my hair. But I lay still, and I didn't look or say a word.

"Baby, are you okay?"

Still, I didn't answer. I didn't even want to open my eyes.

"Tangie, please. I just need to talk to you."

I opened my eyes and took a quick look, but I didn't utter one word. He looked a mess. His eyes were bloodshot, and I could tell that he hadn't been to sleep yet. I turned around so that I was looking right into his eyes, but he said nothing. I wished he would open his fucking mouth and tell me what the hell he had done to me the night before.

"Look, baby, I don't know what to say. I didn't even know what I had done until I woke up this morning and looked over at you."

I sat up so that I could pay more attention to what he had to say.

"Tangie, I know that you are pissed right now, and I know that you are waiting for an explanation, but I'm still trying to put everything together myself. I just remember getting off-stage and going to my dressing room. Shamika came in and asked me if I was trying to smoke with her. The next thing I know, I wake up this morning on the floor next to the bed. When I stood up and looked at you, I panicked and called Tony and Carl. When they got up here, I asked them what happened, and they looked at me like I had lost my mind."

"So what did they tell you?"

"They just went over what they saw."

"Just tell me this, Tay'von. Why did you do this to me? I know that you're saying that everything is a blur and all, but something had to tick you off."

"Baby, I'm telling you. All I remember is that I was smoking with Shamika, and we were talking about what went down between you and Carmello—"

I cut him off once I heard that. "So what did Shamika have to say about it?"

"What do you mean? It was nothing, really."

Tay must have heard the anger in my voice, because he started to back down. I wanted him to tell me if that bitch had anything more to do with last night besides giving him some laced shit to smoke. If I found out that she did, I was going to fuck her whole world up with the biggest dick she would ever come across. I was no killer, but the line between sane and homicidal was very thin when it came to me. That bitch had no idea who she was dealing with. I had been violated in my teens and had vowed never to have that happen again. And if it did, I would make whoever was responsible pay dearly.

"She was just saying shit like what you did was fucked up, and even if you didn't know who Carmello was, you shouldn't have had him in my dressing room."

So that bitch is playing those types of games, huh? I thought. Even with Tay spilling his guts to me, I could still tell that he was holding something back.

"So is that all she had to say to you?" I barked.

He looked like he didn't want to tell me, but he knew that I would just keep on asking until he did.

"Well, she saw how heated I was, so she started telling me that I should whup your ass and how I shouldn't let you get away with anything."

"So you mean to tell me that you did this to me because Shamika told you to? What kind of shit is that? Who the fuck is she to you? She must be something to you if you're doing what she tells you to do. I can't believe this. You have got to be out of your fucking mind! You're so fucking lame, Tay'von. Because Shamika told you to? What are you? Some little boy?"

"Nah, it's not like that, Tangie. Yeah, okay, that bitch was getting me hyped, but she didn't get me to the point where I would do something like this to you. It wasn't until I talked to Tony that I found out that the weed was laced."

I didn't know what to say. Everything that Tay'von was saying to me meant nothing unless he remembered what he had done to me.

"You say that you don't remember what happened last night? Well, *I* do. Before I passed out from the pain that you caused me, I remember having my ass in the air and you forcing your dick into it with no lube. I remember trying to pull away from you, but you held on to me tightly, making sure that I couldn't get away. I remember begging you to use lube, but judging by how my ass feels, you never did."

Tay had a look of terror on his face. Yes, there were times when he could be mean, but this sounded like rape to him, and he would never rape anyone. I stood up and pulled off my clothes. I stood in front of him naked so that he could see what he had done to me.

I wanted him to see every bite mark, every scratch, and every bruise that he had put on me. As he looked over my body, he started to cry, but I just stood there, pissed. The more I looked at myself, the more I wanted to hate him, and my face showed it. He did this to me because of what Shamika had said? Boy, would she pay for hyping him up to harm me. The last man who had taken my body by force was still alive, and well, but I couldn't get to him. Shamika would have to pay for both his and her sins against me. Tay'von wrapped his arms around me and put his head against my stomach.

"Tangie, please, forgive me. You know that I would never do something like this to you unless I was far gone on that laced weed. I would never do anything like this if I was clearheaded. Please, Tangie . . . I am so sorry, baby." The more he talked, the more he cried.

I didn't say anything.

"Tangie, please don't leave me, baby. I love you, and I swear to God that I'm sorry, baby. I am so sorry."

Tay'von held me tight. I was pissed as hell, but something was very wrong with this situation. How did you leave a man who couldn't even remember what he had done to you? At least now I knew the devil that I was with, the devil he could become at any moment.

I stayed in the hotel suite for the next two days, not wanting anyone to see me like this. I steered clear of nearly everyone. Tay'von asked me to go to the last show that they were having in Maryland, but I told him that I didn't have anything to wear that would cover up all the marks on my body. He told me that it would be the perfect time to go shopping with Shamika. I was about to say no, but shopping with her would give me a chance to interrogate her. I got ready as Tay called Black and told him to make sure Shamika was ready by one.

I did the best I could with the clothes that I had there with me at the hotel. The only thing that you could really see was the bite mark on my thigh and the bruise on my right shoulder. Black and Shamika came up twenty minutes early, and as always, Shamika looked a mess. She had traded in the black and pink wig for the red one she used to wear. I sat on the couch, smoking a jay, trying to conceal the disgust I felt toward her.

"How are you doing, Shamika? You want a hit? Maybe not, being that it's not laced with anything." I tried to sound friendly, but my words were dripping with malice.

She looked at Black, then back at me. "Girl, what are you talking about? I don't do nothing but weed," she answered with a nervous giggle. She took the blunt from me and sucked half of it in. I was the only one who had caught the look that Black gave her when I made my comment.

"Are you ready to go?" she asked after exhaling, seeming as if she was dying to leave now that I had made her uncomfortable.

I smiled, stood up, put on my sunglasses, and walked over to Black. I leaned over and gave him a kiss on the cheek before walking out of the suite.

We shopped at CityCenterDC, and our first stop was at Bvlgari, so I could pick up one of my favorite perfumes. Five stores later I was exhausted from not only picking out my clothes, but also picking out all of hers. Given that I hadn't eaten anything for breakfast, I asked her if she wanted to stop and get some lunch. She said yes, so we headed to CityZen in the Mandarin Oriental Washington hotel in Washington, D.C.

We ordered our lunch and waited for the waitress to come back with our DC Apples. The drink had just enough vodka for you to feel it, but not enough to make you drunk, if you paced yourself. It was the perfect drink to loosen her up with. I put my napkin on my lap as Shamika opened up her big fucking mouth.

"Girl, where you get that bite mark from?"

I wanted to give her the Tony treatment by slapping her ass, but I held back. "Before I answer that, let me ask you this. Back at the hotel you said that all you smoke is weed. Well, how come last night you smoked a dippa with Tay? What's up with that shit?"

She sipped her drink and sat back in her chair before answering me.

"Come on, Tangie, you know that I can't let Black know that I still get wet from time to time. He would kick my ass if he found that shit out. Hell, as mad as he's been lately, I just try to fly under the radar with his ass."

"Why has he been so grumpy?"

"What, you didn't hear? The label might be letting him go. They said something about him bringing bad promotion to the label."

"I thought that his album was doing well. It's in the top five right now, isn't it? And how do you bring bad promotion to a label?"

"Damn, Tangie. You don't know shit, do you? Well, two months ago, Black got caught up with some drugs and guns. He thought that the label would stand behind him, but you know how those crackers get. Everything is okay when you're making money for them, but once you do something that can fuck that up, they start acting funny."

"Damn. He really does have a reason to be pissed. I would be too."

She took another sip of her drink and said, "Well, he should have calmed his ass down. He started doing interviews, just so he could talk shit about them. Every chance he got, he blasted them for not standing up for him, and you know that they didn't like that shit. So it's not really out there yet, but people have been talking about it here and there. We're just waiting to hear for ourselves."

I wanted to smile, but then again, I felt sorry for Black.

"So if he gets dropped, what will he do?" I asked, hoping that she didn't have an answer.

"I just don't know. I'm sure he'll find another label, but you know that once a rapper gets dropped from a major label, all the other good ones are gonna think twice about taking you in. They all know that he sells records, but they are gonna be worried about him getting into trouble again."

"Well, I have a friend who deals with a lot of record executives. Maybe I can call and get some info, just in case something goes down."

Her eyes were popping out of her head. I knew that this would have her open. "Girl, call now. I don't want to wait till he gets dropped to make a move."

"I can't have them make an offer without knowing if he's a free agent or not. You know how word spreads, and the last thing Black needs is for the record label to find out that he's trying to get signed by someone else. Let's wait it out, and as soon as the ball drops, I'll make sure that someone is there to pick it up for you. Do you trust me on this?"

She thought about it and still wanted me to act on it now, but then again, I did make a valid point, so she calmed down and sipped her drink.

"Yeah, girl, I trust you. I know that you're going to have my back."

"I always look out for my friends, Shamika, and if I tell you that I got you, then I got you. I'm already thinking of a guy who I heard has been signing all the major rappers, so I'll even get at him for you."

She didn't stop smiling for the rest of our lunch, and I was beaming inside. I may have stretched the truth a little bit, but this was all falling into place. I didn't want her to know who I was talking about, but if she was smart, she would already know. Thank God for dumb people. They make things like this too easy.

As we were getting up to leave, she said, "Well, as soon as I hear something, I'll let you know so you can start making them phone calls, but don't tell Tay that we had this conversation. I don't want it getting back to Black and having him think that I just tell all his shit to everybody."

"Don't worry about it, Shamika. I'm always on top of my game."

After lunch Shamika and I headed back to the hotel. In the lobby, we parted ways. When I got up to my suite, everyone was gone except for Black and Carl. He must have read the look on my face, because Black gave an explanation without me even asking for one.

"Hey, Tangie. I was just waiting for Shamika. Tay said to tell you that he'll see you at the show tonight."

"And where in the fuck is Tay?" I quizzed.

Black and Carl looked at each other, but no one said anything. Well, I knew what that meant. *Fuck him.* I put my bags down and asked Carl to take them in the bedroom for me. While he was in there, I sat next to Black and told him that I had to talk to him. I waited for Carl to come back out, and I asked him to leave us alone. As soon as Carl walked out and closed the door, I went to work. I handed Black some weed and blunts and told him to roll a fat one. I spoke to him as I waited for him to finish.

"So, what's the deal with you and Shamika?"

I already knew their story, but I needed an intro. He finished rolling the first blunt and ran down the same story Tay had told me.

"Did she give you a hard time today?" Black asked, already knowing the response he was about to get.

"Nah, she was cool. Just a little ghetto, that's all."

I smiled, but this was no game. I wanted to put my thoughts into his head, and I was going to make sure that they stuck there.

"Yeah, tell me about it. That's why I told Tay to ask you to hang out with her. Maybe you'll rub off on her."

"Can I be real with you for a second, Black? I mean, I don't want you getting mad if I say something about Shamika that you don't like. And I want this conversation to stay between us."

"Come on, Tangie, you should know that you can talk to me. I'm not going to get mad, nor will I run my mouth. So what's on your mind?"

I didn't really give a shit if he were to go back and tell her what I'd said. I just needed him to think that I was fishing for his trust, and he fell for it.

"I just don't understand what you're doing with her. She's a hot mess. Then I look at you, and you're a smart guy with class. I just don't get how you can put up with someone so ghetto."

It looked like my statement had thrown him into deep thought.

Finally, he said, "You know how things get. A man goes to hit once but gets stuck there. Plus, she's really a down-ass female. All I need her to do is learn to leave that hood shit behind."

I reached over and put my hand on his knee. "So what's going to happen if she can't leave it behind? I'm sure that the hood is all that she knows, well, besides what you have shown her. What I am trying to say is that some people just don't know how to evolve. Look at me. Do you think that shit has always been peachy for me? Hell no, but I knew that there was something else out there. I wanted more for myself and knew that I had to change and become a better person so that I could obtain everything that I wanted. The person has to be willing to change, because you can't make a horse drink if it's not thirsty, Black."

Shit, I had his ass going. I had even put a concerned face on to make my words more believable.

I went on. "What are you going to do when she acts out or flips out in front of some important people that might be able to make or break your career? You're not on the corner anymore, Black, and you have to stop thinking like you are. Don't let one person, male or female, fuck up what you are working so hard to get. Are you really willing to risk it all over some ghetto broad?"

Poor thing. He didn't know what hit him. He was stuck and didn't know what to say, so I just waited until he came up with an answer.

"Tangie, to tell you the truth, I think about everything that you just said all the time. But it seems like every time I'm about to cut her off, I stop myself. I just don't want to be one of them niggas that make it big, then drop the girl who stood by them when they were working to get there."

This dude was too soft.

"Yeah, I understand what you're saying, but I just want you to think of yourself too. Yeah, she's been down with you, but from what I heard, you were always paid. It's not like you were some little corner boy. You were moving big shit. All I'm trying to say is, don't let her fuck your game up. I don't care if it's the corner game or the rap game. She may not always be there when the dough stops coming in."

After I said that, we just sat in silence and smoked. I let the silence go on so that my words could echo in his head. Nothing made you think more than silence and weed.

"What do you think I should do, Tangie?"

"Come on, Black. I'm not in your relationship. I can't tell you what to do. I just want to make sure that you understand your position in life right now. You can either run with what you have and make it to the top, or you can stay where you are and lose it all. I'm not telling you to do anything right now without thinking about it. Just watch her. See how she acts when she's around your fans, your label people, or anyone else that has something to do with the music biz. That will tell you all that you need to know."

I took my last big drag off my blunt and blew the smoke in his face.

I continued. "Just make sure that the smoke has cleared and that you're not being blinded by what used to be. Get your head out of them clouds and watch over your shit. Sit back, think about it, and then make a decision. Either you're going to make the wrong one and fuck your life up or you'll make the right one and move on to bigger and better things."

That was all I had to say. My seeds had once again been planted.

Chapter 8

Thanks For The Dick,
But Pussy Has Nothing
To Do With You

Yeah, shit is about to hit the fan. I am setting her ass up good, and she doesn't even know it. Even today, when I think about it, I still laugh. It seems like everyone around me is so gullible. They all just make things too easy.

At the show, I played nice. I hung with Shamika and acted like I was a good friend, and she seemed to be falling for it. We laughed at the groupies and danced to our favorite songs. I even got her to open up and talk about herself. She told me that she was raised in the South but went to New York because she had heard that there were some big-time ballers there. She said that she wanted to get one in any way, shape, or form. She told me that if she had stayed in Miami, she would have ended up having kids for the thugs she sexed and would probably have ended up on welfare, like most of her friends. I could tell that she was about to tell me something else, but she stopped herself. I didn't even ask her what she was about to say. I knew that I would get it out of her some other time.

Next onstage was this girl named Amira. I was told that her name meant *princess* in Arabic, and I must say that she reminded me of one. She was the hottest thing to hit the R&B charts. She was tall and thick in all the right places. And her voice was heaven sent. Word on the tour was that she was gay, but no one seemed to mind. She was onstage, singing, as Black rapped his featured part.

"That bitch is getting a little too close to my man," Shamika said right on key.

I had been waiting for her to notice how close Amira and Black were onstage.

"Girl, they are just putting on a show for the crowd. Plus, I heard she likes girls," I said with a smile.

"Yeah, well, I heard that she also likes men," Shamika answered as she watched Amira and her boyfriend closely.

"Do you think that I should try to get the dirt on her?" I asked as Shamika turned to me.

"Hell, yeah, you should get the dirt. I don't ever pass up on dirt."

"Okay, well, I'm going to wait for her to finish her set. Then I'll go and talk to her. You stay out here."

She shook her head okay, and we waited.

Amira came backstage after doing four songs and walked by us with a smile. I smiled back, and Shamika just shook her head, as if to say, "What's up?" As I watched Amira walk away, I noticed that she was the only one there who could match my beauty. As soon as she closed her dressing-room door, Shamika was pushing me toward it. I tried to get my thoughts together as I knocked on her door, but before I could even get my mind right, she opened it, with a towel in her hand.

She smiled once she noticed it was me and told me to come in. Once I was in her dressing room, she closed the door and leaned against it. I turned around and faced her, and then I extended my hand to her.

"Hi. I'm Tangie." We said my name in perfect harmony. I gave her a funny look, because we had never been introduced, yet she knew my name.

"Tay'von is always talking about you, so when you came the first night, he pointed you out to me," she explained.

I couldn't speak; all I could do was smile.

"Would you like something to drink?" she asked me.

I said yes, but she didn't move. She took her time to look me over as I watched her watching me.

She licked her lips, then said, "Nice dress." She moved from the door and got my drink.

Her commenting on my dress made me look at her clothes. Her style was a little street, like that of the old Alicia Keys, but there was still something really feminine about it, and it suited her. Anyone looking at her could tell that the style was hers and wasn't some record label's doing.

"Are you going to take the drink out of my hand, or do you want me to hold it up to your lips for you too?" she asked, only half joking.

"I'm sorry. I don't know what's wrong with me." I took the cup from her and sipped it slowly.

"I bet I do," she mumbled, but I didn't think that I heard her right.

"What was that?" I asked her, but she just smiled and didn't repeat herself.

Again, she looked me over, then settled her eyes on mine. I was sure that I was blushing by then, because I could feel the heat in my cheeks. I didn't know what was wrong with me. When I thought back to the time spent in Tay's trailer, I didn't remember it being so intense. Even my hands were clamming up, and I didn't get like that over anyone. When I came back from my thoughts, it seemed like she was standing even closer to me.

"So, what's up, Tangie?"

I took another sip of my drink before I answered. "Um, I just came in to tell you that I really enjoyed your performance tonight. I never really took the time to watch you before, and you were pretty good."

She reached her hand out to me, and I thought that she was going to touch me.

"I'll take that for you," she said as she took the cup from me. "Would you like some more?"

I shook my head no, and she sat down before continuing the conversation.

"Well, Tangie, it is very flattering that you came in here to tell me that you liked my performance. I saw you and that other girl standing backstage. That's Black's girlfriend, right?"

We both smiled at each other.

"Yeah, that's her. Her name is Shamika."

She gave me a look like "Who cares?" and I just continued to stand there like a dummy.

"Well, I'm happy that we had this little chat. Like I said before, I have seen you prancing around here in your fly shit, making sure that everyone knows that Tay is with you. Hell, I've even seen you give out them evil-ass looks of yours. I have been waiting for a chance to talk to you, but you know how things can get around here. Anyways, I'm sorry that I have to cut this short, but unless you plan on joining me, I must ask you to leave."

I could feel her eyes burning through my body. She looked like she wanted me to say that I would join her in whatever it was that she was about to do, but I knew better than to do that.

"Oh, I'm so . . . I'll leave. I don't want to hold you up."

I started for the door. She jumped up and was right behind me when I turned around. My chest was damn near touching hers, and I could even feel her breath.

"I'm just about to jump in the shower. You don't have to run off," she told me.

If I didn't get out of that room, I was going to suffocate.

"Um, it's okay. I'll give you your personal time to do whatever you need to do."

I tried to open the door, but she held the doorknob.

"You really don't have to leave, but since you're insisting that you do, I'll see you around. I hope you drop by again."

She let the doorknob go, and I turned to leave. I could feel her body rub against my ass as I walked past her.

"Are you going to the next city?" she asked once I was out the door.

"Yeah, I'll be there."

"That sounds real good," she said as she closed her door.

Thank God Shamika wasn't out there waiting for me. I had to go and get myself together while Tay closed the show.

There I was on a jet again, wishing that we could take a bus or drive. Shit, we were only going to Philly. I just thanked God that we were almost there. That time around the whole gang was on board. Shamika had been after me for the lowdown on what went down in Amira's dressing room, but I didn't even know myself. I had never in my life felt that way, especially about a woman. I couldn't even get my thoughts together, and Amira had been on my mind ever since.

Her sitting across from me now wasn't helping. She kept sneaking these looks at me, and—I couldn't lie—I was doing the same. I just couldn't figure her out. It was like she possessed some kind of mystery. It was driving me crazy, because I had never thought about being with another woman, but I had these crazy thoughts going through my mind. I didn't know. Maybe I was just overthinking things.

"You better watch out. She keeps giving you those gay looks, like she wants you or something. You know how them dykes get down," Shamika said, trying to whisper but failing miserably.

I wanted to ask her if she was jealous, but I just brushed off her ignorance.

"Girl, you're tripping. She's not doing anything." I paused. "Besides, what are gay looks?" I asked, not really wanting an answer.

She just quietly laughed and shook her head, thinking that I was the dumbest bitch on the aircraft that day.

We landed in Philly and were driven to the Four Seasons Hotel. Tay and I made our way to the presidential suite, while the opening acts headed to their eighth-floor royal suite. All the bodyguards stayed in the superior suites since they didn't need much room. The bellboys brought all our bags up, and I headed to the bathroom to freshen up. All that thinking about Amira had made me realize that Tay had not touched me since that night he fucked me up. He hadn't even looked at me with that hunger for sex that I usually saw in his eyes. I wondered what was up with that. I came out of the bathroom and found Tay fixing a drink.

"Hey, baby, the last thing I want to do right now is to be in a hotel room, so I'm gonna go down to the Swann Lounge and have my drink down there," I announced.

"Well, I'm good up here. I'll have my drink, then rest before the sound check."

Damn. He didn't even ask me to stay with him. What in the hell was going on? I walked over to him and wrapped my arms around him.

"Well, you do know that I could stay up here and *not* get any rest with you."

He smiled and put his drink down. He swung his arms around my waist, then let his hands slide down to my ass. He kissed me passionately, then pulled away.

"It's okay baby. You go ahead. I really need to get some rest before the show."

I gave him a "What the fuck?" look, stepped away from him, and picked up my purse. I stormed out the door to the sound of him calling my name, but I didn't even look back. I made one stop before going to the lounge, and that was at Carl's room.

I knocked on his door and waited until he opened it, without a shirt on. Shock was written all over his face once he saw me.

"Hey, Tangie. Do you need something?"

I pushed right past him and walked into his room. He closed the door slowly, as if an unsettling feeling had come over him. I didn't say anything as I pulled off my skirt and leaned over his bed. My ass faced him, but he was still standing by the door. I couldn't handle rejection for a second time in one day, so I was going to make sure I got what I wanted this time around.

"What are you doing, Tangie? Tay'von is in the hotel, and you take your chances and come down to my room like this?"

"Don't you think that I know that, Carl? You know what I am doing here, and you know what I want, so come over here and give it to me."

I pulled my thong to the side and watched him lick his lips. I knew that as soon as I let him see my pink pussy, he wouldn't be able to resist me. I could tell that he was really trying to hold back, so I leaned a little more on the bed and spread my legs out even wider.

"Come on, baby. Come and give me the good shit that I know you have."

I rubbed on my pussy and watched him walk over to me slowly.

"Do you like what you see?" I asked in a playful way. "Come and give me some of that big dick, baby. Just thinking about it has got my pussy dripping. Come and feel."

I kept on talking shit and stayed in the same position, because I knew that he loved the way my ass looked when I was bent over. I also knew that if I threw in a little masturbation, he wouldn't be able to say no. When he made his way over to me, he stood behind me and rubbed my ass. I looked back and caught him pulling down his sweatpants.

"Nigga, you know that you have to put your tongue in it first," I said as I stood up straight.

He didn't even think twice about it. He just shoved me back down to the same position I had been standing in and dropped to his knees. "Well, open the fuck up, then," he said.

I opened my legs, and he dived right in.

"Damn, Carl. Did Mommy leave you hungry?" I asked as he ate my pussy from the back like a pro.

I lifted my foot backward and pushed him away from me. I was ready for some meat, and he got the message. Carl stood up and walked back over to me. I looked back to see his big black dick coming at me. He took it and rubbed it up and down my wet pussy as we both let out moans of passion. It felt good, but I wanted him inside me.

"Stop teasing me and put it in."

Yes, he had me begging, but he just continued to rub himself on me. "You want this dick? Well, ask me again."

This dude had some balls. Who would ever think that he would have me begging him for dick?

"Come on, baby, stop playing. You know that you're the only one who knows how to make me feel good. Come on, Carl, put it in."

He put the head in, but I could tell that he was still playing games. I pushed my ass to him, which caused his dick to slide all the way inside me. Hearing him moan and feeling the grip that he had on my waist let me know that this was just as good to him as it was to me. I felt him spread my ass cheeks so that he could watch his work as I reached under and rubbed my clit. He fucked me long and slow, but I wanted it hard and fast. So I pushed myself into him at the speed that I wanted it. He held on to me for dear life as my legs started to shake.

"Oh, Carl, baby, I'm about to cum. Keep on going. Yeah, right there. Ahhh," I yelled as Carl lifted my right leg up and gave me his all.

"Ahhh, I'm cumming, baby. Yeah, fuck me, Amira."

Oh shit! What did I just say? I knew that he heard me, because I was always loud when cumming. But he kept going until he busted his nut, and that was when I noticed that he didn't pull out of me when he released his load. I stood up and walked to the bathroom without even a look back at him.

Once I was in the bathroom and was done cleaning myself up, I didn't want to come out. What in the fuck was going on inside my head that would have me screaming out Amira's name? Yes, I had been thinking about her while Carl ate my pussy, but not while he dicked me down. That shit was really getting to me. Or should I say, Amira was getting to me. I knew what I had to do: make a quick exit. But as soon as I stepped out of the bathroom, I found Carl standing there, waiting for me. Damn. I had really thought that I was going to make it out without a comment from him. He even let me get my hand on the doorknob before he opened his big, fat mouth.

"Amira, huh?" he said before laughing in a gloomy tone. "What, is she on your list to be bitten next?"

I looked him up and down and said, "Thanks for the dick, but pussy has nothing to do with you."

I opened the door to walk out and found Tay'von on the other side of it.

"I thought that you were going down to the lounge to get a drink?" Tay asked.

"And I thought that you were having your drink upstairs, then going to sleep?" I asked him back.

We just stood there looking at each other, trying to see who would break first, and I'd be damned if it was going to be me.

"Well, it looks like our thoughts aren't worth shit," I said as I pushed him out of my way. I made my way down to the lounge. Boy, did I really need a drink after that encounter.

A year later, Carl would tell me about the conversation between himself and Tay back in the hotel room that day.

"What was Tangie doing down here?" Tay'von asked.

"Oh, I don't know. I guess she just came down to say, 'What's up?'" Carl couldn't even talk straight as Tay'von looked around the room.

"What were you doing before she came down here?"

"Oh, I was, I was just watching TV."

"Where were you at in the room?"

Carl looked at the bed.

"What were you watching?"

Carl couldn't think of anything to say, because the truth was, before I came down to his room, he had been reading, but he was too nervous to remember this when Tay asked him. "Man, I don't even know. I was dozing off when she knocked on the door."

Tay just looked at him. Carl was not only his employee, but he was also a friend. Tay didn't want his mind to go to that place where the truth rested.

"So what was she doing down here? I didn't know that you and Tangie were so friendly."

"Man, I already told you that she was just saying, 'What's up?' and she told me that she was bored and was about to get a drink." Carl was just repeating what he had heard Tay say to me before I walked off. That was the only thing that he thought could save him.

"How long was she here?"

Carl took a deep breath, then let it out slowly. "She was only in here for about ten minutes or so. It's not like I was counting the minutes. Hell,

I was shocked that she even stopped by. But we just had some small talk, and then she left."

"Yeah, Carl, I know. I know all too well."

"May I have an apple martini?" I asked the bartender as I sat at a table in the lounge.

I wanted to order two off the break, but I opted for one. My body felt relaxed, but my mind was working overtime. Carl had sexed me good, but Tay had looked pissed when I opened that door. But, hey, what could a girl do but deny, deny, deny? I planned on doing that until the day I died.

"May I join you?" a sweet voice whispered in my ear.

Damn. This just must be that kind of day, I thought to myself. I turned around to see a sexy, cornrowed, wifebeater-wearing Amira. The only things womanly on her were the skintight jeans and sexy boots she wore, and I couldn't forget about her killer curves. She had taken off the nice top I'd seen her in before to sport the black tank top, and I started to feel myself staring at her for too long.

"Oh yes, please, have a seat."

As she sat down, her arm touched mine. I tried to get my mind off that fact, but the softness of her skin embedded itself in my mind. She asked me what I was drinking and ordered the same.

"There is something that I have wanted to ask you," she said. "There's a spot that I always like to go to when I'm in Philly that's really laid back, and I thought that maybe you might want to go with me tomorrow. The place is called INK, in case you want to look it up before you make a decision. It's a nice stop, and the poetry is pretty dope." I watched her sip her drink as if she was nervous.

"What about the show? Don't you have to do your part in it?"

"Didn't you hear? It seems that the concert hall needs reassurance that no one will get stabbed, like they did at the New York show, so we don't know if they are going to even let the show go on."

"So why did they even make us come here? They could have told us that when we were in New York."

She shrugged. "Well, we just found out, so I don't know what they are going to do. But, um, what do you think about going out with me?"

Damn. I wondered if Tay'von was going to flip if I told him that I was going out with Amira, especially after finding me in Carl's room. *Fuck it.* I was sure he had plans of his own.

"What time are you trying to go?" I asked.

"Well, they usually start around nine, so we can get something to eat first, or we can go straight from here."

As I thought about it, these two girls came up to her, and I could tell that they were fans.

"Oh, my God! You're Amira, right? Oh, shit. You're, like, my favorite singer? Can you sign this for me?" one of them said, waving a piece of paper.

The girl who had talked didn't look a day over sixteen, but her friend looked a little older. Amira took the paper that the younger girl was holding out as the older one spoke.

"Isn't Tay'von and Black on tour with you too?"

Amira looked at me, and I answered the older girl.

"Yes, they are on tour with her. Why? Who are you trying to see?"

Both of the girls looked like they were about to pass out. I looked them over. The younger one reminded me of Shamika. She was a mess from head to toe, but the older one was holding her own. She was tall and had dark skin and an ass that could be on the cover of any one of the men's magazine.

They both said, "Too Fine," at the same time.

I asked for ID, but only Miss Thick had it on her.

"What are you doing, Tangie?" Amira asked, looking confused.

"I'm making sure that we go out to INK tomorrow."

I gulped down my drink; then I took Miss Thick by the hand.

"Are you ready to see Mr. Too Fine?" I said.

She shook her head yes.

"Well, tell your friend that you'll be back," I told her, and then I escorted her to her dream man.

Chapter 9

No, No, Honey, I'm Not A Bitch.

I'm The Bitch

I know that people think that I am really crazy for doing this. To this day, I still don't know why I took that girl up to Tay'von. Maybe I was trying to show him that I could stop being his girlfriend when need be and could just be a friend. Or maybe I was looking for a way out.

"Oh, my God, I have been dreaming about meeting this nigga for years now. I thought that I was about to pass out when you told me that you were taking me to meet him."

That girl just would not shut up. I wished that she would faint just so I wouldn't have to hear another word from her. Once we stepped out of the elevator, I led her to the door.

"You ready?" I asked her.

"Hell, yeah, I'm ready. How do you know him, if you don't mind me asking?"

I smiled at her. "I'm his girlfriend."

I didn't give her a chance to say anything else. I just opened the door to the suite. When we walked in, Tay'von was spread out on the couch, watching TV. He didn't even look up at us.

"Hey, Tay. Someone is here to see you."

He turned from the TV to see Miss Thick standing beside me. I knew as soon as he sat up that he wanted to know more about her and why she was there.

"This is your early birthday gift. She's why I went down to talk to Carl," I said.

Yeah, that was a good save, if I said so myself.

"And how is she my birthday gift?" He knew, but he wanted me to say it.

"Well, why don't I just let her show you herself?"

He stood up once he heard me say that.

"Calm down, Tay," I said. "She's not going anywhere. Let her go and freshen up first."

I walked her to the bedroom and gave her towels, lotion, perfume, and a nice, new, sexy thong. I didn't want her putting on the same one she had walked in here wearing. I left Tay sitting on the couch so that I could go down and tell Carl what I had just told Tay.

Carl frowned when he opened the door and saw me standing there. "Damn, Tangie. What do you want now? We can't be doing—"

I barged into his room and cut him off before he finished his dumb thought. I ran everything down to him that I had just told Tay. He shook his head, as if I was dead wrong.

"Look, Carl, we can tell him the truth, or you can stick to my story. It's up to you."

I walked away from him, and before I headed out his door, I turned and said, "If you see Amira, tell her I'll be ready and waiting."

I left his room with a smile on my face. I knew that he was pissed, and that would always make me smile.

I went back to the suite to see if Tay and Miss Thick were going at it. To my surprise, he was still on the couch, where I had left him, and she was nowhere in sight. I went to the bathroom and found her fixing her hair.

"Damn, girl. What's taking you so long?"

"I'm so nervous. I never thought that I would be standing in Tay'von's hotel room, let alone in his bathroom."

"Well, don't blow it by making him wait so long."

As we walked back toward the living room area, I stopped and picked up the bag of weed.

Miss Thick stopped in her tracks. "Are you sure that you're all right with this? You are his girl and all. I just don't want to cause a problem between you two."

At least she was nice enough to think of someone besides herself. Most women would say, "Fuck me," and not give it a second thought.

"First, I want you to know that if I wasn't okay with this, then you wouldn't be here, and second, the only way you would cause a problem is if you were good enough to replace me. Let's face the facts, honey. You're not. Now, go on out there."

I was sure I had hurt her feelings, but it wouldn't stop her from fucking my man. And I bet that she would try her best to take him away, that is, if she could. Hell, I would have tried it if I were her, but I guessed you just had to be smart enough to think of it first. I watched her phat ass sway all the way to the living room area.

"Well, don't say that I never gave you anything," I walked into the living room area.

As I said this, Tay'von was looking her up and down and licking his lips.

"Come on over here, girl. I won't bite."

She walked over to Tay as if she was under his spell. I laughed to myself as I watched her. These bitches out here really fell for that "Too Fine" bullshit. I sat directly in front of them and rolled a blunt. I wondered if I was the same way when I was about to fuck my first star. I didn't think I was. I had way too much game to act like that. She wasn't even doing anything. Miss Thick was just sitting on Tay's lap, as if she were ice cold, stiff, and wet.

"Come on, bitch. I didn't bring you up here to just sit and talk. Do what you came to do," I barked.

Tay'von lost his cool and laughed. I even had to chuckle. I kicked off my shoes as I felt the weed kick in.

"Damn, Tangie. You sure did pick a scared one."

"Tell me about it. If I knew that she was just popping her gums, I would have picked her friend," I said as I laughed at her again.

Not that what we were saying was funny. We were just trying to make her do something.

"I ain't scared," Miss Thick said as she rolled her eyes.

I took a deep pull of my blunt, and through my smoke-filled, slanted eyes, I said, "All you're still popping is your gums. Why don't you try popping something else and prove it?"

Tay looked at me with a "Go, bitch" expression on his face, and I smiled back. As if to prove me wrong, Miss Thick stood up and got on her knees in front of Tay. I felt like being mean to her. I wanted to humiliate her for no good reason at all, and the more I smoked, the meaner I got.

"Oh, about to give up some head, huh? Just make sure not to hurt my man's dick with them sharp-ass teeth of yours."

She stopped unbuttoning Tay's pants and looked back at me.

"Why in the fuck are you looking back at me? You should already be slobbing that shit down, you dizzy bitch."

Tay'von was just sitting there with his dick out. Before Miss Thick could respond to my unkind words, he pulled her head down toward his throbbing wood and pressed it against her lips. This made me laugh even louder.

"Pimp hard, nigga. Pimp hard."

She went to lift her head to respond to my pimp comment, but Tay's hand was there to push it back down.

After smoking the blunt, I got up and brought out the camera. I put it on the table so that it faced Tay and Miss Thick. It was a pity that I had to do this, but these girls out here today were fast to scream rape. I sat beside Tay on the couch and held the blunt that he had put out up to his lips after lighting it for him. He took two deep pulls before I took it away from his lips and finished it myself. I had to give it to Miss Thick: she had Tay's ass going. I reached over and played with her hair before I started pushing her head farther down on his dick. She didn't like it, but she didn't stop me.

"Aw, come on, bitch. Don't be scared to make that dick disappear," I said as I took control of her head. "That's right. Suck my man's dick. It tastes good, don't it? You wanna taste that cream, don't you?"

This was starting to turn me on. I leaned over and kissed Tay. The whole time, my hand never left her head. After kissing Tay, I pushed her head away.

"Time to make that ass clap, ho," I told her.

It didn't even take her a minute before she stood naked in front of us. She put one of her feet up on the couch, as if Tay was going to eat her out.

"Bitch, unless you're waiting for Tay to fuck you with your leg up here, you better put it back down. The only pussy he eats is mine."

She put her leg down quickly, as if to make us forget that she was dumb enough to think the he would really go down on her. I still didn't get how low some of these women would go just to sleep with a celeb. Yes, I would have taken this chance, but would I let another woman talk to me like this? Hell, no!

"Break that bitch off from the back," I told Tay'von.

While he went and grabbed a condom, I sat in the seat where he had been sitting.

"Lean her over here," I told him when he returned.

I patted my knees so he knew where to lean her, and she bent over, with her hands in my lap, and got comfortable. Tay wet his fingers with spit and reached down and played with her pussy. She closed her eyes and moaned out load.

"It feels good, doesn't it?" I asked as I reached over and played with her nipples. "You want him to put it in, don't you? You want that dick up in you, huh? Tell me. No, ask me. Ask me for that dick." I was really enjoying this.

I waited for her to ask me, but she said nothing. So I grabbed her hair and pulled her close. Tay'von kept on playing with her, making her want it even more. I looked into her eyes as I wrapped her hair around my hand. I didn't stop pulling on it until I knew I was hurting her.

"Do you think that I am playing? You're not getting that dick without asking for it. I know you don't want to leave here, only being able to say that you sucked Tay'von's dick, right?"

She mumbled a no.

"Well, you better start fucking asking for that dick."

She did as I asked, so Tay'von rammed his dick inside her. She let out another loud moan. The more I watched Tay fuck her, the more I wondered if this was how rough he had been with me that night I passed out. He was being so rough with her that it was getting to the point where Miss Thick was digging her nails into my thighs. Tay reached back under and played with her clit. This took her mind off him pounding into her. Now her moans were dripping with ecstasy. Tay told her to cum on his dick, and I could tell that she was getting there.

"Come on, girl. Let it out. I know you want to cum," I told her in a low tone.

She closed her eyes, and her legs started to tremble. When her legs gave out, Tay had to hold her up as he pounded away. He pulled off the condom and let his cum fly all over her back. After he was done, he put her down and headed for the bathroom to take a shower. He said nothing to her.

"Well, Miss Thick, it looks like your time is up," I said.

She looked at me with a dumb expression on her face.

"What, you didn't think that you were coming to stay, did you? Come on, you're a big girl. You know what this was all about."

"But we just—"

I cut her off. I wanted her to understand that this was just what it was, a fuck. "Don't make this turn ugly. You came here to fuck a star. You did. Now it's time for you to go."

Boy, did she look pissed. What did she think? We were all going to hang out? She cleaned the cum off her back and got dressed. I just watched her as I sparked another jay. She didn't say anything out loud, but she kept rolling her eyes and smacking her teeth. She was done putting on her clothes, so she headed for the front door. Before she walked out of the suite, she turned around and had something to get off her chest.

"By the way, my name isn't Miss Thick. It's Sasha."

"We really don't give a shit," I answered. "Don't worry about locking the door. It locks by itself once people have let themselves out."

She rolled her eyes at me and then called me a bitch, as if it were going to hurt my feelings.

"No, no, honey, I'm not a bitch. I'm *the* bitch. Say it right next time."

She walked out of the suite, and that was the last of Miss Thick. Tay'von was out for the rest of the night. And as for me, I just blazed and watched movies in the living room area until I fell asleep. I wondered if Miss Thick went home halfway pissed but still excited that she had got to fuck the star of her dreams. She and Tay had both got what they wanted, and now I just hoped that all my desires were within reach.

"Tangie, go to bed," Tay said as he tried to wake me up.

"What time is it?" I said, barely awake.

"It's ten in the morning."

I sat up and looked around. I must have passed out on the couch.

"Are you going to bed, or are you going to stay up and have some coffee?" he asked.

"Coffee."

He walked over to the coffeemaker and poured me a cup. I rolled my eyes at him when he came back over to the couch and handed me the cup.

"Someone woke up on the wrong side of the couch," Tay said while smiling.

"Why don't you just shut the fuck up!" I yelled as he laughed at me.

He already knew the deal. I had always been a tad bit nasty in the mornings, so it didn't bother him much. He was used to it.

"I wonder how someone who looks so good could act so ugly?" he said.

He was just trying to piss me off, so I didn't answer him. But if he wanted to play these games, I knew just how to get him.

"I want to go shopping."

"You just went shopping the other day, Tangie. What is it that you need now?"

I smiled, and he caught on to what I was doing.

"Fine. You can go shopping, but you have to take Shamika." Now he was really laughing.

I just got up and went into the bathroom. I took a shower and got dressed. When I was done, Carl and Tony were in the living room area, listening to Tay go on about the night that he had had. Carl was trying to act like he was all into it, but I read his true feelings as soon as I joined them. I sat and listened to them as I smoked a blunt.

Tay shook his head. "Damn, Tangie. How about eating something first?"

"I know you're not talking, Tay'von. You wake up with a blunt in your mouth. Anyways, I'm going to have some breakfast downstairs."

I stood up and grabbed my purse. Tay'von stood up and gave me a long kiss. It had been so strained between us for the past week that I just didn't know how to take his show of affection. I wanted him to take me into the bedroom and give me some of the good dick that he had given to Miss Thick, but I knew that he wouldn't. Instead, he walked me to the door.

"Hey, Tangie, I've been meaning to talk to you," he said in a low voice. "I know that I have been standoffish, and I have been feeling really bad about it. I just can't get over what went down. I have never had a night where I didn't remember anything. I just want you to know that I love you, baby. Now, I know that I really didn't want you to come on tour with me at first, but I have really enjoyed you being here."

He pulled me close and hugged me for a long time. I hugged him back. I knew that he really meant what he had said. I knew that he truly loved me, but I just didn't know where this love would take us. I didn't know why I just couldn't let love be. It was like I could love only the things people did for me or gave me. I had to get it together and find a way to accept it when people really loved me.

On my way down to breakfast, I stopped and asked Shamika if she wanted to go shopping. She said no but came down to eat with me. Once we got to the hotel restaurant, we saw Amira leaving. But she stopped to say hi.

"So what's good to eat?" I asked her.

She told us that all she had had was coffee, so she didn't know. Shamika and I just stood there looking at her as she looked me up and down. I started to blush and wished that Shamika wasn't standing next to me. Her comments before about Amira had let me know that she was too interested in her lesbian lifestyle. I knew that she would have something to say the minute Amira walked away, and honestly, I just wanted to enjoy that moment with Amira and not think about the bullshit that would follow.

"Well, I'm going to head back up to my room," Amira said before getting closer to me and whispering, "Damn, you're looking good. I hope you look this eatable tonight." Then she just walked away, as if everything was normal.

I stood there, wanting to turn around and watch her walk away, but I knew that Shamika was standing beside me. If she caught me staring at Amira's ass, she was sure to make a big deal out of it.

"You two seem to be getting close. You better watch out, Tangie. That bitch is a dyke. I just know it."

"Oh, give it up, Shamika. Who cares what she is? She's just being friendly," I said as I walked to a table.

She could tell that I was agitated and tried to make light of her comments. "Girl, I was just saying, she always acts like she don't like men.

Hell, I haven't seen her with one. And I don't think that she likes me, anyways, so I can say whatever the hell I want."

I wanted to tell Shamika that Amira didn't like her, because she was so cold toward her anytime she came around, but I let it go.

"Did you ever call your friend about Black?" Shamika asked once we were seated.

Damn. I hadn't even realized that with everything that was going on, I had gotten off track with what I had planned for Miss Shamika.

"Girl, don't even worry about it. You know I got you, and when the ball starts rolling for you and Black, trust me, you'll know it," I answered her without a second thought.

We ate our breakfast; then she headed upstairs. I headed to the lobby and told the limo driver to take me to the best shops in Philly.

I shopped hard and got back to the hotel around four in the afternoon, and the bellboy helped me with my bags. When we got up to the suite, I heard some laughter coming from the bedroom. I shushed the bellboy and handed him a fifty-dollar tip. He left quietly, and I made my way to the bedroom without making a sound. As soon as I got close enough to hear everything, I knew exactly who was in the bedroom with Tay.

"Come on, tell me, how much are you pulling in a year?"

I could hear Tay'von laughing at the person's question.

"Why do you want to know? I'm sure your man is making some good money."

"Yeah, but he isn't Mr. Too Fine. I see how everyone treats you like you're a king, and my man doesn't get that. Just tell me how much you make."

I heard movement in the room. Then Tay laughed and said, "You better stop before Tangie comes in here and hears you. You know she'll whup your ass."

"Please, I'm from the hood. I ain't all prissy with my shit like she is. I'll whup her ass before she whups mine."

"Is that right? Well, just because Tangie is proper and all doesn't mean that she isn't nice with the hands. Don't sleep on her. I don't even play fight with her anymore, 'cause she gets too wild and tries to kill me."

Now I heard the person laugh along with Tay.

"Man, fuck Tangie. When are you gonna let me get some of that good shit? I bet Tangie can't get down like I can. I'm not one of them bitches who just lie there and take the dick. I'm going to give it back to you."

"Stop playing around. You know that I don't even get down like that. Plus, with Tangie on tour with me, I'm not even trying to do nothing crazy and have her go off on me," I heard Tay'von answer halfway truthfully.

I just couldn't believe this shit. This was the last person that I would ever think would come at Tay'von like this.

"Come on, Tay. Let me get just a little taste. What, you some kind of bitch or something?"

At first, I didn't hear anything. Then I heard a bang, like someone had been pushed against a wall.

"You're the bitch, and I'm sure you know that. Did you really think that calling me a bitch, nigga, was going to make me fuck you? Hell, having sex with you would make me less than any man that I know. I'm not going to fuck you just to prove something."

"Come on, Tay, let go of my neck. I really can't breathe," the person said, straining to get the words out.

"The next time you think about testing me, you better think again. Now, get your fucking ass out of here. And if you ever try some shit like this again, you will be off this tour and out of a job."

"But, Tay, I was just—"

That was all I heard. I walked back to the door, opened and closed it to make it sound like I was just getting in. I heard the bedroom door fly open, so that it would appear like it had never been closed.

"Baby, I'm back," I yelled as I tried to keep my nice face on. I didn't want them to think that I had heard anything.

Tay came walking out of the bedroom quickly. "Hey, baby, how was shopping? Did you get everything that you need?" Tay was talking a mile a minute.

Then the backstabbing bitch came out second. "Hey, Tangie. I just came up to see if Tay had any smoke. Did you enjoy your shopping?"

I looked at them and held my tongue. "So where's the smoke that you came up for? Did Tay have any?" I asked her.

They both looked at one another, but no one answered.

I broke the silence. "I know that when I left this morning, we had a big bag. Did you get some?"

Tay'von stumbled to find the right words. "I, um, I, I couldn't remember where I put the bag." He chuckled nervously.

I looked over at the coffee table, and the bag was sitting on it in plain view. I didn't say anything. I just walked over to the couch and sat in front of the bag of weed. Without even looking at them, I started to roll up a jay. After rolling it, I lit it and took a deep pull. There was no need for me to say anything. I knew that they knew what I was thinking when they looked at each other with a "Do you think she knows anything?" expression on their faces.

"Well, I'm going to get out of here," the bitch said as they walked toward the door.

"That's funny," I said. "You're going to leave without getting the weed you came up here for? I know Tay said that he didn't know where it was, but now that I have found it, come over here and get some."

That ho-ass bitch looked over at Tay, then walked over to me. You would think that with all that shit they were talking in the bedroom, they would be bolder with their shit. It took everything that I had in me not to fuck this bitch up. But I had bigger plans for them. This bitch held her hand out, and I put a good amount of weed in it.

"If this bag was a snake, it would have bitten you," I said, sounding very sarcastic.

Once that bitch left, I got to thinking. Everything that Tay had told me before I left that morning meant nothing to me after what I had just heard. Okay, so he didn't fuck that ho, but there had to be something in the air that would make someone come at you like that. It never came out of nowhere. I just kept smoking, hoping that I would calm down.

"I was thinking that maybe we can go out tonight. How does dinner and a club sound?" Tay watched me closely as he asked me his question.

"Well, have a good time," I answered him.

"I am talking about you and me going out. I don't want to go by myself."

I stood up and walked right past him. "Nah. I got plans," I said as I walked into the bedroom and closed the door.

I took a long bath and tried to relax, but it was not working. I just didn't understand how someone could have the balls to challenge me, even if I was not there. Although it pissed me off, I was just going to have to put this on the back burner. As I soaked in the tub, I sniffed what seemed like half of Cuba up my nose. I had really been trying to cut back, but every time I felt shitty, that was the first thing I did. I got out of the tub at the same time Tay came into the bedroom and sat on the bed.

"Where are you going?" he asked.

"Out with Amira," I answered him as I started getting dressed.

"Since when have you and Amira started hanging out?"

"Was I supposed to ask you first? Or was I supposed to tell you that her and I have become friendly?"

"Tangie, I'm just asking. It's not like you and her were friends before this tour."

He was getting on my last nerve. How dare he question me? It was not like he walked around here, telling me about everything he did or would do.

"Well, Tay, just be happy that you know now. I just don't see what the big deal is. It's not like I'm going out with another man or anything. Just calm down and roll some weed up for me."

He did as I asked, and I finished getting dressed. As I prepared to leave, Tay handed me two blunts and I gave him a kiss.

"Why don't you call Black and see if he wants to go to a strip club or something?" I suggested.

He told me that he would call, and I turned around and left the suite. I went downstairs and knocked on Amira's door. She opened it, and I took in a deep breath. She could have been Alicia Keys's body double for the "Karma" video. As soon as I laid eyes on her, my mind flashed back to the part of the video where Alicia had on a turquoise one-piece. Amira's hair was long, with bangs just like Alicia Keys's. Her top was even turquoise, but instead of a one-piece, Amira had on a pair of tight jeans. She had dressed up her look with some nice heels. This was the most feminine I had ever seen her.

"Wow! You look really nice," I told her as my eyes searched her body.

"Thanks. I just thought that I would dress it up for you a little," she said as she mimicked me and roamed my body with her eyes.

I had on short denim shorts and a tight black lace top, with thigh-high black lace boots. She asked me to turn around so that she could get a whole-body view of my outfit.

"Damn, girl. You look like you should be walking somebody's runway."

I thanked her as she let me into her room.

"Have a seat while I finish getting ready."

I sat on the edge of her bed and pulled out the weed that Tay had rolled for me. I waited for her to come out of the bathroom and handed her one of the blunts. She took it and leaned against the dresser as she sparked up. As we smoked, she kept giving me these sexy looks. I didn't know if it was the weed, but I gave them right back to her. She smiled, licked her little pink lips, and flicked the ashes from the blunt into an ashtray. I kept thinking about her doing all kinds of nasty things to me, and I couldn't stop as her eyes became sexy small slits the higher she got. The feeling was new to me, and I didn't know if I wanted to fight it. There was a big part of me that wanted to feel something new . . . and she was most certainly that something new.

"What are you thinking about?" she asked, as if she already knew what thoughts had been running through my mind.

I smiled and crossed my legs. "Oh, I was just thinking about how good this weed is," I lied, and she knew it as soon as the words left my mouth.

"Sure you are," she said with a smile.

She came over to the bed and sat beside me. She was so close that every part of the right side of her body touched me. She leaned forward and put her elbows on her knees. She reached over and ran her finger across the part of my thigh that my boot did not cover, and said, "Yeah, that's real nice."

My body was so stiff that I couldn't move it even if I wanted to. My body wanted her to take me, but my mind kept reminding me that I was not gay. She licked her lips and pulled her hand away.

"We better get out of here," she said, as if she needed to stop herself from jumping the gun and doing something that might piss me off.

Yes, I gave off a vibe of interest, but I also clammed up whenever she got too close. She was just going to have to pay really close attention to me, and in time she would test me in every way imaginable. And that day, I didn't know that she would start to do so soon.

When we got into the limo, we sat close together. She lit up a cigarette and made a comment about her having to stop smoking. She didn't want smoking to affect her singing voice. I didn't really have much to say, so I just sat there, wondering where the night would lead us. I stayed this way until we got to the poetry club.

When we pulled up to the club, the people in line broke their necks trying to see what famous person was coming to their well-known poetry club. As soon as we stepped out of the limo and people saw Amira, they wailed with joy. She took my hand, and we walked inside. Once inside, we were seated at a table that I was sure she had reserved over the phone. The host announced that Amira was in the club, then went on with the show.

We sat and listened to people sing their songs and recite their poetry. Halfway through the show, Amira told me that she had to go to the bathroom. The next thing I heard was the host announcing that Amira was about to take the stage.

Oh shit, I thought. *Why didn't she tell me that she is going up there?*

"Hey, everyone. I wrote this poem last night, as I sat in my room, thinking about someone who has been driving me crazy. This person has got me thinking of some wild things that I would love to do to them. So I hope that you all let your imagination run wild, the same way I did last night. The name I gave to my thoughts is 'If You Were Here Right Now.'"

She then pulled out a piece of paper and recited her poem. It went like this.

If you were here right now,
Imagine what we would do.
You'd have your arms around me,
While I'd be kissing you.
Our tongues would play together
Right before I suck your bottom lip.
I'd rub my hands slowly down your back
Until I reached your hips.
Then hold you close while we're still passion-
ately kissing,
Feeling everything that I have been missing.
Thinking about you,
Missing you,
Wanting you,
Needing you.

But what else is new?
Seeking you,
Finding you,
Meeting up with you,
Holding you.
I wish our times together weren't so far and
few.
Seeing you,
Feeling you,
Pleasing you,
Satisfying you
Is just the beginning of what I would do.

The whole time she read her poem, she looked right at me. I could feel every word that came out of her mouth. She read it with such emotion, such truth. Damn, what was I going to do? I felt like the whole room knew that the poem she was reading was about me.

When she finished reciting the poem, she got off the stage and came back to the table, with a smile on her face. She put her hand on my thigh and asked me what I thought about the performance. I turned around and faced her. Again, she was close enough to kiss. She slipped her hand higher up my thigh and slightly massaged it. I held on to the table while I answered her.

"Why didn't you tell me that you were going up there?"

She moved her hand up higher, and I could feel her hand pulling aside my underwear.

"I wanted to see if it would make you wet," she joked, but then again, her hand was now inside my panties and was rubbing my clit.

Fuck, fuck, fuck. What should I do? I knew that I needed to stop her, but this was feeling too good. I spread my legs wider as I looked into her eyes. She just kept licking her lips and working her fingers. I reached under the table and laid my hand on top of hers. I wanted to say something to her, but what?

"I see it worked. It's a waterfall down there," she said and smiled as she pulled her hand out of my shorts. Then she stood up.

I didn't even realize that they had called her back to the stage to sing her latest single. While she was onstage, I went to the bathroom to get myself together. I also needed to powder my nose. Damn. This girl had my head spinning.

A half an hour later Amira and I were back in the car, heading to dinner. If it were up to me, we would be on our way to finish what she had started in the poetry club. But things hadn't gone that way. We went to a restaurant she had chosen and ate dinner. After realizing that things had cooled off between us, I felt agitated and just wanted to go back to the hotel. She paid the bill, and once we got outside, I noticed that the limo was gone and all we had waiting for us was a taxi. Of course, this made me stop in my tracks.

"Uh, where's the limo?"

"Calm down, Tangie. I know that you like to ride in style, but I just wanted to take you somewhere without having someone keeping an eye on us."

"What about the taxi driver? I'm sure he knows who you are."

"Don't worry about it. He's an old friend of mine. He's cool. I trust him with my life."

We got into the taxi, and she handed the driver an envelope that, I later found out, had five thousand dollars in it.

I looked over at her. "So where are we going?"

"Just wait and see. You don't have a curfew, do you?" she joked.

I sat back and enjoyed the ride. Her friend sparked up, and we all smoked. Amira took in a deep pull and covered my mouth with hers. After pushing the smoke in my mouth, she slipped me her tongue. She kissed me deeply and ran her hands all over my body. Suddenly she stopped kissing me but kept her hands on me.

"Damn, girl. You got me going crazy. Stop the car," she told her friend.

He stopped on a dark road, and she got out of the car. As soon as I stepped out, she grabbed me and kissed me. She pushed me against the car as she pulled off my belt. Then she pulled away and led me to the front of the taxi. I sat on the hood and pulled off my shorts. The only light out there was from the taxi's headlights, and it was just enough to let both of us see what we had been fantasizing about. Her friend just sat in the car and watched us, as if what we were doing was done every day.

"You sure you want to do this?" she asked.

I didn't answer her. I just leaned back so that she could pull off my underwear. She pulled it off while I pulled off my shirt.

There we were, in the middle of trees and darkness, and all I had on was my bra and six-inch thigh-high boots. She leaned on top of me and kissed me. It was a long and hungry kiss. She made a trail with her wet tongue down to my nipples, and I moaned openly. Her fingers rubbed my clit without her slipping any inside me. She licked all over my chest and stomach. She acted as if she knew that I wanted her to taste me, but she was making things move at her own speed.

When her lips finally reached my clit, I thought that I was going to die. Her soft little pink lips rubbed my opening. She had my legs spread and had my boots pointing in the air as she pushed her face into me. First, I felt her tongue slide in and out of me, then up and down on my clit. She nibbled on it lightly as I moved my hips with her tongue. I wanted this feeling to last forever.

The noise of her trying to detach my clit from my body was the only sound that could be heard, so I figured it was okay to let loose. I screamed with heated lust as she ate my pussy with passion. Her hands roamed my body as she worked me with her mouth. As my body jerked and moved around, I almost slipped off the hood of the car, but she picked me up and put me right back on top of it. She went back to work. Minutes later, she pulled her head away and held my lips open. Then she pulled off her shirt and rubbed her hard, perky nipple up and down my clit. Shit, she was doing things to me that I had never even thought of. After doing one nipple, she did the other, then went back down and sucked my clit.

Pulling away never crossed my mind. This was different, it was new, and I loved everything about it. I wanted everything that she was giving. She fucked me with her tongue, and I fucked it back. I loved the feeling of something long, wet, and smooth sliding in and out of me. When she stopped and stood up, I leaned forward so that I could tell her to keep on going, but she put her finger against my lips and shushed me. Then she put her hand on the back of my neck and pushed my mouth toward her nipples. I sucked on them, tasting myself. She leaned her head back and enjoyed my touch. I unbuckled her jeans and pulled them down halfway. I wanted to pleasure her the same way she had pleasured me. I got off the hood of the car and got on my knees in front of her. Before I could do anything, she pulled me back up. She got close to me and whispered tenderly in my ear.

"No, not now. I want you to make sure that you are ready to taste me."

And with that, she slid two fingers inside me, while I reached down and played with her clit. She fucked me with her fingers better than any man had done with his dick. She thought that she would make me cum before her, but I got to her first. I could feel her body start to tremble as my fingers became really wet from her juices. She closed her eyes, and I could feel her body stiffen as she stopped moving her fingers and came. When she was done, she opened her eyes and had a look of shock on her face. I figured that maybe she wasn't expecting me to know anything about a woman's body. I pulled my hands away from her and sat back down on the hood of the car. She put her hand against my chest and pushed my back against the hood. She rubbed her finger down my clit, then put one back inside me. She moved her fingers slowly, getting them really wet. She took them out and ran her fingers up and down my asshole. She put her face back into me and flicked her tongue against my clit real fast.

She kept rubbing my ass, and with the other hand, she finger fucked me. My body shook violently as I screamed her name. I opened my legs as wide as I could and let her give it to me. Even after I came, she kept on going. Her tongue moved from my clit to my ass and back up again. She wasn't trying to make me cum again; she just couldn't pull herself away. She loved the taste of me and wanted to savor it. I loved the way she was making me feel, and I didn't mind letting her continue.

Her friend got out of the taxi and came and stood beside her. He looked down at my bare pussy and smiled. Amira just kept on licking, as if he were still in the car.

"I think that we should get out of here. It's getting late," he told her, but she didn't move, so he just stood there watching.

I also sat up and leaned on elbows to watch as I lifted up and wound my hips.

"Damn, A. You're turning her ass out already," the taxi driver said as Amira stood up and pulled up her pants.

She helped me up, and I got dressed. We never made it back to the hotel like we had planned on doing. We ended up at her friend's apartment for rounds two and three.

Chapter 10

I Know That We Had Sex
And All, But I Am Not Gay

That was some crazy night. I know that some people will never understand why or how I gave into her. I am the snake who is known for always getting her prey. I am the sly one, but I just couldn't hold back anymore. I wanted her so badly. She gave me these feelings that were driving me mad with lust. Just the way she looked at me made me wet. I never thought that a woman would bring me to such heights of passion, but my God, she drove me damn near to insanity. There was something about her that drew me to her. She was so smooth with her shit. She never had to say too much. Even when we first made love, she never said more than eighteen words. Instead, she did most of the talking with her body, and I understood every word.

I woke up that morning at Amira's friend's apartment, wondering what the day held for me. I knew that Tay was going to be pissed. And I also knew that last night was something that I would remember forever. I felt the other side of the bed, unable to look. I was not ashamed. I just had that feeling like when you slept with a friend and you had to face them the next day. I felt around on the bed, and no one was there. I got up and headed to the bathroom to get myself together. When I came out, I saw her friend sitting on the couch in the living room, smoking, and I asked him about Amira's whereabouts.

"She went to the store. She said to tell you that she will be right back."

I sat down beside him, and he passed me the blunt.

"Let me ask you something. Are you really feeling A? Or are you just sleeping with her 'cause you need something new in your life?" he said.

I wanted to tell him to mind his fucking business, but he was Amira's friend. Plus, letting us use his apartment was very nice.

"Why would you ask that? She's cool and everything but—"

"*Cool*? That's all you think of her? I happen to know that she's really into you, and from what I saw last night, you think more of her than just her being cool."

I looked at him and really wanted to open up to him. I had been holding back so many things. So many things had run through my mind as far as Amira and I were concerned. I couldn't even figure out if I was now gay, bi, or just curious.

"Okay, I do think that she is more than just cool. I like her, and I find myself thinking about her all the time. She's not like any other person I have ever met."

"So do you think that you want to be with her full-time and not have any other woman or man in your life?"

Man, he was asking hard questions.

"I don't know about all of that. It's not like I think of myself as a gay person," I answered, and it caused him to burst into laughter.

"What do you mean, you don't think of yourself as gay? I watched you last night, you know? You let a woman go down on you, and you wanted to do the same to her. How can you not call yourself gay? Shit, you have to admit that you're at least bi." He did have me there.

"Look, I don't really know what I am when it comes to this relationship. This is all very new to me. I am with a man that I love, and I am still trying to figure things out with him. Then there's Amira. I am starting to feel things for her, but I still have to ask myself, can I really be with a woman?"

"I see where you're coming from, but I think that you should have thought about all of this before you left your man back at the hotel to come and fuck around with her."

Okay, now he was pushing things way too far. He might be right, but no one talked to me like that.

"Hold the fuck up. You don't even know me like that. You know nothing about me or what I'm all about. So I really don't think that it's your place to say a goddamned thing about what I do!"

He didn't get mad, nor did he yell back at me. He just took a sip of his drink that was on the coffee table and said, "All I'm saying is that before you get up and do things with people, you should think not only of yourself but of the other person too. Think about it, Tangie. Do you think that it's easy for A to be in the public eye and not be able to be herself? I remember when she first got picked up by her record label and went to her first big party with her ex-girlfriend. The label made such a big deal about it that it fucked up her relationship."

"Why didn't she just go with a guy? I thought that she likes men too?"

"I wouldn't go as far as to say she likes them. I know that she likes to sleep with men once in a while, but I think that's about it. But it's all good, as far as I'm concerned. I don't know if you know this, but we used to be together back in the day. Then one day she came to me and told me about the feelings she had for women."

"And how did you take it?" I asked, hoping that I could get some insight into how he reacted when he found out about her being gay.

He took another sip of his drink, then took a deep breath, as if it was his turn to unload what was on his chest.

"At first, I was all into it. I thought that having a girlfriend who's into other women would bring something extra to our relationship. But too much of a good thing is never good. It got to the point where we were not having sex on our own. The only time she was up to do anything was when we had another woman in our bed. Once I noticed that, I sat her down, and we talked about how I was feeling and how she was feeling about things. So by the end of this conversation, it was like we both were finding out that she was more gay than bi. She still is. And that's why I think that we are friends today. She told me the truth when she found out her truth."

He had just laid some serious shit on me. Hearing how things had turned out with him and Amira gave me hope for Tay and me.

"So after that talk with her, your relationship just ended abruptly?" I asked, fascinated by his story.

"Well, she would still come around here and there and hit a nigga off with some ass. But I mostly think that she came around because we have that love for each other. I was the first man that she was ever with, you know?"

I just sat there and listened to him talk. He looked like he had spaced out while talking about her. I could understand how he was feeling. Amira had me feeling like that too at times.

"This is why I want you to think things through before she falls too deep into this, Tangie. I know her. She loves too hard. It's hard enough that she has to hide who she is. I just don't think that she needs the added stress that this can end up giving her. She is never good under pressure. And from what she has told me, she is really feeling you, and I just don't want her to get hurt."

Now my mind was spinning. I had to be honest with myself. Was I really the right person for her? I had a gut feeling that I would end up hurting her, and I didn't want to do that. The biggest question that lingered in my mind was whether I could stop myself from sleeping with her or seeing her. I knew for damn sure that I was not going to be able to stop wanting her, so how was this going to work?

As these thoughts ran through my mind, Amira walked into the apartment and made my heart melt. She put down her bag, walked over, and sat on my lap. She pushed my hair out of my face and kissed my lips. I wanted to pull away—God knows I did—but I couldn't. I looked into her eyes, and I saw love. She smiled at me, and I could feel her happiness. I looked over at her friend, and his eyes were begging me to do the right thing. I couldn't take this anymore, and it made my eyes water. She leaned in and kissed me again, and I could feel her love through her lips. This made me pull away. I couldn't let her see the tears in my eyes, so I pushed her back on the couch and went into the bathroom.

Before I closed myself in there, I told her that I wanted to go back to the hotel, to Tay'von. She looked confused. She looked over at her friend, hoping that he could tell her what had just gone down. But he looked away from her, not wanting to see what was in her eyes. She turned back to me and, sad and confused, answered me in a low tone.

"Okay, Tangie. We can go back to the hotel. We can do whatever you want."

On the ride back to the hotel, I didn't utter a word. I sat as far from her as possible, not wanting to feel even a flicker of the fire that had burned between us the night before. At times I caught her friend glancing back at us in his rearview mirror with sadness in his eyes for his good friend. But the pain that I was sure to make her feel would hurt both him and her even more if I hadn't pulled away. I was poison to anyone who got close enough to lick, sniff, or fuck me. I liked her too much to subject her to that much agony, at least I was hoping so.

When I got back to the hotel, I stepped out of the taxi and rushed into the lobby. I looked back before stepping onto the elevator and saw Amira and her friend talking to each other. Neither of them could figure me out, but in that moment, I couldn't figure myself out, either.

I stood in front of my suite door, not knowing what Tay'von was going to do to me once he saw me. I didn't have enough time to come up with anything, so I just walked in and winged it. As soon as I walked in, all eyes were on me. Everyone was up in there, and he even had some bitches that I had never seen before lying around like they belonged there.

"Look who decided to bring her ass back to the hotel," Tay'von said as he staggered his drunken ass over to me. "Where the hell have you been all goddamned night? It's eleven o'clock in the morning, and you're just walking in here? What do you have to say for yourself, Tangie?"

I didn't answer him, because I really didn't have anything to say. I just stood there looking at him, as if he was the one who had done wrong.

"You think that I'm playing with your ass, don't you? How am I supposed to be your man, yet you leave for a whole night, and I don't even know where you're at? That's some real disrespectful shit, Tangie."

I wanted to spit in his face once he said that, but I was not that ghetto. But he did have some nerve talking about disrespect.

"Look, Tay'von, I don't have time for this shit. Now, I understand that you have your little crowd, and maybe you feel like you have to put on a show for them, but do that shit with someone else."

Everyone was waiting to see if Tay was going to let me talk to him like I just had. He was a star who didn't have to put up with no bitch who talked back to him—at least that was how they saw it.

"I just don't understand you, Tangie. Do you know how many bitches will kill to have your spot here with me?"

"Oh, please, Tay'von, spare me the speech. Please don't think that you're the only famous or rich dude I have ever been with. And I want you to know and never forget that if you chose to end this, you won't be the last, and you can bet on that shit."

Tay'von looked at me in disbelief. He threw the bottle of Rémy that he held in his hand at the wall.

One dizzy bitch screamed, and another one said, "Oh no she didn't!"

I turned around and looked at all the faces around the suite and then back at Tay. "I want everyone to get out of here right now, Tay'von."

He laughed, convinced I was playing. "Why do they have to leave? You came and found them here, didn't you?"

"Oh, so you think that I'm playing, right? You're really going to try to challenge me on this, huh?"

I looked at Black. He was the only one who had stood up.

"Uh, we're gonna get out of here and let you two talk," Black said as he yanked on Shamika's arm to leave, but she stood up really slowly, hoping that something would go down before she left the suite.

Black pulled her out into the hallway, with Carl and Tony right behind them. The other three girls just sat there like they were watching a show. I was about to start knocking bitches out, but there was a knock at the door just then, so I went over and opened it. The hotel housekeeper came in with her cleaning cart, and the thought of catching a charge for attempted murder went out the door. I reached down and took the bottle of bleach that was sitting on the left side of her cart and ran over to the girls. I started pouring the bleach on them hoes and anyone else who got in my way.

"I asked y'all bitches to leave, but no, we have to do this the hard way," I said as I splashed the bleach all over their clothes.

Tay'von tried to stop me, but I poured it on him too. He ran to the phone and called Tony and Carl back up to the suite. They rushed back up, but by the time they got there, the bleach bottle was empty and the girls were running out the door. Carl and Tony walked in on me screaming like crazy people, and they looked lost. Tay'von just sat on the floor, unable to believe what he had just seen. I was hysterical. I had been stone cold about everything for far too long, and I had cracked. It had been only a matter of time.

After screaming for ten minutes straight, I ran into the bedroom and began throwing things in an overnight bag. I didn't know where I was going to go, but I did know that I needed to get the hell up out of there. Tay jumped up and came into the bedroom after me. He looked around the room frantically. He came over to the bed and took things out of the bag as I continued to put them in.

"Get the fuck away from me, Tay'von! Don't touch my shit! I'm leaving you!" I screamed like a drama queen.

He took the bag of clothes and threw it on the floor. "You ain't going no damn where! What in the hell is wrong with you?"

"What's wrong with me? I walk in here, and you got all these people in here so they can watch your drunken ass get in my face and talk shit," I said as I cried and talked all at the same time. I was so incoherent that Tay had to concentrate just to understand the little bit that did make sense.

"Fuck all this shit, Tangie. What I really want to know is where in the hell you were all night. What, you and Amira met up with some niggas or something?"

Even through my tears, I had to stop myself from laughing at his dumb question. "Fine, Tay. If you won't let me pack my things, then I'll leave without them." I tried to pass by him, but he grabbed me and pushed me on the bed.

"Didn't I tell you that you are not leaving? You're going to stay here and tell me where you were last night!"

"Fuck you, Tay'von. You can't make me do shit. I don't have to stay here if I don't want to."

He yelled for Carl and told him to lock the door from the outside. The hotel allowed for the bedroom doors to be locked from either side. Carl did as he was told, and from then on, I was trapped.

"Now you can't leave," Tay said as he sat on the bed.

"This is so fucked up, Tay. How are you going to keep me here when I don't want to stay? This is kidnapping, you know?"

"What? Did you think that I would just sit here and let you walk out? Come on, Tangie. We both have put too much into this to just let it go. Me more than you, if you ask me, so no, you can't go. Now that we have that out of the way, you can either tell me where you were or I'm gonna get some sleep. I'll call Carl when I get up to open the door. You might as well get some z's, 'cause I'm sure you didn't get any last night."

"Fuck you, Tay'von."

"Fuck you too, Tangie."

And that was it. He rolled over and went to sleep.

I went into the bathroom and drew a bath. I got one of my baggies and took out my weed and coke. I locked myself in the bathroom and turned on my iPod. I stepped into the hot water, and I made sure not to get out until I had finished everything that had been in my drug baggie.

When I woke up, Tay had already left. I looked at the clock, and it was seven at night. I got up and walked into the living room area. Damn. We were gonna end up paying a hell of a lot of money for the hotel to fix the damage that I had caused with the bleach. I noticed that the same maid whom I had let in earlier was still there.

"Your husband asked me to come back and clean up as much as possible," the older black lady said as I walked to the bar and rolled me up a white boy.

I asked her if she minded that I smoked. She said no, so I rolled up another joint and asked her if she wanted to join me. She sat down, and we lit up.

"It's been so long since I have had one of these," she confided in me.

"Yeah, well, enjoy. If it wasn't for weed, I don't know how I would make it through some days."

She laughed as she choked on the smoke. "*Shit*, my friends and I used to smoke all day and night back in my day. But my husband put a stop to it after we got married."

I looked at the older lady with a "Yeah, right" face. "I wouldn't give weed up for any man. Half the damn time, I have got to be high just to deal with them."

"Isn't that the truth? Trust me, I know. After three husbands and four kids, I wish that I had never given it up."

We shared a laugh as I looked over at her. Anyone could tell that she was one bad bitch back in the day. Hell, she still looked good. Her hair was as soft as mine, but whereas I had a tan complexion, she was damn near white.

"You know, watching you today totally reminded me of myself. I wanted so badly to burst out laughing when I saw you douse them girls with that bleach. Yeah, I had a red-hot temper too," she said as she thought back to her younger days.

"I don't know what got into me. Tay'von was yelling at me, and here were these groupie bitches . . . Oh, my bad. I have to learn how to watch my mouth."

"Oh, child, please. I know all about them groupie bitches myself. See, when I was around your age, I was one of them so-called groupies. I went from singer to singer. We stayed in all the nice hotels, just like this one. I would have never thought that I would end up cleaning them today."

"What happened?" I asked as I got up to fix both of us a drink. I wanted to hear it all. Sometimes hearing about someone else's downfall could save you from your own.

"Well, when you're young, you don't think about putting money away. So when it got to the point that I had been passed around to everyone who would have me, there was no one left. No one wanted me in the end. I was used goods and yesterday's news. I hadn't saved a dime of the money that was given to me by these men. I must have gone through hundreds of thousands of dollars, if not millions. But when you're no longer the 'good-time girl,' no one wants you. But hey, I had a hell of a time while it lasted."

I handed her a drink and sipped my own while thinking about myself. Could I really end up like her? The terrifying part was that any woman in my position could end up like her. Hell, many had.

She went on. "I have seen you around the hotel, but every time I come up here, you are always out. But now that we are sitting here talking, I just have to tell you that in all that you do, make sure to save some money to fall back on. Don't count on these stars to always have your back. That's one of the most important things that I have learned in my forty-six years of living."

We drank and talked for another hour or so. She told me about her life, and I shared some of mine. I vowed never to make the same mistakes that she had made. I learned a lot from her that night and later thought about it as a chance meeting that was meant to be.

Before she left, I asked her for her name. She told me it was Mavis Brown. I got up and told her to hold on. I went to my purse and made her out a check from my own account for sixty thousand dollars. I placed it in an envelope, sealed the flap, and told her to open it when she got home.

I stayed in for the next two days. We ended up having to move to another suite once the hotel found out what I had done with the bleach. I also got a note from Mrs. Brown thanking me for the money. She wrote that she would be taking it and moving down to Florida to be with her mother. She told me that when she saw how much the check was made out for, it made her drop to her knees. She said that she would keep me in her prayers and that she would ask God until the day she died to be by my side whenever I may need Him the most.

A few days later it was time to leave Philly and head to Chicago, and everyone was packed and ready to go. The only person who had seen me since the day I went mad was Tay'von. I walked into the hotel lobby with my shades on and my head held high. "Never let the haters see you down" was my mentality. I walked through the lobby like the queen that I was. I could feel the hatred and envious looks that were shot my way. White, black, yellow, brown, and blue, it never mattered what they were. They all wanted to be me. When I walked by anyone, they stopped what they were doing so that they could take in all that I was giving out. Tay'von watched everyone else watching me with a smile on his face. He understood. My beauty and presence still took him aback at times.

"Damn, girl, you would think that you're the one who's a star," Tay said as he took my hand.

"I *am* the star. Don't you know that by now?"

"You're right. I don't even know what I was just thinking."

With that, we got into our limo and drove away. I didn't even see Amira at the desk in the hotel lobby, but she later told me that she had noticed me and had waited to see if I would speak to her. She said that she had walked away, pissed, thinking that I had meant to ignore her. But she knew she'd get a chance to talk to me in the next city.

During the plane ride, Amira tried to make eye contact, but I pretended to read a book the whole flight. After we landed in Chicago, we went straight to our new hotel, and I did not exchange words with Amira. It was not that I didn't like her; it was just that her friend had freaked me out. Things were different with her. It was not like she was some man whom I wanted something from. I knew that love was what she was looking for, and I just didn't have the time for that, and I was afraid to love. But no matter what I did, I couldn't stop myself from thinking about her. I craved her touch. I wanted her to touch me like she had before. I played the time that we had spent together over and over again in my mind. It was like she got stuck in my head, and no matter what I did, I couldn't get her out.

After hours in the hotel room, I had enough of just sitting around and thinking about her, so I decided to go to Tay's show. I didn't know how things would play out with Amira, but I just couldn't spend another night alone in a hotel room.

When I got to the venue, Tay'von was on his second song, so I rushed past A's dressing room, hoping that she wouldn't see me, but I failed. She came out of her dressing room as if she were a hound dog catching the scent of a fugitive, and stepped in front of me.

"I really need to speak to you, Tangie."

I kept my eyes on the floor, because if I looked at her, I wouldn't be able to stop myself from doing what she wanted. "Can you let me get by so that I can get into Tay's dressing room?"

"No. I need to talk to you, so just give me a minute."

"I don't want to talk, Amira. There's nothing for us to talk about."

She lifted my head so that she could look into my eyes. When she asked again to talk, I was not able to resist. I walked into her dressing room, pissed that I could not tell her no. She closed the door and asked me to sit down. I did.

"So what is this all about?" I asked as she sat in a chair across from me and slid it close to me.

"What's been up with you? I haven't seen you, and you never got back to me. I must have left five to ten messages for you at the hotel desk in Philly. And I didn't get a chance to talk to you the morning my friend dropped us off, 'cause you ran off. I don't know what to make of things."

I wanted to tell her that she had been on my mind like crazy, but I didn't. I just sat there, looking everywhere else but at her.

"I know that this might be hard for you, but don't you think that you should at least give this a try?" she said.

Rage filled me because I knew that I couldn't.

"Give what a try? Do you want me to come to you and say, 'Yes, Amira, I'm gay, and I want to be with you'? Well, that's not going to happen. I could never just be with a woman. I know that we had sex and all, but I am not gay. I am not a gay woman."

She put her hand over mine and tried to comfort me. "Look, I am not trying to push you into something that you are not into. But I do know that you feel something. All that I am asking is for you to be open about things."

I looked down at her hand over mine, then back at her face. Damn, she was sexy. Thoughts of our night together flashed through my mind and turned me on. I crossed my legs to stop myself from taking her hand and putting it down my pants.

"Um, I think that I should get out of here."

I stood up and walked to the door. My body begged for her to stop me. She came over to me and turned me around so that I was facing her. As she pressed me against the door with her body, I felt her breath on my neck. She pressed her hand against the door and just stood like this and breathed, in and out, in and out, in and out. Her breathing started to come harder and faster as desperation snuck into her soul.

"Tangie, please, please just give this a chance."

I felt each word against my neck as she moved her lips. It was as if they were trying to pierce my flesh so that her words could find their way to my heart.

"Okay, fine. You're not gay, but let's not think about it that way," she said.

She moved her lips from my neck and placed them on my lips, but she didn't kiss me. They were just there. She looked at me straight in the eyes, and when I went to turn away, her yelling stopped me, "Look at me, God damn it! Look at me!"

I did as she asked. She knew that the eyes never lied, even though the mouth could tell many tall tales. And right then, she saw it. She saw the need for her in my eyes and knew that she had me. She kissed me with her eyes open.

I kissed her back as our eyes stayed glued on one another. We saw the truth and didn't want to look away. She touched me with her body and lips only. I moaned from her kiss alone and could feel myself wanting more.

There was a knock at the door, but I heard it from afar. Someone was telling her that she needed to head to the stage, but I had her within my grasp and didn't want to let go. She pulled away from me and asked me if I could watch her performance. We left her dressing room and walked to the stage. When we got there, Tay'von was taking a quick break while Amira performed. He'd go back out later and close out the show. He kissed me hello and took my hand so that I could go to his dressing room with him.

"Oh no, I want to stay out here. I'll be there in a minute," I told him.

He gave me a "What's wrong with you?" look and let my hand go. He didn't understand but headed to his dressing room alone.

Amira hit the stage, and you could hear her fans going crazy. She motioned to the sound people to turn down the music as she hit the center of the stage.

"I want to thank everyone for coming out tonight. I have been working on a new song, and I want you all to be the first to hear it."

The crowd went crazy with excitement as the music came back on. It started with a strong and sexy beat. The type of beat that would make you want to do a slow, sexy strip dance for your mate. Then her voice came in low, deep, and full of soul and lust. Her voice oozed sexiness as she started to sing "If You Were Here Right Now." She had turned the poem that she wrote for me into a song. She must have written the rest of the lyrics when I was locked up in my hotel room. I stood there and listened to her belt out the song with so much feeling and heart that it gave me chills. I looked up at the monitors, and I noticed that she had tears running down her face.

The audience was quiet. I had never been to a concert where everyone was that quiet. By the time she was done, most people were in tears, including me. Once she stopped singing, everyone started to clap and cheer. She turned to where I was standing and mouthed, "I love you." She turned back to the crowd and told them that this was her new single and that they would be able to buy it in three weeks on the internet, or they could wait an extra week to pick up the single in stores.

For her next song, Black joined her on the stage, so I left to go back to Tay's dressing room. When I walked in, he was just coming out of the shower.

"Oh, now you want to come and join me, huh?" he said when he saw me.

I walked over to him and put my arms around him. "Come on, baby. Let's not start tonight. Anyway, I came back here hoping that I could get me a little quickie."

"Now, you know that I have to go back out for another set. A quickie would wipe me out."

"What the hell is wrong with you, Tay? You act like you don't want me anymore."

"You know that it's not even like that. You have just been wanting to do it at all the wrong times."

"All the wrong times? Since when has there ever been a wrong time to fuck?"

He pulled away from me before answering.

"Look, Tangie, you don't have to worry about me not wanting you. You turn me on every time I look at you. But with all this traveling that we do, I just get like this at times. This has nothing to do with you. Trust me."

I didn't say anything more about it. He was full of shit, and I knew it. I just sat down on the couch and watched him get ready for his next performance. Some glamorous life this was.

Chapter 11

Will You Marry Me?

"No, Amira, we can't do this," I pleaded, but she wouldn't stop.

She just kept sucking on my clit. I knew that I was telling her to stop, but I really didn't mean it.

"Cum in my mouth, Tangie. I wanna taste your cream," she said as she took her time with me. I watched her tongue slide up and down on me. I let her draw the cum out of me, and I couldn't hold back anymore. She was making it feel too good.

"Ahh, Amira, I'm about to cum. Please stop. Oh shit, I can't take this anymore."

I moaned, but she didn't stop. She just moved her tongue faster and faster.

"Wake up, Tangie."

I opened my eyes and saw Shamika standing over top of me. I was lying on the couch in Tay's dressing room and must have dozed off.

"What in the hell were you just dreaming about?"

"How do you know that I was dreaming?" I asked her.

She looked at me as if I should have known the answer to my own question.

"I know because you were moving around on the bed like someone was laying down some good old dick on your ass."

Amira had really started to roam through my thoughts a little too often. If I wasn't daydreaming about her, she was invading my dreams as I slept.

"Well, if I was dreaming, then I don't remember what about," I lied.

"Well, what's been going on with you and Amira? You two have been staying out really late. I hope you aren't letting her turn you out," Shamika joked, but that only annoyed me.

I didn't answer her. If I did, then that meant that I would have to lie, so I just let it go. Instead, I asked her what she wanted.

"Girl, I came up here to get the dirt. You have been out with that dyke bitch so much that I thought you would have something to tell me. Hell, I want to know what you know."

I looked around the room for something to drink or smoke.

"I really don't think that there is really much to her. We hung out, and she's cool and everything, but that's about it. It's not like I was just going to come right out and ask her to tell me all her secrets."

Shamika sucked her teeth, showing her disappointment. "You should have just asked her if she was gay. Then, when she said yes, that's when you go in for the kill. Well, it doesn't matter, anyway. I know she's gay. I know she be trying to cover it up and dress all fem, but she isn't fooling me."

"So what if she is? It's better than her going after Tay or Black. Don't you think?"

"True, true," she answered back.

I was getting so sick of her that it wasn't even funny. I had to remind myself to get the ball rolling as far as me getting rid of her, but that would take time and opportunity.

Shamika stayed in Tay's dressing room until the show was over. On the ride to the hotel, Amira's song weighed heavily on my mind. She had taken her time and had written a song about me. It was starting to be clear to me that she had more feelings for me than any other man had ever had for me. Out of all the singers and rappers that I had ever been with, she was the only one who had ever written anything about me that I knew of.

After returning to the hotel, Tay and I fell asleep on the bed within minutes. I woke up a few hours later, and the clock on the nightstand let me know that it was three o'clock in the morning. I had just had another dream about Amira, and it was driving me crazy. My heart raced, and my body was yearning. I looked over at Tay, and he was sound asleep. I got up and went into the living room area, hoping to find more air to breathe. I had to get control of myself, but that was hard to do when you were horny and felt like your insides were on fire. I stood in front of the floor-length mirror that covered one of the walls. I was one sexy bitch who should not be wanting for sex. I should have been getting it whenever and from whomever I wanted.

I got my snow out of my purse and sniffed some out of the baggie as I paced the living room. I needed some sex, and there were only three people whom I could get it from. There was Carl, but I had just had sex with him, so I was damn near bored with him. Then there was Amira, but there seemed to be too many feelings growing between us. I wanted to keep things simple with her, but it was clear that neither of us were really in control of our emotional state when it came to our affair. So that just left Tay. The coke that I had sniffed sent a rush through my body and gave me courage. I put the baggie back in my purse and headed toward the bedroom. I turned on the lights and walked over to the bed. Tay'von was on his back, so I just lay on top of him.

"Damn, Tangie. What are you doing, baby?" Tay asked as he opened his eyes.

"What is this? Still not the right time?"

I pulled off my shirt and ground my hips on him. I leaned over and kissed him, impatiently waiting for him to return the affection.

"Come on, baby, don't make me beg," I said.

He flipped me over and got on top of me. I smiled because I was happy to get some love from my man again. He leaned his head down and tongued my chest.

"Fuck all that bullshit. Just give me the dick."

Tay could tell that I needed him inside me badly, and that made him smile. Tay had once told me that when I acted that way, it made him feel wanted and needed, but I didn't do that too often, unless it came to his money. So he slid himself inside me. It had been too long, and both of us were happy that we were doing this. Tay said he didn't even realize how much he missed having sex with me until then. He had forgotten the warmth and tightness my insides provided, but once he was in, it hit him like a ton of bricks. He had been holding himself back from me because of what he thought he had done to me. He had been too ashamed to sex me. He had felt like if he did, I would remember the monster that he had fought hard to hide. I was just happy that my man wanted me again, and I could tell that I was still the best lover he had ever had.

But as good as our sex always was, it still didn't curb my appetite for Amira. It just made me want her even more.

"So did you like the song? I never got to ask you that the other night," Amira said as she walked up behind me at the hotel bar.

"Oh, yeah. Um, that was really sweet. I didn't even know that you were going to do that. I loved it."

She smiled openly, showing her happiness at my approval. "Well, from now on, whenever it comes on, you will know that I wrote it for you."

Every time this girl came around, I had to smile. She just had this glow about her.

"Shouldn't you be getting ready to leave?" I asked her.

"You never keep up with anything. Tonight is our night off. After tomorrow's show, that's when we leave," she said as she pulled my hair from my face and brushed her hand against my cheek.

It sent a chill down my spine, so I pulled away.

"What are you going to do on your night off?" I asked.

She licked her lips and smiled. I knew that my face was turning red, because I was burning with desire.

"Maybe we can spend some time together?" she asked.

I really wanted to, but I knew that if I was alone with her, I would not be able to stop myself from touching her.

"Well, I have some things that I need to do, so I don't know if we will be able to see each other today."

She took my hand and held it. "Well, I'll be in my room if you want to hang out."

She put a hundred-dollar bill on the bar and headed out. I watched her walk away, letting my eyes go from the back of her head to her feet. Damn, she was sexy.

I finished my drink and headed back to my room. Once in the suite, I looked through my purse, but my baggie was gone. Tay watched me and laughed out loud.

"It's not there. I threw it all out. You have been shoving way too much of that shit up your nose. Weed should be enough."

This made me want to jump on him and claw his face, but I didn't.

"That's really fucked up, Tay. I don't walk around here telling you what drug you should take."

"Yeah, well, I'm sick of you doing all that damn coke. You're out of control with that shit. Just smoke a jay or two and you'll be okay."

He threw a ziplock bag at me that was filled with weed. I threw it back at him and told him to roll me up two blunts. I went into the bedroom, undressed, and came back out in my robe. I sat beside him and watched Mr. Too Fine roll up my weed. We had come so far, but then again, I still didn't know what it was that we had. We had never really taken the time to talk about us. I took the first blunt and lit it up. My mind ran wild with thoughts of Amira. My nipples hardened at the thought of her. I got up and told Tay that I was going to take a bath.

The water in the tub warmed my already hot body even more. This was getting to be too much, I thought to myself as I ran my fingers in between my thighs. If soft moans didn't escape my lips, I would have never known that I was playing with myself.

"Fuck it." I got out of the tub and dried myself off. I lotioned my body and put on my Hypnôse perfume. I slid on a thin strapless dress that I liked to wear while I was chilling with no undies. I pulled my hair back in a low ponytail and left the bathroom.

I walked into the living room area, picked up my purse, then noticed that there were two already rolled blunts beside it. I called Tay's name, but he was gone. I walked out of the hotel suite and headed for the elevator. I knew exactly what I wanted and where I was going to get it. I went down to the ninth floor and knocked on door number 912. Amira opened the door with a smile.

"I hate to smoke alone. Would you like to join me?" I asked her as I held my hand out, showing her the two blunts Tay had rolled for me. She stepped aside, and I slid into her room.

Amira had notebooks all over her bed, but other than that, it was neat. She had on a wife-beater and pink boy shorts. I took notice of her hard nipples, and it turned me on. Finding it hard to look away, I lit both blunts and handed her one. She took it and sat on the bed, while I opted for the chair. She took a pull and leaned back on her elbows. Her hair was still styled with the bangs in the front and was still long in the back. Her light skin was shiny, but not in an oily way. It was from being blessed with beautiful skin. I looked at her body openly. She didn't mind. She just stayed there on the bed, in the same position. I loved the way she looked leaning back on her elbows. It was like her body was calling me, begging to be touched by me, but I held back. I just sat in the chair, smoking and looking.

"Come here," she called to me in a low, sexy tone, but I didn't move.

"Come here, Tangie." This time there was more of a demand in her voice, but she kept it low and sexy.

I stood up and walked over to the bed. She slid one of her legs between mine and made our skin touch. I stayed standing while she moved her head closer to me. Her eyes had become red and slanted from the smoke. When she looked up at me, I melted inside. She leaned her head into me, and I could feel one of her hands on my thigh. It made me gasp for air the higher she went. When she reached my clit, she rubbed it softly and slowly. I closed my eyes and enjoyed it.

"Damn, Tangie. I have missed you so much. You're so fucking wet. Damn, Tangie. Damn."

The first time we slept together, she hardly said anything, but now her verbal skills were on full display. I loved the things that she was saying to me. I even loved the sound of her voice.

"I have been thinking about you nonstop. When I'm in here alone, I touch myself as I think about your sexy body," she whispered.

That bitch was turning me the hell on. My eyes were closed, and all I could hear was her voice. My whole body was shaking from her touch. She never changed her pace. She kept it slow and long as she talked.

"All I can do is think about how you feel, how you smell, how you fuck. You're so sexy, and touching you just feels good. You're so soft. You're so, so . . . Shit, you're just you, and that drives me crazy."

After she said this, she moved her fingers faster. She stayed seated, with her head still close to my body, and I couldn't help but moan out her name.

"Damn, Tangie. I just wish that you were mine. I have got to be able to have you anytime I want you. I have got to be able to taste you anytime I want. Yeah, Tangie, I love tasting you. I want to taste that pussy right now."

Oh my God, she had me so hot. She lifted my leg up on the bed and brought my dress up around my waist. She stuck her tongue out and let me see it. She lowered her head and licked

me. Her mouth was as soft as I remembered it.
I moaned loudly as I wondered what she did to
her tongue to make it feel so good. There was
this intensity about the way she did it. She made
me cum in five minutes. I had to push her away
because she wouldn't stop. I pulled my dress off
as she lay back down on her elbows again and
licked her lips.

"Damn, Tangie. You taste so fucking good.
Why did you push me away?"

I got down on my knees in front of her. She
opened her legs slightly wider as I rubbed her
through her boy shorts. I watched her closely as
she slowly breathed in and out. Damn, I really
did like her. I felt like I wanted to be with her
and stay in that room forever.

"Damn, Amira. So many things are happening
to me at once. I know that it's wrong for me to
be with you, but I can't help myself. I want to be
with you. I want to be yours."

I pulled down her underwear and pushed
open her legs. I wanted to eat her the same way
she had just done me. I moved my head close to
her, but she put her hand on my forehead and
stopped me.

"Tangie, I told you before, I don't want you
doing this until you're sure. I want to really
know that your heart is in it."

I looked at her and answered from my heart. "Amira, I am falling in love with you. I know that this will not be easy, but this is what I want right now."

I lowered my head, and she let me love her. I mimicked everything that she did to me. First, I moved my tongue fast; then I slowed it down. I loved the way she felt against it. I loved the taste of her, and it made me fall in love with pleasuring her. As I ate her out, she touched her own nipples.

"Oh, Tangie, don't stop. Baby, don't stop."

She reached down and pushed my face deeper into her pussy. She tried to close her legs and push me away, but I held them open and moved my tongue faster. I got a firm hold on her hips and made her take it. She moved her head from side to side, having no choice but to lie there and scream from pleasure.

"Fuck. I'm cumming, Tangie. Ahhh, I'm cumming."

I kept on going until her body shook uncontrollably. I licked back up her body and let her taste herself on my lips. We moved to the top of the bed and got under the covers. We touched, caressed, and got to know each other's body from head to toe for the next three hours.

***

"Tangie, you know that you don't have to go. Just stay here with me," Amira said as I got dressed.

"Yeah, well, I don't want Tay coming back and getting mad 'cause I have been gone for so long. You know how he can get."

She sat up in the bed and rolled a blunt from her own stash. "I thought you said that you wanted to be with me. Were you just bullshitting?"

"No, Amira, I was telling the truth. I do want to be with you, but I came on this tour with Tay'von. I can't just be like, 'Fuck him,' and move all my stuff down to your room."

She started to get mad because she knew that she wouldn't get her way. But come on. What did she expect? That I was ready to jump out of the closet and start waving my pride flag? I was still getting over the fact that I was actually attracted to a woman. Maybe her friend was right. These were things that I should have thought about before jumping into bed with her, but it was too late to go back. I had tasted the devil's fruit and had become addicted from the first bite. All I thought about was my next meal: where, when, and how was I going to get it. Feelings would have to come later.

"And why can't you just be like, 'Fuck it'? You can do whatever the hell you want to do."

She was right in a way, but I was also comfortable with where I was at, who I was with, and who I thought I was, meaning with being a straight woman. I just didn't know how to break things off with Tay. Or maybe I just didn't want to.

"Come on, A. We just had such a good time. Let's not get into this right now."

"Okay, okay, but we will have to talk about this eventually. It's just not going to go away."

She lit up her blunt and passed it to me. I stayed with her for another hour before going back to my suite.

Over the next two weeks, Amira and I spent every moment we could together. Our days were spent going out in whatever city we were in, and our nights were filled with stolen moments of sexual escapades. Our love for each other grew every day, and I felt like I was getting closer to leaving Tay for her. She filled me with true love. It was not about what she had or what she could do for me. It was just about us. All I had to do was face the truth: I loved a woman, and that was that.

"Where in the hell have you been, Tangie?" Tay asked me when I finally reappeared one evening. I had been out with Amira so much that he really hadn't seen much of me.

"I just been doing my thing and staying out of your way," I said as I sat down and nestled into him. I couldn't even lie; it did feel good to be in a man's arms.

"Yeah, but I miss you, baby. You're always out, and everyone has been asking for you."

I looked up at him and kissed him. His lips were warm and inviting. I had missed him too at times.

"Well, I'm here now. And since today is your off day, let's go out and do something."

He smiled at my happiness to see him. "Where do you want to go? I don't really know too many hot clubs in St. Louis, but I have heard of this club named Plush. Do you want to go?"

I told him yes while enjoying his touch.

As I showered, Tay called everyone up and asked them if they wanted to go. My heart almost stopped when he told me that Amira had said that she would go, even though she didn't like clubs. The last thing I needed was to have to take a car ride with both of them. Well, Amira would just have to deal with the fact that I was going to be all about my man that night.

An hour later we all sat in the limo, and for once, Shamika looked normal. Everyone settled in for the ride and popped bottles. I sat next to Tay and kept quiet. Amira shot sexy looks at me while I tried my best to act like she wasn't there.

Tay noticed that I was quiet. "Damn, baby. It was your idea to go out, and now you're acting like you don't want to be here. What's wrong?"

"I'm all right, Tay. You know how I am. I'm just in my own mind. Pass me a drink." I couldn't wait to get to the club and out of that car. I felt like I was suffocating.

We got to the club and entered through the VIP entrance. At times I hated VIP; sometimes I just felt like being around other club goers. We chilled in there, but everyone started to get bored, which tended to happen when you were locked away in VIP. The DJ made an announcement that Tay, Black, and Amira were in the club, and the club goers went crazy. They set a table aside for us, and we went out and sat among the ordinary people. One after the other, their songs were played, and people started to crowd around us. It was too much for me, so I got up to go get a drink.

It was always crazy being around famous people. Other people didn't know when to leave them alone. Sometimes you just wanted to be able to enjoy yourself without all the things fame brought. When you were famous, it was like you were no longer human. It was as if you didn't belong to yourself anymore. You belonged to the world, and you had no time to just be yourself and do normal things without people running up to you or doing anything just to be near you. People always talked about the fun side of fame. . . . They talked about the money. We all forgot that there was a price you must pay for fame. But as some would say, it was a very small price to pay for a life of luxury. The truth was, though, it might just cost you your soul.

The bartender handed me my drink at the same moment I saw Amira heading toward me. As soon as she got to the bar, I smiled at her and told her to enjoy herself. Then I walked back to Tay—not to be mean, but I needed her to know that I couldn't be all about her that night. During the rest of the time we spent at the club, I hardly looked at her. She didn't seem too happy about it, but I was not her girlfriend. I was Tay's girl, for the time being.

The next morning I woke up to Shamika and Black watching the tape of Tay and me dominating Miss Thick. I gave Tay'von a "What the hell?" look, and he understood.

"Come on, Tangie. It's all good. Plus, it's not like we did anything too crazy, like piss on her," Tay said in his defense.

"It's not about that, Tay'von. You shouldn't be putting our shit out in the street like that."

"Aw, come on, Tangie. We're all friends here," the hood rat had the nerve to say. I didn't even know what made Shamika think that she should open her mouth during my and Tay's conversation, but she did, anyway.

I shook my head. "This doesn't have shit to do with friends. I'm sure R. Kelly showed his friends his tape, and you see how far that got him."

"Okay, okay, Tangie. I'll turn it off."

Tay'von got up and turned off the camera. I pulled out the disk and went and put it in my suitcase in the bedroom. When I walked back out, Shamika was playing with the camera as if she were some ten-year-old. I sat down beside Tay and threw my legs up on his lap. Shamika turned the camera on us, and Tay leaned over and kissed me.

"You two are always all over each other. Don't no two people have that much love in a relationship," Shamika commented.

"Why can't we have that much love, Shamika? I have made Tangie my world. Don't you and Black share that same kind of love?"

I had to stop myself from laughing. I knew that Tay's question made both her and Black uncomfortable.

"Oh, please, nigga. We got that thug love. We're not into all that kissy-kissy bullshit."

I just rolled my eyes at her dumb ass. She didn't know shit about love. She didn't even realize that Black was dying to have this kind of love, and that was why he was getting it elsewhere.

"Well, since we're all talking about love, I have something that I was going to do tonight, but I think that this is the right time," Tay said as he walked over to the phone.

A few minutes later Tony came up to the suite and handed Tay a small light blue box. Tay asked me to stand up. I looked over at Shamika, who was still holding the camera. I wanted to tell her to watch and learn, but I didn't. What was about to go down spoke for itself.

Tay'von got right in front of me and looked in my eyes. "Well, Tangie, we have been together for a while now, and I must say that I have loved every minute of it. I have been with all types of women, and none of them have ever given me the love that you do. You have a spark that has lit my life since the day I met you. I love you, and I want you to be a part of my life till the day I die."

Tay'von got on his knee and took my left hand. "Now is the time for us to stop playing house and to make things legit. Will you marry me?"

In that moment, nothing else mattered. I didn't care about my cars, about Shamika. Not even the love that I had for Amira mattered. It was all about me and that ring. All I could think of was that my dream was coming true. I had been chasing ballers, rappers, actors, and anybody else with money ever since I was old enough to date. Now I had one asking me to be his wife. D-day was here, and all my efforts had paid off.

Tay stayed on his knee until I answered.

"Yes, Tay. I'll marry you, baby."

Tears ran down my face as Black got up and popped a bottle of champagne, while Tony and Carl look pissed. I knew why Carl was mad, but I just thought that Tony was being a bitch about this. Shamika just looked like she had the jealous monkey on her back while Black poured the champagne and made a toast.

"Here's to the beginning of your happiness. And may it last forever. To many more years of love and lovemaking."

After we all took a sip, Black said that we all should go out to lunch. Since I was the only one who was not dressed, I told them that I would meet them at the restaurant.

"That's okay, baby. We can all wait for you," Tay said as he sat back down on the couch.

"No, don't worry about it, Tay. It's going to take me at least forty-five minutes to get ready, so you all go ahead and order drinks. I'll make it in time for the food."

"I'll stop and see if Amira wants to go," Black said right before he walked out the door.

I wanted to stop him, but Tay's lips stopped me. He kissed me and said goodbye. I was unable to move as I watched them leave.

The door closed, and I walked over to the couch and sat down. What was I going to say to Amira? She was bound to flip out. I got up and went into the bathroom. I thought about it as I showered but didn't come up with much. *What will I do? What would a normal person do? Would they give up on their dreams and go with love? Or would they take everything that is owed to them and be with the person that they can learn to love just for the cash?* I just didn't know. Hell, I hadn't been normal for most of my life, anyway.

After getting clean, I got out of the shower, dried off, and sat on the bed to put lotion on. The phone rang, and it was Tay. He gave me the name of the restaurant and told me to take the hotel limo.

"Did Black tell Amira about lunch?" I asked.

"Yeah. She wasn't ready, either, so Black told her to come with you."

"Was she happy to hear the good news?"

I really just wanted to know if she had flipped out when Black told her. I heard Tay asking Black in the background if he had told Amira about the engagement, and I eagerly awaited the answer.

"He says that he didn't tell her. But you can tell her. I'm sure she'll be happy to hear about it."

Damn. Now I had to be the one to break the news to her. As soon as I hung up the phone with Tay, the doorbell rang. I knew who it was and thought about ignoring it, but that would be no use; we still had a car ride ahead of us. I opened the door with my towel on and let Amira know that I would be ready shortly. I tried to go back to the bedroom, but she stopped me.

"Hold up. I want to talk to you."

"Come on, Amira. They are waiting for us. We can't be too damn late."

This was not the truth. I just didn't want to have to face her and tell the truth.

"This won't take that long, Tangie."

I sat on the couch and lit Tay's half-smoked blunt.

"What was with you last night? You hardly even looked at me," Amira began as she took a seat across from me.

I took a deep pull and blew out the smoke. "Things have been heavy between us, and I know that we like each other and all, but—"

"No, Tangie, you told me that you love me. Not *like*, but *love*. And now you're acting like that meant nothing."

What could I say? She was right.

"What is the problem, Tangie? We can't be, because I'm a woman? You have known this since day one."

"Why are you asking so much of me? Why can't we just be? Why must you ask me things that I have no control over? Maybe it has something to do with you being a woman, but then again, maybe it has to do with my love for Tay'von. I just don't know right now."

She stood up and started pacing the room. "This is bullshit, Tangie. You have known that I don't have a dick since before we started messing around. You knew this before you told me that you loved me. Hell no! We can't *just be*. I'm not one of them dumb niggas, Tangie. I can't just fuck you and let things be. I want us to be together. Don't you want to be with me?"

I just sat there. I couldn't say anything to her without it hurting her. So I just smoked.

"Tangie, I can't turn myself into a man. I will stay a woman, and that is what I want to be." By then, she was screaming, and I didn't even have the guts to look at her.

"Fine, Tangie. You don't want to be with a woman, right? Fuck it. I'll do it your way."

She took off running to the bedroom. I went after her, and once in the room, she started going through the suitcases.

"What in the hell are you doing?" I yelled at her as she opened another one of my suitcases and found my dildo. She took it out and shook her head in disgust.

"You're so hung up on dick that you even have to travel with a plastic one."

I just walked out of the room. I wasn't going to win this fight against her, so it was better that I let her be. She had lost her mind, and I needed a drink. There I was in a hotel room with one of the top-selling R & B singers, and she was crying for my love. And at the restaurant was my fiancé, who happened to be a top-selling rap star. You would think that my life was at its best, but instead I was backed up against a wall.

A few minutes later Amira walked out of the bedroom, dressed in Tay's clothes. She even had on one of his fitted hats.

"This is what you want, isn't it? Okay, Tangie, I'm a man. Will this make you love me?"

I looked at her as if she had lost what was left of her mind.

"Don't look so shocked. You can't love me as a woman, so here I am as a man."

By then I was back on the couch, gulping down my drink. She walked over to me and stood in front of me. She unzipped Tay's jeans and stuck the dildo through the slit.

"There it is, Tangie. There's the dick that you can't live without."

She leaned over and pulled my towel from me. I stood up to get it back, but she threw it across the room.

"You're really bugging out, Amira. All this shit isn't necessary."

She reached out and pulled me close. "This is what you want, right? What, you're still not satisfied?"

I was standing face-to-face with her, and even with Tay's clothes on, she still looked womanly. She still held her beauty.

"I will do whatever I have to do to be with you, Tangie. Can't you see that I will do whatever you want me to do for you? Just tell me what it is that you want. Please just tell me."

I pulled away from her with a sordid heart. It sickened me that all I could do at that moment was think about myself. I was too selfish and could no longer stand my own existence. I felt low, unworthy of the love she had for me, and unworthy of the love she was fighting to show me. Maybe if I went about this situation another way, she would get it through her thick skull and finally understand that I was poisonous. With one bite, I would kill the most wonderful thing about her, her heart.

"You know what, Amira? You talk a lot of shit. Here you are, dressed like a man, but you will never be able to fuck me like one. You are a woman, a woman!"

My words dripped with the venom that lurked deep down inside me. It made her face transform, and the rage that was brewing inside her swam through her veins and exploded when it got to her face. Her sweet outer shell became hard and unrecognizable.

"Fine, Tangie. You say I can't fuck you like a man, but there's no harm in trying."

She pushed me down to the floor and put a leg on each side of me.

"Suck my dick."

"What?"

"Suck my dick," she repeated as she took the back of my head and pushed it toward the dildo that was in her pants.

"Amira, you don't have to do this. We can—"

"Fuck that," she screamed. Her whole body was shaking. She lifted her hand, saying she felt pain in her chest. She said she knew that it was not from a premature heart attack but from a broken heart.

"You want a man, right? Well, this is the best that I can do. Now, suck my dick, Tangie."

I leaned forward and wrapped my lips around the dildo as she pushed it deeper into my mouth. After a couple of minutes of this, she pushed me off.

"Now get your ass on that couch," she ordered.

I sat on the couch and tried to talk sense into her. "Amira, you don't have to prove anything to me. My feelings for you are still here, and we can make this work. I just need some time."

"How much fucking time do you need? I've been fucking you for almost a month now, yet you're still asking for more time. Time won't make me grow a dick."

She got on her knees and leaned me back. She pulled me toward the edge of the couch until my ass was hanging off.

"This is one thing I know I do better than a man."

She lowered her head and did what she did best. She had me begging her not to stop.

After a while, she raised her head. "Yeah, I know you love this shit. I knew that once I started, you wouldn't want me to stop. Now tell me that you love me," she said, then put her head back in between my legs.

The more she licked, the more I told her that I loved her. I was dripping wet, and at that moment I didn't give a damn that everyone was waiting for us. They could have waited forever if it were up to me. She stood up and told me to lie down as she climbed on top of me. I reached to pull her shirt off, but she told me no. She took my legs and put one on each of her shoulders. She slowly worked the dildo inside me. I couldn't do anything but lie there and love it. She worked the hell out of me and hit all the right spots.

Amira moved her hips like any man would. She took my legs off her shoulders and spread them apart widely. She pounded me with the dildo. Her eyes look glazed over and demonic. I screamed and moaned with pleasure. I loved everything that she was doing to me, but right before I went over the edge, she stopped.

She had tears streaming down her face and didn't try to hide them. She looked down at me and started to move slowly while her eyes stayed on my pussy. She reached down and rubbed my clit. She knew that this drove me crazy, and she didn't hold back. I reached up and knocked off her hat and ran my fingers through her hair. She came down and kissed me but never lost her rhythm. I came hard, so hard that tears now ran down my face. We both lay there crying, and then she stood up and took off all of Tay's clothes. She got right back on top of me, and we held each other as if one of us was about to die.

Ten minutes later the phone rang. It was Tay asking me why I was still at the hotel. I told him that I was walking out the door and that I would be there soon.

"I'm going to go clean up. We really have to get out of here," I told Amira after I ended the call.

She got up and followed me to the bathroom. Now the panic set in. What would she do when she found out about Tay and me? I put my ring in my purse, and fifteen minutes later we headed to the restaurant. My heart pounded as we were driven to lunch. When we got there, I slid the ring on my finger without her seeing me do so, then reminded her of my true feelings.

"No matter what happens, I just want you to know that my feelings for you are real, and I do love you." I leaned over and kissed her but pulled away and slipped on my sunglasses as the driver opened the door.

"Just remember that I can always change my mind," I said, speaking of marrying Tay, and stepped out of the car.

I took a deep breath and got ready to deal with whatever happened next.

Chapter 12

This Is All Your Fault,

You Fucking Bully

There are some things that will haunt you for the rest of your life. The decisions you make may change your life forever. "If only I knew" just doesn't cut it and will never change what fate has in store for you. The funny thing is, I just can't help but to say . . . if only I knew.

I walked into the restaurant, not knowing what would go down. Things could really get out of hand, although I was praying that they didn't. If Amira flipped out, I wouldn't know what to do. All these thoughts were banging around my head as the hostess led us to our table. I sat down, and Amira sat right next to me.

"Girl, what took you so long? We didn't think that you would make it," Tay'von joked.

"Well, we are here now. Did everyone order?" I said, hoping that the engagement would not come up.

Tay'von shook his head. "No, we were waiting for you. Now that you are here, let's order another round of drinks. I'll call the waitress over."

I moved around in my seat because I knew that the news was about to come out. I was sweating bullets as the waitress came back with our drinks.

"Well, bottoms up," I said, trying to bypass a toast.

Tay'von held up his hand. "Hold on, baby. I want to say a few words."

My body started to tremble as Tay stood up. I knew that the shit was about to hit the fan.

"Tangie, you have made me the happiest man in the world by telling me that you will be my wife—"

Amira damn near jumped out of her seat once the words left Tay's mouth. "What, what happened? She's going to be you're *what*?"

"Oh, she didn't tell you? Tay'von asked her to marry him today. That's why we're here," Shamika said before she faked a smile from ear to ear.

"No, she didn't tell me. I didn't know anything about this."

Amira's face was turning red. I reached under the table and touched her knee. I squeezed it tight, trying to calm her down.

"Yeah, I asked her back at the hotel before we left," Tay said as he leaned over and kissed my neck.

I could feel Amira's legs shaking while I still held on to her knee.

"Well, this is to many years of love," Tay said as he raised his glass.

We all took a sip of our drinks, except for Amira.

"I'm going to go to the bathroom," Amira said as she stood up.

I wanted to go after her, but I didn't want to be so obvious about our love.

"What in the hell is wrong with her?" Shamika asked.

"She said that she wasn't feeling well when we were on our way here. It may be her stomach," I answered, praying that they all would buy it.

"Well, I hope that she feels better for the show tonight. That new song of hers is getting good reviews," Black boasted.

When Amira got back to the table, everyone ordered food and took it easy on the drinks, but not her. She just downed one strong drink after the other.

"You better slow down on them drinks, A. Don't forget we have a show tonight," Tay'von warned.

"Yeah, well, sometimes you just have to say, 'Fuck everything,' and get drunk," Amira answered with sarcasm in her voice.

"I see that we have a party pooper on our hands."

Tay was joking, but she didn't laugh. Actually, she didn't say anything else for the rest of the day.

We all ate, then headed back to our hotel. Amira rode in the other limo with Black and Shamika. Thank God.

"Hey, baby, I'm gonna chill on the couch and watch some TV. If I fall asleep, will you wake me up in an hour so that I can go to the sound check?" Tay'von said as I walked to the bedroom to go change.

It wasn't long before he yelled for me to come back out and watch the tape of him asking me for my hand in marriage. I slipped off my shoes and went to join him. I sat down on the couch as he pressed PLAY. He sat next to me and laid his head down in my lap, and we joked about how corny we thought he looked. I leaned over and kissed him. Things were funny with me. I always found myself loving the person that I was with: it was always an "out of sight, out of my mind" thing with me.

I ran my hands through his hair as I thought about how hard things had gotten. Yes, I loved him, but I also liked her a whole lot, so I was stuck asking myself whom I should pick. Did I go with love for Tay and his money, or did I go with the one I was sure to fall in love with for all the right reasons? Should I pick him or Amira? I just didn't know. I was lost in my thoughts and wasn't prepared for what was about to happen next. I stopped moving my hands through his hair because there I was on the TV, with my towel on. *Fuck!* Everything that happened with Amira earlier that day had been recorded.

"What the hell is this?" Tay asked as his temper started to boil.

I couldn't talk. My body was as stiff as a board. I hadn't even thought to check the video camera after they left. Tay'von watched the whole thing, and I could see his jaw clenching. He heard every word and saw everything that we did. I just sat there as he watched Amira and me make love. The next thing I knew, Tay'von turned around and slapped me clear across the face. I didn't even fight back. I was in the wrong.

"You fucking bitch!" He jumped on me and wrapped his hands around my neck. "I can't believe this shit. You're a fucking dyke? How could you do this right after I proposed to you?"

His hands were so tight around my neck that I was sure I was turning blue. He let me go, then slapped me again. I held my neck and tried to catch my breath.

"I am so sorry, Tay. I just had to follow my heart," I managed to get out.

He smacked me yet again, this time making my nose bleed. "You don't have a fucking heart, bitch. You're just a fucking ho in its truest form."

I stood up, and even though I was a little wobbly, I tried to make it to the front door. "I'm just gonna get out of here. I don't even need any of my shit. Just throw it out."

He came at me again. This time he landed a punch on my chest, and my body flew onto the couch. My eyes felt like he had pulled them out.

"Do you really think that I am just going to let you leave?" he yelled. "Oh, I see . . . You want me to let you go so that you can go and be with that gay bitch."

Tears rolled down my face in an endless stream. He balled up his fist while I rolled my body into a ball on the couch. I couldn't take any more of his punches, and although I told him that, he said he didn't care. He walked over to me and grabbed me by my hair.

"You've been fucking this bitch the whole time, haven't you? All this time you've been bumping pussies with Amira, huh?"

When he slapped me, I almost passed out. He jumped on me, straddled me, and grabbed my neck again.

"Now, listen to me good. I don't care how long this has been going on, but it ends today. You're not going anywhere. I'll fucking kill you before I let you go."

He let go of my neck and walked over to the bar and poured himself a drink. He looked at his watch, then back at me. By then my makeup was running down my face due to the endless supply of snot and tears.

"Shit. It's time for me to get ready to leave," He growled.

He went into the bathroom and washed his face. When he came back out, he looked like an animal with bloodshot eyes.

"Get your ass up," he ordered.

"Where am I going?"

He turned around like he wanted to hit me again. But instead, he just walked over to the couch and grabbed me by my hair for a second round. He pulled at it and made me stand up.

"This is the wrong goddamned time to question me. I'm taking your ass down to end this shit with Amira."

He pulled me to the door and pushed me out of the suite. We took the elevator down to Amira's floor. Thank God no one was in there with us. He kicked on her door, and she opened it with a face full of shock. I wondered if it was because of Tay or because I looked like I had been through a war. I didn't say anything, but Tay'von had much to say.

"What in the hell are you looking so shocked for? I saw your little tape. Yeah, that's right. Everything you did today was recorded. How the fuck could you do this to me? We have been friends since before the tour. I heard that you were gay, but I would never think that you would do this to me. Man, if you were a nigga, I would whup your ass. Since I can't, Tangie has something to tell you."

I didn't say anything, so Amira spoke up.

"Come on, Tay. Just come in so we can talk about this."

"Fuck you, bitch. We don't have anything to talk about," he said as he pulled me out in front of him roughly.

He told me, "Bitch, if you don't speak up, I'm going to break your fucking neck. Now tell Amira what you came down to tell her."

"Amira, I am sorry, but our relationship is over. This can't go on anymore."

He glared at Amira. "There, you heard it. Now, if I see you anywhere near her, I'll kill you."

With that, Tay'von shoved me toward the elevator. Amira tried to push past him and run toward me.

"Tangie, you don't have to do this. Don't let him scare you into staying with him."

I turned around to walk back toward her, but Tay'von pulled me back.

"Are you fucking crazy? I just told you to never go near her. It's over, Amira. It's over," he yelled.

Amira tried to get past him again, but this time he pushed her to the floor. He yelled so loud that I thought the people in the other rooms would come out.

"Get the fuck over it, Amira. She will never be with you. This is the end of whatever you thought you had with her. I fucking mean that shit! Do you hear me?"

The elevator doors opened, and Tay pushed me in. Amira was hysterically screaming my name, but I did nothing. I just looked at the floor like a coward. Tay'von stepped into the elevator and continued his yelling before the doors closed.

"Remember, if I ever see you near her, you won't live to regret it."

As the doors closed, Amira tried to get into the elevator, but she was too late. We rode up to the suite with the fading sounds of her screaming my name.

Once we got back upstairs, Tay opened the door and let me in. Before he turned to leave, he looked at me and said, "Get yourself together. I'm gonna send Carl back to pick you up later for the show."

He closed the door as I fell to the floor. I stayed there for the next hour, crying my soul out. Then I picked myself up and walked into the bathroom to get ready. Amira never came up to my room to try to talk to me, and I didn't go down to hers, either.

Carl came to pick me up, and his eyes popped out of his head. Although my makeup covered my bruises, it couldn't cover up the swelling of my lips and eyes. I stopped him before anything came out of his mouth.

"Please don't say anything," I mumbled.

"What do you mean, don't say anything? Who in the hell did this to you?"

"Who do you think did this to me? Tay did."

"Why would he do this? What did you do?"

"Are you saying that if I did something horrible, this would be justified?"

"Hell no. I'm just trying to figure out what happened."

I picked up the camera and threw it against the wall. "*That's* what happened. Now let's get the hell out of here."

We got to the stadium, and Carl walked me straight to Tay's dressing room. I walked in on him yelling at some man because his microphone was not sounding right. I was sure that his attitude had a lot to do with what had just happened and not the actual mic. The man walked out and slammed the door behind him.

Tay walked over to me and took my hand. He walked me to the couch, and then he pulled out a chair and sat in front of me. At first, he just sat there staring at me and shaking his head. And then he spoke.

"Tangie, I know that I may have taken shit too far today, but I want to be crystal clear. This will not happen again. Man or woman, if you ever do something like this, they won't even be able to find your body, understand?" He leaned in and gently kissed me.

After that, he got up and left the room. I couldn't stop myself from crying. I hated having to hold back and not really react the way that I wanted to. Tay had no idea who he was dealing with, and I was going to let him stay in the dark for a little while longer. I looked through my purse, hoping that I would find some coke. Shit! I had forgotten that Tay threw all my snow out. I got up and went straight to Black's dressing room. I was sure that he and Shamika would have something stronger than weed in their room. I knocked on the door, wanting to have no conversation. Shamika opened the door and gave me the same look that Carl did.

"Look, I was just wondering if you had anything stronger than weed with you tonight?" I said.

"Girl, I told you that I don't do drugs," she joked.

"Cut out the bullshit. As you can tell, I'm having a bad day."

She looked me up and down and then opened the door wider so that I could walk in.

"I ain't even gonna ask who, but I do want to know why. You must have really pissed Tay off."

"Yeah, I must have. Anyway, what do you have in here?"

She walked over to her purse and pulled out a whole bunch of different things. "Girl, I have everything. I have Boy, Girl, X, dippers. Whatever you want, I got it."

I didn't want Ecstasy, because I wasn't in the mood for that. And I wasn't going to smoke a dipper, because that shit would make me flip. I took a little bag of coke and turned to leave but stopped myself.

"You know what? Let me try a little of that H."

"Girl, I didn't know that you got down like that."

"I never have, but I need something strong tonight. Do you want to do a line with me?"

I sat on the couch, and she sat down next to me and took a key and another little bag out of her purse.

"I haven't done any of this in a long time, but I'll do a little bit with you," she told me.

She took the end of the key and put it in the bag. Then she took it out and brought it up to her nose twice, making the yellowish powder disappear. She handed both the key and the bag to me and waited. I did what I watched her do, and it sure as hell wasn't coke. It was like nothing I had ever done before. I didn't do too much, because I hated the feeling. I just sat there for about ten minutes and tried to ride the

wave. I didn't want any more, so I closed the bag
and put it back in Shamika's purse. After a short
while, I got up and left. I went back to Tay's
dressing room and sniffed up all the coke that I
had gotten from Shamika.

The mixture of the drugs left me numb and
wobbly. Now I needed something to mellow me
out. My heart was racing, and I needed to calm
down. I looked around Tay's dressing room, and
I found some weed but no blunt. Once again I
made my way back to Black and Shamika's. This
time I just walked in without knocking. Black
had just come in from doing a set with Tay and
had the same look on his face as all the others
when they first saw me.

"Hey, Tangie. How are you feeling?"

I was sure that he could tell that I was fucked
up. Black then told me my eyes looked frozen
from the glaze the drugs had given them.

"Hey, Black. What's going on? I just came in
to see if y'all had any blunts," I slurred. I could
hardly hold myself up.

"Oh yeah, we got some blunts. But are you
okay? Maybe you need to sit down?"

"No, I'll be all right. Just give me the blunts."

He got up and gave me a box. I opened the
door to leave, but he told me that he would walk
me back. He closed his door behind us, and we

started to walk back to Tay's dressing room. I wrapped my arms around him for support and could feel that he was there for me.

"Hey, Tangie, I heard about what happened today, and I just wanted to tell you not to worry. I'm the only one who knows what the fight was about. Before we went down to the sound check, I went to Amira's room to see if she wanted to ride with me. When I walked into her room, she was a mess. She told me that you and she were having a relationship, and that Tay found out about it today."

I didn't look at him; I just looked at the floor. He must have thought all kinds of bad things about me by then.

"Look, Tangie, I've been thinking that maybe something had been going on between the two of you for a couple of weeks now. I just never came out and said anything, because Amira and I are kind of close, but the best advice that I can give you is to make your own choice. Just remember that nobody can make you do what you don't want to do."

I lifted my head and smiled at him. Then Amira's door opened. She looked just as bad as me, except she didn't have a split lip and a puffy eye. Black and I just stood there. I didn't know what to do.

"Can I talk to you? Please, Tangie, just for a second." Amira said.

I looked at Black, hoping that he would know what I should do. He looked at his watch.

"Tay'von has about two more songs to do," he informed me. "So that means you have about five, maybe eight, nine, minutes. I'll knock on the door when his last song is about to end."

I handed him the box of blunts and weed and asked him to roll it up for me, while I slowly walked into Amira's dressing room.

"So was that really your choice? You really don't want to be with me?" she asked, getting straight to the point.

"Why is everyone talking about choices? I have no choice in this. What's done is done."

Her eyes started to water, and I knew that my own tears were not far behind.

"Come on, baby. Just this morning we were making love. And now you're telling me that you have no choice in this? You told me that you loved me. Doesn't that count for anything?" she said before downing a glass full of Hennessy.

She was making this harder than it was, so I reached out and hugged her.

"I'm sorry. I'm so sorry, but it is over."

"Please don't do this, Tangie. I love you. I'll give all of this up for you. Let's just leave and not tell anyone where we're going."

I tried to pull myself away from her, but she wouldn't let me go. After several attempts, I finally managed to pull away from her embrace, even though I wanted to be in her arms forever.

"There's nothing that we can do. This is the end of us. I'm sorry, Amira."

I left her dressing room before she got ahold of me again. As I took Black's hand, her dressing room door flew open.

"Will you just watch my show? Just do me that one last favor. Please, Tangie. I am going to be performing for you tonight."

"Sure, A. I'll watch your show, but also remember what I told you in the limo. No matter what I say, and no matter where we are, just remember that I love you, and my feelings for you were always real."

A slight smile spread across her face. Then she went back into her dressing room.

As Black held on to me, I felt like I was going to collapse. I couldn't take it anymore. I broke down right there in the hallway, and Black had to carry me back to Tay's dressing room.

"Come on, Tangie. Get yourself together. Tay's set will be over soon, and I know that you don't want him seeing you like this."

"I need some coke," was all that I said.

He looked reluctant but went back to his stash and brought me back another bag. I put it up to my nose, and I took one big sniff.

"Damn, Tangie, slow down with that stuff. What are you trying to do, kill yourself?"

The way that I looked at him seemed to send chills down his spine. He looked as if I had let him know that he had hit the nail right on the head. It wasn't that I really wanted to die; I just wanted to kill my feelings, to kill the hurt. He went to grab the bag away from me, but I pulled it away.

"Give me the fucking bag, Tangie."

I put it up to my nose again and sniffed up as much as I could before handing him the bag.

"Wipe your face off. You got that shit all over yourself," Black said before he left the room.

I wiped my nose and reached for one of the blunts that Black had rolled up for me. Tay walked into the room, sweaty and in a slightly better mood.

"God damn, Tangie. You look fucked up. What have you been doing tonight? Shit, can I have some?" Tay joked, but I didn't answer. I just lit up, took a long hard pull, and walked out the door.

"Where in the hell are you going?" he called from the doorway.

"I need some air. Is that okay, or do you want to beat my ass for doing that too?"

Tay just looked away. He couldn't even face what he had done to me. I walked down the hallway, bumping into the walls on my left and right sides. I made it to the side of the stage, and I asked for a chair. Amira came walking by and stopped once she reached me. She leaned down and kissed me on the lips, and I let her do it without pulling away. Everyone around us looked on but said nothing.

"You asked me to remember that no matter what, your love was always true. Now I want you to remember this. This is and will always be for and because of you," Amira said, then walked out onstage.

The music to the song that she had written for me came on as she hit the center of the stage. The people in the audience could clearly tell that she was drunk, and waited to see what would become of this performance. She was not even singing the words to the song. It was more like she was saying them to herself. It was so sad. The audience was stunned, but no one booed her. They just looked on with pity and curiosity. Toward the end of the song, she looked over at me and told me that she loved me. Then she started to climb up the background to her set. No one stopped her, although we were all wondering what the hell she was doing. She climbed so high that I could no longer see her from where I was sitting.

"As I am up here looking out at the crowd, it feels so good that you all came to see me tonight, but I must tell you that my heart is torn. I know that a lot of people think that I have it all, but you don't really have anything if you don't have love. Tangie, baby, if I can't have you, then none of this is worth it. Life is not worth living without you."

Everyone was silent. All we could hear was her crying. I got up and walked out on the stage just as Tay was coming out of his dressing room so that he could find out where I was. He saw Black, who pointed him to the stage. He got there just in time to see Amira jump headfirst from the very top of her background design. As soon as I saw her jump, I knew that it was all over. It was too high for her to survive. You could hear a penny drop, it was so silent. Suddenly, an outburst of screams was heard, once everyone registered what was going on. As soon as she hit the stage, her head split open. Then the screaming stopped. Everyone was moving in slow motion toward me. I could see their mouths moving, but I couldn't hear them.

I sat down next to her lifeless body, and I put my hand in the blood that was surrounding her head and moving down to her body. I knew that she was dead, but I still tried to make her wake up.

"Amira, come on, baby. Stop playing. You're scaring these people, who paid good money to see you. Just wake up. We can work this all out."

I picked up her cracked head and placed it in my lap.

"See, what you did to your neck? Even your head is bleeding. Now we're gonna be in the hospital all night, trying to fix that shit."

I was still trying to wake her up. I even tried to hold her skull together, hoping that this would stop some of the bleeding. Black, Tony, Carl, Tay'von, and even Shamika formed a circle around me. They all looked like someone had died, but I still wouldn't let myself get it. I refused to believe that it was true.

"Black, she doesn't want to wake up. Tell her that it's okay. Tell her that no one is mad at her anymore. Tell her Black. Tell her," I begged.

No one said anything. I looked out at the audience, and the security was walking everyone out.

"Damn, Amira. You're fucking up. Everyone is leaving because you won't get up. You're going to make them give you a bad review."

She still did not move. Tay bent over and put his hand on my shoulder.

"Baby, she's not going to wake up. I think that she's—"

"Don't you say it, Tay'von. Don't you dare. She's just scared that you're going to hurt us if she wakes up. And don't you fucking touch me. This is all your fault, you fucking bully."

He stood back up and asked Black to talk to me.

"I think that we need a doctor. I can tell that she has hurt her neck really bad. Maybe that's why she's not getting up," I said as I tried to pick her blood up and force it back into her head.

The more I spoke, the more I started to sound like a terrified child who had lost her mind.

"Okay, Tangie, I am about to call him right now, but you're gonna have to let go of her. Why don't you come with me and we can both call?"

"It doesn't take two people to call a doctor, Black. Now please hurry up. The sooner she gets there, the sooner I can tell her that I have changed my mind. I do love her, Black. You are right. I do have a choice. My choice is you, Amira. It's you. Wake up and tell me that you can hear me. Wake up!" I screamed and sobbed all at once.

In that moment Tay'von said he realized that I would never love him the way I loved her. He wanted to pull me off her and hold me until I felt the same way about him, but it would never happen. I loved him in a different way and for a different reason. He became full of anger and hurt because he knew that my heart would always be with the now dead Amira. Although he knew this, he still couldn't and wouldn't let me go. He didn't know if it was his selfishness or maybe his pride. He had to have me, and he would try anything to make me love him. He might not ever get me to be this in love with him, but he would even settle for half.

Black told everyone to just let me be. I held her and sang the song that she wrote for me until the ambulance came. The paramedics put her on a stretcher and checked her for a pulse. She had none. She was dead. They pulled a white sheet over her head and went to zip her up in a body bag.

"What in the fuck are you doing? She won't be able to breathe if you zip her up in that thing!" I yelled at the paramedics.

Black grabbed me before I could run up to the stretcher. Tay'von walked over to the paramedics and told them to leave her face uncovered right up until they got outside. Black held on to me as I watched them wheel her out.

"We have to find out what hospital they are taking her to. We should be there when she wakes up," I told Black.

"Sure, Tangie. We can do that," Black said as he tried hard to hold back his tears.

"Let's go to the car. We can find out where to go from there," Tay said as he started to walk me off the stage.

The last thing that I remembered about that night was falling asleep in the car. We never made it to the hospital. Tay later told me he thought that it was best to take me back to the hotel. I fell asleep thinking that Amira was still alive.

I woke up the next morning in a fog, and my head was pounding. I sat up in the bed, running the dream that I had just had over and over in my mind. I kept dreaming that Amira was jumping from a high building to her death. I shook my head, trying to clear it. I got off the bed and opened the curtains. It was dark and rainy outside, and the weather matched my mood perfectly. I looked at the clock, and it read two o'clock. I went into the bathroom and drew a hot bath as Tay came in and checked on me. I told him that I was hungry and asked him to order lunch for me. After spending almost an hour in the tub, I got out, dried myself off, and slipped into a robe.

When I got out to the living room area, Black and Tay sat watching TV. They turned it off once they saw me. I sat down at the table, and Tay came over and put some food on my plate.

"How are you feeling, baby?" Tay asked as he sat down beside me.

"I'm fine. It's just one of them days. You know how I get when it's dark and rainy out. Plus, I kept having this crazy-ass dream."

"Oh yeah? What was it?"

Maybe I shouldn't tell him that I kept dreaming about Amira, I thought to myself. He might go crazy again.

He watched me hesitate, then said, "It's okay, Tangie. You can tell me. Was it Amira?"

"Yeah, it was. I am so sorry for bringing this up, Tay."

"No. Tell me what your dream was about."

I went over every detail of the wild dream that kept repeating in my sleep the night before. As I ate and talked, I saw Tay and Black looking at each other like I was crazy.

"I know that this must seem a little off to y'all, but it's only a dream," I joked, but they still had this funny look on their faces.

"Tangie, don't you remember anything about last night?" Tay asked as he reached over and held my hand.

"Now, why would you bring that up? Don't you think that I remembered when I looked at my lip and eye in the bathroom this morning?"

Tay lowered his eyes from mine and didn't bring them back up. Black got up and poured himself a drink at the bar, then came and sat with us at the table.

"Look, Tay, I know that you have the right to be mad about Amira, but when I see her, I am still gonna talk and say hi to her. I just want you to understand that."

He lifted my hand to his mouth and kissed it. "Baby, I have something to tell you. I find it odd that you don't remember, because you were there. Maybe you were too fucked up, or maybe you're just blocking it out. But—"

"What is it, Tay? Did you give me something? Am I sick? Did you call off the wedding?"

Tears streamed down his face. My mind was racing as I tried to remember what had gone down the previous day, besides him finding out about the Amira situation.

"Tangie, last night at the concert, um, at the show last night—"

"What is it, Tay? Just tell me, already."

Tay said nothing. He looked at Black, and Black understood that Tay didn't have the heart to tell me, so he did it for him.

"Tangie, what Tay is trying to tell you is that Amira died last night."

My mouth fell open as he talked.

"Yeah, um, she jumped from one of the background designs at the show last night. When she hit the stage, she broke her neck and cracked her skull. She died instantly."

Now I was pissed. Why would they tell me such a lie? Why were they taking my dream and turning it into a mean joke?

"This is so fucked up. I really did think much more of you, Black. What, do you think that what you just said was funny?" I couldn't stop my body from shaking. "This just can't be true," I repeated over and over again.

"Tangie, it's true. Don't you remember any of it?"

"Oh, fuck you, Tay'von. I know that you don't want me to fuck the girl, but this is going too far."

Tay got up, turned on the TV, and put it on CNN. I saw a picture of Amira, and at the bottom it had the date on which she was born and then the previous day's date. What in the hell was going on? Then a caption ran across the screen that said that she had jumped to her death at the show last night. I lost my hearing for a moment. But when it came back, I heard the newscaster say that the network had a tape of her last moments.

My eyes were glued to the television as I watched myself holding her head in my lap. She must not be dead, because I looked like I was talking to her. The tape cut off as fast as it came on. The last words that I heard were, "Rest in peace, Amira." I couldn't hold my food down. I got up and ran to the bathroom just in time to throw up my breakfast. Tay and Black came running after me, but I was able to get in and lock the door before they reached me. After I rid my stomach of its contents, I went to the sink and rinsed my mouth out. I looked at myself in the mirror and couldn't handle what was looking back at me.

I must have been going out of my mind, because I picked up one of my bottles of perfume and rammed it into the mirror. The mirror glass shattered, along with the bottle that was in my hand. I watched the blood that was running from my hand land on the floor. I wanted to be drained of everything that I had left in me. I wanted to be emptied of all the evil that I knew would never leave my soul otherwise. I closed my hand over the broken pieces of the bottle and started to scream. It was a deathly shriek that pierced the ears of anyone who heard it. It was the cry of a broken woman who could never be pieced together again.

I let the blood drain from the deep cuts on my hand and made up my mind. I just had to make sure for myself. Again, I took off running, with Black and Tay hot on my heels. I left the suite and headed straight for the elevator, vowing not to let anyone stop me. I jumped in, and the doors closed right before Tay and Black caught up to me. I went down to Amira's room and damn near kicked in her door, but no one answered. Okay, maybe she was out, I told myself. So I went down to the front desk, bloody hand and all. The clerks looked at me funny, but I thought, *Fuck them.* I was on a mission. I didn't have the time to stop and read their asses right then.

"Hi. I need to leave an urgent message for Amira," I told one of the female clerks, but she just stood there looking at me. I looked at her name tag, telling myself to remember her name. I was going to make sure to get her fired.

"Don't just stand there. Do your job and take down my message and make sure you deliver it!" I yelled. But she just continued to look like she didn't know what to do.

"I am sorry, but Miss Cortez passed away last night," she finally leaned in and whispered.

I looked at her blankly and became infuriated. This joke was being taken to the max, and I didn't find it funny. So I reached over the front desk and pulled her hair as hard as I could and continued to yell. "You better take down my damn message, bitch! Take it down for her. Take it down for her. Take it down for her!" I screamed over and over.

By the time Carl got down to the lobby, my robe was open, my hand was bleeding profusely, and I was now banging her head on the desk. He tried for five minutes to get me off her, but that just made me swing at her more wildly. He used his walkie-talkie to call Tony and tell him what was happening. Black, Tony, and Tay came running into the lobby, and it took all four of them to pull me off the clerk.

"Let me go. She won't take down my message, so I'm gonna fuck her up!" I yelled as Carl picked me up and held me in his arms.

"Take her upstairs," Tay yelled as he helped the desk clerk.

Carl did as he was told, and Tay'von went into an office to talk to the hotel manager and the girl I had damn near killed.

I found out later he walked out fifty thousand dollars poorer. Twenty-five to the hotel and the other half to the clerk. He also made sure to make a call to his lawyer and had him fax a confidentiality agreement and papers stating that he had settled everything with the hotel and its employee. Tay may have been a lot of things, but he wasn't dumb enough to walk out of that office without both signatures.

Carl still held me in his arms as we rode up to my room.

"Why would they tell me that Amira's dead, Carl? That's so mean of them."

"Why are you talking like that, Tangie? You sound like a kid."

I hadn't even noticed that my voice had changed.

"Just tell me what's going on. Why are they saying that to me?"

Carl stood me up and looked me straight in the eyes. "Tangie, this is not a joke. Amira is dead. She's gone, baby. Everything is true."

That was when it finally hit me. It was like a rush of pictures flashed in front of me, and I remembered everything. I stopped breathing and started to gasp for air. No matter how hard I tried to breathe, I just couldn't get any air. I couldn't hold myself up anymore, so I dropped to the floor. Carl picked me up, and I rested my head on his chest. Amira invaded my mind, and all I could think of was her death and the absence of love that it was sure to bring.

I don't remember much more about that day, but I do remember having to go to the hospital. I had to get thirty-three stitches in my hand and fingers and still bear slight scars to this day. Every time I look down at my right hand, I remember both my insanity and my lost love. I didn't go to the funeral. Everyone said that it would be too much for me and that I could possibly lose my mind again.

Tay'von was very supportive during that time. He secretly held the weight of her death on his shoulders too, so he let me grieve for my dead lover, who was at one point his friend. Everything was put on hold while the world mourned Amira's passing, but after two weeks it was time for everyone to get on with the show. Although I told myself that I would finish the U.S. tour with Tay, no matter what, I just couldn't go on. I needed to go home and be around my things. I was broken—my mind, body, and soul.

We were set to leave in the morning, so I sat Tay down in the bedroom to tell him that I was not going with him. Before I could speak, he asked me if I was feeling any better.

"Well, I'm just taking it one day at a time. But things are getting better. And I have also been meaning to thank you. You have really been good with this whole situation. I know that it's hard for you too."

He came over to me and hugged me. I found out he had wanted to tell me that he was filled with his own pain in that moment over what happened, but he had held it all in. He sat back down, and I continued to pack.

"Tay, I called you in here because I wanted to tell you that I am not packing to leave with you in the morning. I want to go home."

"Tangie, you don't have to do that. Plus, I don't think that you should be home alone."

"Baby, I am going home. I don't want to be on the road anymore. I am over this now. I just need to be in my own bed, around my own things. Please don't fight me on this. I am not changing my mind."

He lay down on the bed, and his feet dangled off the side. I got on the bed with him and put my head down on his chest.

"Tangie, I know that we have been through a lot, but we have always made it through the bullshit. Our love has always held strong. Now, when you say you're going back home, is it to our house or to yours? Will you be there when I get back?"

"I'll be there, Tay. I have always been there, haven't I? But if you want me to stay, I need you to understand that if you ever put your hands on me again, not only will I be leaving, but I will also leave with your career, if not your life. The next time you put your hands on me, I am calling the police and the press. Do you understand that?"

He looked like he was taking his time to think about what I had just said. He had never put his hand on a woman before me, and he was ashamed that he'd done this to me. Even though it seemed like I was always pushing his buttons, he knew that losing everything over hitting me was out of the question.

"You don't have to ever worry about that again. I swear on my life that I will never put my hands on you in that way again."

Half of me was happy that I would be there once he came back home, but the other half of me was not sure. There was a hate in me that was cold and empty. It was about the size of a grain of salt, but with every day that passed, it would grow. Eventually, it would grow to take over all of me. It would also grow from being just hate to the need for revenge. It was going to grow and take over me like the plague. An illness that would kill everything and everyone that had or would ever even look at me the wrong way. It was on its way to killing the very heart and soul of me, and in the end result, it would leave me cold-blooded, heartless, and with a lack of remorse.

I lay in his arms and cried the last tears that I would cry for a very long time. I let out all the pain and filled up on hate. The next morning I found myself on a plane, heading home, to our home. This time Tay sent Carl and Shamika to stay with me. As for him, he was on his way to another city to do another show. It would be three months before I saw him again, and I used that time wisely.

Chapter 13

How Dark Is Your Heart?

I have had to come to terms with the fact that I will never be the same. I will never stop missing Amira. I will never stop loving her, and truth be told, I will never stop being angry because I no longer have her in my life. I don't want to have to settle for her just dwelling in my heart. I want her right beside me, right in front of me . . . alive! I also want to go back and tell her that I changed my mind, that she is the one, and that I just want to love her only. I just want to go back. I want to fucking go back and tell her all the things that will forever be unsaid.

After leaving the airport, we stopped and had lunch. We got to the house around one in the afternoon. I couldn't say that I was too happy to have Shamika there with me, but I would just have to deal with it. Carl was an added bonus, although he could be annoying. Tay'von thought that it would be good for me to have a "friend" with me. When he told me this, I had wanted to scream and yell, but then I'd thought, *Hey, this will be the perfect time for me to put my plan in motion.*

"Girl, I didn't know y'all were living as large as this. My God, this house is big," Shamika said as she walked around.

"You and Black should be living just as nice," I answered, trying to downplay everything.

"Black doesn't spend his money. He just got a little town house, and it's nothing close to what you and Tay got."

"Well, that's a good thing. You don't want him to end up like all those other stars that go broke," I joked.

"Girl, please, if you have the money, then you should spend it. It doesn't look like you and Tay have any money problems after buying a house like this. Shit, as much money as you spend on clothes, you all can't be broke."

She was trying to get information out of me already, and I wasn't about to play into her game. I told her that I was tired from the trip so that I could go up to my bedroom without her bothering me.

It felt good to be home, but the death of Amira still lingered on in my mind. Before I'd left the hotel, I gave one of the maids all the clothes that I had ever worn while I was with Amira. They brought too many memories of her. I figured that the best thing to do was to block out everything that had to do with her, but I knew that it wouldn't come easy. Every once in a while, I got this feeling that let me know that I was dying inside, and I didn't know how to make it stop.

Soon after I went upstairs, I fell asleep. I woke up around five in the evening. Winter was settling into New York, and it was dark and gloomy out. The night before I had made up my mind to stop doing drugs. Life was way too short to always be in a fucked-up haze. I wanted my mind clear, and even with all my newfound zest for life, I still couldn't put down the Capris. Maybe one day. I got up and headed downstairs. I could hear Shamika laughing and talking with Carl, so I stopped in my tracks when I was halfway down the staircase.

"You mean to tell me that all them nights you and Tangie were here alone, you two never did nothing?" Shamika asked.

Carl laughed her question off. "Shamika, Tay'von is my boss. What would it look like if I started messing with his girl?"

I walked down a couple more steps, and from my vantage point, I could see her getting really close to Carl as she answered him.

"Shit. As sexy as you are, I would have jumped on that as soon as my man left."

I could see Carl trying to back up, but the wall was stopping him.

"Come on, Carl. Aren't I sexy enough for you? It's not like you're working for Black."

She took one of his hands and put it on one of her breasts. This bitch was worse than me. I at least waited long enough for Tay's scent to wear off me before digging my claws into him. I stormed down the rest of the steps and made it seem like I hadn't heard or seen anything.

"Hey, girl. Did you have a good nap?" Shamika asked, sounding fake as ever.

"Yeah, it was okay. What have you been doing? You find everything okay?"

"I haven't really been doing nothing. I was thinking that we could all go to a club. How about the Voodoo Cave?"

"I don't really feel like going to a club. I would rather stay in," I answered.

She sucked her teeth and walked over to me. "Girl, come on. You just can't stay in the house for the rest of your life. That shit isn't good for you. Let's just go and have a good time. It will help get your mind off things."

I thought about it, and she was right. I shouldn't stop my life because Amira was gone.

"Okay, okay. We can leave around twelve," I said, then went back to my bedroom for a long hot bath.

A while later, Shamika came into my bedroom and watched me go through the jewelry in my safe. I could tell that she was green with envy, but I didn't say anything to her about it. I already knew how she felt about me and how I was living.

I finished getting dressed, and we all got in the car. Carl and Shamika made small talk, while I stayed silent. Both of them were really working my nerves. The sound of their voices made me want to jump out of the moving car. I should have stayed home. My thoughts were still filled with memories of Amira, and I just wanted to be alone to relive them.

We got to the club, and as always, it was packed. Shamika headed to the VIP section, but that night I wanted to be with all the "normal" people. Most were dressed in their best. Everyone was there looking for someone else. I didn't think that people went to the clubs to dance or enjoy the music anymore. Carl went to the bar and got us our drinks while we sat at a table.

"You think that there might be a lot of famous people here tonight?" Shamika asked.

"Who knows? Why are you asking, anyway? You already have one."

"Girl, please, you can always do better."

I smiled. I couldn't be mad at that, 'cause she was right.

Carl came back with our drinks, and I sat back and enjoyed the alcohol. The club scene was and would always be the same, and I was so over it. I looked over at Carl, and he looked like he was feeling the same way. When I looked over at Shamika, she looked like she was having the time of her life, but hood rats always loved going to the club. That was where they could all be ghetto superstars. She was dancing in her seat as she scanned the club for that better man she was just talking about.

"How about we all go dance?" Shamika asked before she headed for the dance floor.

"Nah, you can go on. I don't really like this song," I said before I downed the rest of my drink.

"Come on, Tangie. Don't come to the club and start acting like you don't want to be here. Let's go have some fun," she urged.

This bitch was bugging the hell out of me. Even when I didn't answer, she just kept asking.

Even Carl joined in on the begging. I couldn't take it anymore, so I followed them to the dance floor.

The DJ was hot and knew to play all the good songs. One song turned into five, and I was having fun, like I used to back in the day. Every song that came on found me dancing with someone new. I didn't realize how much I had missed having that carefree feeling. It felt like I was eighteen again, but that feeling didn't last long. The DJ slowed it down and said the words that sent me crashing back down to my low.

"We're going to play this song and show some love for Amira, who passed away just the other day. You will be missed, baby girl."

I stopped dancing and stood still. I should have known that this was going to happen. Her death was still new. I felt like everyone in the club knew who I was, and that they could sense my pain. I started to feel closed in. There were too many people around, and I couldn't get any air. I started to walk off the dance floor, hoping to find a place of refuge. Carl came after me, but I told him to go back and stay with Shamika. I just wanted to go outside and stay there until they stopped playing the very song that Amira had killed herself to. It was kind of cold out, but I enjoyed the chilly wind that was hitting my body.

That was what irony was. I had told Amira that we could no longer be together. I had told myself that I would have to forget her and move on. But now that she had killed herself, I would never forget her. I would always be reminded of her when they played her songs or videos. I laughed and couldn't stop. I wasn't laughing because things were funny; it was just that life had a funny way of working everything out.

"At least the second time we meet, you're smiling," a male voice said suddenly.

I turned around to see who was talking to me. If he hadn't said anything, I would have never known that he was there.

"Carmello. Oh my God! How are you? What are you doing here?"

"I just came to check out the club. What are you doing out here by yourself? And what is so funny?"

I kind of felt silly now that I knew he had been watching me the whole time. I must have seemed crazy.

"Nothing really. I was just laughing at life."

"Yeah, well, I can understand that. So, where's Tay? He's not going to run out here and pull you away from me, is he?"

I laughed. I had to remember to ask him about all the bad blood he and Tay had between them. It had to be something big.

"Tay's not here. I'm out with one of his body-guards and Black's girlfriend. Tay's still out touring."

Once I told him that, he got a little closer to me. Not in a sexual way, but in a friendly way.

"Are you going back in? Maybe I can get a dance out of you?" he asked.

"No, not right now, but I am happy that I ran into you. I was thinking about calling you. I need to talk to you about some things that you may want to help me out with."

He looked like he was interested in hearing what I had to say and couldn't wait.

"Let's go talk in my limo."

I nodded, and Carmello took my hand and led me to the car. He told the driver to step out while we talked.

"So, what's on your mind, sexy?" he asked me once we were ensconced in the limo.

I straightened up and looked him dead in the eyes. "Well, let's say that I have someone around me that has done me wrong, and I am willing to do or fuck anyone over just to get back at this person. Would you be able to help me out with that?"

"I would have to ask who the person is, and I must also ask what I would be getting out of it.

But the number one thing that I would have to ask is, how dark is your heart?"

What he really wanted to know was if I had the heart to carry out my plan to the end.

"Well, this person is not high profile, but their lover is. Plus, you will be getting someone who you have been chasing for a while."

"And what about that heart of yours? With things like this, you can't start and not finish."

This man must have thought that he was messing with a lightweight. He didn't know the darkness my heart contained, so I would just have to show and prove it.

"What heart?" I asked. "Even if I tried to tell you, you would never understand. So let's just do this. Then you will know who I am and will see what I can do not only for myself but also for you."

He smiled. He could tell that I was down for anything, and that was the kind of bitch he liked dealing with. He told me that he would help me in any way he could. So while Shamika and Carl were in the club, dancing, I was in the limo, putting together my master plan. At the end of my conversation with Carmello, he had only one question left.

"Are you sure that I will get Tay'von at the end of this?"

I reached in my purse and lit a Capri. "I swear on Tay'von's life that you will get him in any way, shape, or form that you want him. But I have to get everything that I want first."

Carmello extended his hand, and I shook it. There was no turning back now.

It was about two in the afternoon when I woke up. I had a hair appointment at twelve, which I had missed, so Tasha was coming out to the house. I showered, then went downstairs to wait for her. The maid told me that Carl had gone out with Shamika, and I was grateful to have the house to myself for a while.

Tasha got there around three and started my hair. When Shamika walked in the mini hair studio that was in the basement, Tasha and I could tell that she was drunk. I could feel Tasha stop doing my hair for a second, but she started right back up after taking in an eyeful of Shamika.

"Who is that walking up in your house like she owns the place?" Tasha asked.

I told her that she was Black's girlfriend.

"And who the hell is Black?"

"The rapper who is touring with Tay. You know him. Black Dialect?"

"Oh yeah, I know him. That dude is fine as hell. From the things that he talks about when he raps, I would never think that he would be with a ghetto chick. With him always rapping about getting your mind game right and all, this would be the last thing I would ever think of seeing on his arm."

"Tell me about it. But you know how life is. Men go to fuck but end up getting stuck," I said while laughing.

When I said this, I was halfway talking about Black and Shamika, and the other half of me was thinking about Amira and me. But as I looked at Shamika's drunk ass, I realized that she and Black were truly on a different level. She was trash; he wasn't.

Shamika walked over to us and sat in the chair next to me. "Ooh, girl, you're working the hell out of Tangie's hair. Do you think that you can do mine next?"

I was hoping that Tasha said yes, because Shamika's hair needed to be done. Tasha said nothing, so I answered for her.

"She can do your hair, but it won't be free."

"Well, since you're her mouth for the day, how about letting me know how much it's going to cost me?" Shamika said.

I could tell that she was only half joking, but I didn't have time for her bullshit.

"Since she's at the house, it will cost you five hundred and up."

"I want a fresh weave. People in New York aren't feeling the mixed colors that I have in my hair, so I want it straight-up blond or basic black."

I told her that once I was done, she could talk to Tasha about her hair. She said okay and left us alone.

"I don't like that bitch already." Tasha's and my feelings were mutual, and it made me laugh.

"I can so understand your feelings," I said.

She finished my hair; then I left the house to do some shopping. Carl came with me, even though I had told him to keep his black ass at the house.

While at the store, I took a chance and asked Carl about him and Shamika.

"I see that you're getting close to our guest. How is that working for you?" I said.

He tried to stay cool while answering my question, but I read him like a well-written chapter.

"Why must you always think that something is going on? Can't I just be nice to the girl?"

"Oh, come on, Carl. You fucked me, and my man is your boss. So why even ask those questions?"

A woman who was close to us stopped her shopping and looked at us. What we were saying was more important to her than the three-hundred-dollar shoes that she had in her hand.

"Keep your voice down. All I'm saying is that she's cool once you get to know her. Not everyone is as scandalous as you try to be," he said, hoping that this would get me mad, but I let his words roll off my back.

"Oh please. She's just another low-class ghetto bitch who's not above fucking you. Hell, I am, and I still ended up sleeping with you, so why can't she? But, hey, do you. I was just asking. You don't have to lie. Just tell me that you don't want to answer me."

Carl shook his head at me. Hot, cold, cold, hot. That was how it always was with me, and it was driving him to the line he never wanted to cross, the line that lived between sanity and mental destruction.

"You just can't live if you're not judging someone, can you? You don't even know the girl that well, yet you think you're better than her," he snapped.

"My, my, we sure are getting touchy about her, aren't we? Did I hit a sensitive spot?"

I was only joking, but he was getting mad for real.

"You know what, Tangie? I thought Amira's death would change you for the better, but it seems like nothing will ever change about you. You will always be that same evil bitch that fucked her man's friend and employee."

Normally, his words would have sent me into a blind rage, but I wasn't going to let him take me there.

"Yeah, I am an evil bitch, an evil bitch that you love to fuck and, even worse, that evil bitch that you can't help but to be in love with!" I answered before I gathered my things and headed for the dressing room.

My words spun around in his head and didn't stop until the truth that suffocated him slapped him in the face.

"Are you okay?" I heard a voice ask once I was inside a cubicle in the dressing room.

When I opened the cubicle's swinging doors, I saw the same woman who had been eavesdropping on my conversation with Carl.

"You were listening hard enough to know that I am not okay. So just go on with your shopping," I said in a rude tone without a second thought.

She looked like she wanted to curse me out, but she held back. "Look, I know that this is not my place, but I did hear the harsh words that were said—"

I cut her off with a wave of my hand. "So why does it matter to you?"

"Okay, it looks like you're not in the mood to talk, so I'll just come right out with it. I heard one of you say the name Amira, and I was wondering if you two were talking about the singer who just died."

"Lady, I don't know who you are or what you want. You're talking to the wrong person."

She reached into her purse, pulled out her card, and offered it to me. "My name is Evengeliza Moore. I work for *Tell-All* magazine. If you have any information on anyone famous, please give me a call. It could be worth a lot of money to you."

I took the card and put it in my purse without giving it another thought. On my way home, I stopped and picked up a copy of *Tell-All*. I needed to make sure that I saw her name in it. And, *bam*, there it was. Editor in chief.

I was carrying about five bags, and Carl had a few more, when we walked into the house.

Shamika rolled her eyes when she saw us. "Damn, girl. Did you buy everything that they had in the store? I'm sure you don't even need clothes, as packed as your closets are."

Shamika never knew when to keep her mouth shut. I looked over at Carl, who had been taking up for her, and he knew what the look I was giving him meant.

"A woman can never have too much of anything, Shamika." I paused. "I see that Tasha has your hair braided. Is she going to start putting in the hair now?" I asked, trying to change the subject.

"Yeah, we're about to start. She had a sample of this hair that looks like yours. I know yours is real and shit, but this one looks just as real," she said as she held the sample out me. This bitch was about to pull a single white female on me.

"Why would you want to get hair that looks like mine? My hair is real. That hair won't look as natural." I was trying to get her to change her mind because I didn't need a twin.

"I know it won't look the same, but it will be close. And you ain't got to be throwing your good hair in nobody's face. We all can't be a half-breed like you. Plus, I have always wanted the wet and wavy look."

It took everything that I had in me not to reach out and smack the taste out of her mouth. I was going to deal with her ass soon enough.

***

Tay'von called me two days later, and I told him about Shamika and the hair. He laughed when I told him that she had said that we should start telling people that we were sisters. After that, we made small talk, and I could tell from his voice that he was worried about me. I assured him that I was getting better, and he seemed happy about it. We said our "I love yous" and then hung up. It was not like I was lying. I was sure that after I met up with Carmello in the morning, I'd feel a hell of a lot better.

The next morning I woke up and got dressed in a black pantsuit, a pastel green silk shirt, and my dark alligator stiletto ankle boots. I pulled my hair back and wore small studs in my ears. I loved the fact that I looked good in anything, from my slut wear to my smart clothes.

When I got to Carmello's office, I was told to go right in. As I crossed the threshold, I noticed that we were not alone. The three men turned around and saw me standing in the doorway. One of them asked Carmello if I was the singer whom he had been trying to sign. He told them no. The other man said that he should sign me, anyway. He said that every man would buy the CD if I was on the cover. I smiled and thanked them both. Carmello wrapped up the meeting he was having with them and walked them out of his office. He came back in, and we took a seat at his desk.

"So, Tangie, would you like something to drink, or do you want to get down to the nitty-gritty?"

"What do you think?" I asked.

"Well, like I told you in my limo, in order for us to do this, I have got to have that tape. Have you talked to his girlfriend?"

"No, not yet. I'm still trying to think of a way to bring it up. It's not something that you tell someone every day."

"Come on, Tangie. I know what kind of woman you are. Hell, think about the plan that you have masterminded. I'm sure that you can think of a way to make her do it. She's just another thirsty bitch. She will do anything to make sure her man stays paid."

"Yeah, I know, but I just keep thinking about Black. I keep thinking that maybe I can fuck her over without adding him into the mix."

"I told you that once you started this, you had to finish it. So stop trying to think of a new way. There is no way but the way we said we were going to do it. Step your game up and get me that fucking tape."

He was right. There was no turning back. I stood up and walked to the door.

"Tay and Black will be home for a couple of days in two weeks. I'll have it for you then," I said, then walked out.

I left his office and drove home. The whole time I thought about what I had to get done. It was fucked up, but I had to suck it up. It was a dog-eat-dog world, and I had to eat first. While driving, I called Tay. I forced myself to sound really down. This was the only way that what I was about to do would work.

"What's going on, Tangie? Why do you sound so sad?"

"I need you to come home, Tay. I am going out of my mind. I really miss you."

"Baby, it's not that I don't want to be home with you, but I am about to have some days off, and I know that they will be pissed if I just say, 'Fuck the shows,' and leave early. Can you wait a little while longer?"

I was going to have to turn on the waterworks. I needed him to come home now, not later.

"Oh, I see. The number one–selling rapper, who can do whatever he wants, can't take off early to take care of his girl, who's in need." I made it sound like I was crying while never shedding a tear.

"Come on, Tangie. You know that if I had a choice, I would be home with you all the time, but that's just not how things work."

"Well, I am happy to know that I can count on you being there when I need you, Mr. Too Fine. Money over bitches, right?" I sang, repeating the words from one of his songs.

"Look, I know that it's fucked up that I can't be there right now, but let's not turn this into something that it's not. I'll be home as soon as I can."

He was right. Maybe I was overdoing it. Plus, I really didn't want him to remember this conversation once everything went down.

"I'm sorry, Tay. You know how I get. I'll see you when you get home."

"I am really sorry, Tangie, but I'll make it up to you as soon as I get there. I love you, baby . . ."

While he talked, I thought of another plan. Maybe this would work better.

"Yeah, baby, I love you too. Call me when you can. Bye."

Right before I got home, I called Carmello and told him about my new plan. He was hesitant but said that it was even better than the first one, so we were set to go. When I walked into the house, I found Shamika sitting on the couch, with only her bra and panties on. She was acting like this was her house and I was the visitor.

Who the fuck does that? I wondered. I would never sit around someone else's house, half naked, unless I was fucking them, but again, I let it slide.

"Where did you go so early in the morning?" she asked.

"I am so happy that you're up, because I have some good news. While I was at breakfast, I ran into an old friend of mine who works for that guy that we ran into while on the road. I think his name is Carmello, or something like that. Since I don't really know him that well, I got his card so you can call him. He owns a record label, right?"

Her face brightened up. I knew that she was thinking about Black getting a new deal. She jumped up and took the card out of my hand.

"Do you think that he's at his office now? Or should I wait a few days?"

She was eating right out of my hand, and she didn't even think twice about it. I knew that the saying was "You should never bite the hand that feeds you," but I always said, "You should always watch the hand that feeds you. Your life swings from those fingertips. Poison is always best dealt when it's served on the silver platter that the cook puts down in front of you." In this case, you could call me the Iron Chef.

"No, go ahead and call now. I would think the sooner you call, the better," I replied.

"Good looking out, girl," she said as she walked over to me and hugged me. I fake hugged her back.

As she pulled away, I noticed that she smelled just like me. Now, this was going way too far. It was almost scaring me.

When I walked into the kitchen and got a Coke, I saw Carl sitting at the table. I didn't say anything to him, but as always, he had something to say to me.

"Hey, Tangie, I just wanted to say that I am sorry about what I said yesterday. I know that you're still dealing with Amira's death, and it's not my place to say anything about that."

I took a sip of my drink, then spoke. "It is such a pity that you still don't know your place after all the times that I have put you in it. But you better start staying in it if you like your job, because I won't be putting up with too many more of your comments."

I left the kitchen and went up to my bedroom. When I passed one of the guest rooms, I could hear Shamika on the phone with Carmello. She was talking to him like she was talking to one of her ghetto friends. She didn't care where or whom she was calling. She just didn't know how to turn off her street talk. I went to my bedroom and left the door open. I knew that she would be coming in to tell me about the call she had just made. By the time I took off my shirt, she was walking through my bedroom door.

"I just got off the phone with him. He told me to come to his office on Thursday. I'm gonna make sure to work my shit. I have got to get this deal for Black, no matter what. You wanna come with me?"

"Yeah, I'll go with you. What time do you have to be there?" I wasn't going to pass on seeing her "work it."

"He told me to be there around one, so we can have lunch, then go see what he's talking about."

"I hope that you're able to get a backup deal for Black. You know that you and Black are like family now, and I don't want to see y'all game get fucked up." I walked over to her and put my arm around her while I lied to her face.

"I'll do anything to make sure I get this deal for Black. Shit, I may even try and get one for myself," she joked.

I stood there smiling as she thanked me. I was sealing her fate without her even knowing it. And I even managed to get a thank-you out of it. Boy, I was good.

"Anytime, Shamika. Anytime."

***

I woke up in the middle of the night, dripping with sweat from the dream I had had of Amira and me having sex. I couldn't stop her from invading my thoughts when I was awake or asleep. And for the first time since her death, I felt like having sex.

I slipped my hands under my covers and spread my legs. I was soaking wet. I closed my eyes and thought of the dream that I had just had. I rubbed my clit and moved my hips. I could see Amira's face clearly. I could feel her slide her hands down my thighs and across my clit. I could feel her working me. I could see her lowering her head down to my pussy. Yes, I wanted it. I wanted to feel her smooth tongue fuck me. I wanted her to look up at me, wet lips and all, and tell me that she loved me. I wanted to hear her say that she loved me just one more time.

But she wouldn't, she couldn't, and it made me stop moving my fingers. Damn, I couldn't even masturbate without it being all about Amira. I need to nut, but the thought of her death was now too strong for me to do it myself. I got out of bed and slipped on my short gold silk robe. I was going to get off any way I could. Even if that meant going down to Carl's room and force fucking him.

I walked downstairs without turning on any lights. The last thing I wanted to do was wake Shamika. I opened my robe and slowly turned his doorknob. I started to walk in but stopped myself. Although Carl's room was dimly lit, I still could see Shamika's body on top of his. At first, I thought of walking in and kicking both of their asses, but that would just prove to Shamika that he and I had something going on. So I just stood there and watched them. She was riding the hell out of him, but the more I watched, the more I noticed the lack of emotion. They were having sex, and that was all there was to it. It was just a fuck to both of them. I pushed the door open a little more and sat on the floor silently. I put my back against the wall and spread my legs. I planted my feet on the floor and got ready to bust a nut.

Carl flipped her over, and both their heads were now at the foot of the bed. He reached down and slid himself inside Shamika, and she let out a low moan. As he started to work her again, I played with my nipples and slid my other hand down to my clit. I could hear Shamika telling him to fuck her harder and faster. I fingered myself as I thought of Carl being inside me. Our eyes met, and he stopped moving. I didn't. I was too close to cumming. He just lay on top of her without moving. His heart had to be pounding, because he knew that he had been caught, but I would deal with him at another time. I licked my lips as I thought of him eating my kitty. I could see in his eyes that he was thinking about it too. The thought of it was turning him on more than the pussy he was currently in. Carl later said thoughts of fucking me ran through his mind as he watched me touch myself.

"Come on, Carl. Don't stop. I know that this pussy is good to you. Come on, nigga. Don't front on this," Shamika protested.

Carl started to move his hips again. He long stroked her while watching me. Shamika's moans grew louder, while I had to suppress mine to hide my presence. I could feel myself about to cum. My hands were moving so fast that I couldn't stop even if I wanted to. I closed my eyes, and Carl had to know that I would explode any minute. He knew my body. He looked as if he wished that he could jump off Shamika and run and put his lips on my pussy and catch it. But he couldn't, so he just thought of how soft and wet I looked. I loved the feel of me, and so did he. I opened my eyes and found Carl's eyes still glued on me, but I was done. Yet again, I had used him, and it wouldn't be the last time.

I got up and started to leave, but Carl shook his head no. He wanted me to stay so that he could continue to look at me. I was already on his mind, but me being there made the sex that he was having with Shamika that much better. But I just smirked at him and stuck up my middle finger. I was the one doing the using, not him. I went up to bed and smiled to myself. My only regret was that I didn't get a chance to wipe my cum-filled pussy up and down Carl's face.

Thursday morning came fast. Shamika was up before me and came into my bedroom three times before I got out of bed. I was starting to rethink this whole "no drug" thing. I was missing my high mornings. Hell, I miss my high all day long, but even if I didn't quit forever, I knew that I wouldn't be doing any right now.

Shamika and I had lunch before heading over to Carmello's. She was dressed in some trashy outfit, as always. She had been saying all morning that she was down to do whatever Carmello wanted her to do. She kept saying it like she was trying to make herself believe it more than me. Although I wished that she would just shut the hell up, she did have some ways about her that reminded me of myself. Her fucking Carl was a classic me move.

We walked into Carmello's building after lunch and were taken to his office right away. He had cleared two hours on his schedule just in case Shamika needed convincing. We sat down at his desk as his secretary closed the office door.

"Aren't you that guy Tay'von had some words with?" Shamika asked.

I shifted in my seat. Carmello had said that she would call him out on this, but I just hoped that it didn't blow things. I recited what we had planned, and prayed that it worked.

I looked over at Shamika. "Yeah, that is him, and you know what? I think that I'm having second thoughts. Maybe we should get out of here. Now that I think about it, Tay would flip if he knew I was here."

I stood up and looked down at Shamika. "Come on, Mika. We have got to go. I'm sorry for wasting your time, but we can't stay."

Shamika wasn't about to leave without getting the deal she had come to get.

"What? Nah, come on, Tangie. We're already here. I gotta talk to him."

Carmello had hit it on the head when he said that he knew that she wouldn't leave, no matter what I said.

I picked up my purse and turned to leave. "Look, Shamika, I'm leaving. You can stay if you want, but I can't be here."

I walked out of the office, and I could hear Shamika walking out after me. When she caught up with me, she said, "You can go, but I have to stay to see what I can get out of this. This is a big chance for me and Black, so I can't just walk out. It's not like Tay got to know that you're here." She was trying to get me to stay, but that was not in the plan.

"Nah, I'm good. Like I said before, I should have never come here. But, hey, do you. Don't let me stop you. Go ahead and talk to him. I'll see you at home. Just tell him that you'll need a ride."

She didn't even think twice about going back into Carmello's office. All I saw was her back as she walked into his office. I went home, as planned, and waited for what would be good news for me and me only. I wanted to call Carmello to find out what was said, but she would tell me as soon as she got home.

Shamika came walking in about an hour and a half after me. She came right to my bedroom and sat on my bed. I turned off the TV and waited for her to talk, but for the first time ever, she was speechless. I decided that I would just sit there until she told me everything, and she tried.

"Tangie, now, you know that I'm a whatever-type bitch, but that nigga has asked me to do something that I just don't think I can do. He asked me to do some crazy shit."

I still didn't talk. I wanted her to feel that she could talk to me without interruption. I needed her to tell me how she felt about what he had asked without feeling judged.

She went on. "I know that if Black gets dropped from the label that he's on now, we'll be shit out of luck, but there's just something about this dude that has got me thinking twice about this. I just don't know if I should trust him. If it ever got out that I was behind what Carmello asked for, Black would kill me, because I would be the cause of his rap dreams dying."

I wasn't giving her any input on the issue at hand, because I wanted her to think that she was sealing her fate all on her own. I said, "Well, you know this is your choice. He can't force you to do it. Just take your time and think about it."

"You got to hear what he wants me to do. He asked me to—"

I cut her off. "You know what? Don't even tell me. If it's that crazy, then I don't want to know. If I know what it is, I'm sure I'll want to tell you what to do. I don't want to tell you *not* to do it. and I fuck shit up. Nor do I want to tell you to do it, and it gets you in trouble. This one is all up to you, Shamika."

I didn't want her to blame me when everything blew up in her face. She left my bedroom and went into hers. I was shocked. I had thought that she would be ready to do this. She seemed like the type of female who would set up her own mom to get ahead. Now she was acting brand new on me. I knew that I was going to help her make up her mind without leaving my scent on the situation; she just didn't know it yet.

There was a knock on my door, and I knew that it wasn't Shamika. She would have just walked in.

"Come in, Carl."

Since the night I found out their secret, I had been waiting for him to come and explain to me why he was sleeping with Shamika.

He walked in, closed the door behind him, and strode over to the foot of the bed. "I just wanted to talk to you about the other night."

"You don't have to talk to me about that, Carl. I have eyes. I saw everything for myself," I said as I sat up in the bed.

"Look, Tangie, I know that you saw me fucking her, but it just kind of happened. She just came into the room and got on top of me—"

"Oh, come on, Carl. Man up. Grow some balls. Don't walk in here, trying to play the shit down. You fucked her, and it's too late to try to act like it didn't happen."

"You don't ever give people the time to talk. I'm not trying to downplay anything. I just want you to know that it was just sex."

"I know your story, Carl. I bet you're going to tell me that she just came into your room and raped you, right? But, hey, that's what I always do to you, right? And just like a little bitch, you just couldn't stop her."

I got on my knees on the bed and crawled over to where he was standing. I got close to him and spit my toxin at him as I tried to kill him with my words.

"You will never be a man, Carl. Every time I turn around, you're bitching about something. This is why you will never be my man. Hell, maybe I should start fucking her too. She's more of a man than you are."

He grabbed me by my throat and squeezed. "Bitch, I should kill you for trying to test my manhood. Do you really want to go there, Tangie?"

His grip was getting tighter. I tried to push his hand away from my neck, but I couldn't. He pushed me down and walked around to the side of the bed. He held me down with one hand and ripped my panties off with the other.

"I don't ever hear you calling me a bitch, nigga, when I got my dick up in your ass," he growled.

"Fuck you, Carl. I'm going to call Tay'von on you. How dare you put your hands on me!"

"Call Tay'von, bitch. Fuck you, fuck him, and fuck this job. Call him and put it on speaker-phone. We both can do some talking."

As I lay on the bed, I was thinking that maybe he had lost his mind.

"What, you think you're scaring me? You're just proving my point. Real men don't snitch. You can choke me or do whatever you want to do. It won't change that you're a punk-ass nigga." By now I was almost screaming. I felt so violated. I was so mad at myself for ever sleeping with him. Things always changed either for better or worse when you slept with someone.

He got into my bed and got on top of me. I tried to push him off, but he had all his weight on me.

"If there's anything that I can say, it's that you got some good-ass pussy. Now let's see if your sick ass is going to get wet for me," Carl said as he spread my legs and looked down at me.

I wanted to scream for help, but if I did, that meant Shamika was going to walk in there and see Carl on top of me. That also meant that she would have something on me, and she could hold it over my head in the near future. I wasn't letting that happen. So all I did was take it. I looked down at him as he played with my pussy, and he was serious about what he was doing. He was really trying to see if I was going to get wet.

"You're the sick fuck, Carl. I would have never thought that you would rape a woman in your boss's bed."

He laughed at my statement. "How am I the sick one when you're getting wet?"

I didn't say anything. Maybe I *was* a sick fuck. It was starting to feel good. I hated him, but I loved what he was doing to me. I tried to close my legs, but he pushed them open again.

"Don't try to act like you don't want it. You may try to lie, but your body won't. Look at your legs, Tangie. You can't even stop them from shaking. Yeah, you're a nasty, sick little freak."

He worked his fingers faster, just like he knew I liked it. He was right. My body wouldn't lie to anyone, not even myself. My eyes wanted to close, and my hips wanted to move to the flow of his fingers. There was nothing that I could do. My body wouldn't let me, so I just stopped trying. I opened my legs wider as I pushed his head down to my pussy. He fell right in line and fucked me with his tongue. My hate and lust for Carl merged and became one. The power of

them together ran through me and made me
cum fast. I let it all go in his mouth, and after I
was done, I flipped him over and sat on his lips.
I made sure to rub myself all over his face this
time. And I stayed there until he made me cum
again.

Chapter 14

Girl, I'm About To
Pop Some Shit Off

Two days went by fast. I couldn't wait for Tay to come home today. Carl had been walking around the house with a big, arrogant chip on his shoulder ever since he had got me to want him even when I shouldn't have. What could I say? I was a slave for sex, among other things. I thought that maybe when Tay got home, Carl would step back into his place. I had been counting the minutes until he got home, not only because of Carl, but also because I wanted Shamika to do what she had to do.

Early that morning, I went up to her bedroom to see if she was still in bed. To my surprise, she was up, dressed, and sitting in the chair by the dresser.

"Damn, girl, you're up early. I guess you can't wait for Black to get here, huh?" I said.

She took a puff off her blunt and blew out the smoke. "Shit, I wish I had another week or two before they got home. I don't know if I can do this."

"Girl, don't even think about that. Just spend some time with him and feel things out. If you still feel like you can't do it, well, don't."

I knew that she would have to do it. I had spoken to Carmello yesterday and found out that Black had had a meeting with his label and that they had told him that they were thinking about selling his contract to a smaller label. In the music world, that was the nicest way of telling you that you would be dropped soon. I was sure Carmello had told her all of this, because that would be the only way to help her make up her mind.

I left her bedroom and went into my own. The hours ticked by, and around 3:30 p.m., Tay'von, Black, and Tony got home. I went down the stairs two at a time and jumped into Tay's arms. I could see Carl's jaw clench up, but I didn't care. As much as he was trying to stop loving me, he couldn't, and we both knew it.

"Damn, baby, let me see you." Tay put me down, and I turned around for him. "Your ass looks just as good as I remember it," Tay said as he grabbed my butt. "Looks like Carl's been taking good care of you."

I smiled. That was it; that was all. "Oh yeah, baby, he's been taking good care of both of us."

Tay'von may not have known what I meant, but Carl's eyes stayed on the floor. I knew that all it would take was my man coming home and Carl would lose that chip. Shamika still had not come downstairs, and we all wondered what was keeping her. When Black called out for her, she slowly came walking down the stairs. Once she was in view, Black gasped for air. She wasn't the same ghetto girl he had left behind.

"Damn, Tangie. I can see why she wanted to tell people you two are sisters," Tay joked.

"Hey, Black. I didn't know y'all were here already," Shamika said as she gave him an empty hug.

I was sure Black felt like he wasn't getting any love. The hug she gave him was as cold as an ice cube. Black later shared with me that he had wanted her to be excited and jump into his arms like I had with Tay, but he knew that it would never happen. They didn't have that type of relationship. And every time he thought of leaving her for that very same reason, he always remembered the time they had between them and the freak that she was in the bedroom. At times the outlandish costumes that she would wear as she swung around the stripper pole he had in his basement and her expertise in the act of fucking filled the void Black felt, but it was times like this that the lack of intimacy smacked him in the face. I could tell Tay felt sorry for Black. He led the way to the bar, where we all sat and talked about our time spent apart.

The two men filled us in about the tour and how well it was going. I was sure they left out the stories about hoes they had spent their time with to spare Shamika and me from going crazy. The time was passing by quickly, and Shamika said that she wanted to go out. But Tay and Black were too tired from traveling, so we stayed in for the night. And instead of going out to dinner, we had Tony and Carl go out and pick up the food.

"I'm really feeling that new look, Shamika. It looks really good on you," Tay said as he got up to refill his glass.

"Yeah, it's about time you got rid of all that ugly ghetto shit you've been rocking," Black commented. He was not in a good mood, but after what he had learned about his contract, I wouldn't expect him to be.

"Well, it is a very good choice, Shamika," Tay'von said to her.

Hell, someone had to make her feel better.

The food came, and Black still wasn't feeling better. I thought that maybe after we ate, his frown would turn into a smile.

"Oh, Tangie, I almost forgot to tell you. Our engagement party is tomorrow. Some of my boys thought that it would be nice to do that for us," Tay announced while we all sat down at the table to eat dinner.

"What? Well, okay. That's real nice, baby, but I wish I had known. I would have helped plan it. You must have told a lot of people," I said.

"Shit. I didn't tell you? It has been all over the news and magazines. I got, like, four of them in my carry-on right now." He got up, dug into his carry-on, and brought the magazines over to the table. There it all was. All four of them had our engagement story on the cover. The captions were almost all the same.

"The rapper Tay'von, or as the ladies like to call him, Mr. Too Fine, has gotten engaged to the very sexy star of at least three of his music videos," I read aloud.

When I looked inside that magazine, there was not only a picture of him and me leaving the restaurant where we had had lunch with Black and Shamika that day, but there was also a snapshot of me from one of his videos.

"Wow. They really know how to catch you without you even knowing, don't they?" I observed.

"Man, they'll hide in some bushes or even climb a tree if they have to," Black noted.

"Well, it looks like your face is out there now," Tay'von remarked. "I'm sure everyone is going to try to get you to talk to them. I might just call up a reporter and get it over with. I can get us a two-hour special. That way they can leave us alone after we do one."

My heart skipped a beat when I thought about a two-hour special. That would be the best way to get the word out about the video girl company that I had been thinking about starting. I was going to run everything about that by Tay later on, but I was sure he was going to go for it.

"Oh my God. Yes, we should do that. We can get the house all dressed up and nice. I think that it will be great." I said it as if I was a big kid. I leaned over and planted a big, wet kiss on Tay'von's lips. I appreciated him so much. He was making all my dreams come true, and for that, I loved him.

"Calm down, baby. It's not for sure. All I said was that I'll think about it."

"Yeah, well, I think it's a good idea. At least you would know that you're putting out the facts, and not just sitting back and letting them lie about us. But do whatever you think is best, baby." I leaned over and kissed him again. I was not going to press the issue. I was going to get what I wanted, anyway.

"Look, I'm not hungry. I'm just gonna go to bed. Where's the bedroom?" Black said as he got up from the table.

It was killing me that he was so down. He had been really nice to me in the past. It was a shame to know that things were going to get worse for him, that is, if Shamika came through and did what Carmello had asked her to do.

"I'll show you which one," Shamika said. She got up and walked him to their guest bedroom. I watched them leave, then I turned to Tay.

"What the hell is wrong with Black tonight?"

"He's got a good reason to be pissed. His new single is blowing up, but the label is still giving him shit over what happened. But he'll be all right."

Tay and I ate our food, and I kept reminding him that we had guests in the house. He was telling me how much he wanted to fuck me on the table. I tried to calm him down, but he wouldn't let up, so I ended up saying, "Fuck the food," and pulled him up by his shirt and led him upstairs. Now, I knew that the house was big, but we didn't hear Black yelling at Shamika until we got to the top of the stairs. So I stopped and listened, hoping that I would learn something new about the odd couple.

"How fucked up do you think I feel when I got all this shit going on and I can't even come home to you even acting like you're happy to see me? You could have *tried* to play it off a little bit, don't you think?"

"Come on, nigga. You know that we don't even roll like that," Shamika yelled back. "What, you want me to jump into your arms like we in some type of movie or some shit? That may be Tangie and Tay, but that has never been us. And where are you getting all this new shit from, anyway? You know how we roll."

Shamika had been really thrown off. To her, Black should have known by then that she wasn't an affectionate woman.

"You're such a fucking hood rat. I see not even the new clothes can change you. I am not asking you to be like Tangie. All I am asking you to do is to at least fake like you're with me for more than just my money."

"Black, I have been with you since you were selling just nickel bags of weed. You didn't have any money then. I even held you down when your ass was locked up. Ain't none of them other bitches or so-called friends of yours even come down and see your ass. I was the only bitch to come down and keep your commissary up—"

Black cut her off. No matter what he said she wasn't going to get it. "You kept it up just as much as you kept your ass in the air. Yeah, don't get me wrong. You did hold me down, but I always knew that I was eating 'cause of some other man's money."

I was really getting into their conversation, but Tay'von kept trying to pull me away. I put my finger up in the air, trying to ask him for more time to eavesdrop, but he wouldn't let me stay in the hallway. I gave up after realizing that he wasn't going to stop until he got me in our bedroom. Once we got there, he picked me up and threw me over his shoulders.

"You nosy as hell, girl. Let me find out you wanted to listen to them more than you wanted to fuck me," Tay said as he sat me down on the bed.

"No, that's not it at all. I just wanted to make sure everything was okay with them." I was trying to lie, but he read right through it.

"Well, it didn't look like that to me. Face it, baby. You always want to be in someone else's shit," Tay joked as he laid me down and pulled my panties off. "Damn, baby, that camel toe looking phat as ever."

He was really in a good mood. I was just happy that he wasn't holding what had happened with Amira over my head. As if to prove my thoughts right, he spread my legs like Carl had done two weeks ago and just stared at me.

"What, are you just going to look at it, or are you going to do something to it?" I asked.

He reached down and played with my clit.

"So is this your way of telling me that you missed me?" I asked as I looked up at my Mr. Too Fine.

He looked so damn sexy standing there, with his broad chest and strong arms. His shape-up was fresh, and I loved the way his diamonds sparkled in his ears. His eyes looked like they were lightly lined with a dark brown eyeliner, but you could tell that they were natural. His light eyes had the very same shine as the studs in his ears, and I realized that this man was born to be a star. I hadn't felt that much lust for him in a while. He pulled off his shirt and smiled at me. In some sick, twisted way, even after all that I had done to him and him to me, we still wanted to be with each other. We loved and yearned for each other, and it was something that we just couldn't understand, so we didn't try.

He rubbed my thighs as I looked him over. I let my eyes roam down to his waist. He had that

V cut that some men had at the waistline, and it always drove me crazy. And let's not forget the little trail of hair that led down to their dicks, pointing the way to the treasure like a map. I could see something dark on his chest, but that wasn't my main focus. But wait . . . I rolled my eyes back up, and there it was. My name tattooed over his heart. I sat up and rubbed my fingers over the tattoo.

"Oh my God, Tay'von. What . . . when . . . What made you get this?"

"I just got up one day and did it. This shit is here forever, baby."

I touched it again and then looked up into his eyes. I could see a truth in them that wasn't there before. I kissed him deeply. Then I leaned toward his already hard dick and slid it in my mouth. I sucked the hell out of him. His body was rock hard and defined. I looked down at his legs and got turned on by the structure of them. He looked like a strong, tall Adonis. He ran his hand through my hair and lightly massaged my scalp. He knew that doing this helped me relax so that I was able to take him deeper into my mouth.

"Damn, Tangie. Suck that dick," Tay said as he pulled my hair out of my face so that he could see my headwork.

He fucked my mouth, and I didn't stop him from pushing his dick deeper and deeper down my throat. Soon he tried to pull away, but I held him in my mouth. I wanted to taste his cum. I wanted to suck it out of him. He pushed himself in and out of my mouth faster. He was fucking it like he was in some pussy as I tried to make my mouth feel like a tight, wet one.

"Baby, baby, I'm about to cum. You want me to pull out?" he cried.

I shook my head no.

I looked up at his Adam's apple and watched it move up and down as he gasped for air. I pulled my head back so that his dick was at the tip of my tongue. I flicked it on the tip of his dick and sucked in at the same time as his cum shot to the back of my throat. He moaned as I moved forward and went so deep on his dick that my nose touched his stomach. He pulled himself out of my mouth slowly, and I made sure not to drop even a little bit of his cream. I lay back down as he spoke softly to me.

"Damn, baby. You got me going crazy. I love the way you make me feel."

He just stood there looking at me. He went over my body slowly with his eyes. He picked up one of my feet and brought it to his mouth. He kissed and sucked on it, then moved to the other foot. Then he worked his way down to my clit. I opened wide and enjoyed the head. I soon felt like I was about to cum and tried to close my legs.

"Come on, baby. I want to watch that cum drip down to your ass," he told me.

Just the sound of his voice made me lose it. My chest heaved up and down as I came. He didn't stop until I took my feet and pushed his head away. I thought that he was going to just get on top of me, but he turned me over on my stomach and pulled me up on my knees.

"Hold up, baby. Let me grab a pillow," I said, thinking that I should get comfortable if he was going to hit it from the back.

"Nah, you don't need it yet. Just relax."

He leaned in and slid his tongue from my pussy to my ass. My body tingled with excitement. He worked my ass as if it were a pussy. I moaned more from this than him sucking on my clit.

"You're feeling really freaky tonight, baby. Oh shit. Eat that ass, Tay," I cooed when he moved back to my clit as he began to finger my ass.

The cum that dripped from my pussy and the saliva from his mouth left my ass so wet that I didn't need any lube.

"You gonna let me get some of this tight little ass, baby?"

I didn't even know why he asked. He knew that I would never say no to him sexually, unless I was holding back on purpose.

"Put that big dick in my ass, but get my Mr. Purple. I'm gonna work this pussy while you work my ass."

He did as he was told, and we fucked me right. An hour later we were in the shower, fucking the old-fashioned way, and an hour after that, we were fast asleep.

The next morning I got up around ten and went down to the kitchen for some breakfast. Shamika was already there, without Black. I was sure she was ready for us to go shopping, because Black was driving her crazy, and she needed some time away from him. She asked what time we were leaving, and I told her that after I ate, I would get dressed so that we could leave.

I let her drive while I read through the magazines Tay had brought home, but of course, that didn't stop her from talking.

"Man, Black got so bitchy after Tay brought them magazines out last night."

"Well, he's going to have to cut that shit out. Tay and I are about to get a whole lot of press for the wedding. Then, after that, Tay is going to start working on his new album, so all this hype about us is not about to stop. That's how it is when you're number one in the country."

Now, I know this sounded like I was throwing shit in her face, but I was just telling her the truth. I saw her roll her eyes, but I didn't jump on her about it. I knew that what I had just said stung her a little bit, but that was how the truth felt sometimes.

"Yeah, well, I'm sure that you heard him yelling at me last night. It was all over shit that happened, like, a million years ago."

"Oh, really? I didn't even hear that," I lied. I was sparing her the embarrassment of knowing that I did hear him digging deep into her ass.

"Girl, I know your house is big, but as loud as he was, I'm sure you had to hear something. I just don't know what's up with him. But I'll tell you one thing. If him having problems with his label makes him act like this, then I am ready to do whatever Carmello needs me to do. I just need to stop him from damn near breaking my neck every time he looks at me."

I put down the magazine I was reading and had to stop myself from jumping out of my seat and laughing hysterically. "Well, if you're sure that it will make Black's situation better, then do what you have got to do."

We pulled up to the store, and she gave the valet the car keys. He got in the car and looked at the magazines that I had left on the seat.

"Oh, shit. You're the girl who's with that rapper Tay'von, right? I love his music, and my sister is in love with that dude."

Shamika and I stopped walking and turned around.

"Oh, my bad. I didn't mean to curse," he said, thinking that he was being disrespectful.

"It's okay," I told him. "I'm always pleased to meet one of Tay'von's fans."

He went on to tell me how his girlfriend always wanted him to play Tay's CD every time she got into his car. He even told me that his fifteen-year-old sister had Tay's pictures all over her walls and called him her husband. I loved the love he and his people had for Tay and his music. It was because of fans like him that Tay was such a success and—let's not forget—so rich. He made me feel good about Tay, his music, and his fame.

"Girl, come on. We got other places to go after this," Shamika demanded, with her hands on her hips.

I told him to leave his name and address in my glove box. I also told him that I would send him concert tickets and a couple of backstage passes to Tay's next show in New York. He got them a week later.

I walked into the store without saying anything to Shamika's ignorant ass. She just didn't get the game of fame. It wasn't just on the shoulders of the star; the star's fame also belonged to the people around him or her. You had to know how to carry yourself and definitely how to interact with a star's fans. If you were associated with celebrities in any way, shape, or form, and they're not there, you took their place and had to represent them well. Telling her the rules to the game would have been a waste of time, so I kept my thoughts to myself.

We picked up everything that we needed for my engagement party, which was being held that night. She walked out of the first store seven thousand dollars poorer, while I dropped twenty-six thousand on all my goods. We went to the next store for shoes, then headed home.

We walked in the house, and I told Carl to go and get the bags out of the car. Black and Tay'von were sitting in the game room, playing video games.

"Hey, baby. You get everything you need?" Tay asked as I gave him a kiss and sat on his lap.

I didn't answer him; I just handed him the bill. He looked at it, smiled, and put it in his pocket.

"What's so funny?" I asked him as he wrapped his arms around my waist and pulled me closer.

"Oh, it's nothing, baby. It's just that you can work the hell out of a credit card. But, hey, if that's what it takes to keep your ass looking so fly, then so be it," Tay said before giving me a quick peck on the lips.

He then told me to get off his lap so that he could continue playing his game. I asked him to wake me up in an hour so that I could start getting ready for the party. Shamika got up to go upstairs with me but was stopped by Black.

"Hey, Shamika. Where's your receipt?"

She walked over to him and gave it to him, knowing that he was going to have a problem with the amount of money she had spent.

"Damn. What are you trying to do? Keep up with Tangie?" He tried to make it seem like a joke, but we all knew that he was so for real.

"Calm down, dude," Tay said. "You really got to stop bitching over money. This nigga stays paid, yet he's always crying over dough. Man, fuck it. I'll pay for her stuff. Give me the bill."

As soon as the words left Tay's mouth, I knew that it was the wrong thing for him to say.

"Man, fuck you. I don't need you to pay for my girl's shit. Just because I'm not about wasting my money don't mean I need any of yours," Black protested.

Tay shrugged. "Yeah, okay. I'm just saying. You can't be famous and still be crying over what, twenty, thirty thousand dollars? You make way more than that for one night when performing at a concert."

"I'm not trying to be like all of them other famous people out there, who sit around and talk about how much money they *used* to have. And who said I was talking about thirty thousand dollars? Shamika isn't that crazy."

Tay reached over and grabbed the receipt out of Black's hand.

"Damn, nigga. You're talking all this shit for a total of nine thousand dollars. I wish Tangie would shop like Shamika. It would save me a whole lot of money."

By then, Tay'von was really laughing hard, but Black didn't find it funny.

"Yeah, okay, keep spending up all your money on shit you and Tangie aren't even going to be wearing next year. You'll be calling me to help pay for her fifty-thousand-dollar shopping bill," Black said as he pushed PLAY on the game.

I understood why he felt this way. He felt like he was about to lose everything. I was just happy that they went back to playing the game without coming to blows. I didn't want them fighting, because we had a lot of nice things in the house and, hey, it was not like Black could afford to replace them.

That night I got dressed in a deep red, long silk dress. It had a plunging neckline that turned into a sheer line that ran all the way down the dress. My hair was down and curled. I had one side pinned to the side of my head with a ruby and diamond heart-shaped hairpin, which made the curls fall on one shoulder. I slipped on the Jean Paul Gaultier dress, and Tay zipped me up. I iced up my look with the big rock Tay'von had given me and an invisible diamond necklace. All you saw was a sparkle in the middle of my neck.

I turned around to face him, and he smiled. He had called in a makeup artist and hairstylist to make sure Shamika and I looked our best, and it was money well spent. He looked at me, then gave me a long kiss. I pushed him away playfully, but I was serious about keeping my looks intact.

"Stop, baby. You're going to mess up my makeup."

"Fuck your makeup. You're looking good as hell in that dress."

"Yeah, and I want to keep it on. Just fasten my bracelet and go finish getting ready," I told him.

About ten minutes later we were all ready to go. We got into the limo and were on our way. I must say that we all looked like stars. Even Shamika had herself put together well. She had on the new black Dolce & Gabbana dress that I had picked out for her earlier that day. She had even kept it simple with the jewels. All the men had on nice trendy suits, with a hint of their own style thrown into the mix.

We were getting close to the party when Tay told us that cameras for the top news show would be there. An hour-long segment was set to air the following week. First, they would tape the party, and two days later they were coming out to the house to sit and talk with us. I smiled to myself, knowing that after this, I was going to be just as known as Tay'von, if not more known than him. Hard work always paid off. We pulled up to the rented-out club, and you would have thought that we were at an awards show. There were cameras flashing, lots of celebs, and even a red carpet. The limo driver stopped the car and walked around to open the doors. Tony got out first, followed by Black, Carl, and Shamika.

Tay told the driver to close the doors so that he could have a quick chat with me. He turned to me and took my hand while I waited for him to speak.

"Baby, I just want you to know that you look beautiful tonight. I am very proud to be getting out of this limo with you, and I love you, Tangie, with all my heart, baby." He leaned in and kissed me on my neck.

I could hear everyone outside asking if Tay'von and Tangie were in the limo. They couldn't wait to get a look at us up close, and we couldn't wait to present ourselves. Tay knocked on the window, and the driver opened the door. Tay stepped out and reached back in the car and helped me out. Everyone's mouths dropped, and I heard them gasp.

Tay leaned in to me and gave me the greatest compliment. "See, baby, you're a showstopper."

We walked down the red carpet and talked to the reporters. I was almost blinded from the flashing lights, but I loved every minute of it. We finally made it inside the club, and I was taken aback. Everything looked classy and expensive. You couldn't even tell that you were inside a dance club. On one of the walls was the biggest picture I had ever seen of Tay and me. Thank God it was a cute one. I rubbed elbows with all the major rappers, singers, actors, and ballplayers who were at the top of their game at the time. That night we all let loose and got our party on. By the end of the night, we had so many gifts that we had them packed into two cars.

We made it back home around four in the morning. We all were partied out, so we sat down in the living room before going to bed.

"Out of all the parties I have ever been to, that had to be one of the best. That shit was decked out," Shamika said as she leaned back in her chair.

"Well, you knew it wasn't going to be cheap. Everyone in there was paid," Black answered. He was always thinking about money. It didn't matter if it was someone else's or his own.

"I wasn't even worried about that. I knew my boys were going to hook that shit up right. And did you see my baby tonight? All eyes were on her. Everyone was on her shit tonight." Tay was so proud and was smiling from ear to ear.

"Yeah, I know. People kept coming up to me and Black and asking how you met her, what she is like, or just saying how good she looks. It really was all about y'all tonight," Shamika said as she got up for a soda.

Tay asked her to bring us all back a drink, so she asked me to help. I thought I was just going to help her carry everything, but as soon as we got in the kitchen, she pulled me close.

"Girl, I'm about to pop some shit off."

I looked at her with a dumb look on my face, praying that she was finally going to get down to business.

"You know what I am talking about, Tangie. The thing Carmello asked me to do. I am about to get him real fucked up so that I can get it done," she answered as she took sodas out the refrigerator and glasses from a cabinet.

"How and why do you have to get him fucked up to do it? I know weed don't get people that messed up. If it's as bad as you're making it out to be, then he's gonna put up a fight no matter if you use alcohol or weed."

She walked over to one of the kitchen drawers and pulled out what she wanted to show me. In her hand she held two already rolled-up Js.

"This should get him real fucked up. It's a little bit of weed and a whole lot of other things," she revealed.

I picked up the sodas and glasses she had left on the counter, and put them on a tray.

"Well, if this is what you have to do, then I can't tell you anything to stop you. I just hope that he never finds out what you did. He would kill you for sure," I told her.

"Shit, if you knew what I was about to do, and he killed me, you would say that I deserved every bit of it."

"Like I said before, I don't want to know. I don't want no part in what you're doing. This is even too deep for me."

"Yeah, well, just get Tay up to the bedroom and keep him there. He can't walk out on what I am about to do. The camera is already set up, so all I have to do is press RECORD on the remote," she said.

Shamika and I walked back into the living room, and I handed everyone their drinks. I left my drink on the tray and sat down on Tay's lap and kissed his neck. I knew that this would turn him on and that he would want to head for the bedroom. Black asked Shamika to roll up a J for him as he sipped on his drink. I was the only one really watching her. I was waiting to see if I would miss the switch, because that bitch was slick. She took her time and rolled up a blunt. Then she quickly switched the one she had just rolled for one of the two laced ones. If I had blinked, I would have missed it. Without even thinking about it, she handed the laced blunt to Black.

I really had to get Tay out of here. I didn't want him to say anything about the weed smelling funny. I licked his neck and whispered in his ear. "I want you to take me to the bedroom and fuck the shit out of me. But first, I want you to lick me from head to toe."

He took a sip of his drink and kissed me deeply. I pulled away and stood up.

"Well, what are you waiting for?" I asked as I walked toward the steps.

He got up and followed me like a well-trained puppy. As soon as we hit the bedroom, we got right to it.

Shamika was downstairs, waiting for the laced weed to take over Black's body and mind before knocking him out.

Chapter 15

A Black Heart Is Earned,

Not Learned, Baby Doll

Some will never understand why we had Shamika do what she did, and some may never understand why she herself would even do it. But at times, you make people do things just to see how much power you really have over them. Other times, you make them pay for doing something that brings back the most painful part of your life. Shamika had done that when she gave Tay the drugs that caused him to force himself on me while we were on tour. That bitch had to pay.

I may spill a glass of soda and tell you to clean it up. To some, that may seem small, but the way you clean up that soda will tell me all that I need to know. Did you jump up and

*seem eager to please? Did you show resistance
and give me attitude? All of that matters in
the grand scheme of things. I'll never forget
watching the things she did to Black on that
tape for the first time. A great puppet master
must know their puppets the best! They must
know which string to tug to bring out the best
performance. Dance, bitch. Dance!*

Shamika sat across from Black and watched
him smoke.

"Damn, Tay got some good-ass weed. This shit
got me fucked up already," Black said as he tried
to put it out.

"What, you punking out already? Don't tell me
that you can't handle some good smoke?"

"Girl, please. I could smoke you under the
table."

"Well, show and prove. I bet you can't finish
that one and light up another one," Shamika
said, trying to push him into smoking both of
the laced blunts.

Black picked up his lighter and sparked up
again. With every hit that he took, he felt like
his brain was burning. His mind became foggy,
and he wanted to stop, but there was no way

he was going to let Shamika win. His pride was and would always be his downfall. As soon as he finished the first blunt, she handed him the next. He was way too high to notice that she hadn't rolled the second one in front of him. By the end of it, his mind was frozen. When Shamika called his name, he answered, but she could tell that he was in another world. She picked up the camera's remote and pressed RECORD. She walked over to him and sat beside him.

"Baby, you know that I would do anything for you, right?" she said.

He shook his head yes.

"Well, I was hoping that we could try some new things tonight." She unzipped his pants and stuck her hand in.

"Shit. What are you trying to do? We can try whatever."

She played with his dick and got it rock hard. "I'm tryin'a take our sex to a whole other level. But some guys try to act like they are too scared to do what I'm talking about." She knew that saying this would not only piss him off but also egg him on.

"Girl, you know I'm not scared to do nothing. I'm down for whatever you can think of."

Shamika stood up and started to undress. She took her clothes off slowly, just like Carmello had told her to do. Black rubbed his dick as he admired her body. It was hard for him since he was seeing double, but he managed. She leaned him back, then sat on his face. This would be the only pleasure that she would be getting from this whole ordeal.

After she got her rocks off from the head, she told him that she would be right back. She went to the coat closet and pulled out the bag of things that she had put in there earlier. She walked back over to him with the bag and told him to lie on his back. She kneeled down, took massaging oil out of the bag, and rubbed him down. She did this to relax him and make him think everything was normal. He closed his eyes and enjoyed the feel of her hands. When she was done, she pulled his pants all the way off. She rubbed his chest and worked her way down while letting the oil drip on his dick. She jerked it and slowly moved her fingers lower and lower, until she ran her fingers over the crack of his ass. She felt his body tighten, and her heart pumped with fear as the thought of him going off ran through her head.

"Yo, Mika, what are you doing?" he asked as she stopped moving her fingers.

"I told you I wanted to try something new, didn't I?"

"Man, fuck that. Just give me some head," he said as he reached for her head and pulled it down.

She sucked him off and started to play with his balls, hoping that it would lead her fingers to the promised land. She waited until he closed his eyes again, and then moved her fingers to his asshole again. He opened his eyes, but he did not stop her. It was starting to feel better and better to him. He just leaned back and went with the flow as she worked her lips lower. She went from his dick to his balls; then she tongued down his hole. He let out a gasp as he moved his hips like a female would if she were getting the perfect BJ.

She got him nice and wet, then snuck her pinkie finger in. As she worked another one in, she looked up at him. He started to speak, but then she lowered her head and sucked on the head of his dick. By the end of her head session, she had worked three fingers into his ass. She reached down and came up with a strap-on. He watched her as she stood up and put it on.

He glared at her. "I know you aren't about to use that on me."

"Oh yes I am," she said as she got on top of him. He tried to push her off, but he was too weak from the drugs.

"Come on, Tangie! Stop."

Shamika looked down at him with disgust and hate. "Tangie? My name isn't no muthafuckin' Tangie. You thinking about her or something?"

At that moment, she no longer cared about his reaction to what she was about to do. She was going to make him pay for calling her by the wrong name regardless of what his delayed reaction would be. She slid in between his legs and pushed them all the way back. She leaned down and licked his ass a couple more times, then came up with a quick thrust. She pushed the dildo into his ass so hard that he let out a load moan that I heard all the way upstairs.

I wanted so badly to go down and watch, but Tay would have stopped me. I wasn't tripping; Carmello was going to let me watch the tape, anyway.

Again, Black tried to push her off, but he still was too weak. She pushed his legs so far back that they touched his chest.

"I hope you're ready for a rough ride," Shamika said as she pulled out and slid back in him.

The pain was so strong that Black thought that he was going to pass out, he wasn't used to being the bottom and having to take such a big one. She moved slowly, knowing that he had to get used to it. The more she moved in and out, the more he started to like it. When she noticed that his eyes were opening and closing with pleasure, she moved a little faster and deeper. It was both good and painful for him. He didn't know if he wanted to push her off or to pull her in deeper.

"You like it, don't you? It's okay. I like it too," Shamika said, loving the power she felt from being the one doing the fucking.

Black was now holding his own legs up and was throwing it back. He looked up at her as she leaned in and kissed him. Black humped back like a well-trained whore on graduation day. It was as if he wanted to show off everything he had learned from the institute of fucking back.

That night Shamika fucked him every which way she could think of. It left some questions in her mind about him, though. Why was he so into it? Why was it so easy for her to dive in? Why didn't he try harder to keep her out of what most men would think of as no-man's-land? Although she knew that he was high from the laced weed, he was enjoying himself a little too much for her liking. At least it made the tape seem even more real, and that was very important. Carmello said that it should come off as natural.

***

The next morning I woke up before Tay'von. It was really early, so I tiptoed downstairs, hoping that Black and Shamika were still down there. When I turned the corner, I saw them right away, Black asleep on the couch and Shamika sitting in the chair that faced him.

I tiptoed over to Shamika. "Girl, how long have you been up?" I asked as I looked around the room.

The strap-on that she had used the night before was on the floor beside Black. I wanted to roll on the floor laughing, but I kept it all in.

"I'm scared of what's he's going to do when he wakes up. I couldn't sleep last night, thinking about it."

"What in the hell did you do last night that could be so bad?" I asked, trying to sound like I was totally lost.

She got up, walked over to the dildo, and picked it up.

"I know that you're about to tell me that he used that on you, right?" I said.

She shook her head no while walking over to me. "Tangie, what am I going to do? If he wakes up and is pissed off about what I did to him last night, he's gonna kick my ass, then kick me out. Shit, he doesn't even know—"

I cut her off. Didn't want her to spill her already burnt beans. "Don't tell me any more. I don't want to know anything else about this. Why would you even do something like this? Are you crazy?"

"But this is what Carmello told me to do. I didn't have a choice."

I scrunched up my face in disgust. "Why would he ask you to fuck Black with a strap-on? You know what? Don't tell me. Just pick all this shit up. You're going to have to wake him up."

By then Shamika was shaking. As much shit as she talked, it floored me to see her in such a state. It turned out that she wasn't the bad bitch she had made herself out to be. If she was, she wouldn't be shaking like a leaf. A real bad bitch planned and accepted her fate; she didn't cry when she was staring down the barrel of the gun.

"Don't just stand there," I told her when she just stood in place. "I know you don't want anyone else coming down and seeing all this stuff lying around."

She still didn't move. Fear had grounded her and didn't allow her to take a step.

I frowned at her. "Fine. I'll wake him up, and you get all this stuff upstairs."

I waited for her to do what I had told her to do; then I walked over to Black and patted him on his chest. He looked up at me, then down at his dick. Noticing that I couldn't keep my eyes off his big piece of meat, he jumped up and put his boxers back on. This dude had what I liked to call the Pepsi Challenge between his legs. I smiled at him, and he smiled back.

"You must have had some time last night," I said as I lit a Capri.

"I must have been really fucked up last night. My bad for falling asleep on your couch."

"It's okay. There would be no better time than now for me to catch a glimpse of what you're working with," I said while still smiling.

Yeah, I was flirting, but it was all out of pity.

"Hell, maybe I need something that nice in my life," I added.

"I'm not sure about all of that, 'cause Tay must be doing something right if he's keeping a girl like you around."

"Yeah, you're right. Not all men can handle me."

We shared a laugh over the truth I spoke. Then he looked like something had hit him, something as hard as a big, fake dildo.

"Are you okay, Black?"

"Where's Shamika?"

"I think she's upstairs. Why? What's up?"

I watched him walk away like a man on a mission. I looked to see if he was walking funny, but I couldn't tell. I followed him and got close enough to hear and see everything without either of them knowing. I threw my head back and silently laughed, feeling like if I didn't get it out, it would have been on its way to choking me. I couldn't wait to see the tape. Shamika had just finished washing and putting the dildo away when Black walked into their bedroom. She tried to act like her heart was not pounding fast enough to give her a heart attack.

"Hey, baby. Did you sleep well?" she said casually.

Black didn't say anything. He just stood there, putting his thoughts together. He walked over to her to look her in the eye, but she wouldn't look at him.

"Now, Shamika, I am only going to ask you this once. What in the hell made you think that you could do what you did last night? Take your time and think about it before you open your mouth."

The look that he gave her warned her of the violence that might happen next. If she was smart, she would take heed.

"I, I just thought that we would try something new."

He put his hands around her neck and pushed her back against the wall. "Did you put something in my smoke last night?"

"No, I would never do that. Why are you acting all crazy?"

"Who the hell told you to do that? I saw you in the game room the other day with Tony. Did that nigga put you up to this?"

Shamika was trying to pry his hands lose, but to no avail. When he realized that she wouldn't be able to answer him if she passed out, he let her go. He lit up a Newport while he waited for her to talk.

"Nobody told me to try anything. Why would you think Tony had something to do with this? I was watching a flick, and it turned me on when I saw them doing that. Why are you so mad? You seemed like you liked it. You were really into it, baby."

Black moved so fast that Shamika didn't see the punch coming. Once she hit the floor, she knew that she shouldn't have said what just came out of her mouth.

"What are you trying to say, Shamika? You think you turned me out last night or something?" he asked as he hovered over her. "All I know is that no one better find out about this. Do you hear me, Shamika? Nobody."

Shamika, who was still on the floor, shook her head yes.

"And if you ever try this shit again, I'll kill you," Black said right before he left the room.

Shamika got up, and the only thing on her mind was how she was going to get the tape to Carmello. Dumb bitch!

The next day was so busy for me. While Tay was back at the house, waiting for extra help to come and spruce up the house and yard, I was making sure that I would look my best for our interview the next day. I hit up Fifth Avenue's Bergdorf Goodman in Manhattan and put a huge dent in Tay's credit card. When I got back home, it was a madhouse. There were about ten people running around cleaning, gardening, and rearranging things around the house. They all were there to make sure that everything looked its best. I couldn't wait for Tay and me to be married so that I could demand to pick out a new house.

Tay'von had picked out this house because it was big enough to show off his wealth. I wanted a house that would show off not only our wealth but also the power of the pussy. A house that would make everyone know that I had picked it out. I walked out into the backyard, where

Tay was telling the gardener how he wanted the bushes cut, and gave him a kiss.

"Hey, baby, you're right on time," he remarked. "The makeup people just called, and they wanted to know what time you wanted them to come. You need to call them back and handle that."

I told him I would call, and he let me know he would be in the house soon. I could feel him watching me as I walked away, so I put a little more swing in my hips than I had before.

"Work it, girl," he called out jokingly.

In a crazy way, I felt like my days were becoming mundane. Although this television interview was something that I was looking forward to, I was still lacking something important. The only thing I had going besides this was the thing with Shamika and Carmello, and I couldn't wait to talk to him and go down to his office.

I went up to my bedroom to watch a movie after making my call. I didn't even stop and talk to Shamika, although when I passed her bedroom, I heard her call my name. I just wanted some time to myself. I locked the door and sat on the bed. As soon as I got my feet off the floor, I heard Shamika knocking on my door and calling my name. I just ignored it. I knew that she wanted to talk about Black kicking her ass, but I wasn't in the mood. About an hour later

Tay joined me in the bedroom, and we fell asleep early. It was a good thing, since we had to be up at six in the morning.

I have always hated early mornings. Tay'von had to keep coming into the bedroom to get me out of bed the next morning. I took a long hot shower and then slipped on my robe. When I got downstairs, the makeup and hair people were already there. I walked by like I didn't even see them. Tay laughed at my always present attitude.

"You all will have to excuse her. She's grumpy in the morning." He wanted them to know that it wasn't my fault, but I just rolled my eyes at him and asked the maid to pour me some coffee.

The makeup and hair people took forever to do their jobs. Tay was acting really nervous, but I was so ready for my time in the spotlight. The public saw me only as the girl in his videos. Soon they would know me as Tay'von' s fiancée, who happened to have a brain and something to say. We sat down as Mary Mendel read our bios to prepare herself. Once the cameras started rolling, she talked to Tay about his album that was out and then about the new video, which would premiere at the end of the show. She asked him about his upbringing and how that had affected his music. She also asked him how he felt about being dubbed Mr. Too Fine in the roughneck rap industry. That was when I had to step in and give my input on her question.

"Well, hip-hop has come a long way. It's not just about the saggy jeans and that unkempt look anymore. We are able to show all sides of it," I explained. "You can even find men in suits rapping now. To tell you the truth, I am happy that he's on that side of the game."

Tay smiled proudly.

"So, how is it for you to be with a man who has millions of women dreaming about him every night?" she asked me.

"I take it as it is. I knew who he was when I got with him. There are so many women who won't, can't, shouldn't date or marry famous men, because they would go crazy. You have to have tough skin to deal with this lifestyle, and there is a lot that could mess up a relationship. You just kind of have to deal with it and know that fans will be fans and that most of what you are going to read and hear is lies. And remember that I did say *most*. Yes, there are times that no matter how much trust you have in your relationship, you'll still let your thoughts run wild, and deep down you know that some of what has been said may be true. I mean, come on. How many times do you hear about famous men sleeping with a fan? You just have to have hope and hold on to it."

She was looking like she was really into what I was saying, and I was just getting started.

"And what do you have hope for?" she asked.

I looked at Tay'von, and he took my hand. "You just have to hope that the love that you have for each other will help him or even help you make the right decision. Now, I know that this has been said over and over, but men will be men. Only the strongest of them can turn down a half-dressed, 'willing to do anything' woman who snuck into their dressing room. And if anything happens that shouldn't, well, I hope he's man enough to tell me so that we can deal with it before I see it in some sleazy magazine. And it works both ways."

"Well, since you brought up sleazy magazines, I have one here that has everyone wondering about the death of R & B singer Amira. The headlines read 'Singer jumps to her death after getting dumped by Mr. Too Fine's girlfriend.' What do you make of that?"

I didn't even blink before letting the lie roll off my tongue. I knew that she was watching to see if I would have a reaction, and I made sure to give her the right one. I could feel Tay's hand tighten around mine, but I squeezed it back to let him know that he should relax.

"You know, this really makes me sick," I said. "Here we are in the middle of such a tragic death, and all these people can do is make up lies. This is exactly what I was talking about earlier. We still are not over her death, and to see such trash in this magazine is a shame. I hope that after people see this, they will realize that we should be more interested in how she lived. Not how or why she died. This is someone who touched so many lives with her soul, and she put that very same soul in every song she sang. Let's at least shine the spotlight on that and leave the garbage behind."

I threw her off with that one, and she was impressed from that moment on. The rest of the interview went smoothly. Afterward, we showed her the grounds, and she acted like she loved everything about the house. We then sat back down and talked about the upcoming wedding, and she asked me if I was planning on being a housewife.

"Well, I plan to open an agency for women and men who want to be in music videos or print work," I responded. "Black women and men have a harder time landing jobs outside the hip-hop world. So I want them to have a place where they know I am working just as hard for them as I would for anyone else."

She asked me questions about myself for the next twenty minutes or so, before asking her last question.

"So in an industry that is so overwhelmingly full of divorces, do you two think that this will last?"

Tay leaned over and kissed me, then looked her dead in her eyes and said, "This is for life."

With that, the cameras stopped filming. She shook our hands, and then her crew gathered their things. We walked her to the front door, where Black had been standing and watching. Tay introduced her to him, but she didn't seem that impressed, although she was trying her hardest to fake it.

"Ah, yes. You're on tour with Tay'von, right? Well, keep up the good work. Our next profile just might be of you." She smiled after giving him false hope, then left.

Tay pulled me into his arms and gave me a warm hug. "Damn, baby, you really did your thing. How come you never told me about this agency?"

"It was only a thought. It just kind of came to me. So what do you think?"

"I'm with it. Whatever you need, just let me know."

In his mind, he couldn't get over how well I had come off. He really was proud of me.

"Baby, this shit really is for life," he told me. "I just wasn't saying it for the interview. Now that we have done this, the whole world is going to know what a wonderful woman I have by my side. Niggas gonna hate when they realize you're not just some groupie bitch that's just with me for my money."

"How do you know that's what they ever thought? Has anyone ever said that to you?" I quizzed.

"Come on, Tangie. You know that any man that's in my position and has a girl that looks like you by his side makes people think stuff like that. But we will show them that there is more than that between us."

I was sure that there was something he wasn't telling me, but I let it go. It's not like I gave a shit what others thought, anyway.

He wrapped his arms around me again and squeezed my ass. I knew that he wanted some, so I escorted him to the bedroom.

***

It was Monday morning, and I sat on the edge of the bed, looking down at Tay. I rubbed my hand over his chest as I thought silently to myself, *I am one bad bitch*. I really had everything that I wanted at the time. Out of all the women out there who could have been in my position, I was sitting right in it. My mother had always said that I should make sure that the person I ended up with gave me everything that I needed and wanted. I should be his queen, and that meant that I should live and rule like one. I hoped that I had made her proud by paying attention to the wisdom she had instilled in me. I was so deep into my thoughts that I did not notice Tay'von smiling back up at me.

He brought me out of my thoughts by clearing his throat.

"What's on your mind, Mr. Too Fine?" I asked.

"I'm just thinking about all the shit that we've been through. We have really come a long way, and it kills me every time I have to leave. Do you think that you could come back on the road with me?"

Poor thing. He was pussy whipped. I wondered if this was how the white girls had the NBA and NFL players who seemed to be drawn to them like bees to honey.

"You know that I have to start planning the wedding. Plus, I had all the road time I want for a while."

He laughed, maybe thinking that I just wasn't cut out for the touring lifestyle. "So you're just going to plan the whole thing while I'm gone? I don't get no say-so, huh?"

"Come on, Tay. Even if you were here, I would still be stuck planning the whole thing by myself. Plus, this wedding is going to be all about me."

He pulled me on top of him, and I sat up on his waist.

"Well, since you're going to be doing all of this, you mind telling me the date?" he said.

I really hadn't set one yet. "I'm going to have to get back to you on that."

"Well, you better let me know if you want me to be there," he joked.

Carl knocked on the door just then, walked in, and told Tay that the maid had his suitcase ready. I leaned over and kissed Tay. I did this so that Carl could get a glimpse of my bare pussy. He walked out of the room and slammed the door behind him. I kissed down Tay's chest while making my way to his dick. I dropped some good head on him before he left for the road.

*****

Our goodbye was bittersweet. I knew that I would miss him, but I had to get back to the Shamika situation. We all rode to the airport in the limo, and it kind of reminded me of that Kanye West video, except Tay was the one leaving. When we got to the gate, Tay hugged and kissed me, as if he was leaving forever. People pointed and asked each other if that was really Mr. Too Fine and his girlfriend. Before I knew it, I was watching him walk away with Black and Tony.

As Shamika and I walked back to the car with Carl, she told me that she had "the tape" on her.

"So what are you going to do with it?" I asked her in a low tone so that Carl didn't hear me.

"I'm about to call Carmello and see if I can drop it off at his office now. Do you think that you can come with me?"

"Hell no. I already told you that I don't want anything to do with this. I don't even want to know why you're even giving it to him. Just go do what you have to do. I'm going to go get the Chanel purse that I was put on the waiting list for. I'll see you at home."

She asked me how I was going to get there. I told her that I would get her another car, because I needed to get to the boutique fast. I made the phone call for her and then left the airport. Carl tried to leave with me, but I told him to go to hell. He could either go with Shamika or just take a cab home. I gave the driver Carmello's address and slipped him three hundred dollars. I told him to get me there as fast as possible and to keep his mouth shut later about where he took me. I told him that if anyone asked to just tell them that he took me to Laymen's boutique.

I walked into Carmello's office like I owned the place. There was what looked to be an undiscovered rapper sitting in the office.

As soon as I walked in, he yelled out "Damn!" and grabbed himself. "Who the hell is this?" he asked Carmello.

"Somebody that you could never handle," Carmello answered him.

"Shit. I am known for taming a whole lot of bitches who people thought could never be tamed," he boasted.

I sucked my teeth and looked him up and down. "By the look of them rhinestone studs in your ears, you could never tame or afford me. Now, disappear while grown folks talk."

He didn't like that too much. "Bitch, who the fuck do you think you are? You walk up in here like—"

Carmello cut him off by walking around his desk and yanking him up by the shirt. "I don't give a fuck what you do on your own time, but you don't ever disrespect anyone who walks into my office. Now, are you going to walk out, or do I have to help you?"

Damn! The power Carmello had over the young guy turned me on. I watched him rearrange his pinkie ring while he waited for thug boy to leave.

"You know I could have handled that myself, don't you?" I asked as I took a seat at his desk after the guy had exited his office.

"Yes, I know, but he was way out of line. Anyway, I just got a call from Shamika. You know she's on her way up here, don't you?"

"Yeah, I know. I want to see the tape, so just tell her that she can't stay long. I'll wait in the bathroom for her to leave. You do have one in here, right?"

He got up and opened the door to his office bathroom. The speaker on his desk came on, and his secretary told him that Shamika was there to see him. I picked up my coat and purse, then went into his bathroom and locked the door. I was happy that I could hear everything that was going on in the office. As soon as she walked in, Carmello asked her for the tape. She reached into her purse and gave it to him without asking a single question.

"I didn't watch it, so I hope it's clear. But please promise me that it will never get out. He damn near killed me when he woke up the next morning," she said.

Carmello stood up and walked over to her. "If you don't want me to keep the tape, then take it back. Just know that without it, we have no deal. It's up to you."

"Well, the tape is yours now, so the deal is in effect. You better not fuck me on this," I heard her say as she walked toward the door. She was about to leave when something stopped her. "It smells like Tangie in here. She's the only bitch I know who mixes her perfumes. Has she been here?"

Carmello remained calm as he lied to her. "I'm sorry, but who is Tangie? If you're talking about that girl that came here with you the first time, I haven't seen her since."

Carmello walked her out and asked thug boy, who was in the waiting area, to see her to her car. He then reentered his office, shut the door, and knocked on the bathroom door, letting me know that it was safe to come out.

"Damn. That girl got a good nose. That bitch should have been a drug-sniffing dog," I grumbled.

Carmello laughed and said he was thinking the same thing.

While we were up in the office, putting in the DVD, thug boy was walking Shamika to her car. They made small talk along the way, and we'd later find out about their conversation. When they got to her car, the driver opened the door for her.

"You're way nicer than that other bitch that was up in the office. At least you ain't all stuck up," thug boy told her as she was about to get in the car.

She turned and faced him. "And what bitch are you talking about? What did she look like?"

"Some bitch that looked like she could have been mixed, maybe Indian and Black. But she walked up in there like she was the shit. I didn't like her attitude at all. But she was bad as shit, though."

This was too much for Shamika. She knew she had smelled my perfume in Carmello's office, and thug boy was confirming her thoughts. Someone who sounded very much like me was in that office, and she knew that it just couldn't be a coincidence.

"When did she leave?" she asked.

"I never saw her leave, to tell you the truth. You didn't see her in there?"

"Nope. Well, be easy. I gotta go," Shamika said as she climbed in the car. She closed her door, pulled out her phone, and called me immediately.

"Hey, Tangie. You at the store yet?"

"No, I'm on my way there. Why? You need something?"

I knew that she was just asking me to see if I was really where I said I was. She couldn't trick me on her best day.

"I was wondering if you could pick me up one of them purses."

"Well, I was put on a waiting list, but if they have any more, then sure, I'll get one for you."

When I asked him, the driver of Shamika's car would later tell me that she hung up the phone and told him to take her back to my house. She also told him that she was going to wait and see if I came back with an extra purse for her, and if I didn't, she was planning on showing what ghetto really was.

Back in the office, Carmello had popped in the DVD, and we waited for it to start. We sat down and faced the TV that was on his wall. The sex tape got right into Shamika giving it to Black. I sat there watching with my mouth wide open.

This bitch was crazy. How could she do this? Point for her, 'cause I didn't know what in this world would push me to such a point. Carmello and I sat and laughed at how well Black was taking it. When he held his own legs up and started to fuck back, I lost it. It was so funny that we watched it twice.

When it was over, I stood up and told Carmello that I had to go. When he asked why, I told him about the purses that I had to stop and buy so that Shamika wouldn't suspect anything. He called in his secretary and gave her the names of the purses. He told her to have them delivered within the next hour, and he said that if they gave her any problems, she should drop his name.

I sat back down and pushed PLAY on the remote to watch the DVD one more time. Shamika was fucking the shit out of Black, and I couldn't look away. If I was even a little bit attracted to her, I would have gone home and had her fuck me the same way. It was a shame that just the sight of her disgusted me; we could have had some fun.

"Damn, girl. You're all into that tape, huh? Are you getting wet?"

I had to turn around to make sure that it was Carmello who had just asked that.

"Why would I be getting wet off this?"

He laughed at my question, knowing damn well that I knew the answer to my own question. He walked over to the bar that was in his office and poured two glasses of champagne. He handed me a flute and made a toast.

"To the art of deceit."

We raised our glasses and tapped them together. We sipped our drinks as he went back to his seat at the desk.

"It's not often that I meet a woman with the same kind of mind as mine. You and I seem to be two of a kind."

"Oh, please, Carmello. You have no idea what kind of mind I have."

"Yes, I do, and that's why we are able to do this. Don't get me wrong. I know a whole lot of gold-digging bitches who will do anything for a dollar or two. But none of them are on the level of evil that you're on. A black heart is earned, not learned, baby doll. Always remember that."

I walked around his desk and sat on it, facing him. "I think *evil* is the wrong word. I don't think that I've earned that title yet, have I?"

He smiled and licked his lips. "Tangie, I know evil when I see it. Maybe you didn't start out that way, but evil lives in you now. Your heart is as black as the darkest hour of night."

I looked him dead in the eyes. He didn't lower his. The truth that I always ran away from was staring back at me, and even if I looked away, it would still be there.

"Tangie, you are full of venom. And it looks like it's the deadliest type. But to tell you the truth, it turns me on."

"That's too bad, Carmello, 'cause I never fuck the people I'm doing business with."

"Who said anything about fucking?" he asked as his hand slid up my skirt.

He rubbed the inside of my thigh, and I had to face the fact that we spoke the same language. He stood up and slid me front and center on his desk. He pushed my skirt up around my waist and was pleased to see that I had no panties on. Carmello sat down at his desk as I leaned back on my elbows.

"I have been thinking about tasting you ever since I met you," he said as he spread my legs.

While I took the remote and played the DVD all over again, he played with my clit. He never even put a finger inside me. He had me straight creaming from that good old head. This dude was the pussy-eating champ. He did things with that mouth of his that had to be illegal. About twenty minutes later, his secretary buzzed and told him that the purses were there. He pulled his lips away from my clit and told her to hold them at her desk. I was about to cum for the second time, so I tried to push his head back down.

"It's good, huh? Well, I better let you get cleaned up. You don't want Shamika to start wondering where you are."

"Fuck her. She's not my man. Let her wait."

He smiled as I pushed his head back down. This time I watched him. His mouth and nose were buried in me, and that was just what I wanted.

"Jerk off while you eat my pussy," I told him.

"No. I'm good."

"I want to see you jerk your dick. Now, pull it out and do it," I demanded.

He stood up and unzipped his pants. When he pulled his dick out, I was a little disappointed. It was all right, but for a man his size, I thought that it was going to be massive. Ten minutes later we both came, his first and my second time. I washed up and gathered my things with wobbly legs.

"Well, it's been nice seeing you. I hope we can do this again," I said with a smile as I headed to his office door.

"Tangie, we can do this anytime. You're sweet as honey, and you helped me prove my point."

"And what point was that?"

"It takes an evil woman to fuck with a man her rich and famous boyfriend can't stand. Even if all he did was eat her pussy."

I smiled, because he was totally right. "When you're right, you're right."

I got the purses from the secretary and asked her how much I owed her. When she called Carmello to find out about charging me, he told her to tell me that they were both gifts. I told her to thank him, then left. That was sixteen thousand dollars saved, and I had had fun saving it.

"Did you get them?" Shamika asked as soon as I walked in the door. She was testing me hard.

"Yeah, I got them. Didn't I tell you I would?" I gave her one of the bags, and she looked shocked when she peeked inside it.

"How much were they? I'll give you a check."

"They cost eight thousand dollars each, but don't worry about it. It's my gift to you."

I wasn't worried about it. I would get the purse back once everything went down. It was a good thing that they were different colors. I doubt that I would ever really use it, since she would have been seen around with it, but you never knew what could happen. She looked at me like she was still trying to put two and two together. I wanted to tell her not to bother trying so hard, as she was out of her league. Instead, I just looked at her like she was crazy.

"Girl, don't mind me. I'm just sleepy. Black kept me up all night," she said.

Yeah right. That girl couldn't even come up with a good cover-up, yet she thought that she could tango with me. I just faked a smile and went to my bedroom. There I took my clothes off and drew a bath. Carmello's scent still lingered on me. It was times like this when I would spark up and think about the wonderful day I had just had. But I stayed true to my word—deception over drugs.

During the next few weeks, I started to plan the wedding. I wanted to be married as soon as possible, so I set the date eight weeks from that day. When I called and told Tay, he thought that I was out of my mind for making it so soon. But all I had to do was tell him that I could no longer wait to be his wife and he okayed the date. I then had a meeting with René Brutus. He had planned a lot of high-profile weddings, so he knew how to work with a demanding bride. He assured me that even with the little bit of time

I had given him, he would make sure that I had the wedding of my dreams.

My stops at Carmello's office became more frequent. Different days, same shit. He always ate my pussy while I watched the tape. He never asked me to have sex, and I wasn't tripping. Carl's dick was bigger than his, and to tell the truth, I had been thinking about him lately. All the head that I was getting from Carmello really made me want some dick. I figured that I might as well get it before I officially became Mrs. Too Fine.

Chapter 16

I Don't Know What Made Me Think That I Could Ever Marry A Freak Like You

It was two weeks before the wedding, and Tay'von would be home in another week. That day I was meeting with some singers. I had to pick one soon if I wanted someone to sing at the wedding. They were well-known stars, but I was still having them audition. They all had ill feelings about it, but the pay was great, and my wedding was going to give them a big buzz. As it turned out, I saw about five people. The only one who really hit all the right notes was this white girl who sang with a whole lot of soul. No wonder her single was climbing the charts. The other ones were okay, but she was the only one who made me feel the song she was singing. My mind was made up, so I told her that she had the job.

Even after that, my day was far from over. I had about thirty minutes to get over to the designer who was making my dress. Every time I watched one of those tabloid-like shows, they were all talking about what dress I might wear. That meant that I really had to wow them. And it wasn't that I wasn't excited about all the publicity, but these shows and magazines were harassing anyone who they thought might have some information on my big day. It got so bad that Tay'von had his publicist release a statement saying that the wedding would be held at the house, but it was really going to be in Miami, because it was way too cold in New York for an outside wedding.

It seemed like our pictures were in every magazine, and the paparazzi were working overtime. They even released a story about my mother and how she died. I still didn't know how they found that out, but they always found a way. They were all outside the house, hoping that they would get a shot of a tent going up or the wedding decorations. It was so bad that Tay had to get extra guards for the house. But as I always said, this was a small price to pay for fame. Well, it always seemed small until they got some really bad dirt on you and put it out there for the world to see.

I went up to the home gym and told Carl that I had to leave right away. He would be driving me to my dress fitting, which I was having in an undisclosed location, and I didn't want to be late. I didn't want anyone to know whose dress I was wearing until the last week before the wedding. I was praying that I could keep that information out of the press until then.

Carl took me to the Ritz-Carlton overlooking Central Park, where we had a deluxe suite booked for one day. Carl walked up to the counter and got the key. The room was paid for under the name of Tracy Black. I knew it sounded fake, but that was the first thing that had come to my mind.

A few minutes later, with Carl in tow, I walked into the suite, which was decked out with everything you would need for a comfy stay. I had stayed there many times before, and the hotel had always taken good care of me. My designer was waiting for me in the sitting room.

"Hello, darling. You look wonderful. Please, please sit down," Dominique said as he kissed me on both cheeks.

He was one half of Dominique and Di'lan, the newest and hottest wedding dressmakers. He informed me that Di'lan couldn't be there, but that he and his assistant could handle everything. We made small talk, and ten minutes later I was ready to try on my dress.

I went into one of the bedrooms with Dominique, and he helped me put on my dress. He told me not to look at myself until he was done. The full-length mirror was out in the hallway, so we slowly made our way to it, making sure to protect the dress. As soon as Carl saw me, his eyes got big; then he got this weird look on his face. I turned and looked at myself in the mirror. I couldn't move or talk. It was like I had spent a lifetime not knowing what I looked like and I finally was able to lay eyes on myself.

The dress was white—yes, white—with small yellow crushed diamonds that sparkled at the bottom and at the neckline of the dress. Tay'von had thought that Dominique and Di'lan were crazy when they told him that they wanted to use real yellow diamonds on the dress, but I had thought that it would be perfect. He had almost lost his mind when they told him that the dress would be worth 6.2 million dollars, but they soon told him that they wanted me to wear it for free, so he had breathed a sigh of relief.

"Oh, my goodness! I have never seen a woman more beautiful than you in a wedding dress," Dominique said as he put his hands over his mouth. "As soon as I saw you on TV, I told Di'lan that we had to get you to wear this dress. It was made for you, Tangie. You are the only one who could made this dress even more beautiful."

He walked around me and put one hand over his heart. "Such poise, such mystery, such substance. You are a rare creature, my love," Dominique said with his French accent. "The world will soon be consumed by you, darling. And to think you will be wearing our finest dress," Dominique mused as he came to a stop in front of me.

Now, I knew that he was kissing my ass, but all in all, he was right. I turned around and looked at Carl.

"So what do you think?"

He looked at me for a while, then answered, "You, you, God, you're . . ."

That was all he got out. Right there in front of me, Dominique, and Dominique's assistant, Carl broke down. He didn't sob hysterically, but his weeping was enough to stop him from getting his words out.

The assistant walked over to him and handed him some tissue. He took it and went into the bathroom.

"Well, my dear, if you can bring that big man to tears, then I believe we have done our job. This is the dress for you," the assistant whispered.

I took one more look at myself, then went back into the bedroom and took off the dress. When I came back out, Carl was still in the bathroom. I kissed Dominique goodbye, and he took the dress from my arms for the last of the alterations. I wouldn't see the dress again until my last fitting the day before the wedding.

Once Dominique and his assistant left, I walked to the bathroom door and knocked on it, but Carl said nothing.

"Are you okay?" I asked, not giving any indication that I was pissed.

Once he opened the door, I slapped the shit out of him.

"What in the hell did you do that for?"

I almost slipped into a blind rage, but I tried to contain myself as much as I could.

"Do you know what your little breakdown could cost me? What, you think that people are dumb? Don't you think that they knew why you started crying? Come on, Carl. You're some big-ass bodyguard, yet you start crying at the sight of me in a wedding dress? I'm sure that as soon as they left, they started gossiping about us fucking each other. You're such a fucking dumb ass," I screamed as my whole body trembled with anger.

"Lower your fucking voice, Tangie. Are you that fucking coldhearted? My bad for getting caught up in the moment. And make that the last time you put your hands on me."

"Oh, fuck you, Carl. If I knew that you would get so fucking pussy whipped, I would have never slept with your ass."

Carl did something that I would have never thought that he would do. He hauled off and slapped the hell out of my ass, and it sent me flying into the wall. As soon as he did it, he looked like he wanted to die. I got up and ran for my purse. He ran after me, but I got to my purse first and pulled out my cell phone. At that point, I was willing to tell Tay everything, because Carl had lost his mind and had stepped out of bounds. I started to dial Tay's number, but Carl leaped for the phone and pulled it out of my hand. When he least expected it, I slapped him again, leaving him no time or reason to wonder why. I left him standing in the living room and ran for one of the bedrooms. I tried to get away, but he was right behind me. I damn near jumped over the bed and grabbed the hotel phone. Again, he was there to pull it away from me.

"Get the fuck away from me, Carl. And give me my phone back!"

"Calm down, Tangie. Please, just sit down for a second."

"Sit down for what?" I asked him as I jumped in his face. "You put your fucking hands on me, and now you're asking me to sit down! Eat a dick, Carl."

"You made me do it. You just won't stop. You just can't go around smacking people, and the things that come out of your mouth are real foul most of the time."

I smacked him again, just for thinking that he could read me. "Don't try to explain why you put your hands on your boss's girlfriend. You are so fucking fired, you hear me?"

"Who cares? I'm so sick of you always bringing Tay'von up in everything. We both knew you were his girlfriend when we started fucking, so you don't have to remind me."

"Just give me my phone, Carl. There is nothing else to talk about. If I was you, I would just go home and pack my shit. You won't be there too much longer."

"Tangie, fuck you! That's right! You can get that look off your face. I ain't packing shit. You know what?" He took my phone and threw it against the wall. "You wanna make a call? Well, put it back together, 'cause you're not using the hotel phone, either!" he yelled in my face while holding the phone.

Of all the times that I had told Carl to grow some balls, he picked that day to sprout them. In a way, I was kind of impressed. I walked out of the bedroom and gathered my things.

"This may be over for now, but do remember that I am going to pick it back up when I am good and ready," I shouted.

I looked at myself in the hallway mirror and slid my shades on. Then we left the suite together.

When we walked out of the hotel, there were about ten men waiting for us outside. They took photos of Carl and me leaving the hotel as I tried my best to look away and pull my coat over my head. I think that they still got me, anyway, but to hell with them. They were doing a job.

It was so funny that when I walked in the hotel, I was thinking about maybe getting Carl to give me some of that good dick of his. Now that I was leaving, I was still thinking about fucking him, but not in the literal sense. I just took comfort in knowing that I would one day get him back, and I prayed that he remembered why.

I had been working so hard on everything for the wedding that I hadn't had time for anything else. Tay'von would be home in a matter of hours, so I had one of the maids help me pack the things that I was going to need in Miami. I didn't want to have to be bothered with that once he was home.

In the middle of my running around for the wedding, my visits to Carmello's had ended. He had called me on my new cell phone, but I had always been in the middle of something. So I had just erased the number and had kept it moving. However, I made sure to call him that morning to tell him that Tay was coming home. He knew that he had to stop calling, but he talked me into going down to his office one more time. He told me that he was starving since he really hadn't seen me. Since I was not into leaving anyone hungry, I told him that I would see him within forty-five minutes. Little did I know that this visit would be very different.

When I got there, that rude little thug boy was in the office, but this time he knew the deal. Although he wasn't too happy to see me, he got up and walked out without a word. I thought I saw him snap a picture of me with his camera phone, but then again, he could have just been making a call. Once he was out of the office, I closed and locked the door. There was no need to speak. I knew why I was there. I pulled off my clothes and sat on Carmello's desk, and he spread my legs.

"Damn. I've been missing this," he sighed.

He ate me out as usual. I came, and he kept on going. And for the first time, he stuck his finger in me. I looked down at him, not because I didn't want him to, but because he had never done this before.

"Just relax. I want to try something new," he said in a sexy voice.

I lay back and enjoyed his roaming fingers. I could hear the gushiness of my wet pussy as he sucked on my clit and fingered me. I closed my eyes and took it all in. I heard him stand up, but I still kept my eyes shut. What I didn't hear was him unzipping his pants. The next thing I knew, he was rubbing my clit with one hand as he reached down and rubbed his dick on my pussy lips. I opened my eyes and leaned up on my elbows.

"What are you doing?" I asked, trying to stop my eyes from rolling to the back of my head.

"What, it doesn't feel good?"

I didn't even answer. I just lay back down and thrust my hips at him. This man knew what he was doing. Who would have thought that with such a normal-size dick, he could work me so well? He even managed to make it grow on me. He knew my clit was my spot, and he never let it go. He fucked me until he came, and boy, did

I cum hard. When I finally looked down, I saw that he had no condom on.

"Come on, Carmello. Why would you fuck me raw?"

"Don't you think it's a little too late to be asking that? Besides, I got a clean bill of health from my doctor yesterday," he told me as he pulled up his pants.

He also told me that he had a reason for never having sex with me until that day. He wanted to make sure that he didn't have any STDs. He said that there would be no reason to go there unless he could fuck me raw.

"So, what's your chart looking like?" he asked.

"Don't you think it's a little too late to be asking that?" I said, returning his question to him, but then I quickly assured him that I didn't have anything. I went into his bathroom and cleaned up. When I was done, I came out, got dressed, and opened the door to leave.

"Remember, no more calls until I call you," I told him right before I left his office.

Thug boy was sitting in the waiting area, and as I walked by, I caught him looking at my ass.

"Caught you," I said to him jokingly.

He smiled but said nothing.

I got into one of the cars Tay had bought me and drove home. I sped like hell just to make sure that I had enough time to get Carmello's cum out of me before Tay'von got home. I soaked in the tub and got spick and span. I dressed in a sexy outfit and waited for my man.

Forty-five minutes later Tay'von walked through the door, looking very tired. I was just thankful that he would have some time to rest. He gave me a long, tight hug and kissed me on the forehead.

"Damn, Tay. I have really missed you," I said as I pulled away from him.

"I got a pre-wedding gift for you," he told me.

My face lit up, and I couldn't wait for him to tell me what it was.

"Calm down, calm down. It's not here yet."

I must have looked like a five-year-old child. He took my hand and kissed it, hoping that this would calm me down.

"You're such a brat. It will be here soon. Don't look so sad," he joked.

We went into the kitchen, and I started to show him all the plans that I had for the wedding. About fifteen minutes later the intercom came on. It was someone from a car dealership, asking for Tay'von. I jumped up, ready to go outside.

"Aren't you going to finish showing me this stuff?" he teased.

"Later for that. I want to see what's outside."

I grabbed his hand and tried to pull him up. We got to the front door, and he put his hands over my eyes.

"Now, remember that this isn't too big. It's just a pre-wedding gift," he said.

I heard him open the front door. When he took his hands from my eyes, I just stood there in the doorway, with no emotion. I didn't see what I wanted to see.

"Where are they going with my cars? Why are they putting them up on that truck?" I asked.

"'Cause it's over. I want you out of my life. Get the rest of your shit and get out."

My mouth dropped, and my heart pounded a mile a minute. "Why? What did I do?"

I thought that maybe there really were active cameras in the house and that Tay had seen videos of me getting down with Carl. Or maybe the Amira thing was just too much for him to live with. Or, hell, did he know about Carmello? There were so many reasons why he might want to end things.

"It's just what I said, Tangie. I don't want to be with you anymore."

Tears formed in my eyes once I realized that I was about to lose everything.

"Aw, don't get misty eyed. It's too late for all of that. Plus, I'm just joking. Take a look behind you."

I couldn't move. I felt like I was having a heart attack. He put his arms around me to stop my body from trembling.

"Damn, baby. I was just playing. You're not mad at me, are you?"

"Don't ever play like that. I almost passed out. That wasn't funny, Tay."

"I didn't know you loved me like that. My bad. Just turn around and you'll feel better."

I slowly turned to see that the first tow truck had left and another truck had pulled up in its place. It had two new Bentleys on it.

Tay smiled. "So, are you over my bad joke now?"

"Hell, yeah, I'm over it. Tell him to put the cars down," I demanded as I walked over to the truck. I told the driver myself to put my new babies down.

The cars were out of this world. I felt the same way I had when Tay first gave me the other cars. Everyone came out, and I took pictures with my new cars as Tay told them how he had to have the Bentleys brought up from a California dealership.

I was in the tub when Shamika came rushing through my bathroom door. I looked at her as if she was crazy for just barging in.

"What in the hell is up with you?" I asked, annoyed.

She held a magazine in her hand but didn't show it to me. "You better get your ass out of the tub. Tay'von and Carl are fighting like shit downstairs."

When I asked her what for, she then handed me the magazine. On the cover was a picture of Carl and me going into the hotel, and one photo of us leaving. Shamika guided me to the article in question.

It seems like the soon-to-be wife of Mr. Too Fine has found someone to help her get rid of those pre-wedding jitters and maybe even get over the death of Amira. The hip-hop star Tay'von is soon to marry an ex–video dancer who is known as Tangie. She is pictured here with Too Fine's bodyguard, leaving one of New York's finest hotels. Witnesses say that the duo were holding hands and kissing each other in the lobby and elevator. Photographers were unable to go into the hotel and snap shots of them, but they were caught trying to sneak out. We hope Mr. Too Fine isn't too heartbroken after the famous words he spoke during his latest interview "This is forever." Guess we will see if it really is forever after he sees these photos.

I must have been heaving for air, because Shamika looked scared.

"Girl, just don't sit in the tub, breathing. Get your ass downstairs," she urged.

I threw the magazine on the floor, jumped out of the tub, slipped on my robe, and ran downstairs. The game room looked like they had broken everything in it. Black and Tony were both holding a man back.

"How the fuck are you going to do this to me? You have been working for me from the start. Yet that still don't stop you from fucking Tangie?" Tay'von roared.

"Fuck you, Tay'von. If all it takes is for you to read one thing in one of them trashy magazines, then yeah, I did—"

I cut him off before he could say something too stupid. "Tay, nothing ever happened at the hotel with Carl and me."

"Oh, bitch, please. First, it was Amira. Now it's Carl? I don't know what made me think that I could ever marry a freak like you. You've turned me into the laughingstock of the industry. Well, I guess I should have remembered what they say about turning hoes into housewives. I should fucking kill both ya motherfuckers! At least I would feel a sense of redemption," Tay said, more to himself than to anyone else.

I walked away, got my planner, and returned to the game room. I opened the planner and showed Tay the date in question. I then handed him the designers' card and told him to call them.

"Maybe you'll see how much of an ass you're being," I told him.

Tay pulled out his cell phone and actually made the call. After he hung up, I stood in front of him, with my hands on my hips.

"Well, don't look sorry now. What did they tell you? Was I there on that day for a dress fitting or what?"

He didn't say anything. He just sat there, looking like the jackass he was.

"You know what, Tay'von? I don't know why you're marrying me, either. You don't trust me. And for you to come out of your mouth and call me a freak and a ho is way out of line. How about we just call everything off? I'm not willing to go through this shit for the rest of my life, so that's it. The wedding is off."

"Man, all I know is that my manager calls me and tells me about you and Carl being on the cover of a magazine. When I asked if anyone knew anything about it, Shamika ran upstairs and brought the magazine down to me, and that's when I lost it."

"Where is it? I wanna see it," Carl said, still boiling hot over what had just gone on in the game room.

I glared at Shamika; I couldn't believe what Tay had just said. He had made it sound like she couldn't wait to get that magazine into his hands.

"That bitch just showed it to me. I left it on the bathroom floor. She should give it to you. She was so quick to show it to Tay," I said.

Everyone waited for Shamika to run up to my bathroom and get the magazine. She came back downstairs and handed it to Carl.

I stared at Shamika across the room. "You know what's killing me? How are you going to have this in the house and never show it to me? You would think that since it has to do with Carl and me, you would have brought it up. What were you waiting for? For Tay to come home, hoping that you would start some bullshit?"

The more I spoke, the more upset I got, so I started to walk toward her. "You been in my house, acting like we were cool, and then you go and pull some shit like this? How are you gonna try to set me up like this?"

She didn't utter a word.

"Answer me, God damn it!" I yelled after waiting in vain for her to respond.

When she still didn't answer, I jumped on her and tried to pull out every hair on her head, while not forgetting to try to knock her teeth out of her mouth. By the time Black and Tay pulled us apart, my robe was on the floor, and she had a couple of tracks missing. Tay pulled off his shirt and handed it to me as I spat insults at Shamika.

"You dirty bitch! You walk around here like we're friends, but you're just really waiting for a chance to fuck my shit up. Fucking ghetto trash! Didn't even know how to put an outfit together before you met me. I was just trying to help Black out. He shouldn't have to be seen with such a gutter-butt bitch as you, but I figured, hey, maybe I could change a hood rat into a classy bitch like myself. I should have known that I couldn't extend a helping hand to vermin. A hood-rat bitch will always be just that!"

"Aw, fuck you, bitch!" Shamika shouted. "Ain't nobody trying to fuck nothing up. And I don't have to be in your house. You act like you and Tay are the only ones who are paid around here. My man is just as famous as yours. Why would I have to try to fuck your shit up? We're on the same playing field!"

I tried to jump on her again, but Tay held me back.

"Get your shit and get the fuck out, then!" I snarled. "There's no one holding you here. Take your things and go back to your little town house, or whatever it is that you live in."

"What, you think you better than Black and me just because you live here? You can lose it just as fast as you got it, bitch," she countered.

I crossed my arms over my chest. "Oh, I see. That's why you did this. You were trying to make me lose everything that I have. It's not about where you live. It's about the trash that lives there. You're a hateful bitch, Shamika. You've got half an hour to pack your stuff and leave."

I made my way upstairs, and everyone followed me. I went into her bedroom and took the purse that I had given her out of the shopping bag.

"What are you doing? Put my bag back on the bed!" she said as she reached for the purse. I pushed her away, and Black pushed her on the bed.

I shook my head. "Don't think that I want this after you've had it."

I picked up the bottle of Hennessy that was on one of the nightstands and poured it on the purse. She tried to jump up, but Black made sure that she stayed on the bed. I took the purse and threw it in her bathtub. I took a lighter and set that bad boy on fire. I poured more liquor on the purse to make sure that it was totally torched. I couldn't help but smile when I remembered Left Eye. She had always been my favorite. The thought of her reminded me to make sure I stayed put until the fire was completely out. I said a silent RIP both for Amira, my dead lover, and for Left Eye, my favorite member of TLC.

"Buy your own fucking purse," I said after turning the water in the tub on and putting out my man-made fire.

I walked out of her bedroom and went into my own. Tay walked in after me, amazed by and kind of scared of what he had just seen. The look on my face as the fire burned had given him a glimpse at my very dark side. I didn't even look at him. I didn't know if I should be mad because I had been caught or because he hadn't asked me if I really did it. I sat in the chair by the dresser and lit a cigarette. I decided that I wasn't going to say anything to him until he spoke.

"Tangie, I don't know what to say."

"If you don't know, then don't say nothing at all. You have gone way too far this time. You didn't have to bring up Amira or fight with Carl. You are out of control, and I want no part of it."

He put his hands around his head, as if he were losing his mind. I knew that this was the time to play on his emotions, and I wasn't going to stop until I won. I looked at my watch and got up from the chair immediately. I walked back to the bedroom in which Shamika and

Black were staying and listened at the door. I heard what sounded like hammers hitting the wall. Tay walked out of our bedroom and came over to where I was standing. We listened; then Tay opened the door. Black stood over Shamika, who was lying on the floor. She looked like she had slid down the wall and had landed on her back. Tay pulled Black away from her just as he was about to hit her again. Tay took him into our bedroom and left Shamika on the floor. I ran downstairs and found Carl still in the game room, holding the magazine.

"I knew that this would happen. This shit has me about to lose my job. I have never gotten myself into this kind of situation, never," he grumbled.

"Don't start your shit now. You already know what your choices are, and neither one of them is to tell Tay the truth."

"Your mind never stops working, does it? Here we are in the middle of a shit storm, and you're still trying to keep the stench from all this bullshit off you. I just can't act like nothing has happened. The shit has hit the fan, and something has to be done."

I took a deep breath and tried not to go off on him. "Fine, Carl. You can do anything you want, but do not tell Tay about us. If you do, I'll turn it around on you so fast that your head will spin."

I picked up my cell phone, which I'd left in the game room, pocketed it, and headed for the front door. Along the way, I grabbed the keys to one of my new cars, and once I was behind the wheel, I sped to the gate. I took out my phone and called Carmello.

"What's up, Tangie? I thought you said no more calls for now?"

"I don't have time to explain everything right now. But did you see—"

"Yeah, I saw it. So did Tay go crazy after he saw the magazine?" Carmello said.

I went ahead and gave him the lowdown on what had gone on in the house.

"Damn, Tangie, that's fucked up. What are you going to do to fix this?"

"Well, I hope that you're at your office, because I'm on my way there to get the sex tape."

"You know that I can't give you my only copy. Why would you want it, anyway?"

"'Cause it's time to do what we talked about. I don't need the original. Just make a copy of it. I'll be there in about thirty minutes."

As soon as I hung up, my phone rang. It was someone from the house calling, and I was pretty sure that it was Tay.

"What do you want?" I yelled into the phone.

"Where in the hell did you go? You just can't get up and leave without telling anyone where you're going."

"I just had to get out of there. I have to think, and when I get back, I'll let you know what I want to do."

"What do you mean? What is it that you have to let me know about?"

"Us," was all I said before hanging up.

When I got to Carmello's office, almost everyone was gone. I walked in, wearing only Tay'von's T-shirt and one of my long fur coats.

"Damn, girl. You wearing the hell out of that tee. Why don't you go on and jump on this desk?" Carmello said, half joking.

"You have got to be out of your mind. Tay's back at the house. I can't stay long."

"Aw, come on, Tangie. Just let me taste it."

"Stop playing around and give me the tape."

I walked over to him, and he turned his desk chair around to face me, then slid his hand up my shirt.

"You mean to tell me that Tay is home and he let you leave the house with no panties on? This nigga's buggin'."

"He didn't *let* me do anything. I just kind of, um, left," I said slowly as he hit my spot, but since I wasn't there for that, I pulled away. "Come on, Carm. I need the tape."

"Don't get all new on me, 'cause your 'man' is home. All I'm asking for is just a little taste. You won't get the tape unless you give it to me."

That man always had to have things his way, so I sat on his desk and leaned back.

"Just a taste, Carmello. I can't be here all night," I said as he spread my legs.

I couldn't deny it; the flicker of his tongue made me want more. I looked at the clock behind him and prayed that the five minutes that I was giving him moved by slowly.

Exactly five minutes later, I said, "Okay, baby, that was a taste. Now give me what I came for."

He lifted his head, then licked his lips.

"Come on, Tangie. I can tell that you were close to cumming. Just give me what I want, and I'll hand over what you want."

He was right. I was close. I pushed his head back down, and he pitched a home run.

After I got off the desk, I went into his bathroom and cleaned up. I wanted some dick, but I was going to wait on that. When I walked out of his bathroom, I saw that he had placed the DVD on his desk. I walked over to him and put one of my legs on his lap.

"Now kiss me goodbye," I said.

He leaned in and tongue kissed my pussy, then looked up and said goodbye. I walked out of his office with the DVD in my hand. There was nothing like a good nut on a crazy night.

While I drove, I searched for the card Evengeliza Moore had given me. When I found it, I dialed her number, and she picked up on the second ring.

"Hi. I don't know if you remember me, but I met you some time ago, and you gave me your card at a boutique. My name is Tangie. I'm about to marry—"

She cut me off as soon as she realized who I was. I could almost hear her salivating at the sound of my voice. "Yes, I know who you are. What can I do for you?"

"I'm sorry that I was so rude to you when we first met, but I have something that I think you would want."

"And what makes you think that?" she asked, trying to sound as if she wasn't interested. But curiosity dripped from her voice like water from an ice cube that had been left out on a summer day.

"It's a tape . . . well, a DVD . . . of someone famous getting fucked, and let's just say that it's not a female."

I heard her take a deep breath, as if she was starved for air.

"Wait, are you saying that he is fucking someone or that he's getting fucked?"

"Oh, he's getting fucked. So are you in or out?"

I didn't have time to waste, so she had better act quickly. The sex tape was going to be leaked with or without her.

"Can I meet with you? Where are you right now?" she asked.

"I'm leaving the city. Just give me an address where we can meet up."

She quickly gave me an address. I wrote down the directions, and twenty minutes later I was there. She was already waiting for me when I pulled up, and by the looks of things, she was anxious as hell. She got out of her car and got into mine once I signaled to her.

"Before we start this, I want you to give me your word that no one will ever find out who gave you this sex tape," I said to her as I held the DVD out so that she could see it.

"No one will ever know. We have contracts for these things. You could sue us if your name ever came out in this. Besides, I will be the only one who knows that you gave it to me."

Once she said this, I told her exactly what she was going to find on the DVD. By the end of my explanation, she was damn near jumping out of the seat.

"So how much is all of this going to cost me?" she asked.

"Well, I know that once this gets out, you're going to make a whole lot of money on it. So just make me an offer."

"One million dollars." She said this as if she knew that I wasn't going to take it.

Her doing this, it let me know that she could go a lot higher.

"Well, how about you call me when you really want the tape?" I responded.

"Okay, three million," she offered.

I took my keys and started up my car. "Like I said, call me."

"Well, why don't you just tell me how much money you want?"

"Five million." I blurted out my price with no hesitation.

"Four million," she spat back.

"Look, I can always let this go to someone else. So either you give me four point five million or we have no deal."

She sat in my brand-new car and thought about it, and then she extended her hand. I shook her hand, and the deal was made.

"We have a deal. I'll take the tape now," she said.

She should have known that I was not parting with the DVD until I had my money.

"I'll call you with an account number, and when the funds are there, I'll let you have the tape," I told her.

"Aw, that's some bullshit. I haven't even seen the tape yet, and you want me to trust you?"

"Fine. You don't have to do this. But do you really think that I can get away with scamming you? I am about to be Tay'von's wife. You can always put it out there that I stole your money. So you have a choice. You can do this or not."

Again, she sat there thinking about what I had just said. "So how and when do you want to do this?" she finally said.

I told her that in the morning I would call her and give her all the information. Once everything was right with the money, she would have her DVD the same day. Satisfied, she got out of my car and went back to hers.

I put my car in gear and drove home, feeling like I could conquer the world. Payback wasn't for the faint of heart. Thank God I no longer had one.

Chapter 17

Rot In Hell, You Dirty Bitch

When I got home, Tay'von was sitting on the stairs, waiting for me. I walked into the room as if nothing had gone down.

"Where the fuck have you been for damn near two hours?" he snapped.

"I don't feel like dealing with your shit right now, Tay'von. And why would you care? I'm a freak, right?"

He reached out, grabbed my arm, and pulled me to him. "You just leave, and no one knows where you are. Then you tell me that I shouldn't care? Man, fuck what you're saying. Where the hell have you been?"

I took a cup out of my handbag and showed it to him. "If you would take the time and look, maybe you would see where I was at."

After I left my little meeting with Evengeliza, I had stopped at an all-night ice cream shop. I had bought a milk shake and then had thrown half of it out. I knew that I would need it to throw Tay off.

"So you just ate there in your T-shirt?"

"Oh, I'm sorry for not stopping and putting on any clothes. The freak in me must have gone to my head and clouded my judgment."

"Come on, Tangie. You know I didn't mean that shit."

"Well, while I was out, I did some thinking. I don't think that we should go on with the wedding. There are a lot of things that are not right with us, so maybe we should rethink things."

I could tell that what I was saying was about to make him lose his mind.

"What the fuck are you talking about, Tangie? Don't do this. I told you that I was sorry."

I sucked my teeth as if I didn't care about what he was saying. "If you're really sorry, I can't tell. I'm sure this shit is going to happen every time you even think that I have been with someone else, and I will not be able to take that. For you to even bring up Amira's name is so fucked up. I thought that we were trying to get past all of that?"

"I know, I know, Tangie. Please don't put this wedding on hold. I know that I was wrong. We're only a week away from being married. I'm not even going to have you sign this prenuptial agreement that my lawyer drew up. That's how much I trust you, baby."

"What! You were thinking about having me sign a prenup?" I crossed my arms in front of me and waited for his answer.

"It wasn't me. My lawyer thought that it would be a good idea. It's not about you. It's just a precautionary measure that most people with money take."

"So you weren't going to marry me unless I signed it?"

"Baby, as soon as I saw you, I knew that I wasn't going to ask you to sign it. I know you love me for me and not for my money, so fuck what everyone has to say."

I knew that he had people in his ear about me, but fuck them. I would call off the wedding for real before I signed a prenup. But since it seemed that I had him right where I wanted him, I let everything go and stopped playing with his mind.

"Did you talk to Carl about things?"

He nodded. "Yeah. We're cool."

I walked away from him and said nothing else on the issue. What most people didn't know was that there was an art to deceit. You just couldn't sit around hoping that things would go your way.

You had to make them go your way, without any detours.

I went upstairs and found Shamika still packing her things, and it pissed me off. She should have been gone by the time I got back. But as I thought about things, I realized that I could get back at her a better way. I asked Black if I could speak to him. He said yes and followed me into my bedroom. I told him that what Shamika had done was fucked up, but since we were leaving for Miami soon, they didn't have to leave the house. I also let him know that what little friendship Shamika and I had shared was over. I let him know that I wouldn't be a bitch to her, but that I really didn't want to be around her.

The real truth was that I wanted to see what happened when the DVD got leaked and Black found out that it was all her fault.

The next morning I met with Evengeliza again. Within thirty minutes, the money was in my account, and I couldn't have been happier. I handed her the DVD, and we determined when the best time would be for the story to break. That bitch Shamika had some shit coming her way that she would not be able to handle. After my meeting with Evengeliza, I made sure to stop and get my hair done so that I would have an alibi. Then I went home, and an hour later, we were on our way to Miami.

The weather in Miami was wonderful. As soon as we landed, fans and photographers bombarded us. We fought our way through the crowd with help from Carl, Tony, and airport security, then made our way to the limo.

"How in the hell did they find out that we would be here?" I asked, as if I didn't know.

I had made sure that Evengeliza knew where the wedding was going to be held. I wanted cameras there just in case Black killed Shamika. I wanted everyone to see the madness that happened when you crossed the line with me. I wanted it to be a silent warning. Although no one would know that she had fucked with the wrong bitch, I would know, and that would feed my ego big-time. It would bring me much satisfaction to see that bitch lying there, murdered in cold blood.

I went on. "I made sure to keep everything low profile. I don't know how this could have happened." I was laying it on thick.

Tay laughed because he knew that this pleased me to the core. "Oh, please, Tangie. You know that you're happy that everyone is treating this wedding like you are Princess Diana and I'm the prince. You know how these things are. They always find things out that you don't want them to know."

I wanted to laugh, but I held it in, making sure my face didn't show my real feelings. The press was about to get their hands on the story of the decade.

The house that we were staying in, in Miami was gorgeous. Walking through it made me want to move into it. I knew that I had always said that I'd never move to the South, but this house was calling my name. I thought that maybe I could convince Tay to get me a beach house down there. The week was going to go by fast, so I put that thought on the back burner.

People started flying in, and of course, we put them up in the best hotels. They were all the best players in their field. Singers, rappers, basketball and football players, actors, and even a few talk show hosts came. We had to treat them to the best things a privileged life had to offer. This wedding was starting to look like the event of the year, and we weren't going to let them down.

I really hadn't said much to Shamika lately, and it seemed as if everyone else had been giving her the cold shoulder too. Even Carl's forgiving ass wasn't talking to her, and with all the running around I was doing, I didn't have time to pay attention to the drama that surrounded her.

Friday night had finally come, and Tay'von and I got ready for our dinner party the night before the wedding. Not only was the press hounding us, but they were also after anyone on our star-studded guest list and tried to corner our guests as they flew in. Miami was buzzing outside the norm, and it had everything to do with us. You couldn't turn on the TV or a radio without hearing about our wedding. We didn't think that the week would go by so fast, but the next day we would be married, and I couldn't wait to get that ring on my finger. I put on a scandalously tight little white Dior dress for the dinner party. I dressed it up with a lot of gold bangles and other heavy gold jewelry. I moussed my hair and wore it in a wet, curly look. Hey, I was in Miami, right?

So that meant I had to wear things that I couldn't get away with in New York. Tay's attire was also all white, with his hip-hop swagger on full blast. He looked just as good as I did. He always knew what to wear, and he always made it look too easy to be the sexiest man in the room.

I guess it came naturally to him. When we were done dressing, we looked at ourselves in the mirror and smiled at what we saw. You could say a lot of things about Tay and me, but the one thing you couldn't say was that we didn't look damn good together.

"Look at us, Mr. and Mrs. Miller," he said with a small smile on his face.

"Are you ready for this?" I asked him. "'Cause once we do this, one of us has to die for this to end."

He laughed at my statement, as if I wasn't telling the truth. "Listen to you sounding like me."

I gave him a serious look. "You said that this was for life. I just need you to understand that what you said is true. There is no going back. This is till death."

He looked me in the eyes, then pulled me close. "Till death, baby. Till death," he whispered before wetting my lips with his.

I had hired one of the biggest cruise ships to host our dinner party. It had cost Tay an arm and a leg to guarantee us the entire ship to ourselves, but we didn't care. It was worth it. We got to the cruise ship an hour before our guests, and then I watched the people's facial expressions as they got on the ship. I could tell that they were all impressed as they pointed and nodded their heads at the decor. I overheard a few talk of my exquisite taste.

Before dinner, some of guests sat around listening to the live performers or gambled in the ship's casino, while others stood around sipping on fine liquor and mingling. At seven o'clock we all settled in our seats and ate dinner. While we dined, some friends stood up and wished us the best of luck and much happiness. The liquor flowed, and everyone was having a good time. We even let some of the paparazzi in to snap some pictures. Finally, dessert was served, and it was almost time for the men to leave the ship so that the ladies could get the bachelorette party started.

Over dessert I looked up and saw one of the photographers talking to Black. I watched them talk; then Black scrunched up his face. I could see him mouth the words, "What are you talking about?" That was when the man pulled out a mini DVD player. They stood there as Black watched the footage. On his face was disbelief. He looked from the DVD footage to Shamika and back to the footage again. She didn't even notice him looking at her.

This photographer walked away from Black and approached a man who was working on a computer. The computer guy had been posting pictures of Tay and me on all the flat screens that were around the dining room. The photographer, whom I had hired for this exact purpose, earned his money by plugging the mini DVD player into the computer. And in front of everyone on the cruise ship, the footage of Shamika fucking Black popped up on all the TVs. Everyone watched it in shock, and I made sure to catch all their reactions when Shamika pulled out the big black dildo. I knew that they were all asking themselves what Black had been thinking when he allowed her to film their sex play.

Now was the time for me to put my acting skills on blast. I ran over to where the computer through which the DVD was being played, and I yanked the plug out of the wall. The screens in the dining room went blank, and so did everyone's faces. I thought that Black had lost his mind for the moment. He just stood there, so still, with glazed-over eyes. Then he just charged Shamika like a football player on Super Bowl day, and no one made a move to stop him. Everyone knew and felt that she needed her ass whipped. Finally, Carl stepped up to stop him, but Tay held him back. Tay'von was mystified by what Shamika had done. When Tay glanced at me, I put an "Oh, my God" look on my face.

Black attacked Shamika ferociously, and one of the guests from the party stood up and pulled him off Shamika before he killed her. She lay on the floor, bloody and hurt. Tay let go of Carl, and Carl went over and helped her up out of pity.

"You fucking bitch! I'm going to kill your ass! Let me go," Black screamed as the guest held him back.

I walked over to Shamika and acted like I was going to help her as I told Tay to call for a car. I pulled her hair back from her face and handed her a napkin for her bleeding lips.

"Now, pull yourself together, Mika. Everyone is watching. Don't let them see you break down," I whispered. "Tay'von called a limo for you. I want you to go back to the house and get your things packed."

She looked at me as if she didn't want to leave Miami just yet.

"Now, you know that you can't stay anymore," I told her. "Black is going to try to hurt you if you do. Just give him some time to cool off and get his mind right. But there is one favor I need you to do for me. After all that has happened, there's just one thing that I want you to remember—"

She cut me off before I could make my grand statement. "But, Tangie, I don't know how this got out. I didn't make a copy or anything. The only one who could have put this out is you know who."

I put my arms around her and got real close to her. "You may not know how this got out, but I do."

She looked at me with shock on her face. I wanted to spit in it, but that was too low class for me.

"Come on, Shamika. Don't look so surprised. Try to look like we're having a normal conversation. If you don't, I won't tell you what I know."

She tried her best to keep it together, but her body was shaking uncontrollably under my hands.

"Look at me, Shamika, 'cause I'm responsible for the tape getting leaked. That's right, bitch. I did it."

She strained to pull away from my grip, but I held on tight.

"It fucking hurts, doesn't it?" I said. "I have been setting this up since we were on the road. You fucked me over, so now I'm fucking you with the biggest dick I could find. Tell me, how does it feel? Because I'm feeling damn good!"

"You bitch!" she screamed, but I didn't break.

I still kept the concerned look on my face and made myself look confused and hurt.

"Calm down, little Mika. Don't be so mad. You got to admit that you've had this coming. I'm the last bitch that you should have fucked with. You messed with my life, so now I'm ruining yours. I hope that you never find a man to spend another dime on you again. I hope that life gets so bad for you that you'll need to borrow money just to get a sandwich off the dollar menu at McDonald's. Rot in hell, you dirty bitch, and may you never rest in peace."

She was speechless as I let her arms go. The thought of me getting her first had never crossed her mind. It had just hit her that she had gravely underestimated me, and that bad choice was to her disadvantage. She had lost the game that she thought she played all too well. That was why my motto had always been, "Before you sit down to play a game, you must not only know the rules to the game, but you must also know all your opponents, even if that means skipping a hand or two just to make sure you know their skill level. Having this knowledge gives you an upper hand every time, and an upper hand always wins the game."

Tay came over to us and told Shamika that the car was waiting. I told him to send someone with her to make sure that she took her things, and her things only, from the house. He called Carl over and told him what to do. We all just stood there as I took Tay's hand.

"Well, Shamika, I'm sorry things ended up this way, but take care of yourself," I said as I leaned into Tay. I wanted to show her that while she was losing everything in Black, I was gaining everything in Tay'von. She tried to lunge at me, but Carl grabbed on to her before she made contact.

"You fucking bitch! How could you do this to me? I should fucking kill you! Let me go. Let me go!" she yelled as Tay put his arms around me as I started to cry for show.

"What is she talking about? I have always been nice to her. Why would she say something like that?" I wailed.

People crowded around me and started to console me. They didn't want the bride upset the day before her wedding, so they tried everything they could to make me happy.

"It's okay, baby. She's just crazy. Don't even worry about it," Tay whispered in my ear.

"You know what? I don't even want her going back to the house. Tell the driver to take her straight to the airport. We can mail her clothes to her at a later time," I said as I wiped my face.

Tay'von let me go and helped Carl pull a screaming and cursing Shamika off the ship. When they

got to the limo, Tay later told me that he told Carl
to make sure to head straight for the airport. Carl
had to hold her in the car so that she didn't run
out and make a bigger ass of herself. A few months
later, he would tell me about their conversation in
the car.

"Carl, I'm telling you that bitch Tangie set me
up. She's the one who put the tape out there,"
Shamika insisted.

Carl was thinking that she was off her rocker
by that point. There was nothing that she could
say to make him think differently.

"What reason would Tangie have to do that to
you?"

"'Cause she's an evil bitch, that's why."

"How would she get her hands on the tape?
And why would you make something like that in
the first place? What did you do with it once you
were done taping?" Carl quizzed.

Shamika said nothing. She didn't want Carl
to know why she had taped her and Black or for
whom. She may have been brave, but everyone
who knew Carmello knew never to snitch on him.
Your body would never be found.

Carl went on. "Look, Shamika, it's too late for
you to start blaming other people. You are dead
wrong for that shit. I hope you didn't tape us."

"Why would I tape us?" she asked, as if Carl was dumb to even ask such a question. He was just a broke bodyguard with nothing to lose.

"Why would you tape you and Black? That's about the dumbest shit I have ever seen a girl in your position do. Plus, you can't just go around blaming people if you don't have any proof."

She pulled out her cell phone and called the thug boy whom she had met at Carmello's office. She spoke to him for a minute, then hung up. A short while after, her phone vibrated. She opened her phone and brought up the picture that he had sent her.

"Well, there she is. That's Tangie leaving the office of the person that helped her set me up," Shamika explained as she tilted her phone so that Carl could see the picture.

Carl took the phone and looked at the picture closely. It wasn't very clear. You couldn't tell who or where the person was. The only thing that rang a bell was the outfit the person had on. I did have one just like it, but still, that could have always been a coincidence.

"From what I can tell, this could be just a close-up of Tangie. This won't help you prove anything. You could have taken this at any time."

Once he said that, she started to panic. Maybe he was right. If she didn't have any evidence, her life could really be over. And if it was, what would she do? The word would spread that she was the one who had set up Black. She would never be able to get another baller. Not a famous one or even a street baller. She wouldn't even be able to go back to her hood. She was tarnished and wore something akin to a scarlet letter, the letter *T* for "trifling."

"That fucking bitch." She said this over and over again as tears ran down her face. "I'm telling you, Carl. I'm gonna find a way to get that bitch back. My life is all fucked up now, and it's because of her. I have got to do something to get her back."

Carl looked at her with pity and disgust. He knew that I was not a nice person, but he didn't think that I would take things that far.

Back at the cruise ship, Tay was able to calm Black down. Black was way too ashamed to show his face at the bachelor party, so he left altogether. About a half an hour later, all the men left the ship. It was time for the girls to party alone, and things went down like they did at any high-class bachelorette party: lots of liquor, plenty of male strippers, and women going crazy over them. It was fun as hell. Everyone let their hair down and had a ball. It was always nice to see these celebrities for who they really were, instead of that fake, plastic, "I'm perfect" bullshit they put on for the public.

I partied extra hard and was feeling good because not only had one of my many plans been flawlessly executed, but also when I woke up the next day, it would be the day that I married a millionaire. I didn't get back to the house until four in the morning. Tay'von didn't get in until six. Thank God I was having a sunset wedding, because neither of us would be up before noon.

I woke up to Tay's warm body next to me. I rolled over and faced him. He looked like he had partied just as hard as I had.

"Tay, baby, wake up. It's our wedding day. We have got to start getting ready."

He smiled and slid his hands through my hair. "Don't you mean it's *your* wedding day?"

I laughed because he was right: this day was really all about me.

"It's twelve thirty in the afternoon. We're getting married at six thirty. I got a whole lot of things to do, so we have to get up," I insisted.

"Yeah, well, all that I have to do is shower, get a shape up, and get dressed. After that I'll be done." He glanced at me. "What about you?" he asked jokingly.

I rolled on top of him, and I felt his morning wood. "This is your last morning as an unmarried man. Do you have any last words?" I asked as I moved my hips around on his hard wood.

"I don't have any last words, but I do have a thought running through my mind."

"And what is it that you're thinking about?"

He flipped me over and pulled my thong to the side. He played with my clit and got me wet.

"Come on, Tay, you know that you have to wait till after the wedding. Then you can do whatever you want to me."

He didn't stop; he just added more fingers.

"Why would I have to wait? We've already slept together. Let's just go ahead and let some of this stress out."

He was giving me the "sex" look. It was hard for me to say no to him, but I did. I pushed him off me and got out of the bed. "You'll get some of me tonight. Until then, you can just think about all the things that you want to do to me."

I took off my bra and underwear. I did this slowly, just to tease him a little.

"I'm going to go in and take a bath. Don't come in after me," I told him.

***

I had no mother or father coming to the wedding. I had to make do with old friends from my video days and other industry people. It wasn't what I would have wanted, but that was life sometimes. And although I knew that I would just have to deal with it, it still bothered me. I was pacing the room now, worrying that something was going to go wrong. All kinds of crazy thoughts ran through my mind. I was even wondering if there really was any love between Tay'von and me, not that it should have mattered, but for some reason, at that moment, it did. I wondered, *Could there be*? I had slept with a lot of people while I had been with him, even fucking his enemy.

Sure, I had come into the relationship with my mind only on his money. But now, now I wanted there to be something more than that. I even wondered what it was that he felt for me. I knew that he had slept with other women when he was out on the road. But could he really love me after what went down with Amira? But the more that I thought about it, the more I forced myself to believe that everything that we had been through had fused us together. All the bullshit had to be enough to force two people to love each other. How could he put up with all this shit if he didn't love me? I'd even stayed with him after he had put his hands on me countless times. Shit, this had to be love, and if it wasn't, well, I felt that we could always learn to love one another, right?

I knew what I needed to do. There was only one way to calm myself down. I had to go to Tay'von's room and get some. I made it to the door behind which Tay was getting dressed, and I was about to walk in, but Carl came walking out.

Carl held up a hand to stop me. "Whoa. Where are you going? He can't see you yet."

"Well, I have got to see him. I'm going out of my mind right now. I need him to help me calm down."

Carl could tell that I was upset, and wanted to help out. But he didn't know what I had in mind.

"Okay, let's just go back to your room and get you dressed, 'cause you know if you go in there, you'll have bad luck," he said with a smile.

I looked up at him, and he looked damn good. His hair was freshly cut, and his skin looked wonderful against the white shirt he had on. I let him take me back to my room, with only one thought in my mind, him. He walked in before me, which gave me a chance to lock the door behind me.

"So are you ready to get into your dress?" he asked as he held my wedding dress out to me. I took off my robe and pushed the dress back at him.

"Will you help me get into it?" I asked.

I looked into his eyes and saw that familiar place that only he let me go to. He yearned for me, he needed me, and he wanted me. I knew that place that lived deep in his soul, and at times, I loved being there. I could feel his hand on certain parts of my body as he helped me into my wedding dress, and it seemed as if he hoped that I thought that it was all by accident, but his lingering touch told me that his actions were on purpose. Once he had zipped me up, I turned around and faced him.

"So, do I look as good to you as I did that day I tried on the dress in the hotel room?"

"You look even better, Tangie."

"Aw, Carl, you're so sweet. Well, these are my last hours as a single woman. After today I'll be Tay'von's missus."

"Yeah, I know. Well, um . . ."

Carl was acting as if he couldn't think of what to say. He seemed as if he wanted to let me in on his pain and grief, but the words wouldn't leave his lips. I knew what he was feeling without him having to utter a word. I got close to him and hugged him tightly. His hands ran across my dress and pressed against my body. It sent chills through me, as if I were in an ice-cold room. We stood there and hugged longer than we should have. I kissed his neck and made my way to his lips. I tasted them as he kissed me back.

"Tangie, what are you doing?" he asked before slipping me his tongue.

I didn't answer him, but feeling his hands lifting up my dress let me know that he understood. Once he got it up around my waist, he slipped his finger in my panties. I moaned and enjoyed his touch.

"Tangie, you're about to get married, and Tay is right down the hall," Carl said with his mouth, but he didn't stop moving his fingers.

"Come on, Carl. This is our last chance. Just bend me over right here."

He took his time and looked at me while he worked me over slowly. He leaned in and kissed me before turning me around. I held my dress up as he unzipped his pants. He entered me with the force of passion. I held back what would have been a loud moan as he pounded me. I savored the feeling of him inside me. I knew that this was crazy, but I loved it, standing there in my wedding dress while he sexed me up.

Twenty minutes later I was getting cleaned up so that I could walk down the aisle. Yeah, that was fucked up. I knew that a sane person would never do that. But I had to get it out of my system. Hopefully, I wouldn't feel the need to do it again.

The time had come to get the show on the road. All the guests had arrived on time to the Miami estate. Everyone stood up as I walked toward Tay'von, but for some reason, my eyes stayed on Carl. I wondered if anyone else could see the look of sadness mixed with satisfaction on his face. For a split second, I asked myself if I should be marrying Carl instead. I knew that he loved me with all his heart, but what about Tay? Was I the woman of his dreams? Would this really be forever? *Fuck*. I had to stop tripping. I took a look around, and I saw what my life was going to be. It would be filled with jewels, famous people, and lots of money. *Fuck it*. I forced the crazy thoughts that I was having out of my head. This was what I had always wanted—and not a life with a bodyguard who made just a little more than minimum wage.

The ceremony lasted forty-five minutes. I thought Carl was going to pass out when Tay and I started to recite our vows. Carl tried to hide his true feelings from the crowd, but I knew why those tears ran down his face. He realized that all the thoughts he had about him and me falling in love and spending the rest of our days together were all a dream.

"You may now kiss the bride," I heard the priest say.

I must have gone so far into my own thoughts that I missed most of what had been said. Tay came close and tongued me down.

"I would like to introduce Mr. and Mrs. Miller," the priest announced.

We turned around and faced our guests. Everyone had that "aw" look on their face, but I still felt the same thing—nothing. Then I started to wonder if this was what married life was like. Would every day be the same? Who the fuck was I trying to fool? None of my days were ever the same. There would always be someone new to fuck, trick, or lick.

By the time Tay and I had changed into our reception clothes, all the guests had ambled to the back of the estate and were under the tents. We had had large white tents erected and one hundred tables set up to accommodate our guests. The tables and chairs were white and gold. There were big pillars with white candles, gold-colored roses wrapped around them. Everything was candlelit. We had no lights on, nor did we need them. The five hundred big and small candles lighting the area gave the night a romantic glow.

Tay and I made our way across the back lawn and took our seats at the head table. The evening went on as expected. Friends made speeches and toasts as everyone else listened. The liquor was the best, the food was out of this world, and we had the best live music, followed by one of the best DJs Miami had to offer. While Tay and I were having our first dance together, the music stopped.

"Okay, everyone, I just want to stop the partying for a second or two," Tay said as he turned to me and took my hand. "Now, you didn't think that I would let this day pass without giving you a gift, did you? It's nothing too big, it's nothing too small, and it's just right for you. I hope that we are able to spend many happy days with this gift."

Carl walked over to him and handed him an envelope. Then Tay handed it to me. I just stared at it.

"Well, go on and open it," Tay said as he waited impatiently. "This is the longest she's ever taken to open anything," Tay said, joking with the guests.

When I finally opened the envelope, I almost fainted. It contained a check for twenty-five million dollars.

"What, what is this for?" I asked as I read the numbers over and over again.

"Well, you're always saying how much you hate the house that we live in. Now you can use this money to get us a new one, or two or three."

Tears ran down my face. It was funny how the wedding did nothing to me, but a check for twenty-five million made me cry instantly.

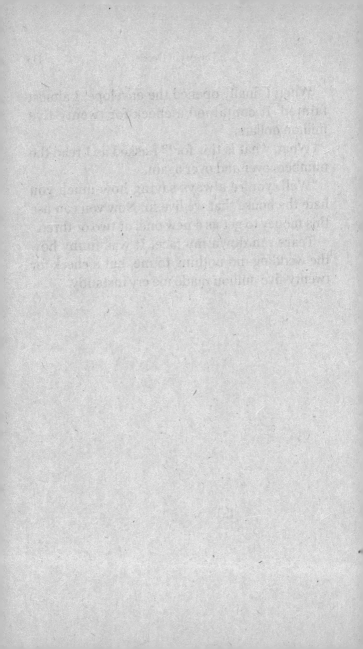

Chapter 18

Congratulations.

You're Going To Be A Father

We arrived at São Paulo–Guarulhos International Airport around twelve the next day. I was so ready to hit the beach that I couldn't stop smiling. Everything had gone exactly the way I wanted it to go. The wedding was a hit, I got my last taste of Carl, and now I was in Brazil. Who could ask for more? Probably me. A driver picked us up and took us to Natal, the city of the sun. We had rented a beachfront home there called simply "the Beach House." It was a five-bedroom, 10,763-square-foot house with an ocean view. It came with everything, including a cook, a maid, and a driver. This was just what I needed for the next seven days. I was so happy to see that it had an eight-foot wall that went all around the house, to keep out those peeping eyes of fans and paparazzi.

Tay and I settled in the biggest bedroom that had an ocean view, while Carl and Tony settled in downstairs. I jumped out of my clothes and put on my bikini.

"Damn, girl, aren't you tired from all that traveling?" Tay asked as he came up behind me and wrapped his arms around my waist.

"Yeah, but I have got to put our little private beach to some use. Why don't you come with me? We can get our tan on," I suggested seductively.

"Only if we can get our freak on too."

He was always thinking about sex, but in a way, so was I.

"Well, meet me outside, and I'll see what I can do," I said as I pulled away from him.

I went downstairs and asked the cook to make a nice cold, strong drink for me and Tay. Carl and Tony were already outside on the porch, enjoying theirs. I joined them.

"Why don't you two go for a swim? There's a pool out back, and we have our own beach," I said.

Tony said that he didn't like to swim, which was so typical of him.

"What about you, Carl? Want to get wet?" I said. Anyone who was out there could hear the sexual undertones to my question, and I did it on purpose.

"Oh, uh, I'm black enough," he said as he took a big swig of his drink.

Tay'von came out and picked me up. It was clear that he had overheard our conversation. "Girl, you know that these niggas ain't getting in no water. They probably can't even swim. Black folks," Tay said as he walked off the porch with me still in his arms.

He put me down once we reached the sand, and we walked close to the water. Everything was already set up by the house workers. They made sure we had everything we needed and that we were very comfortable. Finding the section on the beach that was arranged for us, we took our seat on the lounge chairs, and the maid brought our drinks out. Tay told her to keep them coming, and I asked her to put on some nice calming samba music. A minute later we were downing our drinks, lying back, and listening to some sweet samba grooves.

"So how does it feel now that you're Mrs. Miller?" Tay asked a while later.

"I have been Mrs. Too Fine since the day we met. You just didn't know it," I joked, but he took my hand and squeezed it hard, a little too hard.

"No, Tangie, I'm not joking. This isn't about me being Too Fine. I am talking about me as a person, without the fame, money, and everything else. Are you happy to be with me, and nothing else?"

I could see that this question burned deep down in his soul. He really wanted to know; he needed to know the truth. In that moment, there was no longer any doubt about the love I had for him. It might not be the conventional love that the world felt was proper, but it was the way I felt, what and how I felt about him. From then on, I was going to leave all the bad and sad in the past. Everything may have been money driven at first, but love had found its way in. It had slid its way through the cracks, and for once, I was happy that I hadn't stopped it. I had found love and hadn't even known it until then. I got off my towel and sat in his lap.

"Tay, I never let myself love anyone before you. Before you, the closest I ever came to letting someone in ended with me being hurt. I know that we have been to hell and back, but I am so happy that we fought our way through it and stayed together. I won't lie to you. When I first met you, sure all I saw was the glitz and glamour that come with being with you. But with the time that has passed, I now realize that the only real thing in life is the love that we have for each other. Baby, I love you. And I love you for you.

Sure, I love the life you work hard to give me, but above that, I love the person that you are. This is for life, remember?"

He looked deep into my eyes while I watched tears form in his. I leaned in and kissed him deeply. I pushed him down on his towel as I pulled off my top. The question of his love no longer loomed in my mind, and that turned me on to the max. Knowing that Tay really loved me did something to me. It was as if some parts of my frozen heart had actually started to melt. It touched me; it made me wish that I wasn't such an ice queen. It made me yearn to be normal. And although I was grateful for that part of me that he made human, I knew that I was a long way from full rehabilitation, if I was even capable of fully recovering. But it didn't matter if some parts of me remained the same. I would be eternally thankful to him for reaching in and bringing alive the part of me that I thought was forever deceased.

"Damn, baby, you make me so happy. I can't believe it took me so long to find you. And you're sexy as hell, on top of it. What would I do without you?" Tay said as the sun kissed my body.

He untied my bikini bottom as I straddled him. I looked deep into the eyes of the man I loved and let him enter me slowly and lovingly.

I rode him and let my hips sway to the smooth sounds of Brazil. We made love on our private beach until sundown. We even forgot that Tony and Carl were on the back porch, watching us, and even if we did remember, we wouldn't have cared.

Our honeymoon sizzled. With my newfound love for Tay'von came days and nights that were filled with back-breaking, nasty, sweaty, and delicious sex. We couldn't keep our hands off each other, and I didn't want it to end. I couldn't face the emptiness that was waiting for me. Brazil was like my very own little make-believe world, and I loved living in it. But as our time there came to an end, the reality of Tay going back to work set in. I wanted to ask him to stay there with me forever as we waited for dinner on the back porch, watching the evening waves roll in.

"Well, Tangie, this is our last night. Is there anything that you want to do before we leave Brazil?"

"God, this went by so fast. I feel like we just got here. Maybe it's because we didn't go out."

"Well, you have about three hours to shop before our flight leaves tomorrow."

"Yeah, yeah, I know, but how about we go out dancing tonight? You know how much I have gotten into the samba music here. What do you think?"

"We can do whatever you want," Tay said. Then he got up to tell Tony and Carl that we were going out.

After dinner we got ready to party with the Brazilians.

The club was off the hook. The Brazilian women and men were some of the most beautiful people on earth. Most of them even came up to me and started speaking Portuguese. I had to let them know that I was not a native. People even recognized Tay and asked him to rap for them. I was having such a good time that it saddened me even more to think we were about to leave paradise. The night was young, and it had an aura of sex. The freedom I felt from that place was beyond words. I was a woman in love, and it felt like a wonderful new world out there. The attention and love that Tay was showing me made my insides burn, and I was in love with being in love.

After another round on the dance floor, I headed to the bathroom to freshen up. As soon as I got in there, I heard someone walk in after me.

"Looks like you're having a good time, Tangie."

I knew exactly who it was once I heard him speak.

"Carl, you have got to get out of here. You're in the ladies' room."

"I know where I'm at. I just need to talk to you. Just give me a minute."

Oh hell, no. I didn't trust myself alone with him in that bathroom. I had to get him out of there fast. This "no cheating" thing was all new to me, and I didn't want to lose the fight so quickly.

"Okay, Carl, we can talk. Just let me tell you something first."

I went on and told him about my plans for a fresh start, and about my newfound love for Tay'von. I tried my best to make him understand that we would no longer be sleeping together.

"Oh please, Tangie. We both know that this won't last. You may want to make yourself believe that you love Tay, but you know what I think? I think that you really love me."

I laughed in his face. He was really delusional.

"Carl, you are crazy. I have never loved you. It was all just sex."

"Yeah, laugh all you want, but it was me that you were looking at while you walked down the aisle, not Tay." He was telling the truth about me looking at him, but that didn't mean that it was him that I loved.

"Okay, I'm getting out of here, because you seem to have lost your mind." I had started to walk away from him when he pulled me back.

"You can walk out of this bathroom, but you can't walk away from the feelings that you have for me."

He let me go, and I left him standing in the bathroom with unanswered questions.

The next morning we woke up, packed our things, and checked out of the house. Tay took me shopping and then to a late lunch. Before I knew it, I was saying goodbye to Brazil.

About nine hours later we were home. As soon as we walked through the door, I was ready to hit the bed. It wasn't really the traveling that had made me tired. I was just sad that it was all over. My comfort of paradise was gone, and I missed it already. Tay and I headed to the bedroom and turned on our phones. We had promised to leave the real world behind while on our honeymoon, and surprisingly, we did.

When I called my mailbox, it instantly told me that it was full. I pressed ONE to listen to my messages, and that was when the craziness began. I sat on the bed once I realized that the first ten messages were from Shamika. She sounded like a madwoman. In between Shamika's voicemail rampage, there was a message from Carmello.

"Hey, I know you told me not to call you, but I had to have 'her' thrown out of my office. She came up here screaming that we set her up and that she is going to kill us. Give me a call when you can."

I laughed. I was so happy that Shamika was feeling the effects of what I had done to her. *Never underestimate a bitch with a brain*, I thought. I looked over at Tay, who was also checking his in-box.

"This bitch is crazy," he said as he put his phone on speaker.

"That fucking no-good bitch is dead, you hear me? I'm gonna kill her ass," I told him.

"She filled my whole in-box with this bullshit," Tay said as he shook his head. He was just as over her craziness as I was.

"I tried to tell you that she's crazy, but you just brushed it off."

He picked up the house phone so he could see if she had left her scent on that too. Let's just say that she didn't let him down. The robotic voice told him that we had sixty-six voicemails waiting to be heard. He found the situation to be so out of hand that he called Tony and Carl into the room so that they could hear her rant and rave about my death. I didn't care to hear any more of it, so I got up and headed for the shower. She didn't scare me one bit.

I was so bitter that Tay was leaving that I half-way lost my mind. It made me go into this crazy crying fit that I couldn't control. I didn't want him to leave. Married life had been wonderful. I could go with him, but I wasn't in the mood to go on the road again. A part of me was also fearful that if I did, thoughts of Amira would rain down on me. The road would bring back too many emotions that I knew I was pushing to the side, and I wasn't ready to face them.

I stood at the front door, holding on to Tay so tight that I was choking him. I felt that we hadn't had enough time together. And I didn't want to have to look for our new house without him. In fact, with my newfound love for him, I didn't want to do *anything* without him, not even breathe.

"Honey, I'll be back as soon as I can. You're gonna make me late, baby," Tay said as he tried to push me away from him.

Tony had to step in and help, because I wasn't going to let go. Tay kissed my forehead and told me not to fret, because I would see him in no time. He walked out the door as I ran upstairs. I didn't come out of my bedroom for the next three days.

For the next three weeks, I felt so alone and lost. And although it was a new feeling for me, I soaked in my loneliness, not knowing when I would snap out of it. Tay'von was gone, and I felt like he had taken my soul with him. I rarely emerged from my bedroom. I spent days at a time not eating, and then I'd end up going downstairs in the middle of the night and eating everything in sight. I even refused to talk to Tay when he called. I felt that he shouldn't have left me. We had just married, for crying out loud.

By the third week of me doing this, Tay was worried, and he told Carl to do anything he could to get me out of the bedroom. He knew that I was slipping into a deep depression, and that was the last thing that he wanted to happen to me. I was in bed when Carl started banging on the door. Just the sheer thought of Carl being the person who was knocking on my door rubbed me the wrong way.

"Come on, Tangie. Open up. Tay says that he really needs to talk to you," Carl called.

I didn't answer. I just waited for him to go away, but the banging just continued and even got louder.

"I am told to kick the door open if you don't unlock it. Do you hear me, Tangie?"

Still I said nothing.

"I'm going to count to ten, and if it's not open, then I'm going to have to open it myself."

I didn't think that Carl was really going to kick open the door, so I just rolled over and pulled the covers over my head. But as sure as the sky was blue, he counted to ten, then kicked my door in. He walked over to the bed and pulled my covers off my head. He held the phone out, but I didn't take it. He told Tay that he was holding the phone up to my ear and that he could talk.

"What in the hell are you doing, Tangie? This is not like you. I have left plenty of times, and you have never acted like this. What's up, baby?" Tay's voice dripped with concern.

I wanted to tell him that I hadn't loved him all those other times he left. I wanted to let him know that I had just started to really love him. But before the words left my mouth, I had to run to the bathroom. I had been throwing up for the past week and had been trying to convince myself that it was from my bad eating habits, but that was just me trying to run away from the truth. The two home pregnancy tests that I had taken both came out the same way. Two lines meant that I was pregnant.

Carl walked into the bathroom after me, and I could hear him telling Tay that I was throwing up. Then he stopped and zeroed in on the two pregnancy tests that were lying out on the counter. He picked them up and saw the same two lines that had been haunting me for the past week or so.

"Oh shit," he said out loud without even realizing it. I could hear Tay yelling through the phone for Carl to tell him what was going on, but Carl was speechless, and for good reason.

"I think that Tangie better tell you," he finally said before he handed me the phone.

I took it from him and told Tay the truth. After doing so, I handed the phone back to Carl and got back in bed. I heard him tell Tay exactly what he had seen in the bathroom. Once Carl hung up, he walked over to the bed to deliver Tay's message.

"Tay's going to call back and let me know when he'll be able to come home. Once I know, you'll know."

I showed no emotion, even though I wanted to scream and yell. I was not ready for this, by no means. I needed more time before I started having kids. I was too damn young. And whose baby was it? I had slept with both Carl and Tay'von around the same time, and let's not forget Carmello. *Oh shit, shit, shit, shit.* I ran into the bathroom and looked at the calendar on the wall. Indeed, everything had happened in the same week. I had slept with all three of them too close together to even try to guess who the father was. *Fuck!*

The phone rang, and Carl picked it up before the first ring was even finished. He spoke for a minute or so, then hung up.

Carl stuck his head in the bathroom, where my eyes were still glued to my calendar, and said, "Tangie, Tay will be home in three days."

I didn't answer him. Not because I was being rude, but because my mouth had gone dry. My vision became blurry, and I could no longer see the dates on the calendar. I couldn't take the madness. My body suddenly became too heavy for my knees to support it, so I just let it go and fell to the floor.

I woke up in bed, with a cold washcloth on my head. Carl was in a chair beside the bed, looking like he had been through hell.

"What happened?" I said weakly.

"You passed out, so I picked you up and put you in bed."

It all started to come back to me with the force of hurricane winds. I touched my stomach, then pulled my hand away quickly. Carl picked my hand up and put it back on my stomach.

"It's okay to let yourself feel, Tangie."

He put his hand on top of mine, and we let our hands rest on what was to be.

Tay'von showed up three days later, at 11:00 p.m. I was in bed, half asleep, when I felt his body next to mine. Knowing he was there made me happy. I needed him, and although it took a few days, his presence made me so damn content. He wrapped his arm around my waist, and we slept that way until morning. I woke up to Tay'von kissing me on the neck and whispering in my ear.

"Tangie, wake up. I made an appointment for you at Dr. Webber's."

I turned around and faced him as he smiled at me lovingly. Seeing his face first thing in the morning heated my insides.

"I'm so happy you're home, Tay. I have missed you so much," I said as tears ran down my face.

"Yeah, well, you don't have to worry about that.
I have canceled all my shows—"

"For how long?"

"For as long as it takes," he said.

That was when I really started crying. Tay
really loved me, and that was very different for
me. Men always loved my body. They loved
having sex with me and being seen with me. But
Tay'von seemed to love *me* . . . the person.

He picked me up and took me into the bathroom as if he were my superman. He stood me
up and undressed me slowly. Once done, he
helped me into the tub, which was already filled
with warm, calming water. I took my time and
enjoyed everything he was doing for me. After
washing my back, Tay went downstairs, then
came back up with a tray that had eggs, bacon,
and orange juice on it. The sight of the eggs
made me want to throw up, so I just ate a slice of
the bacon and drank a little of the orange juice.

Tay never left my side that morning. He
helped me in the tub and then helped me get
dressed. I didn't tell him that I could still do
these things for myself. I could tell that he found
joy in helping me. He smiled the whole time and
was so caring. And sometimes in life, just letting
someone help you brought them more joy than
you helping them.

***

"So, Doctor, is she pregnant?" Tay asked as he paced back and forth.

I sat on the examination table, unable to make up my mind. Tay seemed so happy at the thought of having a child, yet I was so unsure on the subject. *What if it's not his? What will I do?* I had so many questions.

The doctor read the chart and then smiled at Tay. "Congratulations. You're going to be a father," he said as he shook Tay's hand.

"Baby, we're pregnant," Tay said as I flashed a fake smile.

"Can we leave now?" I asked as I headed for the door.

I didn't say much on the ride home. Tay asked me if I wanted to go shopping for bigger clothes, but I just told him to take me home. Once inside my bedroom, I stripped down to my bra and panties and climbed into bed.

The phone had been ringing nonstop since we came back from the honeymoon, and it had been driving everyone crazy. It rang again now. Tay picked it up and heard a still upset Shamika on the other end.

"Didn't I tell you to stop calling here? Don't make me have to call the police on your ass," he said before hanging up on her. But it didn't stop her. She just kept on calling.

If there was one thing that I could say about her, it was that she could hold a grudge. It had been over a month since I leaked her tape, yet she still wasn't over it. I turned off the ringer on the phone and pulled the covers over my head. Tay looked down at me, as if he was puzzled and wanted answers that I just couldn't give.

"Tangie, what's going on with you? Aren't you happy about the baby?"

I didn't answer him, and that pissed him off even more.

"I know it's kind of soon and all, but it's not like we don't have any money. We're going to be able to give this child everything."

"Can we please talk about this some other time, Tay'von?" I asked, with the covers still over my head. He pulled them off me so that he could see my face while he talked to me.

"What the fuck is wrong, Tangie?"

I sat up and decided to tell him the truth, since he wasn't going to stop until I did.

"I didn't hear you ask me if I even wanted to keep this baby. It's my body, and it's my choice. But you just come home with your mind already made up without even talking to me."

"Are you losing your mind? What do you mean, it's your choice? You're having this baby, Tangie!" he yelled out of disbelief.

Tony knocked on the door and told Tay that Shamika was on the phone again. Tay yanked the phone out of Tony's hand and slammed the door shut.

"Bitch, stop calling my fucking house!" Tay yelled before throwing the phone down on the bed.

He turned back to me. "What is it that you're lacking, Tangie? Tell me what would make you question having this child. This baby is here for a reason, and I will not let you take that away from me or yourself."

I felt like I was going crazy. I had started to feel like I wasn't in control of my choices, and it was fucking with me hard. It was like no one understood me.

"I don't have to tell you shit, Tay'von! I am going to do what I want to do, so just leave me alone about it."

He walked over to the bed, and for a second, I thought that he was going to hit me. Instead, he touched my face gently.

"Look, I don't want to upset you, so please calm down. All I'm asking is that you don't get rid of my baby. Don't get rid of the little person that's growing inside you. I love you, Tangie, and I want you to have my child."

Tears ran down his face, and it opened the floodgates for mine. While we stayed in our bedroom, arguing and crying, neither of us paid attention to the phone, and to whether Tay had properly hung it up or not.

Chapter 19

The Beast That Came
To Drag Me To Hell

The phone rang, waking me out of a deep sleep. I looked at the clock, and it read 7:30 p.m. I reached over and picked up the receiver, and to no surprise, it was Shamika.

"Get a fucking life, Shamika," I said before hanging up.

As soon as I laid my head back down, the phone rang again. I picked it up, ready to give Shamika a royal cussing out.

"Bitch, if you—"

A man's voice interrupted me before I could really unleash the bullets I used as words. "Tangie, it's Carmello—"

"What are you doing calling me here?"

"Shamika's on her way to your house, and she has a—"

"I know you didn't just say that Shamika's on her way over here." I thought that maybe I was dreaming. That bitch had to have some major balls if she was thinking about coming to my house.

"Look, she showed up at my office, talking all types of crazy shit. She even tried to pull a gun out on me, but I saw it coming."

I sucked my teeth at the thought of Shamika's empty threats. "Fuck her. She won't be able to get through the gate, anyway. I'll just call the cops when she gets here."

"Is your code one-oh-three-one-two-three?"

My heart skipped a beat, which caused me not to answer.

"Tangie, is your code one-oh-three-one-two-three?"

"Yes, it is. Oh my God! I gotta go get Tay," I said out loud.

"Look, I'm on my way over there. Just hang up and call the cops," Carmello said before hanging up.

I opened the bedroom door and slowly walked down the stairs. I walked past the living room and peeked into the kitchen. The only person I saw was Tony.

"Where's Tay?" I asked as I tried to stay calm, but my voice was a little shaky. If Tony was paying attention, he would, or I should say *should*, have picked up on it.

"Oh, he said to tell you that he and Carl went out to get your favorite dinner, so calm your ass down. He'll be back soon," Tony said in a hateful tone.

I took a long look at him and decided not to tell him what was going on. I hated his ass and thought that I could wait for Tay to deal with things. I went back upstairs and called Tay. He picked up, but his cell phone was breaking up something bad. All I heard him say was that he would call me back. I hung up and called Carmello back.

"Is she there?" he asked, concerned.

"No, but I just called Tay. I couldn't really hear him, so he said that he'd call back."

"Did you call the cops?"

"Oh shit. I for—"

There was a loud noise that caused me to stop talking. A few seconds later, a louder bang rocked me to my core.

"Tangie, was that a gunshot I heard go off?"

"Oh, shit. I think she's here!" I told Carmello as I gripped the phone.

"Look, hang up the phone and call the police. I'm almost there."

He hung up as I heard footsteps coming up the stairs. I looked around the room, hoping that I could find something to use to knock this crazy bitch out. Nothing. I ran into the closet and grabbed the first thing I saw, Tay'von's bat. I waited behind the bedroom door, with a heart that raced a million miles a minute. I got in position to knock her head off, but the footsteps stopped coming my way, and soon after, I heard them heading back down the stairs. I took a deep breath, opened the bedroom door, and walked into the hallway. I slowly made my way down the stairs, hoping to go unnoticed. I couldn't hear anything, because Shamika had turned on the music full blast. I walked into the living room and saw Shamika standing over Tony.

"Where the fuck is she?" she yelled as she paused the music with the remote.

"Look, I don't like the bitch, either, but this is my job—"

Shamika cut him off, not caring to hear any more of his bullshit. "Nigga, if you were doing your job, I wouldn't be here. Now, tell me where Tangie is, or I'll shoot you dead."

I tried to move slowly and quietly to the front door, but as we all know, people make the most noise when they're trying to be invisible. As soon as I turned the corner, the bat hit the vase that sat on the piano. It was as if everything went in slow motion. My eyes followed the vase as it hit the marble floor. I gazed at it in disbelief. How could I have been so stupid? When I looked up, I was staring into the eyes of the beast that had come to drag me to hell, and in those eyes was the danger that I had thought I could ignore.

She had nothing to lose and was 100 percent invested in completing her own mission, which was to kill me. That bitch was on fire and lusted for revenge. She walked over to me. I swung the bat, missed, and she ended up slapping me with the gun. I fell back, and she yelled for me to get up. I moved too slowly for her liking, so she came over and kicked me in my stomach. I fell back down and clutched my baby.

"Yeah, that's right, bitch," she snarled. "I'm going to kill that unborn muthafucka. Then I'm going to kill you."

I looked up at her and wondered how she knew about the baby.

"You and Mr. Too Gay should really make sure y'all hang up the phone next time. I heard his bitch ass begging you to keep his baby. What, did you think that I was going to let you fuck me over and not try to get you back? Please, I'm a bitch from the hood. We just don't let shit slide like that." She smiled and looked like an escaped mental patient as she grabbed me by my hair and sat me down by Tony, who had a puddle of blood forming around him.

She waved her gun in the air. "Now, you have one minute to tell me why and how you and Carmello set me up."

I thought about it and weighed my options. I could try to fight her, but the crazy nut had a gun. So I tried to lie my way out of it instead.

"Shamika, I don't know—"

She didn't even let me finish. "You must be out of your fucking mind, Tangie. Now I know that you're high saddity and shit, but this is a fucking gun. So how about you try telling me the truth, because my trigger finger is a fast-moving bitch. You get me?" she said as she waved the gun in my face.

I told myself to forget the bullshit and give her what she wanted, so I did. I told her everything. I told her that I knew she really hated me. I told her that what Tay had done to me because of the drugs she gave him, and because of the talk they had, was her fault. I told her that a man had violated me in my youth, and that I had vowed that if it ever happened again, I'd deal with whoever was responsible. I didn't leave anything out as I told her of meeting up with Carmello and planning her demise. I explained that I was sorry that Black had had to take the fall, but that bringing him down had been necessary to take away the little bit of fame and shine that she had by being with him. He was just the fall guy behind her downfall.

I knew that I was taking a big chance, but I made sure to take my time when telling her what had really gone down. I was hoping that Carmello would get there soon. She just laughed and rocked back and forth the whole time I spoke. Even Tony's eyes grew big as he listened to my story. I was nearing the end of it when I noticed Carmello at the front door. Shamika didn't see him, so I just kept on talking, as if he was not there.

"So you mean to tell me that you did all of this to me over some drugs that Tay and I smoked?" she asked as she wondered whether I was really the one who was insane, and not her.

"That, and for the things that followed. I am good at reading people, Shamika. I have always known that you wanted to be me. It killed you that I was the one in my position. You always thought that you were going to be the queen bitch, and not only did I step on your toes, but I stepped out and got in front of you too."

I said this because it was true, but for the most part, I just wanted a reaction out of her.

As soon as she turned and faced me, Carmello charged her. The gun flew out of her hand, and he held her down while I grabbed the gun. What Carmello didn't know was that Shamika had a knife in her back pocket. She slid it out while they rolled around on the carpet, and stabbed him in the arm, which forced him to let her go. She tried to hurry to her feet, but it was too late. I pointed the gun at her and told her to sit down in a chair. I had some things I needed to say and do before I killed her ass.

She did as she was told, and then I told Carmello to keep an eye on her. I walked over to Tony without taking my eyes off her so that I could check on him.

"Are you okay?" I asked him.

"Yeah, but she shot me in the back," he said in a faint voice.

"I am so happy to hear that. Now I have the pleasure of killing you myself," I said.

He twisted his face in confusion, but I was going to make things crystal clear for him.

"You know too much. And as much as you love Tay, I know that if I let you live, you'll tell him everything."

"No I won't, Tangie. Please just call nine-one-one and get me some help."

"You can get that thought out of your head. You're not going to live to see a hospital."

His bitch ass started crying like a baby. All that did was make me smile.

"Don't cry now. You weren't crying that day I heard you in Tay'von's hotel room, telling him that you could fuck him better than me."

The whole time that I spoke, I was looking right into Shamika's eyes. I wanted her to see what a real crazy bitch looked like.

I went on. "That's right, Tony. When I showed you a little pussy, it wasn't because I wanted to fuck. It was because I wanted to see if you were the queen that I had you pegged to be. And sure enough, you turned me down. No straight man turns me down, Tony."

He didn't even bother to say anything, but for some reason, Shamika did.

"So if he told Tay that he could fuck him better than you, how do you know Tay didn't let him try? I knew that nigga was too pretty to be straight."

Shamika was trying to get a reaction out of me the same way I had done to her, but I was way too smart for that. I just smiled and answered her.

"'Cause Tony is the one who has been fucking Black. Always has and probably always would, that is, if Tony wasn't a dead man. See, Shamika, I watched Tay and made sure that he wasn't going around fucking men. No, Tay's not gay, but Black, he loves to fuck men, and Tony here was one of them. Isn't that right, Tony?"

If looks could kill, I would have been a dead woman. Shamika had murder in her eyes after my comment, but it wasn't worth shit anymore. I had the gun. I just laughed and continued my conversation with Tony.

"So now that you know what I know, do you still think that I should let you live, Tony?"

"Please, just let me explain. Yes, I was fucking Black, and I even tried to get at Tay, but he wasn't having it. I swear that it will never happen again," he mumbled as tears dripped down his chin and landed in the puddle of blood that had formed from his bullet wound.

"This isn't about you trying to fuck Tay. This is about you knowing too damn much to live. Plus, I never really liked you, anyway."

"Tangie, please, you have to let me live. Just let me explain."

I stood there and pretended to think about letting him live. Then, with one quick move, I turned the gun from Shamika to him.

"I don't have time for explanations."

Bang, bang.

He died as soon as the bullets hit his skull. I quickly turned the gun back on Shamika after taking care of Tony, and for the first time since walking into the house, she had fear in her eyes.

"So I know that this is a big cliché, but I just can't help myself. Do you have any last words?" I said.

As soon as she opened her mouth . . . *bang, bang*. I pulled the trigger twice; both shots went straight to where her brain should have been. I was not going to give her the pleasure of any last words. She didn't deserve them.

"Damn. You're nicer with that gun than I thought," Carmello said as he pulled out his cell phone.

"Don't call yet. We gotta move the bodies, remember?"

Movies and TV shows on how to get away with murder came in handy. We moved the bodies to make it look like Shamika had killed Tony. Then I sat in the puddle of his blood and scooted on my ass and made a trail of blood, as if I had been backing away from her as she walked over to me with the gun. That was where Carmello came into the story. Thank God she had stabbed him. She made the story we were going to tell the cops even more believable. Now we could say that I had thought that she was going to stab him to death, and that was why I'd shot her. After standing her body up and letting it hit the floor, I put another shot into her head, hoping that the blood splatter would match my story.

"You don't even want to know how nice I can get with a gun or a setup, trust me. Now call the cops," I said while standing there, admiring my work of art. It had all gone down so well.

I had truly created a masterpiece of deception.

I called Tay on the house phone and put on my hysterical voice as I told him what had just gone down. He told me that he was about ten minutes away and that he was going to speed until he got home. In his hurry to get to the house, he even beat the cops there. He and Carl ran into the house and came over to where I was sitting in the living room.

"What, what . . . who? Where's Tony? That nigga is supposed to stop shit like this from happening," Tay said as his eyes searched the room frantically.

"He's dead," Carmello answered him, while I played too shocked to speak.

That was when Tay took notice that he was there. He looked at Carmello and then back at me. I knew what he was thinking as soon as I saw the expression that was on his face. I started crying and talking at the same time.

"Shamika ran up in his office, yelling and asking him for a ride over here. When he told her no, she said that she would come here on her own and kill everyone in the house. If it wasn't for him rushing over here to stop her, I would be dead right now."

Tay sat down next to me, put his arm around me and looked over at Carmello. He gave him a "thank you" nod as I sobbed in his arms. I even pretended to be shocked and started screaming when I faked realizing that the gun was still in my hand. Tay'von took it from me and stood up.

"Freeze!" I heard a bunch of voices say. This part was certainly not in my plans.

"Sir, put the gun down and put your hands in the air," a single voice said.

Tay'von just stood there, too shocked to move. There were about six police officers in the house, with their guns drawn and pointing at him.

"Wait. I live here. I just got here. My name is Tay'von Miller."

The cops weren't trying to hear that shit. All they saw was a whole bunch of niggers, who they assumed were out of place. They saw that we were in an affluent neighborhood that was predominantly white, that we were covered in blood, and that dead bodies littered the floor. Tay was a well-known star and the owner of that house, yet they still thought that we were intruders. It made no difference what we did;

we were shit out of luck. I stood up and tried to make them understand that we were the ones in need of help, not knowing that it would all fall on deaf ears.

"No, he didn't do any of this. She's over there. It's okay. We live—"

That was all I got out. Something hot hit me in the arm. Then I started to feel it in other places. Maybe the cops had misunderstood my actions. I had just wanted to take the gun out of Tay's hand, not shoot them. I fell back, and Tay fell after me. Carl jumped on top of me to stop any more of the bullets from hitting me, with no concern for himself. I looked over at Tay'von, and he was out cold. I didn't know what stopped me from passing out right away, but the longer I stayed awake, the stronger the urge to sleep came over me. I just lay there, staring at Tay. I heard a cop yelling for the paramedics, but the more he yelled, the quieter it got.

"They're the ones who called us. Fuck! You all shot the wrong people. That's the rapper Tay'von and his wife. They live here," I heard what sounded like a black cop say.

I could feel Carl getting off me before searching my body for bullet holes. Miraculously, he hadn't been hit.

"She was hit twice," Carl yelled to the police.

I was in shock. I thought for sure that the heat that I felt all over my body was from more than two bullet wounds. Carl finished searching my body, then went over to Tay. I tried to hear what he was saying, but my hearing was gone. All I got from reading his lips was that something was seriously wrong with Tay. I looked down and saw a big puddle of blood. I couldn't tell if it was just from me or if my blood had merged with Tay's. After a minute or two, I just stopped trying. My mind wouldn't work right. I started to see red and pink spots everywhere I looked, and found it too distracting to concentrate. As my sight failed me, my hearing came back for a brief moment. The last thing I heard caused me to give in and not fight so hard.

"We're losing him," someone said before I slipped into darkness.

Chapter 20

When Shit Hits

The Fan Unplanned

The next ten minutes of my life came in spurts. People, people all around, but there was only one face that I knew. Stress dominated Carl's normally soft features. It was bleak, scared, and worried.

Beep, beep, beep. That annoying sound went on and on. My body burned with anger and with pain. Flashes of the night's events and the blood that hypothetically stained my hands were a constant reminder of my lost soul.

"Tay, where's Tay?" I asked as I pulled at the cords that seemed to be coming out of my body.

"Tangie, we're going to need for you to calm down. Tay'von is fine. Don't worry about him. We have to get you and your baby stable."

I looked into the face of the cute, young white guy who was working on me as if he saw pregnant women with bullets burned into their flesh every day, and I realized where I was.

"Fuck, fuck, fuck me. That bitch shot me, didn't she? Oh my God! What about my baby? Oh, God, my baby!"

I touched my stomach and prayed that I hadn't fucked up the mistake that I once wished hadn't happened. I remembered cursing myself for fucking so many men with no protection. I remember the pure anger I had had for the extra person I was now carrying around with me. Why did this happen to me? I had asked myself. "He or she is only going to slow me down. I don't want this. It isn't part of the plan, I had once said, trying to convince myself. But in that moment, I wanted my baby more than ever. I wanted to make Tay'von happy; I wanted to make him a father.

"Just tell me, Carl, is he dead? Did she kill him?"

Carl had been sitting beside me the whole time, silently saying his own prayers.

"Who is 'she'?" he asked.

"That fucking bitch Shamika. Did she kill him? I swear, Carl, I didn't want it to go down this way. I had no fucking way of knowing this would happen." I screamed out in pain. "Ahhh!" It was becoming unbearable. There was so much blood. Blood seemed to surround me, and it was too much to just be all mine. Carl was bleeding too.

"Shamika didn't shoot you, Tangie. The cops . . . they shot you . . . me . . . and Tay."

"Sir, sir, are you saying that you've been shot too?" another white guy asked frantically. "Oh my God! Okay, I'm going to cut off your pants. Just lean back for me, okay?"

It was a madhouse inside the ambulance. While the cute white guy worked on me, his partner checked Carl's bullet wounds. As my eyelids grew heavy, there was so much I wanted to know. There was so much that I wanted to say. There were so many apologies I wanted to give, but I couldn't. I was too tired, I was too weak, and it was too late.

"Wait. He's bleeding from somewhere else too. Look for another puncture wound," said the cute white guy.

My eyes closed and opened over and over again. The more time that passed, the longer they stayed closed.

"Here, I found one. He's been hit in the chest. Alert the hospital that we have two in critical condition," said the cute guy.

Carl let out a loud groan as they applied pressure to his chest wound. Before my eyes closed for the last time in that ambulance, I saw a gut-wrenching scene. Carl's body stiffened, then started to shake. I couldn't tell what was happening, but I did know that it wasn't good. I gathered all the strength in my body and reached for his hand. And as our fingers met, I regretted everything bad I had ever done to him. His love for me was pure and without malice. He had wanted nothing from me but love and respect, and I had been too selfish to give him that.

When my eyes opened again, I was in the hospital, with a brand-new set of faces staring down at me.

"No, wait. Where's Tay? Get all this shit off of me. I can't breathe. Give me something quick," I screamed, fighting the doctors and nurses as I tried to get my thoughts together.

"Tangie, we need you to calm down. We won't be able to help you if you keep this up. You need to keep your oxygen mask on," a doctor told me.

This was not how I had envisioned everything going down.

"I just need to know about Carl and Tay. Are they okay?" I asked while trying to suck air into my lungs.

"Just lie back and try to calm down. We have to make sure everything is okay with you," a nurse said, trying to make it clear that it was about me in that moment.

My chest felt like a rock was lying on top of it, and it felt like it was slowly pushing all the life out of me. My eyelids started to get heavy again, and I wanted to go back to sleep.

"You cannot go to sleep, Tangie. You have to stay up for you and the babies."

"What about Tay? Where is he? Is he okay? I need to see him. I have to tell him that I am sorry. Wait . . . What do you mean, babies?"

My jumbled thoughts seemed to get lighter as my eyes closed. I felt like I had nothing left in me to give. My energy was fleeing fast. I was weak—mind, body, and soul. All I could do was pray that my fuckup didn't cost me my life, Tay's and Carl's lives . . . and the life of the baby inside me.

I woke up three days later in a private hospital room. It was cold and lonely. How could it all have gone so wrong? Everything had been planned to the tee. I reached down and touch my stomach. My baby still felt like it was inside me, but I wasn't sure. I pushed the call button, and a voice told me that a nurse would be in shortly, but I need someone right away. My mouth was dry, and I got a sudden urge to throw up. As I somehow managed to get out of bed, Carl walked into my room with a hospital gown on.

"What are you doing, Tangie? You need to stay in bed until the doctor sees you," Carl said as he rushed to my side and tried to get me back into bed.

I tried to tell him that I was about to throw up, but my words didn't make it out. What was left in my stomach ended up on the floor and his shoes. Being the caring and gentle man that he was, he just got me back into bed and rushed to get a doctor to my room.

"We cannot have you getting out of bed just yet, Mrs. Miller."

I looked at the young white doctor and almost asked for someone else, but he let me know that he was the one who had operated on me, so I stayed calm and heard him out. I was told that they had rushed me into surgery after I almost lost enough blood to kill me.

"What about my baby?" I asked him, still holding on to my stomach.

"While we were getting you prepped for surgery, we found two heartbeats. We were worried, because one had a very faint heartbeat. After further testing and an ultrasound, we came to the conclusion that we would have to take a chance and get you into surgery."

"What do you mean, you found two heartbeats? I was gonna have twins?" It didn't hit me that I may not be pregnant anymore until I said "was."

"Not *was*, Mrs. Miller. You are going to have twins. You have little fighters in there," he said as he patted my tummy.

I breathed a sigh of relief as he assured me that my babies were still inside me. He went on and told me about my surgery and how they had managed to get all the bullets out of me. I heard most of it, but my mind was more on my babies and Tay.

"Where is my husband, Dr. Cohen? Is he okay? I need to see him now," I said. I had got a weird feeling in the pit of my stomach.

"We have you on total bed rest right now for the safety of your babies. I understand that you want to see him, but your husband is not as lucky as you. We don't know when he will be—"

"I don't give a shit about no bed rest right now, Doctor. I am not *asking* you if I can see Tay'von. I am *telling* you that I need to see him. Call an orderly in and tell him to bring in a wheelchair, or I'll walk to wherever he is."

I hated letting the bitch out while I was lying in a hospital bed, but I had to make sure that my man was okay. The doctor stood there and looked around the room like he was unsure. When he saw me move to get off the bed again, he walk out of the room and called for a nurse and an orderly. When an orderly came in with a wheelchair, I climbed in the chair. Then Carl walked behind me and pushed me to Tay's room.

"Am I going to lose it once I step into this room, Carl?" I asked when I came face-to-face with the door to Tay's private room.

"I don't think that you should. The doctors are saying that he is stable. He just hasn't woken up yet," Carl answered.

I could tell that he wasn't just saying that to make me feel better. But maybe he should have just held his tongue.

I was wheeled in to find a woman sitting in a chair next to my husband's bed. I racked my brain, trying to figure out where I had seen her before. She was tall, fatter than she should be, dressed to kill, and cute.

Where, where, where do I know her from? I asked myself. *The tour! It's that fat bitch that I would see hanging around backstage.*

"What in the hell are you doing in my husband's room?" I asked, having to be held down in the wheelchair by Carl.

"I'm here to make sure that the man that I have been with for the past fifteen years of my life lives to see the birth of his child," she answered, as if she was Tay's wife and I was the woman on the side.

"Bitch, I know that you have lost your fucking mind. He is my husband, and I don't give a shit what relationship you've had with him. The day he became my husband was the day your bullshit affair ended," I threw her way, while using my feet to inch the wheelchair closer to Tay's bed.

I looked over at Carl. "Carl, you need to get back on your job and get this crazy bitch out of here. As if her relationship with my man matters at this point. She's probably making this shit up, anyway," I barked.

"Oh no, honey. This is not a made-up relationship. Isn't that right, Carl?"

We both looked at Carl, waiting to see whose side he was going to be on.

"Connie, what are you doing here? I thought that they weren't letting anyone in?" Carl said.

"Oh, so now I'm just *anyone*? What, you don't know me now, Carl? Damn, you must be fucking that ho too, since I'm just anyone now. Y'all niggas kill me. Start fucking a ho-ass bitch, and *boom*, next thing you know a nigga is turning her into a housewife. But we all know what they say about trying to turn a ho into a housewife, don't we?" Connie said, with her face screwed up, as if had she smelled something awful.

That bitch had to be out of her fucking mind speaking of me that way. The only thing that saved her from getting the taste slapped out of her mouth was the fact that I couldn't get out of that wheelchair fast enough to do it. I was trying to stay as calm as my temper would allow me to be, but she was pushing it, and I was running low on calm.

I crossed my arms over my chest. "Well, you know what they also say? Maybe the better ho won . . . And it looks like I did. Just because you get fucked by a star, it doesn't mean that you'll be the one to marry him. Remember that next time you find yourself under another woman's man."

She turned to me and leaned forward. "*Better*? I wouldn't say that. You just made all the right moves to hook a dumb, pussy-whipped nigga. But this isn't all about you right now. Although I must admit that I was a little stupid to have gone along with his stupid-ass plan to use you as arm candy in the first place."

What was this fat bitch talking about? First, she was in there talking about a relationship that

I was pretty sure never existed. Then she was insinuating that she went along with something. All I knew was that my head was starting to hurt, and I could feel my blood pressure going up.

"Do you know her, Carl?" I asked.

I watched him shuffle his feet around before he looked at me blankly.

"Answer the fucking question, Carl. Do you know her?"

She answered for him. "Don't look so uneasy, Tangie. I know that this has got to be hitting you a little hard, but I'm sure it's not as hard as hearing on a show that the man that you have been with since middle school just up and asked a bitch who was just supposed to be his arm candy to marry him. But you know what? I'm sick of being in the background just because I don't look like you. Fuck a record label, fuck a magazine, and fuck whoever feels that just because I'm not a size two, I can't be around or spend time with my man in public. I don't care if he is a rapper or not. Shit, he wouldn't even be where he is today if it wasn't for me working my ass off and giving him studio money when he was shelved by the first label that ever signed him.

So yeah, Carl knows me. He knows who I am and why I'm here. It's 'cause *my* man is laying up in the hospital, and I got to make sure that he pulls through for me and his baby."

The word *calm* had gone out of the window now. My face was bloodred and hot. I was ready to kick a new hole in that girl's ass. I jump out of the wheelchair so fast that Carl was unable to hold me down. I staggered toward her fast. My heart was pumping a mile a minute as the palm of my hand slid across her face. Before she could react, Carl was between us.

"Fuck you, bitch. My man isn't tryin'a live for you. *I* am his wife, and *I* am the one who is pregnant with his children. Even if what you are saying is true, it's too damn late. I have the ring, so now I have the all the rights," I spat at her.

I waved my ring in her face. I could see the hurt in her eyes, and I stood proud in my wifely glory. Once a woman realized that she had lost the race to another, she knew that there was nothing else that she could do but pop her gums.

"Bitch, that ring doesn't mean a damn thing. I have his heart and always will."

I cock my head back and let out a long laugh. "*His heart*? You think that you have his heart? Girl, please, I have had that since the first time I fucked him, and my marriage license proves it," I shot back.

"That's what he lets you think, since he needed you to stay around and look good on his arm. You ain't nothing but a high-priced ho that should have been shelved, like Tay was the first time around." She looked like she was really trying to believe the words she spoke, but the weakness in her chest showed itself in her eyes.

I sat back down in my wheelchair, knowing that when it was all said and done, I had the upper hand. There was no point in me engaging in a fight that I had already won. As soon as I saw the tears in her eyes, I knew that she had lost, and so did everyone else in the room, including her. But I was sure she would continue to fight. So I didn't let up.

"Where was his heart the day he asked me to move in? Where was his heart when he asked me to go on tour with him . . . ?" I said.

"From what I hear, he didn't ask. You begged," she said, standing up.

I wondered if this was said to make herself feel better, because her words weren't hurting me at all. Facts were facts, and she couldn't change history.

"Where was his heart when he asked me to marry him? Did you have it then? Or, let me guess, his reps told him to do that too? Girl, don't fool yourself. This may have started because he needed 'arm candy,' as you put it, but please know that it ended with him forgetting about you and loving me. Tell me, how can you say that you have his heart when you had to hear about the wedding on an entertainment news show? That's not love, honey. He just didn't know how to tell you that he is over you. He has found something better, and you are just going to have to deal with it," I said, adding to the tension in the room.

"Okay, ladies. I think that we all need to calm down and try to talk about this without all the insults," Carl said, seemingly still feeling the heat from my earlier question.

I shook my head and frowned at Carl. "What we *need* to do is get this shit straight. She needs to stop walking around here thinking that she and Tay still have something. And you still didn't answer me. Do you know her, Carl?"

I already knew the answer because of how he was acting, but I wanted him to look me in the eye and say it. That time, his feet didn't move. He just left his head down and answered.

"Yeah, I know her, and most of what she is saying is true. She has been with Tay since they were young, and he was still with her while he was with you."

"And what about the 'arm candy' statement? Is that true too?" I asked, wanting to get up again and slap his ass too.

I could tell that he didn't want to answer that one, but we both stayed quiet until he did.

"I can't really speak for Tay'von, but I know that he does love both of you—"

"That's not what I asked you, Carl. Is Tay only with me so that I can be his arm candy?"

"It started out that way, but he really did fall in love with you. And, Connie, well, he just didn't know how to tell you," Carl answered, finally telling the full truth.

I got some satisfaction from Carl's answers, but I was already planning on giving Tay hell when he got better.

Carl's words hit Connie hard. She pulled out the chair that she was once sitting in and fell into it. She went on to speak to Carl as if I wasn't in the room. She said she wasn't going to jump to any conclusions until she talked to Tay, but she also knew that if anyone knew the truth, it would be Carl. She said she had been sitting at her "man's" bedside, praying that he had a good explanation for what he had done. She had been there for three days. She had played this fantasy she had constructed over and over in her mind. He would wake up, tell her that he was sorry for everything he had done, tell her that she was the only one that he loved, and beg her to marry him as soon as he got a divorce. She had been through too much with him for him to do otherwise.

"What am I going to do about the baby?" she asked.

I looked over at Carl and gave him a "What the fuck?" face.

"It's *babies*. I just found out that Tay and I are having twins. Plus, they or we will have nothing to do with you, so you don't have to worry about us or them," I informed her.

"Who gives a shit about you and yours? I am talking about *my* baby, Tay's baby," she answered, staring me in the eye.

"Now, if there is one thing that I know, it's that Tay has no kids, so don't even try to pull that shit," I said matter-of-factly, getting heated all over again.

"I wouldn't go off of what I know right now, because it seems like you don't know too much. I'm talking about our baby that is still in my stomach," the fat bitch proclaimed.

I got a sharp pain in my chest. I knew she didn't just mention a child that was still in her stomach. That bitch was really trying to steal my shine. I should be the only Mommy to be.

She continued. "He was over my house three nights ago, when I told him. If only he had stayed when I asked him to, he wouldn't be in this mess he's in now. I told him that fucking with you wouldn't bring him anything but pain, but he just wouldn't stay. I should have known then that something was wrong. What was I thinking? I saw all the signs a long time ago. Hell, I've been the chick on the side for a long time now. I was just in denial. I saw how he was with you when we were out on tour. He kept on telling me that it was all for show, but I knew—"

I really was not interested in her sob story, so I cut her off. "He was over your house three nights ago?"

If I had heard her right, that meant that Tay was with her the night of the shooting. I looked from her to Carl. If Tay was really over at her house, then Carl would know, since he was with Tay that night.

"She's not lying, Tangie," Carl said quietly. "We went over there so that Tay could talk to her about the wedding, and to let her know what was really up with you and him, but she had some news of her own, and that's when he found out that she was also pregnant."

"You mean to tell me that as I was at home with that crazy bitch Shamika, who was holding a gun to my head, while you and Tay were over that bitch's house? I could have died, and Tay would have been spending time with the other woman, who happened to be having his baby too? Oh, hell no! This mothafucka needs to wake up and start answering some questions."

I rose from the wheelchair, walked over to Tay's bed, and stood over him. I held him by the shoulders, and I shook him hard. It had just hit me that I had been in the dark the whole time. Not that I hadn't been running game on Tay and sleeping with other people, but I had always been the one with the upper hand. All that time I had spent thinking that I was running shit was a lie. My plan with Carmello hadn't even gone down right. Was I slipping?

I sat back down once I started to feel light-headed, and I let it all sink in. I looked around the room, and my vision seemed foggy all of a sudden. I wasn't sure if it was my anger or the fact that I had just been shot. One thing was for sure, and that was that I needed to get my shit together and step up my game. Tay had a whole other life that I knew nothing about. I had always known that he was fucking around, but this nigga damn near had already had a wife when he married me. If my game had been tighter, none if this would have fallen through the cracks.

To deal with Tay, I was going to have to wait until he was up and walking. Carl would be put on the back burner until I was healthy enough to really get in his shit for keeping all that info from me. But Miss Connie . . . she was about to get taught a tough lesson. The lesson went, "No matter what, always make sure that you are the one standing with the ring on that left hand when it is all said and done. If not, you'll be fucked." Just like she was about to be.

"Carl, I want you to get me and my husband twenty-four-hour security. No one—and I mean no one—will be allowed to see us unless I say they can. From here on out, if anyone gets into this room without my knowledge, not only will they be removed by force, but you will also lose your job. Do you understand me?" I said, speaking directly to Carl.

All that soft shit I felt for him in the ambulance had flown out the window the minute I found out he had been holding out on me. That nigga had had the chance of a lifetime, and that was fucking me. The least he could have done was to warn a bitch about who her man really was.

"You can't keep me away from Tay'von," Connie objected. "I am carrying his child—"

"Bitch, so am I . . . and that doesn't make anybody special but me. I am his wife, and what

I say goes. You will be placed on a no-visitation list. If you even come close to this room, I will have you arrested. And, Connie, you do not want to fuck with me, because if you do, you will end up having that little bastard child of yours in a jail cell."

Connie stood up and put her hands on her hips, as if she had found a new jolt of strength. I looked her up and down before settling for the "I don't give a shit about what you're thinking" expression.

"You can't keep me away from him. I love him."

"Honey, your love holds no weight over here. Your time has been up with Tay for a while now, and your time is up with me now. Carl, do your fucking job and see to it that I do not ever see her around here again. Please let the nurses know that she is not to even be on this floor."

Both Carl and Connie waited to see if I was serious. All he had to do was look into my eyes and he knew that his job was on the line. He got up and walked over to Connie. She seemed as if she couldn't believe what she was hearing or seeing.

"You gonna put me out, Carl? I have known you too damn long for you to just put me out because that cold-hearted bitch is barking out orders!"

Damn. If I had had a heart, I would have felt bad for her. She looked broken and hurt. Someone should have told her not to try to go toe to toe with me, but it was too late. Maybe if she had gone a different way about things, I would have been a bit nicer. She should have known that if I walked in there and found everything out the way I had, not only would I bark, but I would bite her ass too and leave a goddamned mark.

"Carl, you have ten seconds to get this fat bitch out of here," I said, meaning every single word.

Carl took her arm and tried to lead her to the door without a fight, but I already knew that it wasn't going to be easy, especially with Carl being hurt.

Connie waved a fist in the air and yelled, "Shamika should have killed your ass when she had the chance. She used to tell me that you were an evil and worthless bitch while you were out on tour with Tay, but I . . . I just didn't think that Tay would stoop this low. You have no—"

"Get her the fuck out of here now!" I said, my voice raised slightly.

Carl had to damn near drag her out as she kicked and screamed. I had had enough of her lip, and I was happy to see her go. I waited for Carl to get back into the room before I spoke again.

"I need you to get on top of the twenty-four-hour security *now*. Make sure that there is a no-visitation list drawn up, with that nutjob at the top it," I said as I looked around the room. "And one more thing. I need to be moved in here with Tay. It seems to me that I haven't been at the top of my game, and that's going to change starting today. Me moving in here is the first thing that I need to do. And remember that no one, not even a nurse or a doctor, can come in here unless I say so." I "barked," as Connie had put it. I gave a couple more orders to Carl and then waited for him to leave me alone in the room.

Well, I hadn't seen that one coming at me, but I thought that I had handled it okay. I looked over at Tay and watched him sleep while I thought about things. I really wished he had been up while the whole Connie thing went down, but most of all, I just wanted him to wake up. If he died because of me . . . I wasn't even going to think that way. I knew that Tay had just as much fight in him as I did, and his babies did too.

As I got settled beside my man in my new hospital room, all I could think about was how I was going to deal with the Connie situation. If she really was having his baby, I was just going to put a plan together to make sure that my kids, my man, and my whole life were better than hers. And it would be on every level. The boss bitch was back, and I was going to make sure that nothing got past me from that moment on.

Another week would pass by before Tay woke up. I didn't bother bringing up Connie right away, since I hadn't heard from her or about her since the first day I walked into this room. The first thing Tay did when he woke up was call my name. And that bitch thought that she still had his heart. I was half asleep when I heard him softly call out, "*Tangie.*" I jumped out of bed and sat beside him.

"Baby, I'm here. How do you feel? Let me call for a doctor," I said as I pushed the call button.

My baby looked so out of it. I didn't know how long it was gonna take him before he was back to his old self again. For a couple of days while waiting for him to wake up, I felt like I was well enough to go home, but I wasn't leaving my baby alone. I needed to be the first face he saw when he woke up, no matter the time. I was still very upset about Connie, but that wasn't the main focus in that moment. I remembered what it was like to wake up in that cold-ass place by myself, and I didn't want that for him.

When the doctor came in, I stepped to the side, and he checked everything out. Whereas I had been shot three times, Tay's unlucky number was five.

I couldn't wait to get out of here, just so I could start the paperwork and sue those fucking policemen. The news had been pretty much on top of their shit. All the entertainment news shows, along with the major networks, had been reporting on the shooting, Tay's condition, and my progress. I had made what seemed like fifty calls to magazine and TV reporters. You couldn't let anything die down in this business. It didn't matter if you got shot, stabbed, or killed. People would want to know the when, how, and why. If you were the lucky, one of those things would push your career even further, especially in the rap biz.

While the doctor examined Tay, it hit me. I didn't have to wait to do an interview. No. I was going to call Evengeliza Moore and ask her to come out to the hospital with her film crew. Tay and I would give interviews right there in our hospital beds. Not only would the world show sympathy for us and direct anger at the cops who had shot us, but I would drop the Connie bomb and turn her into a monster.

The world would look at her as the side chick who came to the hospital to antagonize Tay'von's wife while both her life and his hung in the balance. Not to mention, dropping my baby news would have the world talking, and it would also make me look like even more of a victim. They were going to drag her for filth, and I was going to use the public uproar to my advantage. I was going to ruin her, while allowing our situation to soften the blow of another woman being pregnant by my husband at the same damn time as me. It wouldn't matter what she took to the press after that. The court of public opinion would have already judged her and sentenced her to shame and humiliation.

Oh yes, the bitch was certainly back, and I had some new missions to accomplish.

Books by the Author

Rebel's Domain: Scarred for Life

Porn Stars Porn Stars 2

Niya: Rainbow Dreams

Truth or Death
(eBook)

The Bully Bangers

Pricey: Playing in Traffic The TurnOut Queens

To Contact the Author

Facebook: Fabiola.Joseph3
Facebook Like Page: @FabieTheDreamer
Twitter: SoulOfAWriter
Instagram: TheArtOfBeingFabie
Email: WriterFabieJ@gmail.com